This book is dedicated to God,
The Master Storyteller
who knows all ends from
their beginnings.

It is also dedicated to all the readers of this book.
May you be strong and courageous
in these difficult times.

"HAVE I NOT COMMANDED YOU?
BE STRONG AND COURAGEOUS. DO NOT BE AFRAID;
DO NOT BE DISCOURAGED,
FOR THE LORD YOUR GOD WILL BE WITH YOU
WHEREVER YOU GO."

JOSHUA 1:9

CONTENTS

PROLOGUE

Long ago, the first people came to Niclausia following the orders of Abba, the Most High God. They came from a place of darkness and evil, where those in power fought with all they had to retain it, unmindful of the cost; those who led the faithful often acted no better than the secular princes; and those who professed holiness led services in solemnity but then engaged in acts of debauchery. Many people had no sense of security about this life, and only the faintest sense of it about the next. Daily survival was a constant battle for common folk, but those in power mostly ignored the less fortunate. In the midst of this madness, several communities bound by ties of sincere faith and led by truly holy leaders sent a heartfelt plea to God to save them.

And He answered.

He opened a pathway to a completely new realm where the people could live, flourish, and govern themselves according to His principles. Eventually, five sovereign kingdoms were founded. While these kingdoms also struggled with the power-hungry and evil, in the end, unlike in the other world, God's goodness and truth usually prevailed. Because of this, he came to be more often called Abba, Father, and in time it was the only name the people knew him by. He was their Father, who loved them and had brought them to this place.

This place was quite different from the one they had left, full of strange creatures as well as familiar. In the old world, many of these had been called monsters and existed only in myth. To help the people establish themselves and remain mindful of his laws, God opened the pathway between the worlds for a second time for a new people to come through, a race of people called Brenwyds.

In the old world, Brenwyds had fallen into legend, driven into hiding by fear and hatred. Most of the stories that spoke of them spoke of a cunning, Otherworldly folk with whom ordinary people should deal warily, of witches, magic, and mischief. Only a few stories remained that spoke of their true purpose as guardians of Earth in the service of God, protecting the ordinary folk from the unseen evils that walked the land. Gifted by him for remaining faithful in a previous time of darkness, they possessed exceptional beauty, were marked by pointed ears, and could heal with song. Some spoke to animals; others could read and communicate with the minds of people. Their true power and purpose, however, was in using their gift of song to fight against evil, darkness, and magic. It was because of these abilities that many had come to fear them, and eventually, to hunt them. The few true stories about Brenwyds mainly persisted because they were tied up with stories dear to the hearts of many people, those of a king named Arthur who stood for a time against the darkness and mayhem resulting from the fall of a mighty empire once called Rome. Those who cared to remember and think about such things wondered if the darkness in which they lived was connected to the disappearance of the Brenwyds.

For they had disappeared. No one knew how or when, but one day they were gone. Some said they had all been killed, others that they had been destroyed by the hand of God, or that they had set sail upon the sea into the west, never to return. Few except those who hunted them suspected the truth: they had gone into hiding in the very communities that had come to despise them. Hiding their ears and relegating their healing and guardian activities to the deepest secrecy they persisted, but in ever decreasing numbers.

Their hunters were vigilant and led by a man rumored to be immortal and invincible.

So God opened the door for a remnant of Brenwyds to seek refuge in Niclausia. There, in time, the Brenwyds and humans became staunch allies, fighting against the monsters and working together to forge a society of peace centered on God. A difficult task, but enough people kept fighting for it as the generations passed that it became realized across all five kingdoms.

The smallest of these kingdoms, and the last to be founded, was a realm on the eastern coast of the continent called Ecclesia, separated from the others by a vast forest. It was founded by a woodcutter and his family who had traveled to the other edge of the Anianol Forest in search of more trees to support themselves. They found the trees, and in time they also found themselves the beginning of a ruling dynasty. Ecclesia hugged the coast, which was mostly made of jagged, rocky cliffs against which the waves below pummeled furiously. In the south, however, the coast gentled to beaches of pale sand. Inland, the kingdom's center contained vast plains that developed into gently rolling hills and valleys as one traveled northward, which slowly became larger hills, which became still larger and steeper hills and eventually turned to vast mountains on the northern border. These mountains were almost exclusively made of bare rock and earth, their tops rising high enough that snow covered them almost the whole year. Few people lived so far north; instead, most made their homes in the south and east, among the plains and hills. To the south and west, the farms and villages gave way to the Anianol Forest separating the kingdom from the rest of the continent. Many stories abounded about the forest, telling of strange monsters not seen elsewhere living within it, for its remote and mysterious depths easily lent themselves to such tales. Only the boldest woodsmen and hunters lived within its fringes and dared to journey far within its reaches off the established roads. Despite its relative isolation, Ecclesia grew and prospered as the years went by, and eventually gained a reputation as the most peaceful of the Five Realms.

Several centuries after the kingdom's founding, that began to change.

The reigning king's queen died after birthing a daughter, Nivea by name. Some years later, the king married a woman from the northern island nation of Lamasia. Several years after that, the king died and his queen revealed herself as a powerful sorceress, a servant of the Shadow Angel himself, the first creature to ever rebel against the Creator. A great battle ensued as Nivea fought with an army of Brenwyds to defeat her stepmother and prevent her from casting Ecclesia - and all of Niclausia - into darkness. It was the greatest battle between Light and Dark that had ever taken place in Niclausia. Nivea and her army were victorious, and the queen, Morrian, cast herself into a river and drowned.

Nivea was crowned and began her rule. As the years passed, the terror of Morrian and the scars of battle faded from the country's memory. Indeed, across all Niclausia was a time of relative peace. Two hundred and fifty years later, Nivea's descendant, King Cayden, ruled Ecclesia with his queen, Alyessa. Their only child, a daughter named Calissa, became betrothed to a prince of their neighboring country, Darlesia. They were to wed on Calissa's twentieth birthday, the day she officially came of age according to Ecclesian custom. But six months before the wedding, her betrothed, Prince Rhodri, vanished while en route to his family's lands in Darlesia as he passed through the Anianol Forest. Not a trace of him could be found, despite thorough and exhaustive searches by his men, his parents' men, King Cayden's men, and all the Brenwyds that could be mustered. Calissa was heartbroken, and even her dearest friend, a half-Brenwyd girl named Aislinn, could do little to cheer her since she, like everyone else, was at a loss as to Rhodri's whereabouts. In hindsight, the disappearance was the first sign of the curse that was to come. But it had been so long since the country had faced a serious magical threat that no one had any inkling of what was hanging over their heads until it had already fallen...

BEFORE THE CURSE

I was in the forest, I could tell; none of the woods near Kheprah had trees with girths that large. The canopy was a mix of new leaves shadowed in shades from emerald to deep hunter and blossoms flushing from white to pink. I could feel the sun on my face from where it could peek through the spring foliage. Furthermore, I discovered that I was gathering forest moss mushrooms, Lissa's favorite. As I moved toward another likely looking patch, I stubbed my toe on something hard. But before I could see what it was, my surroundings changed. Images flashed before my mind's eye, too quick to make any lasting sense of: a woman in a dark, bare room, back turned toward me, bent over something on a table; the same woman in the familiar rose garden, offering Lissa a beautiful white rose; Lissa taking the rose, one of the thorns pricking her finger, Lissa starting to sway as if about to swoon; a pathway in the forest, leading somewhere I couldn't identify with strange, tall buildings and objects that sped past too quickly to be seen clearly; a small island with a dark stone fortress built on it, with three people fighting on top of the tower...finally the images slowed. Now I stood outside the city at night, but there was something wrong. I tried to enter through the front gate, but found the way barred by a thick wall of thorns. I drew my dagger to cut my way through, but when I started to hack off the limbs barring my way, they immediately grew back, the thorns looking even larger as they came within inches of my face. Suddenly I found myself running backward with panic sweeping through my body, the thorns chasing me, trying to spear me on their cruel points. I ran faster, trying to reach the open plain I could see beyond the barricade of thorns...and then suddenly I was on one end of a mountain valley. There was a small pool against the mountain face to my right, framed by clusters of maroon and crimson roses. I walked over to the pool to get a closer look, but as I drew near, I became aware of a large presence behind me. I whirled to face it and found myself looking at a giant form covered all in black....

I woke with a start, feeling a great weight on top of me. Still bleary with sleep, I jerked up, right hand flailing around for some sort of weapon, certain I was being attacked. Being violently woken from sleep in the middle of a disturbing dream makes one rather disoriented. "Aislinn! Come on, get up! The ball's tomorrow and Mother needs your help."

Recognizing my attacker, I groaned and relaxed back into bed. "Aiden, must you jump on me to wake me? Isn't that childish to you now? How did Elva let you get past the door anyway?" I turned my gaze toward the door, expecting to see one of our two Brenwyd wolfhounds who usually slept by my door. Now, though, the doorframe was empty.

My thirteen-year-old brother grinned at me, his blue eyes dancing in merriment. "Never. I enjoy it too much. Elva went with Father and Conall this morning, so it was a golden opportunity. Besides, you've slept late."

"I have?" I looked out the window and jolted back upright when I saw how far the sun had risen in the sky. "Grindles and spindles, Aiden, why wasn't I woken sooner? I need to ride out today to find those mushrooms for Maude." I leapt out of bed and went about getting dressed. Aiden turned around, but he didn't leave.

"You complain about my waking you, but then you complain that I didn't wake you sooner? How is that fair?" he asked. "Did you have bad dreams last night?" He sounded serious on the last question. Brenwyd dreams were rarely just dreams.

I sighed. "I'm not sure what sort of dream I had last night, to be perfectly honest. It was very...strange more than anything. The scenes I was Seeing kept changing every few seconds to something new. I started out in the forest gathering mushrooms, then I Saw Lissa in the garden with an old woman giving her a rose, then I was outside Kheprah with a wall of thorns chasing me, and you woke me up as a very large figure completely dressed in black appeared on a mountain plateau."

Aiden had turned around to stare at me as my narration continued. Fortunately, I had finished dressing. His blue eyes were big. "You Saw all of that?" I nodded, grabbing my brush and starting to drag it through my thick auburn hair. I grunted as it hit tangles. For a brief moment, I envied my friend Calissa. As a princess, she had her lady's maid to help her brush her hair out every day. I had no personal lady's maid; the closest I got was that on special occasions, my mother's maid came to help me. For every day, however, I was on my own, unless I could find and persuade a housemaid to help me.

"Are you going to tell Father? Did it seem to be anything about Rhodri?"

I frowned and sighed. "No, nothing about Rhodri. Whatever knowledge or wisdom Abba wants me to gain from this dream, it's not at all clear. I suppose I should tell Father, shouldn't I?" I mused, then gritted my teeth as I hit a particularly snarled bit of hair. I had only recently started having true dreams like this, and they usually meant trouble of some sort was on the way. They were a result of my gift of Second Sight and were signs from Abba of what was to come. Often, they were shrouded in metaphors and symbolism and hard to understand. I counted myself fortunate that so far, my dreams had been fairly straightforward, like when I had dreamed last year while at Ecclesia's southern port that a hurricane was coming in from the sea. This dream had broken that trend.

"Where is Father?"

"Mother said the king was sending him out today to oversee the transport of the last nobles coming for the ball. He's supposed to be gone much of the day. He took the dogs to help carry messages."

I sighed again. "Of course. Well, hopefully none of what I saw indicates an imminent disaster. I'll speak with him this evening." I finally finished brushing my hair and twisted it into a braid. "Now, you said something about Mother needing my help, yes?"

He nodded. "She's in the great hall with the queen. I think she wants to ask you about roses from the garden. Maybe you could talk to someone else about the dream, like Sir Ethelred or Lady Ailith."

It was a sound suggestion, but...it was going to be an extremely busy day and I was already getting a late start. Not to mention I had a feeling that the two Brenwyds my brother named, both good friends of my family, would also be caught up in transport duty today as my father was. It would be simplest to wait until it was convenient to talk to Father.

"If I come across them, perhaps." I ushered Aiden out the door. "Now get going. I'm sure you have tasks set before you as well today. I'll see you later."

He released a dramatic groan. "Why must you remind me?"

I grinned. "You did ambush me in bed this morning. Go on with you!"

"Alright." He left my room with deliberately dragging feet, but I heard him adopt a bouncier step once out of sight of my door. Clearly, despite his dreaded chores, the heightened energy around the castle as a result of the preparations for Lissa's birthday ball had infected him. Once he'd well and truly gone, I opened the door beside my bed and entered a small room lit with the cheery light of morning. I took a moment to let my eyes soak in the colors springing out at me from all the canvases on the walls and to inhale the smell of the oil-based paint that I made myself. My small art studio was one of my favorite places in the world. Painting on canvases with oil-paints as I preferred was an unusual hobby, but I had discovered at an early age that I had a talent for it, and fortunately my family supported me in pursuing it. At the moment, instead of letting my gaze drift fondly over my past works decorating the walls, I focused my attention on the painting currently standing on my easel, studying it critically.

It was a painting of Lissa's favorite rosebush, and I had spent a lot of time trying to get the roses to look just right. I decided that the days spent in painstaking experiments to discover exactly how to create the right shades of white for the petals had not been in vain. The white petals showed the variation in hue evident in a real flower as light plays across it, from cream to ivory to almost pure white. I smiled in satisfaction at the painting. I had only put the finishing touches on it late the night before by candlelight, and had worried my brush-strokes in the dark would mar the work. Usually, I only painted during the day when I had the light of the sun, but to finish in time I had needed to take extra measures. Now, I thought it would have just enough time to dry before I presented it to Lissa late tomorrow afternoon. I opened the window before leaving the studio so the early spring breezes outside could make their way into the room. This would both help the painting dry completely and let the room air out. The fumes from my paints could become quite overpowering in enclosed spaces, and they could also be poisonous if the proper precautions weren't taken, as my mother constantly reminded me. So I kept the windows open as often as I could, though I also made sure to draw the light curtain across the window before leaving the room so the bright sunlight wouldn't cause the colors on my other paintings to fade.

When I reentered my main bedroom, I looked myself over in the mirror to make sure I was suitably presentable, since it was likely I would run into the queen. Were this a day when the king and queen formally held court to hear complaints and legal cases, I would have donned one of my finer dresses, but since everyone was in a tizzy over the ball I had opted for a more practical outfit. Over a pair of close-fitting russet breeches, I wore a smalt blue linen undertunic with long, billowing sleeves gathered in at the wrist and was topped by a sleeveless sage woolen jerkin-style overshirt, both garments ending halfway down my thighs and belted at my waist. The fine fabric, bright colors, and detailed embroidery (which I had done myself in silk thread) around the tunic hems and sleeve cuffs made it good enough for royalty on a casual day, but work-like enough that I could go ride later without having to come back and change. I brushed flyaway wisps of hair away from my green eyes, tucking them behind my slightly pointed ears. Though my mother was not technically a Brenwyd (she said that she had Brenwyds in her ancestry, but it had been so long ago that she had no discernable Brenwyd traits), the fact that my father was a full-blood meant that I had the full range of Brenwyd talents and traits, which was reflected in my outward appearance. Well, mostly.

Out of habit, I rubbed a finger over my cheeks as if trying to wipe away the small brown spots that dotted them. My freckles most definitely came from my mother's side of the family. Unfortunately, the rest of her family had died in some sort of accident before I was born so I had never met any of them, but she had told me that both her mother and one of her brothers had had freckles. When I was younger, I had heartily wished them away as I knew no other Brenwyds with freckles, and the young noble girls around the castle (who tended to be jealous of Brenwyds' natural beauty) pounced on them as a point of ridicule. Over the years, however, and with constant reassurances from my mother, Lissa, and others, I had come to accept them, and even like them. Now, I grinned at them in the mirror. Satisfied with my appearance, I left the house where my family lived, located in Kheprah's noble quarter, and walked toward the castle gates. Though most Brenwyds lived in country villages, preferring open spaces, those who directly served the king and queen, like my parents, had to live in the capital, and so we were granted generous living quarters only a stone's throw and a step from the entrance to the castle proper.

After weaving my way through the chaotic courtyard, I located my mother where Aiden had said she would be, in the great hall helping Queen Alyessa direct the decorations going up. A princess's birthday is a special occasion in and of itself, but when a person in Ecclesia turned twenty, they came of age, so this celebration was of special significance. However, there was also a wistful, sorrowful look on many faces, for tomorrow was supposed to have been Calissa's wedding day as well. Not for the first time, I closed my eyes briefly and Searched for Rhodri, but as usual, I had no luck. Only blackness appeared in my mind's eye.

"Aislinn, you're up. Good." I opened my eyes and stepped to Mother's side.

"I'm sorry, Mother. I didn't intend to oversleep."

"It's alright. Were you having a dream?"

"Yes, but I don't think I need to worry about it at the moment. I'll talk to Father about it when he returns. It could mean simply that the roses resent my pruning work." I smiled and made a joke of it so she didn't worry.

Mother raised her eyebrows, then chuckled a little. I had a feeling she knew I was deliberately downplaying the dream so I wouldn't have to go into it in depth at the moment. Her green eyes held a humoring look. "Well, I don't blame them for that. You spend almost all your free time in there with Calissa, and they certainly seemed in a sorry state when I was last in there. There's hardly any bit of plant left!"

She affected a shocked tone, but I knew she was teasing me. She was the one who had taught me how to tend roses in the first place, and that the severe pruning was necessary to keep the flowers looking their best. Roses were her favorite flower, and when I was young she had often taken me to the small garden plot we had behind our house that she used for growing them. In fact, it was this garden that had inspired the queen to install a rose garden in an interior courtyard in the castle, and that was the one Lissa and I now tended with zealous attention.

I smiled. "I only copy what I see you do first, Mother." Then, to hurry along the conversation, "What do you want me to do? I did promise Maude I'd go and gather forest moss mushrooms for the feast, and that will likely take me much of the afternoon."

"Are you sure it's safe?" the Queen asked, blond brows scrunched lightly in worry. She's the worrying kind, and after Rhodri vanished, she'd gotten even more wary of trips into the forest.

"I'll be fine, Your Majesty. I've been to the grove many times, and it's not far from the road. I thank you for your concern."

"When do you plan to leave?" Mother asked.

"Right after luncheon, I think."

She nodded thoughtfully, running a hand across her blond hair as if to be sure every strand was still contained in its bun. "Alright. You should still have plenty of time for what I have in mind. You know the early-blooming roses that have opened in the greenhouse?"

"Of course."

"I'd like you to find some of the more plentiful boughs of blooms and make some rose wreaths for the high table and garlands for the others. It wouldn't do to have every flower but the princess's favorite present in the decorations."

"As you wish, Mother."

"And if you could convince Calissa to help you, I would appreciate it, Aislinn," Queen Alyessa said. "She's rather...depressed today, and she needs you to cheer her, and a task to busy her mind." She sighed, her blue eyes sad.

"Of course, Your Majesty. Mother, Your Majesty, good morning." I curtseyed and prepared to walk from the hall.

"Aislinn, wait a minute," my mother's voice halted my progress, and I turned back around with brows raised in question. An anxious expression not unlike the queen's had come over her face. "Before you leave today, please ask around and see if someone could go with you to the forest. I know," she raised a hand in the face of my immediate protest, "that you've been to the forest many times by yourself and are perfectly capable of defending yourself if need be, but better safe than sorry, yes?" The phrase was a favorite of hers, and also unique to her. My mother had a whole host of phrases and turns of speech that I have never heard anyone else use, save my father on occasion.

I stifled a sigh. I knew the suggestion was good sense, but I had been looking forward to some alone time. There was precious little of it to be had within Kheprah's walls, and even less in the castle. "Yes, Mother. But what if I can't find anyone available?"

"Then just be extra cautious, alright?" She stepped toward me and wrapped me in a brief hug. "I know it's probably a bit silly, but I'm your mother. I can't help it."

I smiled and returned the hug. "I know. I'll be careful, I promise. And I'll get those wreaths to you quick as dragonflight."

"Good girl." My mother turned and went back to her current task. It looked like seating arrangements. "Now go on with you. This is not a day for dawdling." With that, I turned and walked from the hall, neatly avoiding the decorators, maids, footmen, and other people filling the hall in preparation for the feast tomorrow. I took a back way to Lissa's rooms, wanting to avoid running into any and all foreign nobles and dignitaries who were visiting for the event. Since I was often in attendance on Lissa, I was a known face in and out of Ecclesia and I didn't have any desire today to be stopped by well-meaning strangers with questions about Lissa's health and the search for Rhodri. Familiar servants and friends I could deal with, but they were all too busy with their own duties to give me more than a brief smile and "Good morning" as I passed them.

I reached Lissa's door and knocked. "Come in," she said, her voice sounding muffled. I walked in. She sat on the window seat of her sitting room, gazing out at the view of the city and the fields beyond. At first glance, Calissa is the perfect image of a princess. Her honey-golden hair reaches nearly to her waist, she has sapphire blue eyes framed by dark lashes, her skin is clear and smooth, and she almost always wears lovely dresses, except when she works in the garden (she does still wear dresses when she does, just plain ones). But on closer inspection, one realizes her features are too prominent and irregular for classic beauty. She takes more after her father than her mother, and her features would be handsome if she was a boy, but are not very suited to a girl. However, her personality more than makes up for her lack of looks, and indeed the knowledge of that personality often causes me to forget them. Lissa is the most loving, patient person you will ever meet. Certainly more patient than me, but she sometimes teases me that my temper is because of the red in my hair. "Good morning, Aislinn."

"Morning, Lissa. How does it feel to know it's your last day of being nineteen?"

She smiled, but her eyes were distant, like she was thinking of something else. Or, rather, someone else. It was a look I'd grown quite accustomed to over the past few months. This morning, though, there was a focused energy to the look that I hadn't seen before. Her air also seemed a bit distracted, like she had just learned something important. Or maybe it was just because of what tomorrow was – and should have been.

"Oh, the same as every other day. I am surprised you were not here earlier. Were you working on a painting?"

"Ah, I overslept, actually."

She raised her eyebrows. "You overslept?"

"Hmm. It happens occasionally, you know. And you're a fine one to cast stones; you do it regularly."

She smiled a bit. "But you do not." She patted the seat beside her. "Do come and sit down. You have been rather scarce over the last couple of weeks. I have missed you."

"Ah, well." I sat beside her. "I've been busy. You want your present, don't you?"

"Oh, I suppose." She gazed out the window again, her expression much too sad. "Though there is only one thing I really want..."

I sighed. "Oh, Lissa. If I could find him for you, I'd do it in a heartbeat."

"I know you would. In fact," she hesitated a moment, "there is something I would like to speak with you about. An idea I have formed. Concerning Rhodri." The name tumbled from her lips in a rush. I looked at her in surprise. It had been months since she had said Rhodri's name in any tone but a sad wistfulness.

"Oh? What?"

Lissa stood up and began pacing around the room, which showed me just how agitated she was. Lissa did not pace. She had in fact been emphatically trained not to pace by her mother. "Well, I have grown tired, you see, of sitting about waiting for any news to come in, and whenever news does come in, it is no news at all, so I decided to put my own mind to work on the matter. He is my fiancé, after all. I should be the one working hardest to find him instead of relying on everyone else." She paused.

"Alright. Go on," I encouraged, my curiosity very much piqued. In the last few weeks I had buried myself in my studio to work on the painting, but I had been aware that Lissa had been engaged in some sort of intent activity of her own. Olwen, one of our housemaids who always kept an ear out for castle gossip, had mentioned that Lissa had been spending much time in the library. Given her proclivity for self-assigned research projects whenever something new caught her fancy, I had figured she was doing one to distract herself from the upcoming ball and Rhodri's absence. Apparently, it had been quite the opposite.

She went on. "The problem is that there is no reasonable explanation for what happened. We do not know where he went. His parents do not know where he went. The people he was traveling with say he simply went into the forest to relieve himself and never came back. The search parties sent through the forest and the Brenwyd patrols who questioned the animals ruled out an animal attack or foul play from any person, whether magical or otherwise. And since no monsters have been seen in nearly a century, it seems logical to rule out an attack from that quarter as well. Therefore, logically, if all the reasonable explanations have been discounted, one must start looking at the unreasonable ones." She paused again, looking very nervous.

I could feel my eyebrows making their way up my forehead. Lissa was, by nature, practical and logical to a fault. It was how she had been trained and schooled as the future queen of Ecclesia. I was usually the one who reached first for wild ideas and information, not her. Then again, her reasoning to get there was sound, and Abba knew I was the last person to judge a person reaching for unreasonable ideas.

"Alright. Pardon my impatience, but could you please hurry up and get to the point?"

She took a breath as if mentally preparing herself. Then, in a slow, measured, and definite tone she said, "I believe that it is possible that the pathways Abba opened for our ancestors to come through to Niclausia are not sealed as everyone believes. I think it is possible that they might operate randomly and Rhodri may have accidentally fallen through one."

I stared at her, open-mouthed. Unreasonable explanations were one thing, but this? "I beg your pardon?"

She repeated herself, then added. "Aislinn, I know it sounds mad and just the sort of thing a grieving fiancée would come up with to ease her own mind, but I tell you, I truly do think it is plausible. I have been researching pathways, going over all the old, original accounts, stories, and histories, and not one of them ever really says they were irrevocably sealed. Only that any further travel between the realms was forbidden. But one writer intimated that Brenwyds still used the portals from time to time, and there are those stories that we liked so much as children about the wonderful inventions and stories of the old world. They have to have come from somewhere. And you know as well as I the reports of people vanishing without a trace from time to time, both in and outside the forest. Do you know anything else?" She looked at me hopefully.

I simply continued staring at her. This sort of theorizing was so unlike Lissa...but then, she and Rhodri had been very much in love. And not the silly, infatuated kind either. It came from a deep and intimate understanding of each other, not from personal charms. It came from knowing the other's flaws and accepting them. They had known each other since she was ten and he was eleven, when Rhodri's family had come on diplomatic business to Ecclesia. He was the youngest son of the current Darlesian king's younger brother. Rhodri had come upon Lissa and me in the rose garden, where we were trying to help a kitten descend from a high tree. My arguments about safety and the gripping power of its own claws had done nothing to dislodge the kitten. Rhodri had given us his assistance by climbing up to the kitten, which put him high in our favor. (Not to mention the kitten's, who subsequently adopted Rhodri. Christened Boomer, he was ten now, a handsome long-haired grey tabby with a white chest and mittens. For the last six months he had been more in despair than I ever thought a cat could be.)

Rhodri had then lived here in the castle for five years as a fosterling of Lissa's father when he turned thirteen, and during those years the friendship between him and Lissa had slowly changed to something far more serious. The match was approved by everyone. Lissa's parents liked it because Rhodri would bring wealth and good connections to the kingdom, but was far enough down the line of Darlesian succession that there was no danger of Ecclesia becoming part of Darlesia. Rhodri's parents liked it because Lissa was an only child and so the heir to the throne, which meant that Rhodri would one day become king. Everything had been going perfectly; the proper gifts had been exchanged, the betrothal announced the prerequisite year in advance, the contract signed, and Rhodri had been on his way back home so that he would not be in the same house as his future wife for the six months leading up to the wedding. That's when everything had gone wrong.

I myself had had an inkling almost immediately that something was wrong with Rhodri, for my father had woken me in the middle of the night several days after Rhodri left, asking me if I had had any dreams or presentiments about Rhodri. When I gave him my sleepy denial and asked why, he only brushed me off with a smile meant to be reassuring but overshadowed by the worry in his eyes. Several days later, a messenger presented himself to King Cayden, Queen Alyessa, and Lissa with the dreadful news: Rhodri had disappeared while the group was traveling through the Anianol, and though they had searched the area thoroughly, he had not been found. No one could say how he had vanished, and many whispered of witchcraft. The king had ordered the Brenwyds to perform a sweep of the kingdom and forest, to try and ferret out any possible witch or wizard and figure out what had happened to Rhodri. They had found nothing either, even those of us gifted with Second Sight. The only comfort given by the ones with Sight was that they sensed he was not dead. Darlesian relations had been suffering since his disappearance as well, since it was unclear if he had been within Darlesian or Ecclesian borders when he disappeared (the border's nebulous that far into the forest), and so Ecclesia had gotten the blame. Poor Lissa had stayed in her rooms for nearly a week, and even now she rarely laughed or smiled, and there was always sadness in her eyes. When you spoke with her, it was like part of her wasn't there, was always looking beyond you to try and glimpse her prince.

"Lissa, those are fairy tales. There's a reason they're only told to children. All the histories say that those pathways were specifically opened by Abba, and then closed when our ancestors came through. There is no passage between here and the old world, and from all the stories I've heard, it's a good thing. And think of all the strange things they claim to exist over there: horseless carriages and flying machines and a dozen other things that sound like magic, yet all the stories insist it's not. How can they be anything but stories?"

She frowned at me. "All stories had to come from somewhere. Think of what your mother has said often: even the most absurd tales usually start with at least a small grain of truth. Think about it seriously for a moment. I would think that you of all people would at least admit it could be possible. With magic ruled out, what other option is there?"

She had a point. My mother did often repeat the saying when she told stories, and I had the reputation of constantly throwing out ridiculous theories. However, simply because I said silly things didn't mean I believed them. I sighed and closed my eyes. *At least honor her request, Aislinn,* my mind scolded me. *Think about it from her viewpoint. She's exhausted every logical option, that much is true; she wouldn't be Lissa if she didn't.* So I thought about it. And, to my surprise, as I did, I realized it might just make some sense. If the pathways were still open, and if there was one near where Rhodri had disappeared...

"Alright, I see your point," I said at length. "I've never heard of Brenwyds still going through them, but I can ask my father when I see him this evening, if you like."

"Really?" Hope brightened Lissa's expression and she threw her arms around me in an embrace. "Oh, Aislinn, thank you." She sobered for a moment and pulled back to look me in the eye. "You are not saying that merely to placate me, are you?" As the crown princess, she was well used to that sort of patronizing.

I looked at her indignantly. "When have you ever known me to agree with you out of deference to your position? Don't insult me. I might have to challenge you to a duel at dawn."

To my delight, she actually laughed. "I know, I apologize; I had to ask. Will you go ask your father now? I have done all the research I can in the library. I am afraid Master Ferghil has grown quite tired of me disturbing his carefully arranged records, but I have taken notes of everything that seemed important." I rolled my eyes at the reference to the castle's master librarian. He was a brilliant man and completely dedicated to his work, but he did not like others, even members of the royal family, searching through the records themselves. He thought it reflected poorly on him as a librarian if others had to go searching through the stacks that he knew by heart. I tried to avoid him whenever possible. I found him too fussy.

Lissa opened the small book she'd been holding on her lap. It was one of the many blank books she kept on hand for research notes. "Apparently, only Brenwyds could sense the pathways and really work them because there is something musical about them, but I thought that perhaps they open at random, and if Rhodri was in the right place at the right time – or wrong place, rather. Perhaps we can investigate where he disappeared, and you could see if you sense anything unusual. I am afraid I do not know how to direct you any more than that, but-"

"Easy," I laughed, putting a hand up to stop her flow of words. While I still maintained some skepticism about the idea, I was starting to really hope that she was right, for I would hate for her to be disappointed in her theory. Besides, it was the best theory I'd heard about Rhodri's disappearance for months. "Yes, I agree, we must investigate where he disappeared, but if you recall, there's a rather large ball being held here tomorrow and everyone, including me, is tied up with tasks today. My father is busy monitoring all the transports, so I won't see him for a good while. I'm afraid you'll have to wait a little longer."

She sighed and sat back down on the window seat beside me, visibly deflated. "The ball. Of course." She turned her gaze out the window. "I suppose I cannot ask Mother to cancel at this late date."

"No. But be easy. I'm going into the Anianol Forest today, to find some of your favorite mushrooms for Maude. If I have time, on my way back I'm sure I could find where Rhodri's party camped for the night by asking the animals for directions, and I could take a quick look and listen around. Does that sound alright?"

"Oh, would you?"

"Of course. What are friends for, if not to go hunt for evidence to support mad ideas?"

She laughed again. "Oh, Aislinn. I am so glad you live here. How would I survive court without you?"

I embraced her. "I'm sure you'd find some way. Imagine, rather, me trying to survive court without you. There would be a disaster within the first hours."

"Surely not. It has been ages since you tripped on anyone's gown."

I groaned. For several years after I entered adolescence and suddenly shot up like a beanstalk, I had gone through a period where it seemed like all the grace I should have from my Brenwyd ancestry deserted me. "Don't speak of it, please! You'll end my graceful streak." We sat there for several long moments in each other's arms, taking solace from the companionship and memories.

"Quite the pair we have been," Lissa murmured finally. "The plain princess-"

"And the freckled Brenwyd," I finished for her. The epithets had initially been given to us by others in scorn, but we had long ago decided to turn the phrases around and use them in fun. We were neither of us quite what people expected for who we were. I gave Lissa a final squeeze and then released her. "Let's go down to the greenhouse. My mother wants me to make rose wreaths and garlands for the tables, and you can help me."

"Of course. Let me change first. I do not need another lecture from Mother about ruining my good dresses in the garden." She rolled her eyes.

"It really is too bad that your mother is so against princesses wearing breeches. It's not as if it's an uncommon practice among women, even if they aren't Brenwyd," I said. "They are eminently practical."

"The consequences of being royalty," she commented wryly as she rose from the seat. "But no matter; and if you help me, I will change faster than if I ring for Marin, we can get to the greenhouse and finish sooner, and you will be on your way to the forest faster than dragonflight."

I got up behind her and bowed. "I hear and obey, Your Highness."

Later that day, I was in the barn tacking up my bay gelding, Dynin, in preparation for my mushroom gathering expedition. As it happened, I would be getting my alone time after all, for I had found no one available to accompany me. Even the dogs were still busy helping Father, and Boomer had decided that his place in Rhodri's absence was firmly in Lissa's shadow. He had only been absent this morning to roam through the various guest rooms and make sure everything was in order, as he put it, which really meant he was listening for any gossip that might be helpful for Lissa. He made an astonishingly good court spy. The thought cheered me. I didn't like making my mother worry, but I knew the Anianol Forest, and had been there many times alone. Besides, since I was alone, I would be better able to keep my promise to Lissa to investigate the possibility of a pathway. It would have been a bit awkward to explain that to someone. I pondered how I would know a pathway was a pathway. In all the stories I'd heard they operated through music as Lissa had said, which didn't surprise me as only Brenwyds or Abba could allegedly operate them. But how exactly? What should I listen for? *How long will we be gone today?* The query from Dynin interrupted my musings.

Until four past noon at least. I'd like a long ride today, so I think we'll ride for a bit before transferring. And I need to check on something for Lissa. Is that alright? I asked him. Without a doubt, one of my favorite parts about being half Brenwyd was my ability to talk to animals, which was much more desirable than mind reading, in my opinion. My father was a mind reader, and he often grumbled about people's thoughts entering his head when he didn't want them to. Although when I spoke with Dynin, or any other Brenwyd breed of animal, the ability was rather a moot point since they could speak with any person they chose regardless of that person's ability – or lack of – to talk to animals.

Dynin stretched his neck out and shook his mane before letting me put the bit in his mouth and guide the bridle into place. *A run would be nice,* he said reflectively.

I thought so. I finished with the straps and led Dynin out into the stable yard where there was a mounting block. Since the place where the particular species of mushroom I was in search of was a week's ride away under normal circumstances, I couldn't go the whole way straight, but Brenwyd horses had a unique ability that allowed them to travel almost instantaneously from one place to another by getting up to a gallop at top speed and then thinking about their destination. Brenwyd history holds that the ability, along with the general ability of Brenwyd animals to speak to whomever they wished, had been granted to them by Abba when he had blessed us with our unique abilities so we would be able to fulfill our duties more easily. No one is really sure as to how and why transferring works; whenever I've asked Dynin about it, he's only said that he runs with the destination in mind and so he gets there. He doesn't understand why it's such a puzzlement to me.

I mounted and rode out the castle gate, calling a cheerful farewell to the guards on duty. I wound down through the city at a leisurely walk, looking around at all the shoppers and the decorations that many of the citizens and merchants had set up in front of their homes and shops for Lissa's birthday. I smiled at the clear public support for her. The Ecclesian royal family was mostly loved by their subjects, but especially by the people of Kheprah, who had more contact with them. Lissa and the queen often made a point of shopping in the Kheprah markets for things they needed instead of importing fine goods from other countries, and Rhodri had often joined them, so I knew many of the citizens felt his loss on a personal level. As Dynin and I waded through the people, many greetings were tossed my way by people I knew, and even some people I didn't but who recognized me as Lissa's special friend. People asked me about Lissa's mood, the decorations at the castle, and a few even whispered queries about the search for Rhodri the several times I had to stop Dynin to wait for people to cross the road. I generally didn't mind the city people's attention and enjoyed answering their questions or exchanging bits of news, but today with every small delay I felt a burning impatience grow within to get out of the city to the solitude of the forest. In fact, I felt the desire to leave so keenly that it surprised me a bit. I decided it was just a sign of the length of time since the last time I had been out of the city alone for an afternoon.

Finally, Dynin and I made it out the main city gate. Once we were clear of the people clustered about the gate, I squeezed Dynin's sides to urge him into a trot, intending to send him into a gallop as soon as we cleared the people on the road before the city with their wagons and carts. However, for an inexplicable reason I found myself instead sitting back and signaling him to halt as we reached the crest of the first large hill after the city, which Dynin didn't appreciate. He wanted to run.

Nonetheless he did halt, and I looked back at Kheprah. It looked as it always had; the city was built up around a broad hill, with the castle at the top, though the city itself sprawled out in all directions. The wall encircling the city had about half a mile of space between it and the nearest city structures to account for growth; there were two other walls within Kheprah that marked its previous boundaries in the past. The houses were made of light grey stone, and the roofs of wood. As I sat there gazing at my home, a cloud passed over the sun, causing darkness to cover the city for a moment. I abruptly remembered my dream from earlier, of thorn bushes surrounding the city, barring me from entry, and a chill shuddered its way down my spine. What did it mean?

But the cloud moved on from the sun, light poured over the bright, lively city, and the feeling left. *Can we run now?* Dynin demanded impatiently.

I shook the remnants of the somber mood from my mind and looked eagerly at the long, mostly empty road ahead. *But of course.* I gave him his head, and he took off.

The Curse Falls

Are you done yet? Dynin's plaintive query came to my mind. I grinned at his tone, careful to guard from him how much I was amused. He wouldn't have appreciated it.

Not quite. There are a lot of people coming to this feast, and I need to make sure Maude has enough. And I promised Lissa I'd look about for any possible pathways. We'll be leaving soon enough; be patient. Dynin made his opinion of that statement clear by snorting loudly, but I noticed he drifted away to an area with some grass and started munching with contentment. I had a feeling he was complaining more on principle than anything else, as he always appreciated trips on which he could eat grass. They took excellent care of him in the royal stables, but pastures were rather hard to come by in the middle of Kheprah. All the horses were rotated to pastures outside the city on a regular basis, but according to Dynin, his turn was never long enough.

I continued my mushroom picking. It had really been a relaxing afternoon, I reflected. No brothers playing pranks, no parents assigning chores, no visiting nobles and dignitaries one had to be polite to no matter the provocation – only the quiet forest and Dynin, with some visits from local forest denizens to catch me up on the latest gossip about who had mated with whom and who had had babies since the last time I visited. I was always privately amused by how much the animals enjoyed sharing such news with me. As gossips go, animals are almost worse than people, though not quite; they never share gossip with malicious intent.

However, the memory soon made me frown thoughtfully, for the animals had shared other news with me. I had asked them if they had seen Rhodri or anyone like him around the forest recently, and let them know how long ago he had disappeared. Animals tended to have a hard time understanding the concept of time beyond the change of seasons and how many matings or litters they had gone through, but they remembered that incident well enough. A squirrel had told me he remembered Rhodri's party coming through the forest, and that soon after they stopped, he had sensed something bad in the forest and promptly ran home to his hole to hide. Several songbirds and a deer said the same. Then they said the feeling had passed, and the next notable thing they remembered was all the search parties coming through. (The squirrel had been especially put out, as he was convinced all the people would find his nut stashes and he would subsequently starve in the coming winter. But by the grace of Abba, his stashes had remained undisturbed and he had come through the cold season just fine.)

I had heard such reports from other animal speakers who had gone to the forest soon after Rhodri disappeared and inquired of the animals if they had sensed anything unusual. But the animals hadn't been able to confirm what kind of bad feeling they had had, and none of them could shed any light on where Rhodri could have gone.

Abruptly, I was shaken from my wool-gathering by the feeling of an unexpected pain in my right toe, and I yelped. "Ouch!" I balanced on one leg and gently massaged the injured toe. As I did so, I felt the strangest sense of familiarity, as if I'd done this exact action in this exact place before, though I knew I hadn't.

What is it? Dynin asked, raising his head from his grazing.

"Oh, nothing. I stubbed my toe, 'tis all." I frowned at the ground. "But on what?" I knelt and carefully probed the ground for the hard object I had hit. My fingers found it before my eyes saw it, and I let out another hiss of pain. "Ack! What in the Five Realms..." my voice trailed off as I finally uncovered the object. I stared at it, disbelieving my eyes. Carefully, I ran a hand down the thin strip of metal until I reached the broad end of it. It was a sword. And not just any sword. I knew the crest etched into the metal that I could make out under the rust. I had helped design it, every line and stroke. Lissa had been so proud of the combination of the Darlesian and Ecclesian royal crests that we had concocted.

This was Rhodri's sword, the one Lissa had given him as a betrothal present a year ago.

My mind reeled. This was the first concrete evidence anyone had found of Rhodri since he'd disappeared. And it certainly didn't bode well. He would never have left his sword in the forest to rust away unless he had been forced, and if he had been forced to give up his weapon...he must have been attacked by something, but what?

What is it, girl? Dynin's voice startled me. He had abandoned his grass patch to stand behind me, worriedly nuzzling my hair. He could sense my tumultuous emotions.

"It's Rhodri's sword," I said aloud, trying to get a handle on my thoughts. "It's his sword. He must have been here. This must be exactly where it happened...whatever it was." I stood up and began to look around, willing myself to see a detail, any detail, that could explain what had happened. *Like what, Aislinn?* I asked myself harshly. *Any blood would be long gone. Do you want to find his bones? So you can go back to your best friend on her birthday and tell her that her fiancé is undisputedly dead?*

If I have to, I decided grimly. *Lissa more than anyone deserves the truth.* I moved out of the mushroom grove and found myself up against a thick hedge of thorns and bushes. I frowned. I didn't remember such a hedge being here before. Where had it come from? Then again, the last time I had been here was last year.

Excuse me, a small voice entered my mind, startling me. *Are you here about the witch?* I looked down. A little forest mouse was sitting by my boot, looking up at me with round black eyes and trembling whiskers. I knelt so I was closer to the tiny creature, though I knew better than to hold out a hand to pick her up. That was considered very rude by wild animals, unless they were sick or injured.

What witch? I asked the mouse, alarmed by her use of the word.

Her nose twitched nervously. *The one that put these briars down and blocked my hole entrance! I was trapped for days! I finally managed to get out when a relative happened by and we coordinated chewing. I knew a Brenwyd would come eventually.*

I blinked, absorbing the information. *A witch made this hedge?*

Undeniably, the mouse said emphatically. *There I was, minding my business and coming back to my hole after gathering food for the cold, and suddenly she was there! There was another human with her, I think they were fighting, but I did not really see what was going on. I scurried to my hole like any self-respecting mouse, and then next thing I knew, all these briars were springing up out of the ground and I was trapped!* The mouse sounded very indignant.

I felt my heartbeat rising at the account. Had I just discovered what happened to Rhodri? If the mouse had been trapped for days after this altercation, it was possible that other animal-speakers might have missed her in their rush to find information from the animals about Rhodri. And after the first week or two, they had stopped coming to this part of the forest, believing that they had learned all there was to learn. *What did this other human look like?* I asked. *Did you see what happened to him?*

The mouse thought for a moment. *It was a male, a young one,* she said finally. *And...he smelled sweaty. And horsey. But not as bad as most humans that come here. The fur on his head was dark, and his skin was darker than yours.* I knew that was as complete a description as I was likely to get. For one thing, something the size of the mouse would have trouble seeing the detail of a person's face from their vantage point, and for another, I knew that mice, like most animals, couldn't see all the colors that people could. Their descriptions tended to focus on the smell of a person, and Brenwyds had learned to interpret smell-descriptions animals gave them into more practical identification measures. The description the mouse gave could very well fit Rhodri. After traveling for many days on horseback, he would certainly be sweaty and smell of horse, but since he was a noble, he bathed more frequently than peasants and so overall wouldn't smell as bad to an animal. His hair was dark brown, and his skin was darker than mine. His mother came from a family that lived in the far south of Darlesia on the edge of the Great Desert, and those families tended to have skin that looked permanently tanned by the sun. Rhodri had inherited the trait. *Oh! Do you think it could be that prince you humans are all looking for?* the mouse queried suddenly.

Quite possibly, I said, not too surprised that the mouse had made the connection. While usually animals this far into the forest paid little heed to events in the human world, the search for Rhodri had brought people into their territory and so made it common gossip for them. *Did you see anything else?*

Well, not much, the mouse said, *but I did creep to the opening of my hole once I reached it to take a peek. He seemed to be trying to fight her, but she pushed him back, and then I could not see him anymore. Then she put out a hand and said some awful words, and then those horrible thorns trapped me!* The mouse trembled at the memory.

Where? Where did he disappear?

It was in the clearing that way. The mouse turned to indicate the hedge. *But the hedge is blocking it now.*

Thank you, thank you.

Of course, the mouse sniffed. *But what are you going to do about that witch?*

Well, finding her would probably be a good start. I reached into the small knapsack I'd placed some food and a water flask in and pinched off a small piece of the cheese I'd brought as a snack. *Here. You have earned it.*

The mouse took the cheese excitedly. *You just be sure to get that witch!* she said as she scurried off to put it safely in her hole. I stood, staring at the hedge, my mind whirling more than ever. Finally, an answer. It *was* a witch. But a witch no Brenwyd had been able to find or even hear a whisper of in the last six months. She must be powerful and canny, then. Extremely so. But what had she done with Rhodri? And why take him in the first place? Turning on my heel, I whistled for Dynin, who came at a trot.

"Dynin, I think Abba has just blessed us with an answer to what happened to Rhodri. We must go back to Kheprah to tell Mother and Father and the king and queen." I grabbed my sheathed sword from where it hung from my saddle and headed for the hedge. "Just as soon as I get through this hedge to find what's on the other side, that is."

Shouldn't we go tell them first?

"I'd rather give them a full report. We're here already; we might as well take an extra few minutes to investigate." Using my sword to cut away the thick hedge, I quickly made myself and Dynin a path into the clearing. As I entered, the sense of familiarity I'd had about stubbing my toe came back to me, stronger than ever, and I stopped, taking stock of my surroundings carefully. Slowly, the memory of the clearing came to me, and my eyes widened. "Dy! I saw this place in my dream this morning! And I stubbed my toe at the start of it! Abba *was* trying to tell me something about Rhodri."

What else was in this dream?

I scrambled to remember. "There was a woman...a woman in a dark room, and then with Lissa in a garden. She gave her a rose...

Lissa pricked herself on it." I paused for a moment. "That woman I saw must be the witch! I Saw her! I could draw her, send the description across the Five Kingdoms. Someone must know who and where she is."

That is good, Dynin said, *but why did you see this clearing? You stubbed your toe back there.*

I took a deep breath to steady myself. I hadn't felt so optimistic about Rhodri in months. "This clearing...I remember, it was strange. There was something else here, some sort of path that led somewhere I'd never seen the like of before. But," I looked around with some bewilderment, "I only see forest here. But I'm sure this is the clearing. The path was so clear it was like a..." I gasped, and breathed out the next words in a whisper, "like a pathway."

Like the princess suggested?

"Exactly. Oh, why didn't I make the connection when she was telling me about it this morning?" I asked myself ruefully. I closed my eyes and began to listen with my Brenwyd sense to the songs around me. My first lessons from Father as a small child about how to use my gifts had involved him taking me to the fields and woods outside Kheprah and just having me listen to the songs that were embedded in the trees, grass, flowers, animals, and every living thing, placed within them by Abba at Creation to constantly give praise. As I grew older, he had taught me how to sift through the melodies carefully, looking for any aberrations or discordance that could indicate injury or some other hurt. That was what I listened for now. Though I had never faced a magic user or fought spells myself, I knew from my lessons that magic left a taint in the area where it had been practiced, and that it was possible to find this taint even months later if one listened carefully. Or, barring any magic, if a pathway truly was involved, I might find it instead.

After several minutes I came across a melody the like of which I had never heard before. It came to my attention because usually melodies in nature tended to blend together harmoniously, but this one went against the natural musical flow of the grove quite obviously. My first thought was magic. In all the lessons my father and other teachers had given me, they had emphasized that magic could be identified by how it grated against the natural melodies designed by Abba. But as I kept listening, I realized that, despite the seeming discordance, there was another underlying melody like an echo. It did correctly harmonize with the natural melodies, and it seemed to me that I could sing it and correct the discordant melody. So, I started to sing.

Like most Brenwyd songs sung in healing or fighting magic, I didn't sing words, just moved my voice up and down the scales to the correct notes. Curious as to what might happen, I opened my eyes. As I saw what formed in response to my singing, I almost stopped in amazement to gape. Right where I sensed the melody to be, a gap opened in the forest, just like in my dream from that morning. Although, now I could see that "gap" wasn't a very accurate description. It looked much more like a passageway opening in the middle of the forest.

I finished the melody and allowed myself to gasp. *What is that?* Dynin asked.

"I think...it must be a pathway. Lissa was right, this has to be what happened to Rhodri." I felt elated. What a development! Pathways did still exist. So why was it said that they were closed?

I forgot the question as I studied what little I could see through the pathway. On the other side I glimpsed a grass-covered area with a thick hedge of bushes immediately in front that obscured most of my view. Above the tops of the bushes I could make out the heads of people walking by and beyond them...were those buildings? I had never seen such architecture or building materials, let alone anything built that tall except for castle and church towers which these did not look like at all. Whatever they were built with seemed strangely reflective, like it was almost all glass. Was it all glass? How peculiar. However, I didn't have long to look as the gateway closed itself after a few minutes.

I turned with wide eyes to Dynin, who was looking back at me with the horse equivalent of the expression – nostrils wide and flaring, the whites of his eyes showing. *That place smells strange*, he said. *Dangerous.*

"Just because a place smells strange doesn't mean it's dangerous, Dy."

It does not mean it is not, either. He turned so his left side was closest to me, a clear invitation to mount. *Come. We need to go tell the others.*

"Yes, yes, but wait just one more minute. I think I might have heard something as I was singing." It had been when I was almost done with the melody that I had noticed a slight disturbance in the other melodies, something that definitely had not sounded natural. It was very subtle, but it was there. And as I listened to it, I realized that this...this was magic. Unlike the gateway, there was no correct melody hiding behind the chords, and the way it grated against the other melodies in the grove made me grit my teeth. *Alright,* I thought, *now I really need to go get my father.* Magic had indeed been practiced in this grove some time ago. And as I listened, a scene formed in my mind:

I saw Rhodri about to walk from the clearing, presumably to rejoin his companions, when something caught his attention. He turned back in the direction he came from, hand dropping to his sword hilt. His lips moved, but the vision had no sound. Abruptly he drew his sword and stepped forward into a fighting stance, but his sword flew from his hand as if it had a will of its own and he stood as if frozen into a statue. Then came the magic. I couldn't see the wielder, but to the side of Rhodri I saw the passage open. Another figure appeared in my vision, but her back was to me. She made a pushing gesture with her hands and Rhodri flew through the passage, apparently unable to resist. Once he had gone through, the pathway closed.

The vision faded. I blinked as I opened my eyes and the clearing in the here and now reappeared in front of me.

Aislinn? Dynin's voice asked carefully. *Are you alright?*

I nodded slowly. "I Saw what happened to Rhodri. A witch pushed him through the pathway, to the other world." I quickly crossed to Dynin. "We must get back to Kheprah now. Who knows what Rhodri might be going through in that other world? We have to send people after him." But before I could say or do anything more, another vision fell upon me, this one much more intense and all-encompassing. It was so intense, in fact, that for a few brief moments I wondered if I had somehow transferred back to Kheprah without Dynin.

I Saw Lissa sitting on one of the benches in the rose garden, bent over with her hands to her face, her body shaking in silent sobs. Boomer sat in her lap, purring and rubbing his face against hers in comfort. I half-tried to reach out to her, but at that point I fully realized it was a vision, the like of which I had never experienced before, only heard of. It was a waking vision, and Abba only sent such omens to people in times of direst need, when they needed to observe something far from them as it happened. I felt myself quail on the inside as I remembered the fact. What was going on?

A voice entered the vision. "Poor child. You've lost someone you love, haven't you?" It was kind, warm, sympathetic.

Lissa looked up, alarm showing on her face. The speaker was a woman, hair white with age and face lined with wrinkles. But her grey eyes were sharp with intelligence. In her hands she carried a slim wooden box. I felt a bad feeling settle in my stomach at the sight of her.

"Oh...um, yes," Lissa answered, her words halting. Clearly, she was surprised to see someone there whom she didn't know, which made sense, for there were guards posted at the entrances into the rose garden that restricted entry to only the immediate members of the royal family and certain appointed friends, of which this woman was neither.

The woman sat down next to Lissa. She made a motion as if about to take Lissa's hands in a comforting gesture, but Boomer puffed himself out and hissed, so the old woman dropped her hands back into her lap. Boomer's behavior made me feel more on edge. The cat had an uncanny ability for reading people. "I know how it feels, and I know there are no words anyone can say that make it feel any better. In fact, I suspect you're rather tired of people trying to be so kind and considerate, aren't you?"

Lissa, after quelling the cat, looked at the woman with a confused expression, as if trying to place her, but she responded to her words. "Well, yes, to be honest, but they all mean well. They are trying...as best they can." She was taking deep breaths to try and settle herself, though tear tracks were still visible on her face.

"Of course. But with such a grievous loss...they can't really understand, can they? What it's like to feel as if you're missing a piece of your very self?"

Lissa nodded slowly. "You describe it well. Have you, too, lost someone close?"

"Oh, I've lost everyone," the old woman said sadly. "All my family has preceded me to the grave. Call it the curse of old age. But of course, I am old, so it is to be expected. But you...you are so young, your life still ahead of you. This is not the age to be losing people." Lissa's face started to crumple again, though she was obviously trying to maintain her composure. I knew she hated showing such emotion in front of other people, and as a general rule, she couldn't because of her position. She only rarely did so in front of me. The woman moved to embrace her but was again rebuffed by Boomer. He was full-on growling at her now.

"Boomer! That is quite enough," Lissa said. She tried to dislodge him from her lap, but he didn't budge, hooking his claws firmly into her dress. He stared at the old woman with unblinking green eyes, a ferocious expression on his face I had rarely seen. Lissa looked at the woman apologetically. "I am sorry, usually he is very amenable. He is my fiancé's cat, you see, and he has been severely affected by his absence."

"Of course," old woman said agreeably, but I caught an annoyed expression flash across her face. "Cats can be sensitive creatures, I understand. And here I am making you cry again instead of being of help. I do apologize." I was finding this whole situation odder by the minute. The woman should not have been able to enter the garden. That aside, Lissa didn't usually seek solace in strangers. She hadn't even asked the woman's name yet. Nor had the woman offered. And why wasn't Lissa paying attention to Boomer's signals? He clearly sensed something off with the old woman.

Lissa let out a noise that sounded like a feeble attempt at a laugh. "No, please, do not apologize. It is only that you do understand so well, and not many other people do. They...they try but they cannot...they cannot really understand." She blinked and shook her head slightly as if trying to rid herself of an unwanted thought.

The old woman picked up the box and laid it on her lap, in full view of Lissa. "Be that as it may, I must make it up to you for my own sake. And besides, it is still your birthday tomorrow, is it not? One must still find some reason for happiness amid the grief. I doubt your prince would want you to be forever unhappy."

Lissa shook her head, eyes distant in the way they always were when recalling Rhodri. "No...he most certainly would not. One of his favorite things to do is make people laugh."

"Laughter is a valuable gift to have," the old woman agreed. She held up the box, drawing Lissa's attention to it. "Now, I don't know that what I have in here will make you laugh exactly, but I hope you find some joy in it."

Lissa dipped her head in a formal acknowledgment as she took the box from the woman. My bad feeling grew even worse at the sight of the box in her hands. If I had really been in that garden in body, I would have run up to Lissa and torn it away from her. But since only my mind was watching, I could do nothing.

Lissa lifted the lid, and gasped, her lips forming an O of astonishment. "Why, it's lovely! I've never seen a rose that color so full this early in the season. How did you know what my favorite rose color is?" For it was, indeed, a rose in the box, a white rose in full bloom, as if it were summer and not only just turned spring. We had nothing like it in the garden at the moment; all the bushes were bare, trimmed back nearly to the ground to prepare them for the profusion of blooms that would appear in a couple of months. The roses Lissa and I had worked with earlier had all come from the large greenhouse located behind the castle kitchen.

The woman smiled. "Is it really? How wonderful. I had no idea at all. I'm so glad you like it. I've heard of your rose garden here, and I thought that, though I only keep a few bushes, you might accept such a gift."

"Indeed, I will."

At the sight of the rose, my mind flew to my dream from this morning. The woman...the rose...the garden...Lissa...my new knowledge of a witch abroad...*Dear Abba, no!* My instincts started screaming at me to spur Dynin into a gallop and transfer back to Kheprah at all speed, but I was powerless to end the vision and couldn't move until it ended.

Boomer could move, however. With a loud yowl he sprang up and batted the box and rose from Lissa's hands to the ground. He jumped to the ground, kicked it farther away for good measure, then turned toward the woman and began preparing himself to spring at her. Lissa caught him in midair.

"Boomer! For shame. What is wrong with you?" Boomer struggled in her grip, meowing loudly. I could tell he was trying to tell her something was wrong. But Lissa ignored him. "Again, let me express my apologies, mistress. I have no idea what has possessed him." The woman made an appropriate reply, but I could see anger flaring in her eyes, directed at Boomer, as Lissa bent down and picked the rose up with her free hand.

She suddenly let out a cry and released the rose; a bright red bead of blood was forming on her index finger. "Oh, dear me, did I leave a thorn?" The old woman asked. She appeared to ask out of genuine concern, but I thought I caught an almost triumphant look cross her face. "I'm so sorry." Boomer stopped struggling and looked at Lissa in concern.

Lissa smiled, but a wavery one. "No need...It's...easy...to miss the ones...up near the petals." As she spoke, her words became slurred and labored. Her eyes grew wide, as she began to realize that something was amiss, but before she could do anything else her eyes closed and she slumped. Boomer twisted out of her arms as she fell to the ground in a faint. He walked up to her face and batted at it, making a low, worried sound deep in his throat.

I'll admit it, I was not proud of my initial gut reaction. I knew that Lissa had a fairly low pain tolerance (the first time she'd stubbed her toe I had honestly thought she'd broken something), so my first thought was, *Really, Lissa? There's not nearly enough blood to warrant such dramatics.*

Then the woman stood, staring down at Lissa with a definite triumphant look on her face, and a cruel joy lit her eyes and smile. Boomer turned toward her with an angry yowl, springing towards her again with claws extended, but she made a motion with her hand and suddenly Boomer's cry turned to one of pain as he flew through the air in the opposite direction as if being kicked – although nothing had touched him. The woman scowled in his direction. "Disgusting creature. Try to ruin my plan, did you? Foolish. I've come much too far to be stopped by a *cat*." She turned back to Lissa. "Still, that was easy. Princesses are simply so gullible, aren't they?" She sniffed as if in disdain. "Almost takes all the enjoyment out of it, really. Ah, well, soon enough the true challenge will begin."

I barely had time to register the comment before my vision began to change. Instead of viewing Lissa and the woman in the rose garden, I now viewed Kheprah from above, like a bird. But something was dreadfully wrong. The streets that had been so loud and bustling when I had left for the forest mere hours ago started to become silent, as people dropped to the ground in the middle of whatever they were doing and remained there, motionless. I watched with mounting horror and fear as my Sight took me out of Kheprah and to other towns in the kingdoms, and in all of them I saw men, women, children, and even the animals fall over as if in a faint...or dead. Behind it all I could now sense a spell, a huge spell such as I had never imagined being possible, washing over the land and spilling into every nook and cranny like the giant waves that sometimes hit coastal regions after earthquakes. It moved from populated areas and into the forest, coming closer, closer, closer....

Suddenly my vision broke off, and I fell to the ground, abruptly aware of the loud sound of thunder overhead, wind roaring through the trees, and flashes of lightning nearly blinding me. I knew what it was, though I had never seen it before: Creation itself reacting violently to the great torrent of magic loosed upon it. And the storm sounds were coming closer. "No, no, no," I muttered frantically under my breath. "Can't let it catch me. I have to help!" In the background, I was vaguely aware of Dynin whinnying in fright and various forest animals streaking toward me, looking for some safety in the company of a Brenwyd. After several moments of terror that the spell was upon me, I began to register that I felt no sleepier than I had before, and that the storm the spell had triggered calmed as abruptly as it had begun.

I took several deep breaths to steady myself. Around me, I could sense the forest animals that had gathered frantically trying to figure out what had just occurred. Dynin was blowing hard through his nostrils, his every muscle rigid and his eyes rolling so the whites showed. The mouse who had spoken with me earlier had retreated deep into her hole, and now that I had the presence of mind to look about me somewhat calmly, I saw birds, rabbits, squirrels, deer, foxes, a few turtles, and even a couple of bears as part of the animal congregation currently surrounding me.

What just happened? Dynin asked. *Something big just happened. Something with magic.*

I forced my mind to calm, knowing that as I did so the animals around me would also calm. It was hard for me to focus with their panicked thoughts flitting through my head. Most of the rabbits had come close enough to press up against me, and I began to stroke their heads, knowing in this situation that my touching them was acceptable. The motion helped to calm me further as well. "Yes, it did. I saw Lissa in the rose garden. She was crying. Then this woman came upon her, someone I have never seen before. She offered her comfort, and then gave her a box that had a rose. Lissa took it, and she pricked her finger on a thorn. As soon as she did that, she lost consciousness and fell over, like she fainted. Then I saw this...fainting spell, whatever it is, spread into Kheprah, and then across Ecclesia. It entered the forest, but then...it stopped before it got here, thank Abba, though I don't know why. Maybe she hadn't the energy to push it farther."

Maybe it could not cross your border, a hawk suggested from his perch almost directly above my head. He was trying to appear completely unaffected by the events of the past few minutes, but the image was ruined by the way his feathers kept fluffing up. *Your kingdom's territory ends some wingbeats away.*

I considered the idea. "It is possible, I suppose. I've always thought this grove was technically in Darlesia."

But what will you do now? a rabbit asked. *I have family on that side. Can you wake them?*

I...I don't know. In fact, I very much doubted it. The spell was very powerful, and I was not, by Brenwyd terms. For one, I was only half Brenwyd. For another, I was an alto, and the more powerful Brenwyd women tended to be sopranos with their higher range. And, last but most definitely not least, I had never dealt with magic, real magic, in my life. Yes, I had learned my lessons as well as anyone, but I had never used them in a real situation, and had always imagined that when and if I did, I would have others to help me. But now...was everyone in the kingdom dead? My throat closed at the thought and I rejected it desperately. *Abba, what do I do?*

Girl, we should go to Darlesia. Get help from there. If the spell stopped at the borders, the other kingdoms should be unaffected, Dynin suggested, nudging my shoulder. It made sense, of course. But as I pondered the idea, I knew I couldn't go just yet.

No. I took a breath and looked at all the frightened animals around me. I hoped fervently that I sounded braver to them than I felt. *I will go back to Kheprah and see what really happened, what damage the spell caused, gather information. Based on what I find there, I...I will try to break the spell, or go for help.*

Spying on a Sorceress

I studied the city from the cover of a small stand of trees half a mile from the walls. Even at this distance, normally I should have heard noises from the lively capital. But now, everything was quiet, eerily so, with the late afternoon shadows starting to stretch across the landscape and not a single bird's song winging through the air. There wasn't even any wind breaking the stillness, as if nature had summoned all its strength for its initial stormy protestation but now was as ensnared by the spell as everything else. I took a breath to steady my nerves and cautiously reached out to listen with my song sense, praying I would at least still hear the songs of the animals and people I knew were nearby, and fearing more than anything that I would not. To my relief, the melodies and harmonies I was looking for reached my mind and, though distorted due to the spell, never had any music sounded so sweet. Everyone was still alive. Encouraged on this point, I dismounted.

Dynin, stay here. I can move around undetected more easily without you. I began to move off, trying to leave before he could raise much of a protest. The effort was in vain.

You are not going there alone, Dynin said, grabbing my tunic sleeve between his teeth. *Who will guard your back?*

I will, Dy, and I have to. With you along, I'll never sneak up on her. I'll be careful, I promise. It will only be a reconnaissance trip. She might even have left. I would much rather have taken him along, but I needed to be quieter than quiet, and despite Dynin's many sterling qualities, stealth wasn't one of them.

And she might have not. What then? I will not have you killed in a battle.

I don't want to be killed in a battle, either. But I need to gather information, and the only way to do that is to go into the city. I love you, Dy, and there's no one I'd rather have by my side in a fight, but you would just be too conspicuous. I'm sorry, but I must go alone. I made my mental voice firm, hoping to reassure him.

He stared at me. *Promise me you will not fight her. Not unless forced. You have never encountered anything magical before. It would not be wise to try and pit yourself against something of this scale alone.*

I looked at him. On a logical level, I quite agreed with his reasoning. The mere thought of encountering this powerful sorceress in a head-to-head confrontation made my limbs feel shaky – and yet. I was a half-Brenwyd, and I had been trained on how to fight magic and its wielders my whole life. I had always longed for an opportunity to prove myself, had sometimes wished the times I lived in were not quite so peaceful. I wanted adventure, excitement, to feel like I really accomplished something with my life. Now the chance was here and, despite my fear, I could feel a slight bloom of excitement along with it. If a real chance to take out the witch presented itself...could I really ignore it?

Aislinn. Dynin saying my name recalled me to his presence. He only ever really said my name when he was being very serious. *Killing yourself trying to help will not help anyone. If you know she is too strong for you, promise me you will come back here, and we will go for help from Darlesia.*

"Dynin-"

Promise. He kept a firm grip on my tunic, and I knew there would be no pacifying him. He did have a point, I admitted. If I died fighting the witch, then when would help come for Ecclesia?

"Very well, I promise," I told him. "I won't fight her if can help it. I'm afraid that's the best I can do, Dy."

He released my tunic begrudgingly. *Alright. Be careful.*

"I will be." I drew an arrow from my quiver and set it on my bow. I crept toward the city, moving quickly but silently. As I walked, I prayed silently, reciting verses from Abba's Word. It helped my mind stay calm despite my elevated heartbeat, and I knew I needed to remain calm to concentrate on keeping quiet. The familiar phrases heartened me, and my fear began to recede somewhat.

The gates were still open and I slipped inside, grateful to once more be in the cover of a shadow. However, I did almost trip over one of the collapsed guardsmen lying in said shadow. Steadying my stance, I looked down. It was a man I recognized, Rhyan, I thought his name was. He had waved a cheerful salute to me on my way out earlier. Wanting to confirm what my song-sense had already told me, I knelt by him and placed two fingers at his throat to feel for a pulse. It thrummed clear and strong against my fingertips. My next step was to shake him in an effort to wake him up. Despite my best efforts, the man remained unconscious, even when out of desperation I eventually kicked him. The only thing that did was further bruise my already tender toe.

So, the spell only put everyone to sleep, I mused as I rose and began to slip through the streets to the castle. Indeed, now that I knew what it was, I could hear all the rustlings and whisperings of the sleepers breathing in and out, and even some snores. But why? What purpose could this serve? What in the Five Realms was this witch's grudge against Ecclesia? Was the spell designed to be permanent or only temporary? I supposed that, since the witch had seemed quite old, she might have been defeated by Ecclesian Brenwyds some years ago and now sought revenge. But still, against the whole kingdom? And what did this have to do with Rhodri? Not to mention, I would surely have heard stories about such a woman being defeated fifty to seventy years ago, but no stories stood out to me as likely candidates.

These questions occupied me on my trip through Kheprah's side streets and back alleys as I made my way to the castle. I was glad of it, for it helped distract me a bit from the strangeness of my surroundings. Usually, Kheprah was buzzing with activity. Just now was the time of day that merchants would start to pack up their wares and make their way home for the night, while wives and servants began preparing dinner. Not so now. I stopped occasionally to reposition people lying in uncomfortable or awkward positions, but kept up a quick pace and soon reached the castle.

I didn't approach the castle by the main entrance; instead, I opted for a smaller, lesser- known door in the wall separating the castle complex from the city that was often used by servants or food sellers going to and from the kitchen. It was open. A man I recognized as the man Maude bought many of her vegetables from had clearly been on his way out when the spell hit and now his body acted as a doorstop. I moved past him and peered cautiously inside. There was still no sound except for people breathing and snoring. Satisfied that if the witch was still about, she wasn't anywhere in my immediate vicinity, I took the time to drag the vegetable man from the doorway and laid him along the wall instead – something that required a fair bit of effort on my part, as he had a rather large girth. As I dragged him to his new position, I marveled at how deeply he slept; he nary twitched an eyelid.

Since I was close to the kitchen entrance, I decided to enter the castle that way and use the servant passageways, designed to let people move about unnoticed, to check the castle over for the witch and find out what I could about this spell. As I approached the kitchen, delicious smells filled my nostrils and for a moment it was as if everything was normal. But then I detected a burned tinge to the odors, something the fastidious Maude would never allow in her kitchen. I saw Maude herself almost right away upon entering the kitchen, slumped over a batch of dough she had obviously been in the middle of kneading for bread. I put my bow and arrow down on a table as I set about securing the kitchen. Several fires were burning, and I put them out, worried that with no one tending them they would escape their hearths and set the castle on fire. Then, as I had done in the city, I moved people into more comfortable positions. As I was rearranging a couple of little servant girls, I looked up and saw Aiden with his head on the counter. My throat constricted and I felt my heart thud almost painfully inside my chest. Up to this point, I had forcefully ignored how the sight of my home city asleep was affecting me. But this I could not push away. This was my baby brother, caught in the clutches of a spell like everyone else, and I was alone. Knowing it would do no good, I still couldn't help shaking his shoulder.

"Aiden? Aiden, can you hear me? Wake up. Please." Of course, he didn't respond. He just remained sitting there with his head on the table with an unconcerned look on his face. He had probably come to the kitchen to wheedle treats from Maude. Being Maude's official taste-tester for feasts was a highly prized position among the younger residents of the castle. I decided to try and wake him. Perhaps, if I couldn't break the whole spell myself (which I knew I couldn't just by the sheer size of the thing) it would be possible to wake individual people. If so, I could wake key people – my parents, the king and queen, Lissa, some other Brenwyds – who could then figure out what to do next.

Hopeful, I listened for the spell. I found it easily and it was so loud and overpowering that I recoiled mentally and shut off my sense, gasping. When I had collected myself, I tried again, more cautiously this time. But as I listened, I grew dismayed, my hope vanishing like morning mist in the sun's heat. The spell grated in my mind, full of discord, and seemed to spill over in all directions like a snarled ball of yarn. It was far beyond my abilities. As my father had drilled into my head again and again, fighting magic could be quite risky for Brenwyds. If they set themselves against a magic too strong for them, the energy and effort required to defeat it would drain them completely of vigor and end in death. I had no wish to chance such a thing. This spell was made of well-nurtured hate, malice, and cunning, and it told me I could in no way defeat this sorceress by myself. She had more power than I had ever dreamed a witch could have. The bit of excitement and courage within me at the chance to actually battle magic withered like a rose bush in a frost, and the full impact of the situation hit me. This was no minor spell cast by a middling magician that would be easy for me to break as a first true test. This was something that experienced Brenwyds would likely wish to never encounter.

I sat down. Though I tried to fight them, tears began to leak slowly from my eyes onto my cheeks. *So much for dreams of heroics*, I thought somewhat bitterly. I lifted my gaze skyward. "Abba, why is this happening? Why did you let this happen? Why am I the only one to escape? What good can I do? I can't defeat this spell. You must know that. Father says you have a plan for everything. Is this one of your plans? What for? Why was there no warning? Why? *Why?*" I demanded, anguished, but also a bit angry. Surely Abba could have left the realm more equipped to deal with this sort of attack, or sent more warning instead of just a vague dream to a young half-Brenwyd girl who had never fought any sort of magic before. He was our Maker, our Father, who works in everything for our good. What was so good about this?

My demands got no answer, but when my initial burst of anger flared out, I forced myself to breathe more deeply and calm myself. *You must be able to control your emotions in a combat situation*, I heard my father's voice echo in my head. *Emotions will lie to you and cause you to make mistakes. Breathe deeply. Trust your training, trust your instincts, and trust Abba. Then make the best decision you can.* Trust. Trust was key. This was a test, I slowly realized, a test of faith. I knew my lessons from the Word. The people Abba chose for tasks never had easy ones. He always gave them things they couldn't accomplish without His help. That was faith, as my mother had told me many times: trusting that Abba did truly know what was best, and making the choice to believe all His promises and act as one knew was right even when everything was hopeless.

"I'm sorry, Abba," I whispered. "But please, help me. Help me keep believing. I can't do it on my own." I received no obvious answer, but slowly a peace entered my soul and calmed my emotions. I remembered a verse I had always particularly liked from the book of Joshua, when Abba (or Yahweh, as the Israelites called him) spoke to that great leader before commanding them to go to Jericho: "Haven't I commanded you: be strong and courageous? Do not be afraid or discouraged, for the LORD your God is with you wherever you go."

"Be strong and courageous," I whispered aloud. "Be strong and courageous." As I repeated the phrase, I felt a bit of courage rise up in me again. I was not alone. Abba was with me, and I would stand on that promise with all I had. To do otherwise would be to surrender to despair, and if I did that the battle was over before I even started to fight. Aiden stirred slightly, and the movement brought me back to the reality of the kitchen.

With my personal crisis resolved, at least for the moment, I realized that I needed to listen to the spell again, more carefully this time, so that I could tell the Darlesian Brenwyds exactly what to expect and how it might best be accomplished. That was the whole point of my current excursion, I reminded myself. Gather information on the spell so I can tell the others. I could do that. I'd trained for it. So, I listened again.

This time, I could paint a mental picture of the spell in my mind as I followed the discordant melodies and harmonies with my song-sense in a way that seemed almost tangible. It was like an untended rose bush, I decided. It went out wildly in all directions in a tangled mass of thorns and branches, but I slowly realized that there was one main melody that underlay it all and traced back to a particular starting point, like the main stem meeting the roots of the plant. If one could undercut and break that main melody, I thought, then the whole spell would die and everyone would wake. The small amount of courage that had entered my heart earlier grew and became accompanied by a strong sense of hope. No, I could not defeat this spell myself. But if I gathered more Brenwyds and we all bent our energies to defeating that main branch of the spell, we could break it. I was sure of it. *Thank you, Abba.*

I placed a light kiss on Aiden's brow and walked from the kitchen into the rest of the castle. Though I now had the information on the spell I needed, I still wanted to do a quick survey of the castle. It would also be useful to be able to tell the Darlesian Brenwyds exactly where certain people were, like Lissa and her parents. And I did need to determine if the witch was still in the castle. If she was, I would try to get to Darlesia and rally at least a Brenwyd company of twenty as quickly as Dynin could run, on the chance we might still catch the witch before she left Kheprah. And if she was not...well, then I would have to figure out where she had come from. *And,* I thought with a further frown, *I need to determine what in the Five Realms her purpose was in sending Rhodri through a gateway.* In the chaos of the last hour, I had nearly forgotten about him. Although, I had thought that the vague image of the woman I had seen pushing him through the gateway had indicated a younger woman, not one as old as the woman who had been with Lissa in the garden. Could there be two witches working together? That might explain why the spell was so powerful.

I was so busy mulling thoughts about in my head regarding the witch that I briefly forgot that I was looking for her, and consequently, I drew up short as I neared one of the servant entrances to the great hall and heard someone speaking.

Idiot! I chastised myself. I crept to the door cautiously, straining my ears, and dared to take a peek through the partly open gap.

There she was. She stood at the far end of the hall by the royal thrones, looking immensely pleased with herself, and she held something in front of her that she placed on the floor as I watched. It looked like a mirror. I felt my brow furrow slightly in puzzlement. What good was a mirror when laying a curse like this? A mirror...a memory began to stir in my mind, a story I had heard many times before. Before I could think too hard on it, she spoke again, the same litany I had heard before, for I recognized the cadence of it, though not the words themselves. Before, I had assumed it was because of the distance and barriers between us. But now, I realized that she was reciting a spoken spell in a tongue unknown to me. The words hurt my ears and reverberated around the room, words full of dark power that almost seemed to settle in the hall's corners as deep shadows.

Smoke billowed up from the mirror and fanned out into a circle, turning to grey, then white, then clear, like a bigger version of the mirror. Her voice changed, and now she spoke in the common tongue, chanting.

"Master of Darkness, heed my call,
The fools have fallen, one and all
The kingdom is now ready for you
Come and let us claim our dues."

The hall darkened, and my skin crawled. Whatever she was doing and whoever she was calling, it was evil. The clear fog darkened as well, and a figure appeared in it. It was a dark, nebulous figure, the outline never clearly defined for all the swirling darkness, but it was big, and I thought I made out two wing-like shapes behind it. The figure's eyes were clearly defined and burned red like fire. I trembled, a cold sweat breaking out on my body. I knew that one wrong move now would mean my death. *Abba, protect me,* I prayed, instinctively crossing myself as well.

The figure spoke, and the voice was surprising melodious and pleasant to listen to. He must have a wonderful singing voice, I thought abstractedly. "You have been successful? Ecclesia sleeps?"

"Yes, my lord," the woman said. "As I suspected, it was rather too easy for someone of my talents. The loss of her precious fiancé made the princess vulnerable to manipulation." She snorted derisively. "Though I believe she would have done anything for the rose. The centuries of security have made the people much too trusting."

"As we planned," the figure said. "To get what we want, we have to be very careful. No more mistakes." His tone held a firm note of warning.

The witch bristled. "Of course not, my lord. I learned from last time. No big battles. To achieve our goal, we must be discreet."

"Yes. You must take no chances. Now, are you certain all the Brenwyds have been ensnared? What about the Brenwyds who were traveling to bring guests for the festivities?"

"Yes, my lord. Everyone within the kingdom's boundaries sleeps. Once the princess pricked her finger, there was no escape. And the reason I waited so long in the day was to be sure all those Brenwyds were back. My informant within the court assured me they were."

"And you trust him?"

"Yes. Because I also kept watch. They had all returned, with the guests in tow. And he had a very good incentive to be truthful. I told him that if he helped me, I would spare him and his family from the curse." She had an informant within the court? Who would possibly provide a witch with information in Kheprah's court?

"Ah. And where are they?"

"Sleeping. He was a fool to really think I would let a few people go untouched."

"Indeed. And you're certain the fiancé will not be a problem?"

I blinked. Why would Rhodri be a problem? He couldn't break spells. He wasn't a Brenwyd. The woman laughed. "Perfectly certain, my lord. The dear prince is struggling now on Earth, and it would require a Brenwyd to open the portal. As you know, Brenwyds were driven to extinction in that realm centuries ago, and here they believe the pathways no longer exist." I felt my eyes widen. Yes, I had found that strange melody in the forest and assumed it was a pathway, especially given my brief vision, but to hear actual confirmation of it was something else again, even if from an evil sorceress.

"Hmm. It might have been better to kill him. Your information about Brenwyds on Earth is outdated, Morrian. There is one. She killed a powerful servant of mine several years ago."

The woman was quiet for a few minutes, and I saw her shoulders tense. "I was unaware of that, my lord. But Earth is vast, and I sent him there six months ago. I plan to bring him back so he can see his beloved and her kingdom die before I kill him. I want them both to see how flimsy love is." Her voice was venomous.

The smoky figure laughed. "Flimsy, Morrian? You seem to forget how a mere kiss became your undoing all those years ago. If you're not careful, it could happen again. Love is ever our enemy."

"I remember it well, my lord. Don't worry; there is no one to get him or warn him. And besides, I designed this curse to be self-sustaining after the first few hours. After that time, even if he somehow gets back and kisses her, only she would awaken. I did not make this curse for it to be broken so easily."

The figure laughed again. "Ah, Morrian, I should not have doubted you. You are a loyal servant. So, is it time to call forth my legions to conquer this world? You have prepared everything admirably."

"Not quite yet, my lord. I was quite particular about timing in the design of the curse. In a month, those caught in it will wake, but they will wake disoriented and sick, and the Brenwyds will be powerless. Then your legions will come and conquer this land, while the Brenwyds watch helplessly. Once entrenched here, the other kingdoms will easily fall." It took everything in my power to keep from gasping. How was it possible such a plan and spell could have come into being without being noticed? Had we really grown so blind? Why hadn't Abba told us? My doubt started growing again.

"Why a month? That runs a great risk of discovery, especially considering how many foreign nobles are here."

"There are many powerful Brenwyds here, my lord. The curse needs time to work and draw all their power from them, or we will fail. But the month also gives us time to gather our forces. And don't worry about the other countries noticing. I kept any other monarchs from attending, and they will soon be too busy with problems in their own countries to worry about others. I will wake the ancient monsters and activate my servants in the other realms. And I will set up a barrier around Ecclesia's borders to keep everyone out."

"Good. Do not fail me, Morrian. The consequences would be most unpleasant. I've waited a long time for this opportunity and would hate to be disappointed. Again." The words were spoken in a seemingly mild manner, but there was a coldness underneath that caused me to shudder.

"I will not disappoint you, my lord, have no fear," Morrian vowed.

"And take off that revolting disguise. I would much prefer to look at your beauty." His voice had lowered and become seductive.

"As you wish, my lord." Her tone matched his. She muttered a few words, there was a brief flash, and when my vision cleared, she was taller, her face was young and her hair had become a rich black that fell to her waist in curling waves. Her skin was quite pale, like someone who lived in one of the northern countries. All in all, she was a very striking woman.

The figure smiled. "Ah, the centuries have not diminished your beauty, Morrian. You should visit me more often."

"It would be my pleasure, my lord," Morrian said. "But I must go now to lay the barrier."

"Report back to me when you do." The figure disappeared and the smoke grew clear once more. I was trembling violently, and my heart was pounding so hard I was surprised she didn't hear it. Could this be true? Was I having a nightmare? I pinched my arm. No. Definitely awake. But now what should I do? It seemed that going for help was the only option, but who was the smoky figure? And who was this Morrian? Had that figure implied she'd been alive for centuries? How was that possible? Morrian spoke the strange words again, and another image formed in the smoke.

I saw a young man standing in a room behind an odd-looking counter. The whole room looked strange, really, completely covered in white with lots of people in unfamiliar clothes standing around or sitting on stool-chair things that were white and silver. Honestly, the whole room seemed excessively bright. However, I quickly shifted my focus from the room as a whole to the young man behind the counter. My view of his face had been obscured by a woman standing in front of him, who had just moved away with a small container in her hand that clearly had food in it, as she started to eat whatever it was with a spoon. Now, with the clear view of his face...I had to stifle another gasp. It was Rhodri, clearly alive and well, but I recognized the sadness in his hazel eyes. I'd seen it countless times over the last few months on Lissa's face. His brown hair was cut short, and he was wearing clothes that in general style matched what everyone else in the room wore.

Morrian laughed. "Well, well, my young prince, how is life on Earth going for you?" she said softly. "How ironic. The prince forced to play the servant. Well, that will end before the month is up, and then you shall wish for it." She waved her hand through the smoke and it dissipated. She picked up the mirror, put it back in her pack, said more of those strange words, took a hold of her cloak, spun in a circle – and vanished.

I remained behind the door, trembling, for another five minutes. I finally forced myself to my feet, supporting myself with the door, and stumbled into the hall. My thoughts were whirling around my head like a hurricane. I braced myself against a table and took some deep breaths to try and calm myself, despite having just heard someone planning the end of my country. And quite possibly my whole world. I definitely had to go and get more Brenwyds. As quickly as possible, and much faster than dragonflight. But I found myself sliding into a chair, and realized that sitting outside the door listening had seriously drained me. I would take a few minutes to recover, I decided. Organize my thoughts. Figure out a way to explain things as quickly as possible to the Darlesian Brenwyds. But where in Darlesia to go? My father had many friends around the capital and in the king's court, but it would take precious time for me to get to them and explain the situation. And hadn't Morrian said that she would put some sort of barrier around Ecclesia to prevent other people from coming? Time was a resource I did not have.

I decided it would be quicker to go to Rhodri's father's lands and contact the Brenwyds there. My father had a good friend there, a Sir Eiwas, who also knew me. And since this Morrian was the witch responsible for Rhodri's disappearance, his father would waste no time sending messages to the Brenwyds in his lands and gathering them. Yes, that would likely be the best course. But as I sat there, I remembered how both Morrian and the shadowy figure had concerns that Rhodri might foil their scheme. Morrian had sent Rhodri to the other world, Earth, because of them. How had Morrian known of the portal? Why was she so set against Ecclesia? What could Rhodri, who was completely non-Brenwyd, do to disrupt the spell? What was it Morrian had said he'd do? A kiss?

My mind stilled as things began clicking into place. A powerful witch, with a mirror. A magic mirror. The figure mentioned how love had defeated her once before. She sent Rhodri away...so he couldn't kiss Lissa. I realized why the elements seemed familiar. The story was one every Ecclesian learned in childhood: the story of Nivea, one of our greatest rulers who had reigned two hundred and fifty years ago. Her mother had died birthing her, and her father had later remarried a beautiful woman who'd turned out to be an evil sorceress, a sorceress reputed to have a magic mirror that showed her things happening all over the kingdom. Nivea's stepmother had tried to kill her multiple times, once by ordering a huntsman to kill her and once by poisoning her into an enchanted sleep leading to death, a spell that had only been broken...by true love's kiss. Nivea had gone on to defeat the evil queen...who, according to history, had drowned. But had they actually retrieved her body from the river to confirm that?

Oh, please, Aislinn, I told myself. *Even if she wasn't killed, that was over two hundred years ago. She'd be long dead by now, anyway.* I frowned, my mind continuing to work. *But if that shadowy figure is her master...had that been the Shadow Angel? He had implied she'd survived for centuries.* My blood ran cold as I considered the possibility that I had just seen the Lord of Evil and Darkness. I was grateful I hadn't thought of that possibility at the time. *He might be able to grant his followers long life, mightn't he? Or is this witch simply copying the methods used by the evil queen?*

"Grindles and spindles," I whispered. "I've got to get Rhodri back here." That much seemed clear. If, *if* by some incredible chance Morrian was the queen from Nivea's day or a copycat, and if the sleeping spell was similar to the one used on Nivea, true love's kiss could break it. I knew from my lessons that the shadowy figure had been right about one thing: love was a powerful thing. Darkness didn't understand it, because the Dark Angel's servants were inherently selfish, and love made one act selflessly. Then I recalled something else: Morrian had intimated that if Rhodri kissed Lissa awake soon enough, the whole spell would break. But only if he got to her soon.

Galvanized by the thought, I jumped to my feet. I had a direction. I would go back to the forest clearing, open the pathway, find Rhodri, and bring him back to break the spell. Morrian didn't know I was still awake. She would be taken completely by surprise. And once the spell was broken, the Brenwyds of Ecclesia could gather, fight her, and defeat her. A relieved smile curved my lips upward. *Praise Abba. There is a way out of this.*

I ran from the hall, but when I exited, I hesitated a moment, then turned so I walked, not toward the castle entrance, but in the opposite direction. I wanted to check on one more thing before I left.

I opened the door to the rose garden. It had been created in an interior courtyard of the castle, and the roof was open to the sky to allow the sun and rain to fall into it. It was shaped in a circle and was completely private, for no windows from surrounding hallways opened into it. It was part of why Lissa and I liked it so much. The queen had allowed the two of us full reign over the design of the garden, and we had decided on a spiral that ended in the center with a small gazebo surrounded by rosebushes of several different colors that the gardeners had created. The other rosebushes in the garden were aligned so that the palest roses in colors of red, pink, yellow, white, and purple surrounded the exterior of the spiral. As the walkway circled toward the gazebo, the rose colors gradually increased in intensity so that the ones in the center bloomed in full saturation. It greatly pleased my artist eye.

Right now, however, my eyes went straight to where Lissa lay just as I had seen her in my vision, collapsed across the garden walkway halfway into the spiral, an arm stretched into the dirt. "Oh, Liss," I murmured. "Why did you do it?" Her face was calm, but her brow was slightly wrinkled, like she sensed something was wrong. I wished I could take her up to her bed, but I couldn't carry her that far. And I didn't have much time. The witch hadn't given an exact timeline, just mentioned "the first few hours," and who knew how long it would take me to find Rhodri in this other world? So I got her up onto the garden bench, retrieved some pillows from a couch to put under her head, and arranged her as comfortably as I could.

Then I searched farther down the path, looking in the bushes until I saw a still, grey lump. I picked Boomer up, checking him for injuries. He slept like everything else, but in listening to his song below the spell I heard discordance. It seemed the force the witch had used to swat him aside had broken ribs. "You brave cat," I murmured. "I'm sorry I wasn't here to translate for you. You did your best." I healed him as much as I could, considering the spell, and took him to Lissa, tucking him close to her side as I knew he often slept. These duties completed, I left the garden to go back to Dynin.

As I walked, I mulled over the image of Rhodri in my mind, trying to pick out any clues that might help me locate him in the other realm. He had been wearing a single white tunic, and beige breeches, though in quite a different style than any I had seen before. Instead of the tunic falling past the waistband of his breeches, the tunic looked tucked into them, and there had been no overshirt or doublet. He had seemed to be working in some merchant's store, but I had seen no clues in the brief image I'd seen that might help me find it. As I crossed the castle courtyard, I decided to make a quick detour to my house. I had painted a small portrait of Rhodri before he left six months earlier at Lissa's request, but with his subsequent disappearance I had kept it in my studio, fearing it would upset Lissa further. Now, I thought it could be helpful in locating him. Hopefully, he would not have traveled far from where the pathway opened in the other world and I would be able to ask after him in the nearest village or town.

I opened the door to my house and ran to my studio. I opened the trunk where I kept finished parchment paintings and dug through it. There! I fished the small piece of parchment from the trunk and placed it in my pocket. As I went back through my room, a thought struck me and I crossed to my wardrobe instead of the door. I opened it and looked through my clothes, trying to see if there was something that looked more like the clothes I had seen than what I was currently wearing. It had seemed to me when I watched through the mirror that I had seen such clothes somewhere before...though, clearly, I concluded several minutes later, not in my closet. Then where? I sighed and closed the doors, leaving the room. No matter. Hopefully my clothes would not be strange enough to incite comment. I frowned. What if there were laws against women wearing breeches? While there were no such laws in the Five Kingdoms anymore, per se, I knew that the older, more traditional kingdoms tended to frown heavily on the practice. Perhaps I should change into a dress. But that could hamper my movement if I ran into trouble. I would find a hat, I decided, and stuff my hair up into it. My father had one that might work.

I walked down the hall to my parents' bedroom. No one was in it. No one would be in mid-afternoon. Both my parents served in the castle — my father as one of the king's advisors and my mother as an aide to the queen. Their bedchamber had an actual closet attached to it, and I took a breath before entering it, memories of previous trips to the room coming to the front of my mind. When I was younger, I used to come watch my mother dress for balls before I was old enough to attend them myself. I'd loved watching her brush her long, dark blond hair and she had let me help pick out her jewelry and gown. I smiled slightly as I remembered how proud I had felt to dive into the midst of Mother's clothes in search of the perfect dress for the occasion, and I ran a hand over the gowns now in remembrance as I scanned the other side of the closet looking for the hat I had in mind. I was sure it was in here somewhere. "Where did you leave it, Father?" I murmured under my breath.

The next moment, my toe connected with something hard for the third time that day and I tripped over a small wooden trunk jutting out from the wall into the center of the closet. "Ouch!" I yelped, reaching a hand down to massage my foot. "Not my day to be graceful, apparently. Maybe Lissa did jinx me." I frowned at the offending trunk. "And what business do you have in the middle of a closet where people can trip over you?" Predictably, the trunk didn't answer. However, my frown turned from one of annoyance to one of thoughtfulness as I studied it. The trunk was my mother's, containing belongings of hers from before she had married my father, and I had often come across it in my hunts through the closet for gowns. I had only opened it once, and what I had found inside...Suddenly I remembered why the clothes Rhodri and the other people I had seen in Morrian's mirror had worn seemed familiar. I hastily opened the trunk now and smiled at what I found, though it also puzzled me.

Clothes. Foreign clothes, the like of which were not worn anywhere in Niclausia. There was an ash grey, collared tunic with very short sleeves made of a soft fabric I didn't recognize which buttoned up the front, and breeches that were dark blue, made of a stiff-feeling fabric with small pockets in the front and a couple of larger ones in the back. Instead of the loose bags of fabric sewn inside clothing, the pockets were small and tightly sewn on the outside of the pants. They didn't look very useful to me; I doubted one could fit more than a couple of small items inside them. And they weren't the only clothes in the trunk. There were several other tunics of various colors and patterns that were unfamiliar to me, more breeches, though I was shocked to see that some of them were extremely short and when worn would only cover one's leg down to mid-thigh. I could not imagine my mother ever wearing something so revealing, but I knew all these things belonged to her. I remembered now that, one day when I was helping her dress, I had come across the trunk and decided to open it out of curiosity. I had pulled several of the garments out to show her. Her eyes had widened and she'd quickly repacked the clothes in the trunk and closed it. She had said that the clothes were from her youth, and that it served no purpose in bringing them out again. Then she'd sent me to my room. At the time I had been rather upset with her, but now I realized that the emotion that had crossed her face back then had been pain. But why did my mother have these clothes? Had she known that the pathways were still open? And she couldn't have been the only one, I realized. She wasn't Brenwyd. She'd have needed someone else to open them for her. My father must have known. Why hadn't they said anything when Rhodri went missing?

Well, Aislinn, if you want to ever ask them about it, you need to stop standing around asking yourself questions and get moving, I told myself sternly. I grabbed the gray-colored tunic and one of the pairs of blue breeches and changed into them. Fortunately, my mother and I were about the same size.

The breeches were stiff, but no doubt I would get used to them. The tunic was shorter than any I had ever worn, just coming past my waist, and did nothing to hide how the pants clung to my thighs, which made me a little uncomfortable. The absence of the usual layers I dressed in also added to my discomfort, so I rummaged around in the trunk for other clothing items. I found something I initially took to be a shawl, but it had buttons on the front of it and sleeves and was made of woven wool. Since it was still early spring in Ecclesia and it was clearly some sort of warm garment, I decided to wear it as well, in case the other world was chilly. I didn't know what kind of shoes they wore in the other realm, so my boots would have to do, and I pulled the leg of the breeches over the part of the boot that came up my leg.

Thus attired, I looked down at myself. While somewhat similar to what I usually wore, everything as a whole was tighter-fitting and just felt foreign and strange. "Get over it, Aislinn," I told myself aloud. "It's only to find Rhodri. It will be fine." Recalling my original reason for entering the closet, I started looking again for the hat and found it behind the trunk. Moving out of the closet, I twisted my braid up on top of my head and pulled the hat on over it. I surveyed the result in the bedroom mirror and frowned. I went back into the closet and found a baggier tunic to put on. Now I looked more convincingly boyish. Recalling what Morrian had mentioned about Brenwyds being extinct in that realm (which wasn't very reassuring) I found a strip of cloth from my mother's sewing basket and tied it around my head to conceal my pointed ears. It looked a bit strange, but the hat covered most of it. I also grabbed a bag to pack my regular clothes in, and a small dagger that belonged to my father that I could hide under the tunic, since the sleeves on this one came down to my wrists and fit loosely. Thus prepared, I went from the house and made my way back to Dynin. As I went back through the silent city, I looked at the sun's position in the sky and was relieved to see it wasn't as late as I had thought it was. That meant I had more time to spare looking for Rhodri.

Dynin nickered in relief when he saw me. *What have you been doing?* he asked.

"Eavesdropping, mainly. I heard the witch talking with someone she called her lord, and she's planning to take over the kingdom and kill everyone! The sleep is to drain all the Brenwyds of their power, and she's the one who made Rhodri disappear. But I found out where he is, so we're going after him. He'll be able to help." I realized my words didn't make too much sense, but Dynin didn't question it. What he did question were my clothes. (I love my horse, but sometimes he gets hung up on the littlest things. Animals think humans somewhat strange for wearing clothes anyway, but really, the kingdom is in mortal peril and he questions my attire?)

What are you wearing? It smells strange. It looks strange, too.

"Some clothes from Mother's closet that I think they wear in the other realm. I want to be inconspicuous." I mounted. "Now we've got to go back to the mushroom grove, and quick. Morrian said something about throwing up a barrier around the kingdom to keep people out."

Is this other realm safe? Can I come with you?

"I don't know. But let us go! If there is any hope of breaking the curse soon, I have to find Rhodri and get him back here as soon as possible." I kicked him to get his attention, and he took off. A minute later we were back on the road near the mushroom grove. I guided Dynin back through the trees until we reached the pathway location. I dismounted, shouldered my bag, and went to stand in front of the passage, wasting no time in singing to reopen it. Once again, the narrow pathway opened in the forest glade and I saw the other world through it. Dynin moved to be behind me, and I sensed his intention to follow. I knew he wouldn't like what I was about to say.

"Dynin," I said, a sudden thought grabbing my focus, "I need to be able to move around without attracting undue attention. It might be best for you to stay here. A horse tends to attract attention anywhere."

He snorted his displeasure. *And who will look after you?*

"Myself. It shouldn't take long. It can't take too long if we want this curse broken today. Once I go through, I'll Search for Rhodri. I doubt he'll have traveled far from the portal opening, not if he's been hoping for us to find the pathway and then find him. Once I find him, we'll come right back through the portal." I put a hand on his warm neck, taking a bunch of his mane into my hand and squeezing it. I gave his muzzle a kiss. "You wait right here. I shan't take any longer than I have to." And then, before he could put up any objection – or my resolve could falter – I stepped into the pathway.

ANOTHER WORLD

Going through the pathway did not, in truth, feel too strange. It was as if I was going through one of the many doorways at the castle, though I did feel as if I had traveled a great distance in a few short steps, which was a bit disconcerting. The only odd thing was, as I passed through, I heard a lot of indecipherable chatter in languages I didn't recognize. It was a shock to me, because across Niclausia there was only one spoken tongue. I had heard in the old histories that there had been several different languages spoken originally when the first people came to Niclausia, but over time one common one had developed, though there were still regional dialects. I hadn't even considered the possibility that people in the old world might speak a different language. What if I couldn't make it out at all? As I continued through the passage, though, the words slowed down and I found I was starting to understand them, though they still sounded foreign.

Just as the words began to settle comfortably in my ears, I emerged on the other end of the gateway. I stumbled a couple of steps and braced myself against a tree, feeling a touch disoriented. I looked behind me in time to see the pathway closing and caught a brief glimpse of Dynin waiting on the other side. Then it vanished, and I was alone in this new realm.

The first thing to hit me was the noise. It was the noisiest place I had ever been, and I winced, clapping my hands over the sides of my head. Sometimes, having keen ears isn't a good thing. They were sounds I didn't know, either – honking sounds that reminded me a little bit of geese, but no geese I had ever heard; a constant rushing sound like wind through the trees, but too consistent to be any sort of wind; the occasional wailing noise that I guessed might function as some sort of alarm, but for what, I had not a clue. Beyond that, my immediate vision was obscured by the large hedge of tall bushes surrounding me. The bushes looked purely ornamental to my eye, and were pruned carefully into box-shapes. They almost completely encircled the area around the gateway, except for one narrow opening to my left. Behind me was a bench made of metal. It almost looked like someone had purposefully surrounded the gateway with a screen to offer protection to any people who might use it. Did that mean that people in this world did have knowledge of gateways? How, if there were no Brenwyds here?

I walked over to the gap in the bushes and peeked out cautiously. It looked like I was in some sort of planned park with trees and walkways and a lake nearby, with people everywhere. I had seen similar landscaping ideas at the country estates of some Ecclesian nobles. But I had never seen a park designed right next to a city. My gaze was immediately arrested by the sight of the buildings lying beyond the park. They were of varying heights, but some were so tall they seemed to scrape the sky itself. Were they homes? Merchant shops? Extremely large inns? Turning around in a circle, I could see that the park was quite large, and that it wasn't just next to this city; it was completely surrounded by it. I felt my mouth open a bit as I realized the scope of the city. If it was big enough to have a large, landscaped park within its boundaries, how could I find Rhodri in time?

Well, you're not going to find him by standing in this park all day, I told myself logically. *You have to go out and start looking.* I took a deep breath to settle myself and walked from the circle of bushes, feeling exposed and hoping it wasn't too obvious to the people walking by that I was a foreigner. I was reassured, in looking around, that at least the clothes from my mother's closet did, in fact, match what was worn here. The sky was overcast, and a chilly breeze tugged at my frame. I was glad to see at a moment's glance that it appeared extremely common to see women wearing trousers and so I took off my hat, stuffing it in the bag. Much better. However, I was shocked to see some women and men wearing trousers that were cut off very short, exposing much of their legs. Was that customary here? I could think of several people I knew who would faint at such a display. For myself, I felt a bit uncomfortable, but I did wonder how they felt warm enough wearing such short trousers. Beyond that, the different colors and patterns of the clothes amazed me. At home, people wore things that were mostly dyed all one color, with only the very wealthy able to purchase garments with multiple colors. But here, many people wore patterns of different colors on their clothes, and many tunics had strange symbols on them that I couldn't make anything of. Was everyone in this world as rich as kings?

I walked to the nearest path and looked both ways, considering my options. Fortunately, no one seemed to take much notice of me. Some people were running along the path with small threads coming from their ears and disappearing into a pocket. I frowned as I tried to figure out what they were running from. No one else seemed alarmed. Were they running simply because they liked it? How strange. Perhaps they were training for something. They all wore similar, tight-fitting clothes that made me feel a bit embarrassed to see it. Since no one around me seemed scandalized by their attire, I assumed it was normal. Shaking my head, I scolded myself. *Focus, Aislinn*, I chided. *You have to find Rhodri. Quickly. You do not have time to gawk.* However, my looking both ways on the path offered no help as to which way to go. I retreated back and leaned against a tree, trying to think. Upon being shoved into a foreign world, what would Rhodri have done?

Well, he would have tried to get back, first of all, but of course he wouldn't have been able to. So then what? He would have tried to get help. But from whom? There weren't any Brenwyds here...though that shadowy figure had mentioned one, a woman, I thought. Might he have found her? Not likely, I decided, or else he would have come back already. He would likely still be in this city, waiting and hoping for a rescue party...so hopefully he wouldn't be far from the pathway. But how could he be sure that any rescue party would be able to find him? Rhodri was a practical person. He wouldn't just disappear into a large, unknown city without leaving some sort of clue to potential rescuers. I pushed myself off the tree and hurried back to the bushes around the gateway. In hope of people coming through the pathway after him, Rhodri would have left something near it to indicate where he might be found, and he would have left it someplace protected from the elements. Somewhere in the bushes made the most sense.

I arrived back at the clearing and began searching the bushes. "Where did you leave it, Rhodri?" I muttered under my breath. "Where?" I spied a rock from the corner of my eye and, next to it, I made out the impression of a footprint, the right size to be Rhodri's. I grabbed the rock, and smiled at the small hole revealed underneath it. In the hole was a leather letter tube. "Thank you, Abba," I muttered under my breath. I snatched it up and opened it...and frowned. "Bother it all, Rhodri, why did you have to write so small?"

I glared at the paper. It was very fine quality, which seemed to indicate to me that this world had been manufacturing paper from trees longer than Niclausia. It also had lines going horizontally across it to differentiate the different lines of writing, which I did appreciate. What I did not appreciate was how Rhodri had apparently tried to fill every spare margin with letters. Very tiny letters. For almost any other person, they would be able to read the penmanship without much trouble – Rhodri actually had very good handwriting – but I was not most people. Where most people looked at a written page and saw letters and words, I saw scribbles that if I squinted at, I could slowly make out as words. For some reason, my eyes scrambled up letters and rearranged them so it was hard for me to read. I could do it with concentration, but not quickly. And the smaller the letters, the harder it was for me to read. I had been hoping that Rhodri would have written in big enough letters that I could read it without too much trouble, but apparently he hadn't considered that I might be coming through the pathway on my own to retrieve him. I sighed.

I walked out of the hedge grove and found a bench near the pathway to begin scanning the letter. Slowly I started to work through it. The first part of the letter gave assurances that Rhodri was well, then gave an account of how he had been pushed through the gateway. Most of that I skipped over, because I already had a good idea of how it had happened and didn't want to waste time on the details. Then it seemed to go into detail of how he had been living in this world. Here, my progress slowed almost to a stop. Many of the words themselves were foreign, likely because he was explaining how things worked here, but it meant I had no references in my mental dictionary to help me figure them out. I let out a groan. "Oh, Abba, help me," I muttered. I flipped to the last page in frustration, thinking maybe the pertinent information about how to find him would be near the end. I focused on two places above the signature that were specifically set off by themselves in the middle of the page. In each indentation, there were several short lines. The first was a combination of numbers and words, and then the next lines were just words. I scrutinized them. Could it be some sort of direction or address? It looked similar to how people were starting to give directions to newcomers in the bigger towns and cities at home. I scrutinized the lines and made out that several of the words referenced a specific street. So, it *was* an address. Good. Perhaps if I showed just the address lines to people, they would be able to direct me to the place specified. And there was one more thing I could do.

I closed my eyes and called on my Sight. I pictured Rhodri as I had seen him in the mirror, in the shiny white room. This time, unlike the countless times I'd tried before over the past six months, I was successful, and he appeared in my mind's eye, clear as diamond. He was dressed in the same clothes I had seen in the mirror – some sort of uniform, I realized – and still behind the counter, along with another person, a young woman. I watched Rhodri for a few minutes, trying to figure out what he was doing. One part of the counter was clear, and I realized it must be completely made of glass. Behind it, I Saw tubs of brightly colored...something? I had never seen anything like it before, but based on the amount of people eating out of small bowls around the counter it must be something edible. Whatever it was, a person would come to that section of the counter, point to one of the colored tubs, and then Rhodri or the other person would scoop some of the...whatever it was...into a small cup or a triangle-shaped, brown colored odd bowl. Then whichever of them was doing the serving would hand it to the person across the counter. That person would hand over several slips of paper, and leave to start eating the...substance. Maybe it was some sort of sweet? It did look a bit like the whipped cream that Maude sometimes put on her pies and cakes. And I now noticed that other people were eating different things as well, more familiar-looking cake and pastry type items. It must be a sort of bakery specializing in sweets, and Rhodri was working on behalf of the merchant who supplied the food.

He was clearly currently at a place where he worked. I supposed that he couldn't exactly tell people in this world that he was a prince from another one, and given he'd been here some months he would have had to have some way to pay for food and lodgings.

I opened my eyes and began scanning the crowds for a likely person to tell me where I might find the addresses in the letter. To help myself, I decided to listen to the songs of the people walking by, hoping I would find someone with a deep commitment to Abba. Unfortunately, most of the people walking by lacked the melody strain in their songs that indicated such a thing. In fact, most people had holes, rents, and discords in their songs, indicating everything from indifference to outright rejection of Abba. I couldn't believe the number of people with such indicators. Yes, at home one ran across the odd person every so often who didn't believe, and the old stories of this world said it was very corrupt, but still...the overall absence of Abba's active presence in these people's lives made me want to weep.

Suddenly my attention was caught by the sound of not one, but two songs with the connection to Abba loud and clear. I turned my head to the left, and identified the songs as belonging to a boy and girl walking up the path toward me in the middle of a conversation. Both looked to be about sixteen or seventeen years of age. The boy had black hair and blue eyes. The girl was shorter by a few inches, with hazel eyes and long, curly brown hair and had a bright smile on her face. They were holding hands, and I got the impression that they were a courting couple. So where was their chaperone? Did they not have those in this world? The question so preoccupied me that they nearly passed me before I remembered to hail them.

I maneuvered around the other people traversing the path and came up a little behind them and to the side. "Excuse me," I said. They both stopped and turned to look at me with questioning expressions. "I'm terribly sorry to inconvenience you, but might I ask you for directions?"

The boy looked me over, but it was more of a critical appraisal than an admiring one. I would have given a similar look to a stranger at home who asked me for directions. The girl had more of a welcoming expression. However, quickly enough both their expressions changed to something like surprise. "Uh, sure. Where are you trying to get to?" the boy asked. Though the words sounded strange in my ears, I was able to understand them, and they understood me.

I held up the letter, which I had folded so only the section with the addresses was showing. "I need to get to an address written here, but I'm afraid I have no notion whatsoever of how to navigate this city, and it's urgent that I travel quickly. Could you read it for me and tell me how to get there?"

"Of course," the girl said. She narrowed her eyes at the letter. "Can't make out the handwriting, huh? Don't blame you, whoever wrote it writes even smaller than my brother." She raised a hand as if to take the letter, but I resisted.

"I'm sorry, but I need to keep holding it. It contains...private information."

"Oh. Okay." She gave me a curious look, but scanned the lines nonetheless. "Well, you know there are two different addresses there, right?"

"Yes, I had gathered that. Does one seem more like an address for a place of work? I believe at this time of day that would be the better place for me to search. Or perhaps whichever is closest?"

"The second one says it's for the dessert bar in Harrod's," the boy said. Interestingly, they had two very different accents. The boy's reminded me of the accents from the older kingdoms in Niclausia, but the girl's accent wasn't familiar at all. "That's just the other side of the park. Are you looking for someone who works there?"

"Ah...yes. Yes, I'm trying to find a good friend of mine, and it is imperative that I do so quickly. You say it's quite close?"

He nodded. "Yes. It's...hang on, I'll get the exact directions for you." He reached into his pocket, and pulled out a very thin, small black box. One of the long sides looked clear, and he drew his finger across it rapidly, then kept tapping it. I looked at it in astonishment. What in the Five Realms could that be? Abruptly he looked up. "Hey, why don't you pull out your phone and enter the address? There'd be less chance of you getting lost."

The black box must be called a "phone," but that did not help me in determining what its purpose was. They must be fairly common here, though, or he wouldn't assume I would have one. "Oh, I...I, um, don't have one, I'm afraid."

"You don't?" He looked shocked.

Surprisingly, the girl offered up an explanation. "Oh, are you from out of the country?" she asked.

I nodded, smiling. They had no idea. "Yes, rather. As I said, I have never been here before."

The girl turned her head to the boy. "Then her phone won't really work over here, same as mine, William. No wonder she's having trouble navigating."

"Oh. Right. Sorry, you just sound like you're from somewhere in the UK. You must be from Ireland, then," he said.

Despite having no idea what or where this "Ireland" was, I decided to follow along with it. "Yes, so I do not have access to a phone." I pronounced the word carefully. "This is only a short trip."

"In that case..." the girl said, a sly look coming into her eyes. It made me wary. "Why don't we walk with you to Harrod's? That way you definitely won't get lost."

I blinked. While I needed help to find the store, I wasn't sure I wanted them along. That would mean more questions and conversation and I didn't know how well I could keep up the charade that I was from this world. "That is...exceedingly kind of you, but I wouldn't want to inconvenience you. I'm certain that I can find my own way if you instruct me as to the direction."

"But London is confusing if you've never been before," the girl protested. "Besides, I'd be worried that after we left you that you got lost after all and then spent hours wandering around. I would feel better being sure of your having gotten there safely."

I gauged her words, and decided they were sincere. I had a feeling I would not be able to sway her and would end up just wasting time. Time was one resource I did not have to waste. Besides, it did make sense. Given the total foreignness of this world, it would be quite easy for me to lose my way. I smiled at her. "Very well, then, if it's no trouble."

"Not at all." She returned the smile and extended her hand. "By the way, my name's Sarah, and this is William."

I took her hand. Fortunately, we had this greeting at home. "I am Aislinn."

"Aislinn. That's a pretty name," Sarah commented.

"Thank you." We turned and began making our way through the park. Now that I had guides taking me to where Rhodri was, I allowed myself to fully soak in the new and strange sights around me. And I decided to take advantage of having native guides to ask some questions. "Tell me, are parks of this size common in your cities?"

"Well, most towns and cities have parks of some sort, but they aren't generally this big," William answered. "Where in Ireland are you from? No offense, but I'm guessing you're not from a large city."

I considered my answer carefully. "Um...it's not the largest of towns, but the largest of the settlements nearby. I live...in the west. It's not as populated as the rest of the...country." Which was true, to a point. Kheprah was the largest city in Ecclesia, but the smallest of the capital cities in Niclausia, and Ecclesia was the most sparsely populated of the continental kingdoms. I gestured around at the buildings I could see encircling the park. "But there is nothing like this."

"Yeah, I've heard that part of Ireland is pretty rural," William responded. I felt relieved that what I had said matched up with the facts of this world. "So, who is it that you're looking for? I think you said it was urgent."

"Yes..." I wondered how I could describe the emergency in terms they would understand, then decided not to bother. "I'm here to collect the fiancé of my dearest friend. He's been away some time...to earn money for the wedding...but something's happened and it is imperative that he return. I'm sorry, but I can give no more details."

"That's alright," Sarah said, nodding in understanding. "We get it. But wouldn't calling him on his phone have been easier?"

Grindles. Apparently these "phones" were some sort of communication devices. That also gave directions? "Well..." I looked around as I scrambled for an answer. We had come out of a section of the park with a lot of trees and were now walking around a small lake. There were many more people in this area, and it looked like there was a tavern at the end we were walking toward where people were eating. It was noisier in this area of the park, and the extra sounds of people talking and laughing cut into my concentration on my own conversation. "It, um, it simply wasn't possible. Someone had to come in person."

"I'm sorry. I hope that whatever it is, it ends well," Sarah said sympathetically.

I smiled a bit, my worry starting to cloud my mind again. "As do I. As long as I reach Rhodri quickly, I have every hope it will be." I could see their curiosity, so I quickly turned my gaze away to the sky, and noticed the low position of the sun. "What time is sunset?" I asked. If it was soon here, it might be best to wait until nightfall to open the pathway back up.

"A little after six," William said, glancing at something strapped on his wrist. Its surface reflected the sunlight, and I blinked at the sudden glare. It looked like a miniature, portable clock. "So, in about an hour from now."

"Ah. Thank you." By this time we had rounded the end of the lake and I could see better what the environs around the park looked like. There was a street out in front of us, and on it were conveyances I had never seen the like of before. They looked somewhat like the enclosed carriages used for traveling large distances, but incredibly, they seemed to move of their own volition. No horses or any other sort of animal pulled them. I noticed that the rushing wind sound I had heard upon arrival into this world increased dramatically as we approached the road, and it was accompanied by a low droning sound that reminded me a bit of a large swarm of bees. It was all I could do to keep an expression of absolute astonishment from overtaking my face. Did they run by magic? Was it really so common in this world? Worried, I listened for a moment to the songs in the area to determine if there was any magic. While I heard nothing that struck me as magical, I again ran into the large discordances that indicated the lack of a commitment to Abba, and the Creation song in the area was sadly depressed. I winced at both the regular noise and the underlying noise. Clearly, I thought, this world has suffered from the lack of Brenwyds.

"Are you alright?" Sarah's voice asked, and I quickly shifted my concentration back to my companions.

"Yes, perfectly. 'Tis only that it's rather noisier than I'm used to, is all."

She gave me a rather odd look then, as if trying to study my face intently, and I had the strange feeling that her focus was settling on the headband that concealed my ears. "Have good hearing, do you?"

"Ah, yes. Sometimes it's rather helpful, but at other times, not at all."

"Is that what the headband is for? To muffle the noise?"

I felt my eyebrows scrunch down in puzzlement. Why would she directly question the headband? There was no way she could know what I was really hiding. "Well, partly I suppose, but it's more for keeping my ears warm. It is a bit chilly here today, after all," I dissembled with a shrug.

"Hmm. It is," Sarah agreed. I had a feeling she wasn't about to let the headband go, but then we reached the street with all the... whatever they were. I supposed I couldn't ask without revealing my total unfamiliarity with this world. I had to keep myself from wincing again as a fresh wave of noise washed over me.

"Is it much farther?" I asked, wanting to change the subject.

"No," William said, glancing at the phone in his hand. "Just a few minutes more walkaway." He looked up and down the street. "Come on, the crosswalk's up here." The sidewalk beside the street had considerably more people on it than the walkways in the park, and I kept a tight grip on my bag. It was worse than market day in Kheprah. To cross the street with all the moving not-carriages, there was a specified walkway for people, and I observed that the not-carriages, as I decided to call them, were controlled by a light system that seemed to work very effectively. I wondered if I could suggest such a system be implemented in Kheprah. We could use it on market days.

From then on, I deliberately steered the conversation in neutral directions, not wanting any more probing questions, and asked about Sarah and William's day in the city. I found out that they were in the city for the day accompanying William's mother, who had the charge of a large number of children and had brought them here on a special trip. They had left her and the children for some time of their own, and were due to rejoin her very soon, which reinforced my suspicion that they were a courting couple. I was also able to divide my attention between the conversation and looking at the buildings around me. I marveled at them, noting how different they were from the stone cities, castles, and wooden villages I was used to. Most buildings rose multiple stories into the sky and were made in so many different styles and materials that I could tell this was a very old city that had seen much change. In fact, I became so engrossed by my surroundings that I was caught off guard when William came to a stop ahead of me and I accidentally bumped into his back.

"Oh, my apologies," I said hastily. "I'm afraid I've been rather distracted."

"No problem. I've had harder knocks, believe me," he said dryly. Sarah giggled a bit, and I assumed he referred to a specific event they had both experienced.

I looked around and noticed we were standing in front of a large building on a street corner. It appeared five to six levels high, with the first level consisting of large glass windows behind which there were various displays of what I assumed were the goods for sale. Though I recognized the items as clothes, bags, jewelry, and the like, the styles and even the colors themselves were totally foreign. My inability to easily recognize the colors disquieted me more than anything, for as an artist I am well familiar with (or so I thought) all the shades of red, blue, green, orange, yellow, purple, pink, and more that make up the world. I was used to looking at a green leaf and noting it was hunter, or a yellow bolt of cloth and seeing the underlying ochre tones. Here, blue was simply...blue, not celestine or lapis.

I took a deep breath and shoved the feeling away. It would do me absolutely no good to continue those thoughts. I needed to stay focused. Above each window was a green (malachite? moss?) awning, and I saw a word printed on it in gold. I squinted at it and determined it began with an H. "Is this it?"

William nodded. "Yep. Fanciest department store in London."

"Ah. What is it they sell? I believe you said Rhodri is in the...ice cream department?" I tried to pronounce the words correctly.

"What don't they sell would be the better question," Sarah said. "It's an everything sort of store, but all very high-end and pricey." She sighed. "Unfortunately pricey."

William was giving me a curious look. "Don't you know where your friend works? It says so in the letter."

"Ah. That. Well..." I sighed a bit myself. "It might sound a little hard to believe, but I have a hard time reading. All the letters and words get scrambled in my head and they're hard for me to make out. It's easiest for me to have someone else read to me." I braced myself for the usual look of skepticism and disbelief I received when I gave this explanation. Most people I had met thought I was simply making up the disability.

To my complete shock, however, an understanding light suddenly broke across William's face. "Oh, you're dyslexic. That's why you showed us the written address in the letter."

I stared at him. Dyslexic. My mother had sometimes used that word to describe my condition, but I had never heard anyone else use it until now. "You've heard of it?" I exclaimed.

Both William and Sarah looked a little surprised by the vehemence of my question. "Well, sure. It's a pretty well-known learning handicap. Is it not common where you live?"

"Not at all. Most of the time people think I'm making it up!"

"That's awful," Sarah said.

I nodded agreement. "But this is the place?"

"Yes," William assured me. "The letter definitely said at the ice cream place. It's on the second floor, I think."

"Have you been here before?"

Sarah laughed. "Yes, I made him come here with me last time we were in London. Most of the stuff in there is way more than my spending budget, but I wanted to say I at least visited. We visited the dessert bar, as a matter of fact. Really good. Do you think your friend might give out free samples?"

I blinked. "Um, I'm not...that is, I don't know."

Sarah was giving William a sideways look. "Maybe we should go in to help direct you." I was about to assure her it wasn't necessary – I would prefer to find Rhodri on my own, since he would be considerably surprised to see me – but just then a shrill ringing sound split the air between us. Taken by surprise, I flinched a bit from the sudden loud noise. It seemed to be coming from the phone William still held in his hand.

He looked down at it. "There's Mum. Probably wondering where we are." He slid a finger across it, and then started talking into it. I watched, fascinated. Was it some sort of long-distance communication device?

"Well, it sounds like we have to leave," Sarah said, breaking my train of thought. She sighed regretfully. "Rats. I was starting to look forward to ice cream. Or, I think it's technically gelato." The technicality was lost on me. She continued. "Sorry the volume was turned up so loud on his phone. It has to be, or else we can't hear it in the city. Usually he has it turned down fairly low, especially... around this one friend of ours. She has pretty sensitive hearing, too." She looked at me intently as she relayed the information, as if looking for a specific reaction. I merely returned her gaze steadily. She was clearly fishing for some sort of information, but what?

"Don't worry yourself about it, 'tis no great bother." I looked toward the store again and felt the sense of urgency kick in full force. I had to go find Rhodri. Now. "I thank you a thousand times for your help. Time is of the utmost importance to my errand."

"No problem. We're glad to help."

By this point William had finished his conversation and had turned back to us. "Sarah, we have to go. If we don't get to the rendezvous at Kensington Gardens in the next few minutes, we'll make everybody miss the train."

Sarah's eyes widened. "Is it that late? I hadn't realized."

He nodded, and looked back to me. "It was nice to meet you. Hope everything turns out well."

"So do I. Goodbye." I turned toward the store entrance, and they began walking back the way we had come. As I reached the doors, I paused for a moment and turned back to look at them. I had the sudden urge to run after them and explain myself more, but I resisted. They would think I was mad, and I could not waste any more time in finding Rhodri. Ecclesia depended on it. So I turned back and stepped through the door.

My jaw immediately dropped. What was this place? There were so many people, the place was full of shelves, and on the shelves were many things that were vaguely familiar yet wildly different from anything I had seen before – bags, clothes, and more items I couldn't really identify at all. I could tell, though, that as Sarah had said, this store obviously catered to the wealthy. It was like a market someone had built indoors, as many rooms opened off the hallway I was standing in, each with different things inside. I wandered around aimlessly for a few minutes, trying to take it all in. There was so much. How was I supposed to get to the second floor? Fortunately, in turning a corner I spied a set of stairs that people were going up and down on. Or rather, the people weren't moving, the stairs were moving them. My brow furrowed. That was curious. I walked over to it and looked at it with fascination. The *stairs* were *moving*. They rose out of the floor and carried the people up with them. I cautiously stepped onto one, putting a hand on the railing. Sure enough, the step carried me upward without me walking a step. Now this would be useful in the castle, I thought, thinking of all the long staircases. I wondered how it worked. I decided that if this sleeping spell got broken, I would come back here and investigate this world further. It seemed to have many useful inventions.

I reached the top of the stairs and stepped off. Turning back around, I saw that the stairs disappeared into the floor. Did they get transported all the way back to the bottom? I wondered. Then I shook my head slightly. "Remove your head from the clouds, Aislinn, you've got to find Rhodri and then get home." I turned around and almost ran over a young man standing in front of me.

"Careful there," he said, putting a hand out to steady me.

"My apologies," I said.

"No problem. Can I help you?" He seemed very eager to be of help. I had to stop my eyes from rolling. I recognized the behavior. I got it often enough from all the young male nobles around the castle – and some of the older ones, too. Apparently, there were some things common between the two worlds after all. Still, he was wearing garb identical to many other people in the store, and I assumed it was the uniform of those who worked there, so he should be able to help me locate this ice cream parlor.

"Yes, actually. I'm looking for the dessert bar? I believe it's located on this floor. Can you direct me to it? A friend of mine works there, and I must find him."

He nodded. "Sure, but it's not on this floor. It's on the next."

I frowned. "It is? I thought...I was told it was on the second."

"It is. This is the first floor."

I blinked in puzzlement and involuntarily glanced back at the stairs I had just come up. Did they count differently here? "But...I came up to this floor..."

Now he looked a bit puzzled. "I'm sorry, are you American? I assumed you were from somewhere in the U.K. from your accent. I know the U.S. has a different floor numbering system than we do."

American, Ireland, U.K....there certainly seemed to be a lot of kingdoms in this world. I simply shrugged off the question. "I'm not from this area, that you can be sure of. Now you say this dessert bar is on the next floor? Where?"

"Yes." He narrated the directions to me and I locked them into my memory. I thanked him and went on my way before he could trap me in a flirtatious conversation. I had neither the time nor patience for it. I fixed my mind on finding Rhodri, hoping my Sight and the directions I had received would help me locate him.

I glanced back to see if he was following, but an older woman had approached him and was asking him a question, so he was distracted. Thank Abba. I quickly found the next set of moving stairs and got on them. Then I turned right, and in a couple of minutes, on my left, I could see the place I had glimpsed through the mirror – the white and silver-colored design of the room I found almost blinding, but it was obviously the place, as I could clearly see the display of sweets on a counter. I quickened my step toward the entrance, straining for a sight of the people behind the counter and praying Rhodri would still be there.

I was so focused on it, in fact, that I accidentally bumped into a young man coming out of the parlor. My first awareness of him was as a solid mass that abruptly halted my progress. "Oh, I'm so terribly sorry," I cried immediately. "Do forgive-" And then a hoarse whisper stopped me in my step.

"Aislinn?!?"

Startled, I really looked into the face of the person I had nearly run over, and my eyes widened. My eyes were staring into familiar hazel ones of honey and umber, framed by a handsome face several shades darker than my own pale skin and capped with brown hair that I knew quite well. "Rhodri?" I squeaked, suddenly feeling like there wasn't quite enough air in my lungs. He simply continued to stare at me, blinking slowly. I put a hand on his arm and squeezed, hardly able to believe he was really there after being missing for so long. I felt a huge smile turn the corners of my lips upward and deep into my cheeks, and I threw my arms around him in an impulsive embrace. "Rhodri! Oh, thank Abba I've found you."

He seemed to be coming a bit out of his shock, as after a moment he returned the embrace tightly. Then he pushed me away to arm's length and stared at my face as if...well, as if he hadn't seen it in months. "It's really you," he breathed out. "Thank Abba. You're here. In London." He glanced down at the rest of me, and a puzzled expression crossed his face. "Where did you get those clothes?" Before I could formulate any sort of answer, he shook his head. "Never mind that. How did you find me? Are there others with you?" He released the grip on my arms and looked past me. "I've tried to get back. Every day I've gone back to the park and tried. I've felt terrible, knowing how you all must be desperate to know what happened. I left a letter. Did you find it? Of course, you must have to know to come here." He looked back at me. I was scrambling to keep up with all the words tumbling from his lips. I had never heard Rhodri speak so swiftly. He started looking puzzled again. "But how did you read the letter? I'm sorry, if I thought it would be you specifically coming through the passage I would have written much more legibly. You know, there's a name for your problem here, it's called dyslexia, just like-"

"My mother said," I finally interrupted him, holding up a hand. "Peace, Rhodri. I can't answer your questions if you continue firing them at me like arrows from a bow."

He actually smiled, and then laughed a little. "Sorry. It's only..." the smile faded, "I was beginning to rather lose hope. Is...that is, how's Lissa?" He looked at me anxiously for my answer.

I let a solemn expression cross my face. "At the moment, she is...fine, physically, I suppose, but we have a problem. A serious problem. We need to speak someplace privately, and quickly. There is no time to waste. Where can we go?"

Rhodri frowned and glanced around. "Here. We can use one of the benches. No one ever listens too carefully, and fortunately I just ended my shift so I don't need to go back in." He guided me over to an empty bench and we sat. "What's wrong?"

I took a breath. "I went into the forest to gather mushrooms this afternoon, those ones that Lissa likes so much. That's how I found the pathway, and I also ran across a mouse who saw you in a confrontation with a witch, and so learned you had been pushed through to this world."

He nodded. "That's true. She surprised me." He shifted and looked at me intently. "She attacked Ecclesia, didn't she?" An anguished expression crossed his face. "She threatened to do so; she said she'd go after Lissa and there was nothing I could do to stop it."

"Almost right. She did attack Ecclesia with a spell, and she enacted it through Lissa. The whole country's been put under a sleeping curse, like the one Nivea experienced, I think." His eyes widened and he opened his mouth to say something, but I stopped him with a raised hand. "But Rhodri, I think that you can break it."

He blinked. "Me? How? I'm not a Brenwyd."

"As I said, I was out in the mushroom grove, but I Saw a vision of Lissa in the rose garden. An old woman came into the garden with a rose she said was a birthday present for her, a white one. Lissa picked it up and was examining it, then she caught her finger on a thorn and pricked it. Then she simply...slumped over and fell asleep. That action triggered the sleeping spell. Everyone within Ecclesia's borders is asleep. I wasn't affected because it stopped at the borders and apparently the pathway is actually in Darlesia. After I Saw the spell strike, I raced back on Dynin to Khephrah. I found the witch still in the castle, and she summoned this...figure she called her lord. She discussed the curse with him, and that's how I found out why she sent you here. She needed to get you out of the way." I paused then, not quite sure how Rhodri would react to the next part. "Rhodri, I think – though I know it sounds impossible – that she's the evil Queen from Nivea's time."

His brow furrowed. "Aislinn, that was over two hundred years ago. It's impossible that she's still alive, and anyway, she was defeated and drowned in the Hellwyl."

"I know, I know, but.... it's her, Rhodri. You must believe me. She sent you here because you can foil her spell. Do you remember, in the story of Nivea, how she was awakened from the sleeping spell when her true love kissed her?" He nodded, and I could see the light starting to dawn in his eyes. "The same will work with this. If you kiss Lissa, the spell will break. But it has to be within the first few hours. The witch, Morrian, the figure said her name was, said specifically that she designed the spell so that once enough time passes, the only one who will wake is Lissa. But in these first few hours, if you get to her in time, the whole thing will come apart."

He stared at me. "Are you sure?"

"I heard it from her own mouth." I stood, and he stood with me.

"How long has it been?"

"Almost two hours, I think. We should still have time, but we must hurry." I turned to go, but he caught my arm.

"Wait." I raised my eyebrows in inquiry. "I've got to go by the place I've been living and collect my things first," he said. Before I could protest, he went on. "I know time is of the essence, but my Darlesian clothes are there, as well as my dagger, and I need to write some sort of explanation for my friend, Ian. It shouldn't take too long, maybe twenty minutes, thirty at most, and we're back at Hyde Park. If we really do have a several-hour window, we should still be well within it."

"But what if we're not?" I argued. "What if it's really less time than she said? This is our best chance for ending this spell. Rhodri, it's only the beginning of something. She's planning something with that figure, something that will happen in a month's time. She said by then the spell will end naturally, but it will drain every Brenwyd caught in it of their abilities so they will be powerless to fight what follows. Ecclesia wouldn't stand a chance against any sort of magical attack if that happens."

He pressed his lips together in a set expression. "We won't let it." He looked at his wrist, and I saw he was wearing a portable clock like William had. "Okay. Ian should be back at the flat by now, so I'll call him and have him meet us at the park with my stuff. Would that work?"

"Can this Ian meet us there quickly?" He nodded. I sighed. "Very well."

"Good." He pulled out one of the phone things and started tapping the screen. "You know, this world really has the most useful inventions. This is a phone, and it lets you talk to people who are far away. This will just take a moment." And it did. Rhodri instructed his friend to meet us, and then put the phone away. "Alright, let's go. And while we're walking, why don't you give me a fuller version of exactly what happened today?"

To Wake a Princess

On our way back to the park, I did just that. Once we reached the park, we had to wait for his friend, Ian, to get there, so we discussed what our full plan should be once we were back in Ecclesia. I hadn't thought much beyond getting Rhodri back to kiss Lissa, but he pointed out that the witch likely wouldn't take kindly to our interference and, given that she was so powerful, would probably know when the spell broke. Assuming it took some time for the people caught in the sleep to understand what was going on, we had to have a plan in place to deal with her immediately upon its breaking. Unfortunately, our options were limited. The best we could come up with was to take preventative measures. It felt like ages before Rhodri's friend appeared, and when he finally did, he apologized for being late and said something about construction on a tube. I didn't see how that was relevant to reaching the park, but Rhodri assured me he would explain later.

His friend looked at me incredulously almost the whole time we conversed. Apparently, he had thought Rhodri a bit mad with all his talk of another realm and the kingdoms, but I was living proof. I didn't let them linger over goodbyes, as I fairly dragged Rhodri back to the pathway once Ian had given him the bag with his belongings. Though the sun was setting and dusk was starting to fall, there were still a fair number of people in the park, so when I sang to open the pathway I was sure to pitch my voice low so as not to attract attention. For a few moments I feared that Ian might want to come with us, so entranced he looked with the view through the pathway, but then he backed up, wished us luck, and agreed to come to the wedding. Rhodri had invited him several moments earlier, promising to send someone through to get him. I went through first and released a breath of relief when I reached the other side. I was glad to be back in my own world.

Dynin was standing mere feet from the gateway, and he whickered with delight and reproach when I appeared. *What took you so long? You said you would be back while the sun was still out,* he scolded. I could see from the trampled grass that he had actually been pacing instead of eating, indicating his highly agitated state.

"Sorry, Dy, we came as fast as we could." I wrapped my arms around his neck and inhaled his scent deeply.

He nuzzled me, and then turned his attention to Rhodri, who had just stepped through the gateway. Once he had done so, the pathway and the strange world of London disappeared. *It is good to see you again,* Dynin told him. As a Brenwyd horse, he was able to communicate directly to Rhodri on his own initiative.

"Good to see you, too," Rhodri said. He breathed deeply of the cool twilight air, and I saw him relax, looking around with bright eyes, a smile breaking through on his face. "Oh, it's good to be back."

It is good you have come back, Dynin said. *You must see it.*

I frowned. "See what?"

Follow me. He turned and started walking in the direction that would eventually get one to Darlesia. Puzzled, Rhodri and I followed him. When we had gone only twenty horse lengths from the clearing, a thick fog suddenly rose up in front of us like a wall, and as I stopped directly in front of it, I could see that in the midst of the fog was a more physical barrier of thorny briars that reached up past the height of the treetops. I stared at it with my mouth slightly agape. It had definitely not been there when I had left.

"How in the Five Realms did that happen?" Rhodri breathed.

"Magic," I said, frowning as I listened. "A very strong magic." Suddenly I realized what it was. "Of course! A barrier. Morrian mentioned putting up a barrier between us and Darlesia to prevent the other kingdoms from interfering." Tentatively, I put a hand out toward it. The fog felt almost physical, like a slippery force that kept me from quite reaching the thorns, and it extended far above the thorns, from what I could tell. I squinted up through a gap in the leaf canopy, trying to see just how far up it extended. "This might be a problem with our plan to send a bird to Darlesia to tell them."

"Couldn't they just fly over it?" Rhodri asked, also craning his head back to look upward.

"I'm not sure. It looks too high." I used my gift to reach out to the birds in the area. I found a hawk willing to help, the same one whom I had spoken to earlier, and he took flight to try to get past the barrier. But only a few minutes later, he returned with disheartening news. The fog continued up for as high as he could fly, and he could not go through it. There was a force repelling him. I relayed the information to Rhodri.

He looked grave. "We have to get a message through, somehow. We'll need their help in the immediate aftermath while the Ecclesian Brenwyds are still gathering their wits." That was the plan we had landed on in the park. We had decided that, once we got back, I would send word through the forest animals to Rhodri's father's province to tell the Brenwyds there what had happened and ask for help. Animals could relay news almost faster than wildfire, and as long as Rhodri and I gave the message a bit of time as a head start, it was sure to reach them in time, as his father held lands just the other side of the Anianol. That way, when Rhodri broke the spell, I would have help on the way who wouldn't be struggling to wake. In the meantime, our plan was to try and hold the sorceress at bay as long as possible and, Abba willing, the Darlesian Brenwyds would reach Kheprah quickly and the Ecclesian Brenwyds would recover nearly as fast. But now?

I kicked the trunk of a tree in frustration. "Why did I not think to send a message through when it first occurred? Or even just before I went through the gateway? Idiot!" I chided myself.

"Don't kick yourself too badly," Rhodri said. I blinked at the odd turn of phrase. I hadn't heard him use it before. Then again, I had noticed he seemed to be speaking much less formally overall than he had last time we'd spoken. I supposed he had picked up the local Earth way of speaking. "You were trying to do the best you could. And you brought me back. That was smart thinking on your part to put everything together, and then to actually find me in London. Most people would have been so fully distracted and overwhelmed by being in a different world it would have taken them hours to find me, if they did at all."

"But I should have-"

"Should haves won't help us at the moment," he said, cutting me off. "We'll just have to go on as we planned and pray to Abba that the spell wears off quickly on the Ecclesian Brenwyds."

I nodded, feeling a bit bleak. We didn't have much of a choice, really. "And hope that they still have their abilities intact." That was also worrying me. I had no idea how this spell was taking away my people's abilities, and what if we broke the spell only to find we had done so too late?

Rhodri merely grunted in agreement before returning to the problem of the thorns, tapping his fingers against his thigh as he thought. "Could you tear it down?"

I considered the melodies for a few minutes before answering. "Perhaps...but the effort would likely exhaust me, given its scope. I think we would be better off saving my efforts for when we get to Kheprah. We can simply transfer past the barrier on Dynin anyhow." What I didn't say was that though I knew all the theory of spell-breaking, I had never truly done it before, and the idea made me nervous. I had always thought that whenever I did encounter magic for the first time, it would be with other, older Brenwyds beside me, but instead I was alone. "Hmm, good point. Well, let's get going then. You should go first. It would be awkward if I went first, ran into the sorceress, and got turned to stone or something." He actually gave me a smile at that, one of his usual jokester smiles.

I stared at him. "Are you really jesting at this moment?"

He shrugged. "Thought I'd try." Seeing my frowning expression, he added, "I know it's serious, Aislinn. I just...I think I'm still trying to absorb it. An hour ago, I was thinking the biggest challenge I'd have today was making dinner."

I saw his point. Still, the last part of the sentence caused me to raise an eyebrow and lift a corner of my mouth. "You've learned how to cook?" The idea struck me as rather funny.

He smiled ruefully. "Sort of. Badly. I'll be glad to return to Maude's cooking."

"I'd imagine so." I swung up onto Dynin. "Very well, then, I'm off. Dynin will be back in a few moments. Don't go anywhere, now." I tried my own attempt at humor.

He chuckled. "I won't."

I turned Dynin around to give him room to run, and he picked up speed quickly. Dynin and I arrived outside Kheprah - and I immediately pulled Dynin up hard. So hard that he reared up as I turned him to the side. *Hey!* he protested. *Do not haul on my mouth. Would you like it if I hauled on your mouth?*

"I'm sorry, Dy, but would you have preferred to be impaled by thorn bushes?"

He focused on where he had been heading before I'd pulled him aside. *I suppose not.* He still sounded surly. Apparently Morrian had decided that Kheprah needed still more protection from would-be interferers. A guard of thorn bushes surrounded the city, several feet higher than the outer wall and about twenty feet thick. Fog concealed most of the city from view, save for a few castle towers and roofs that were occasionally visible through gaps in the mist. In the darkness of the night, it looked almost unreal. "Grindles and spindles," I whispered. "How are we supposed to get through all that?"

Your swords? Dynin suggested in a sensible tone.

"We have exactly one sword and two daggers, Dy. I don't like our chances with such a meager number." *Abba, please help us*, I prayed, for what seemed the hundredth time that day. I dismounted and sent Dynin back for Rhodri, warning him to transfer back farther away from Kheprah.

I walked up to the wall of thorns. I sensed the same spell here as the one at the border, but this thorn patch was smaller and so might not be such a large spell...which meant I might be able to break it without exhausting myself. However, there was still the chance of alerting Morrian to our presence by breaking one of her spells, and I knew I couldn't defeat her by myself. I heard Dynin return and Rhodri take in a sharp breath as he beheld the thorns.

"So, now what?" I asked him without turning around.

"Well, I don't fancy trying to cut through all that with only a sword and a dagger. Can you break the spell?"

"I think so. But that could alert her..."

"If your idea works and I wake Lissa, we already discussed how that will probably alert her. Which is why Dynin will be waiting outside the castle to take us to Darlesia for help. If you break this spell, we'll just have to move more quickly, is all." That wasn't all and he knew it, but it was our best option. At least I was fairly confident I could hold the witch off enough – Abba willing – so Rhodri and Lissa could get to Darlesia and raise the alarm. I swung my sword experimentally at one of the thorn branches. It hacked the limb off, but several seconds later it regrew before our astonished eyes. I was reminded of my dream that morning, with the regrowing thorn bushes. Apparently, it had meant something after all.

"That settles it. There's no other choice," Rhodri said, a bit grimly. "I wonder if she designed the spell so the only way to get past the thorns is to break the enchantment and so alert her."

That was a lovely thought. "Give me a few minutes." I closed my eyes and listened to the tune of the spell. The melody was loud and twisted in my mind, composed of slightly discordant minors that wound around each other and grated on my nerves. It reminded me very much of the tangle of thorns it was responsible for. I decided the simplest way to break the spell was to call up the Creation song, which I heard faintly – the spell suppressed it. The Creation song was the song from the beginning of time that Abba had created the world around, and Brenwyds counted on it often to set things right when dealing with spells. It was pure and holy. Some parts of it were soft and low, like a mother's lullaby, while others were grand and majestic like the northern mountains. The melodies were intricate and interwoven into each other like a large, living tapestry, yet there was never any discordance. Listening to it all at once often made a person start to shed tears, it was so beautiful. I began singing softly with the melody. This I knew how to do well, for my father had often had me listen and sing to the Creation song in training for just this sort of situation. Here around Kheprah, the melody was mostly straightforward and clear, with some crescendos, fitting as Kheprah was situated in a part of the kingdom that consisted mainly of gentle hills. I didn't sing words, as it was the melody that was the important part. My voice swelled in volume and strength as the song went on, and my confidence grew as I sensed the spell weakening.

It weakened slowly at first, then faster and faster as I continued singing, finally breaking as I reached a crescendo. I stopped singing and opened my eyes. The thorns shriveled up, shrank, and crumbled to the ground, leaving only dust, and the mist dissipated in the suddenly bright starlight. After listening and singing to the Creation song, the eerie silence of the night, absent of any usual city or animal sounds, was amplified in my ears.

"Well done, Aislinn," Rhodri said admiringly, looking toward the city with eagerness and longing. I nodded in response, a bit in awe of what I had done. I had never done anything like it before. I also felt a sense of immense satisfaction, and (if I was honest) a bit of delight. I had actually broken a spell. *Thank you for the Song, Abba,* I thought heavenward. I leaned against Dynin, feeling a bit tired. "Are you alright?" Rhodri asked.

"Yes. Just a bit tired." I fumbled with the fastenings of my waterskin, which I had attached to Dynin's saddle before leaving the castle earlier. I worked it loose and drank some of the water, feeling a bit parched. "Let's go. We shouldn't dawdle." We went through the gates, Dynin following, and hurried up the main cobblestone road of the city. The only sounds to reach my ears were mine and Rhodri's footfalls and Dynin's hoofbeats. We couldn't go especially fast, though, because of all the sleeping bodies in the street that the darkness only obscured further. Rhodri was completely dependent on me for direction.

Halfway to the castle, that became a serious problem. I had been half-listening to our surroundings with my song-sense since we'd entered the city, hoping I would get a forewarning of Morrian's approach that way. Consequently, I was nearly knocked over by a wave of anger and disbelief that sounded along nature's chords announcing her approach just as I was starting to think she hadn't noticed my breaking the thorn spell after all. I lurched against Rhodri, who steadied me. "What is it?" he asked, but I could see in his face that he knew.

"Morrian," I gasped. "We've got to run. You get on Dynin. He'll get you to the castle. I'll run after you. I shouldn't have too much trouble keeping up."

But what about the people? Dynin asked. *They are blocking the road. I cannot trample them.*

"I know. Avoid them as best you can, but go as quickly as possible. Go!" Rhodri vaulted up onto Dynin without a word. Dynin took off as soon as he felt Rhodri settle on his back, breaking into a slow trot so he could avoid the people. It was faster than we had been traveling, but to my fretful eyes didn't seem near fast enough. I followed them at a run, at first keeping up without too much difficulty. I'm light on my feet. Still, Dynin outdistanced me a few minutes later as we crossed into the wealthier section of Kheprah. It was higher up on the city's hill within Kheprah's original wall, and because it was upper-class homes, not as many street-hawkers and peddlers loitered there with their wares on a daily basis – which meant there were fewer people lying asleep in the street, and Dynin could accelerate to a canter. *Tell him Lissa's in the rose garden*, I called to Dynin as he and Rhodri were about to disappear around a bend in the road. I had told Rhodri that already, of course, but I wanted to be sure he remembered.

I could sense the witch coming. I didn't know how she was traveling, but I guessed it was by magic, since the Creation song at first got stronger to fight the magic, and then weakened because of the strength of her evil. There wasn't much time, and the fact that she repressed the Creation song did not bode well for me if – when – I had to face her. *If only I had a flamestone blade*, I thought. That would help even the odds.

Flamestone swords, arrows, and spears were weapons forged from stars on fire that fell from the sky and landed on the earth. According to the stories, the smiths who'd forged them had found a way to retain the stars' flames in the blades, and their bearers could then call that fire forth when needed. The blades were also said to be able to cut through spells like other swords cut through flesh. They had once been widespread, as they were the favored weapon of choice of Brenwyds in fighting magic, but starting about a hundred years ago they had disappeared. Families who owned them began reporting that their houses had been robbed and the weapons taken. By the time enough robberies occurred so the Brenwyds realized what was happening, nearly a third of all the known weapons had gone, and they had never been found. As a precaution, Brenwyd leaders at the time had gathered up all the remaining weapons and taken them to a safe hiding place somewhere in the northern mountains until the culprits could be caught. Unfortunately, the party that went to hide the weapons disappeared, and their remains were found months later at the base of the mountains. No one knew where the weapons had gone, or whether they had been safely hidden or stolen like the rest. The last battle story containing flamestone weapons was the Monsters' War, which had ended just before the weapons started disappearing. The two most famous (in story, anyway) flamestone blades had been called Seren and Caliburn, but the stories concerning them were fairy tales, speaking of a king called Arthur and his cousin Caelwyn.

Of course, many people over the years had tried to find the weapons in the mountains, but no one had been successful. Many people nowadays doubted if they had even existed at all, but Brenwyds knew the truth of them, and believed that Abba would lead someone to them when the kingdom needed them. If I had one, it would give me a much better chance against Morrian.

I reached the castle gates and crossed into the courtyard, catching sight of Dynin standing before the castle doors, riderless. Rhodri must have gone in already. I drew my bow and an arrow from my quiver, setting the arrow on the bowstring. I didn't want to meet Morrian without a weapon in hand. If I was lucky, I might even be able to shoot her before she realized what was in my hands and so end the problem. Somehow, though, I didn't think she would be defeated so easily. My father had told me that powerful witches and wizards constructed shields around themselves so weapons couldn't harm them, and those shields had to be destroyed before they could be killed. Morrian definitely qualified as a powerful witch. Dynin snorted anxiously, his eyes rolling so the whites showed, but he didn't speak. He felt her coming too. Animals were more connected to the Creation song than people, and could often sense disturbances in it. A thunderclap from overhead startled me, and I looked up to see a bank of ebony clouds rising up from the northwest and heading toward Kheprah, blotting out the stars. My blood ran cold. My father had taught me that great works of magic and magic-users sometimes could cause disturbances so large that they caused huge storms because of the laws of nature that were being broken. This was not looking good at all. "Dear Abba, please help and protect us," I prayed.

"I'm afraid it's far too late for prayers, my dear," a voice hissed from behind me.

✿✿✿

Rhodri jumped off Dynin and raced for the palace door, glancing up at the developing storm. He didn't like the look of it. He stepped into the castle and paused. Despite the urgency of the situation, he couldn't help it. It had been so long since he had stood here. He had been losing hope of ever seeing it again. If he had not literally run into Aislinn walking out of work, he would have assumed he imagined her. He opened his bag and dug out the electric torch he'd instructed Ian to put in it. He allowed himself the luxury of a brief moment to play the light over the dark hall and let his gaze drift over the high, vaulted ceilings and portraits on the wall, remembering how he and Lissa had made fun of the old clothing styles as children. More recently, they had joked about wearing their most ridiculous clothes when the time came for their portraits to be painted. In fact, it had been the topic of their last conversation when she had seen him off to Darlesia – or rather, that was where he had been supposed to end up. Lissa...the thought jolted him back into action, and he ran the rest of the way to the rose garden, pausing here and there to readjust the position of several sleepers. Obviously, the curse had caught the castle in the middle of preparations for Lissa's birthday ball – what should have been their wedding ball.

Enough of that, he told himself severely. *It will be, once we break this curse.* He reached the entrance of the garden and pushed open the door. His eye immediately fell on Lissa lying on the bench, her pale hair spread out on the pillow behind her and a peaceful expression on her face. The sight of her after so many months literally stopped him in his tracks. He had always been aware that Lissa was not, strictly speaking, conventionally pretty, but in that moment, she was the most beautiful thing he had ever seen. *Oh, Abba, thank you for Aislinn.* He approached the bench slowly, aware of a tightness in his throat and tears coming to his eyes. He knelt when he reached her, and raised a hand to her face, just to make sure she was really real. It also told him that her sleep was definitely the work of magic, because she was a light sleeper and had told him she was often awakened by wind blowing outside or her mother giving her a light kiss. Now, however, she didn't even react. His gaze moved to the cat placed against her, breathing in and out with a familiar rhythm. He stroked him, the familiar motion soothing yet heartbreaking as Boomer's eyes stayed firmly closed instead of cracking open, and no paw appeared to bat his hand away.

"I'll wake you up, Boomer," he said, turning his attention back to Lissa. "I hope." He briefly looked up in supplication. "Please let this work." Then Rhodri bent his head to Lissa's and kissed her soundly. He poured six months of separation and desperation into that kiss, willing her to wake up with every part of his being. And he felt her stir.

He broke off the kiss and raised his head, watching her intently. Her head moved, and she shifted her position on the bench. Her hands began moving toward her face, likely to rub the sleep out of her eyes, but her right caught at his torso, and he took it in his hand and squeezed it gently. That brought her eyes open immediately.

Sleep still clouded her blue irises, but her gaze latched onto him and froze. He grinned. "Hello, Liss. Miss me?"

He felt her hand return his grip tightly. "Rhodri?" Her voice was scratchy from sleep and slightly squeaky from surprise, but never had it sounded more like music to his ears.

"Well, nobody else had better be kissing you. And if they are, I want to know about it." He gave her a brief mock scowl.

"But...but how?"

"Our wedding is tomorrow, is it not? Would be rather embarrassing to miss my own wedding, don't you agree?"

"Oh, Rhodri!" She sat up and threw her arms around him and he wrapped her tightly in his embrace, relishing the moment. He had dreamed about doing this countless times over the last few months. Her face found his and he kissed her again, hard, for several long moments. Every other thought was driven from his mind. She drew back, gasping slightly. "My heavens."

"I've missed you."

"And I you." She gazed at him, her eyes moving over his features as if to reassure herself it was truly he. She reached a hand up and laid it on his head, moving her fingers through his hair. Her touch felt heavenly to him. However, he did not predict her next comment. "You cut your hair." She sounded...surprised? Amused? Bemused? Rhodri couldn't tell, but the words – so different from anything and everything he'd imagined her saying to him when they were finally reunited – made him laugh.

"Yes, well, where I was...it's the more customary fashion. It'll grow back out, you know."

Her hand slipped down to clutch at his tightly. "But where in the Five Realms were you? Not even the Brenwyds..." Her eyes suddenly lit up, and she shifted her gaze to move about the garden as if looking for something. "Aislinn! Did she find you? Was I right? Was it really a gateway to the old world?"

"Yes, it was," he answered, smiling at her. "You were right. Aislinn found me." At that moment, thunder boomed and lightning flashed overhead. It reminded him that Aislinn was likely outside fighting the witch. His feelings of euphoria vanished. "Aislinn!" He turned. "Come, we must help her." He looked at where Boomer lay, suddenly realizing he had remained silent. He felt a sinking feeling in his stomach as he saw the cat lying still on the bench. *Abba, no, please...*

"With what?" Lissa looked around and seemed to realize where she was for the first time. "Why was I sleeping here? What is going on?" She frowned at Boomer. "How is he sleeping with you back? Do you know, he was acting most strangely-"

"Come on, Liss," he interrupted her, only half-aware of what she was saying. "We have to check on everyone else...surely they must be waking." He pulled her to her feet and led her from the garden, she silencing her questions at his strange behavior.

They reached the passage Rhodri had entered from, and what he saw caused despair to clench in his gut. *No...*everyone was still sleeping. There were no signs of waking. "We were too late," he breathed out. "But how?" Aislinn had thought they'd had several hours. They were well within that. Why was no one else waking up? Had she heard wrong?

"Rhodri? What is this? Why is everyone asleep?" Lissa's voice broke through his dismay. It sounded shaky, and as he met her blue eyes, he saw the fear in them. She had knelt next to one of the maids and was shaking her shoulder with no success.

He exhaled a breath. "Aislinn told me she Saw you accept a white rose from an old woman, and that you pricked your finger."

"Yes...I did," she said. "It seems like a dream."

"That woman was a witch. Your pricking your finger set off a spell that swept over the rest of Ecclesia and caused everyone in the kingdom to fall asleep. Aislinn was able to escape it because the mushroom grove is over the border. We don't know who the woman is, exactly, but Aislinn overheard her talking with someone and the end goal of the spell is to strip all the Brenwyds of their abilities so the woman can take over the kingdom with demon servants."

Now horror joined the fear in Lissa's expression. "What? I caused -"

"You didn't cause anything," Rhodri said. "You were only a tool. Now we must hurry to help Aislinn. I'll explain more later, I promise you. We thought...never mind that now. If we're to have any chance, we must get to Darlesia and come back here with Brenwyds as soon as possible."

He could see the myriad questions still filling her eyes, saw the nervous swallow she took, but when she opened her mouth to answer, she merely said in a steady voice, "Very well." With that, he led her down the hallway toward the gates, praying they weren't too late.

6

$\mathcal{F}$ighting a $\mathcal{S}$orceress

$\mathcal{I}$ whirled, caught a glimpse of her, and released the arrow. It should have pierced her neck. Instead, it hit an invisible barrier about six inches from her and fell to the stone ground of the court-yard. She laughed. "An impressive effort, but it would take more than a mere arrow to kill me." Her silver eyes fixed on me. I read hatred, anger, pain, and triumph in those eyes, all shaded in tones of malevolence and power. I realized that until that moment I had never truly been terrified. My stomach felt empty and hollow, and fear turned my limbs to stone. What I saw in those eyes was a person who could kill me at the flick of a finger, and would not hesitate to do so. *Oh, Abba, help and protect me,* I prayed again.

"Who are you, Brenwyd girl? How did you get past the barrier?"

"I...I think I shall keep that to myself, if you don't mind." My voice sounded small to my ears, but a part of my brain that wasn't focused on feeling terrified told me to keep her out here, and to keep her talking. I had to give Rhodri time.

"I do mind, as it happens." Her voice sounded colder than icicles, and I shuddered involuntarily. "How did you get here?"

"I rode."

She frowned, looking around the courtyard. Dynin had pressed himself against a wall, trying to blend in with the shadows, and she spotted him. "I see. Your devil horses. Well, that's easily enough taken care of." She raised her hands.

"No!" I yelled. "Don't hurt him! Please! What does it matter? You've already taken the kingdom. What does one horse matter?"

She lowered her hands and looked back at me. "In the grand scheme of things, nothing most likely. But I have learned that even things that most likely mean nothing can become important. And it's not my fault he's here." She raised her hands again and started chanting. I heard thunder, and saw that the storm clouds were now right over us. Dynin whinnied shrilly, almost screaming. The danger to my horse shook me from my immobility. Nobody, *nobody*, hurts my horse. And that includes powerful witches. Knowing I couldn't hurt or kill her with weapons, I charged her, slamming into her at full speed and knocking her to the ground. She gasped, and we rolled over, then away from each other. I ended up near Dynin.

Morrian looked at me as she pulled herself back up. *Rhodri, please hurry*, I thought. I got back to my feet. "You have spirit," she said softly. "Does a horse really mean so much to you?"

"Yes," I said, staring back at her. The fall had jarred some of the fear from my mind, allowing me to concentrate and think. I listened to her shield. I could tear it down. But for that I needed time. I couldn't give myself time, because I couldn't talk and sing at the same time. Maybe if Rhodri came back out soon... "Why have you put everyone here to sleep?" I asked.

"Why should I answer you?" she asked. "It matters not. It is enough for you to know that I have. And now, you shall die." Grindles. She wasn't talkative. She began the chanting again. Thunder crackled and lightning flashed overhead. The winds whipped up, nearly knocking me over. I started singing the Creation song, willing the melody to life in my defense. Dynin snorted and stood behind me, supporting me. With the song, I prayed to Abba, asking for his protection, asking for victory, praising him. I knew that such things were anathema to evil.

Morrian's brow furrowed and the pace of her chanting increased. Good. The Song was affecting her. I kept singing, the adrenaline pumping through my body making me feel bolder, stronger. My voice rang out and that, combined with the thunderstorm overhead, drowned out Morrian's chanting. Movement caught the corner of my eye. Rhodri stood in the castle doors, staring at the scene in the courtyard, dagger drawn. To my relief, Lissa stood behind him, fully awake, staring at the courtyard in horror. She gripped Rhodri's hand tightly. Good. Hopefully I would be joined in my efforts momentarily.

Suddenly I sensed the strength of Morrian's shield increase, distracting me from looking around the courtyard for waking people. I kept singing, concentrating on forcing power from my vocal cords and not just volume. Still, I knew I couldn't keep this up indefinitely. With no Brenwyds supporting me, if she continued to bring all her power to bear against me, she would wear me down. *Dynin, tell Rhodri to get behind her and try to knock her out. And start moving toward Lissa. You two need to go for help.* Dynin sent me mental assent and started walking toward the castle door. I saw Rhodri begin to move. Lissa stayed in the doorway, her lips moving in what I assumed was prayer. In the back of my mind, I registered that I heard and saw no signs of anyone else waking. There were no movements from other parts of the courtyard where I knew people lay, no sounds of shouting from people trying to figure out what was going on. A chill crept up my spine. Had no one else woken with Lissa? Had we been too late?

The storm rose to new fury as Morrian threw more and more power into her shield. I realized she was also starting a new spell, one I knew was designed to kill me. If I failed in my song now, I would die. Rhodri crept up behind the witch, raised the dagger above him in preparation for bringing it down on her head hilt-first...but somehow, Morrian sensed him. She abruptly stopped her chanting and spells, turned around, and grabbed Rhodri's wrist just as he started to bring the dagger down. He cried out in pain and the dagger slipped from his grasp. The storm died and I fell to my knees, feeling like a puppet cut from its strings with the sudden cessation of what I had been fighting against. The moon and stars reappeared overhead, brightening the courtyard with their cold light.

"So," Morrian said, her eyes fixed on Rhodri, "this is what you were hiding, eh, girl? You were hoping to keep me out here so this prince could wake his princess and break my spell. Was that it?" She looked back at me. I didn't respond, but then, I didn't have to. She saw Lissa in the door, frozen in the act of preparing to mount Dynin.

Morrian smiled. "How disappointing, then. I designed this spell with the possibility of this scenario in mind and guarded against it. The princess was the starting point, true, but once the spell was cast, it immediately began growing independent of that starting point so that even if this princeling..." She tightened her grip on Rhodri's wrist, and I heard a distinct snap. His face twisted and paled, and he let loose a gasp of pain. "Even if this princeling made it back from Earth to awaken his sweetheart, it would awaken only her. The others still sleep, and the spell goes on. The Brenwyds will awaken at the end of the month to find themselves powerless. Once darkness fell, there was no stopping it." She spoke in a cruelly triumphant tone. It was a repeat of what I had heard before, but of course, she didn't know that I knew the information already. What I wanted to know was why we hadn't gotten there in time to break the whole thing. From what I'd overheard earlier, we had arrived in plenty of time. Perhaps her mention of darkness falling...

"But why?" Lissa's voice asked, interrupting my train of thought. I looked at her. Her eyes were wide in fear, and she gripped Dynin's saddle with white knuckles. "Why would you do this to the kingdom? What have we done to you?"

"What have you done to me?" Morrian cried. She released Rhodri, and he went to his knees, cradling his wrist. I blinked, and realized his wrist was broken. "This kingdom and its Brenwyds took everything from me! I am taking my vengeance! I have waited over two centuries for this opportunity, princess, and this time, nothing shall stop me from taking this puny kingdom. You will all become slaves."

"But...but who are you?" Lissa looked bewildered. "I've never seen you before."

Morrian laughed. "Are you so sure, princess?" Somehow she made Lissa's title a derogatory term. Her form blurred and changed to the old woman she had been when she tricked Lissa into pricking her finger. Lissa gasped and backed up a step from Dynin, her face white. "Do you recognize me now?" She paused. "I see that you do. But you ask who I am." She changed back to her true form. "Have I been so remiss as to not introduce myself? Let me rectify that." She bowed mockingly. "My name is Morrian. No doubt you have forgotten what that name means, but I shall remind you soon enough."

"That won't be necessary," Rhodri said, standing. His face was drawn in pain, but he spoke steadily. "You will leave now and never return." He gripped the dagger in his uninjured right hand.

Morrian laughed. "So says the powerless prince. It would have been better for you to remain on Earth. As it is..." She extended a hand toward him, and he stiffened. After a moment, I realized she had actually immobilized him with magic. "Your princess will watch you die."

"No!" Lissa screamed, coming down the castle stairs around Dynin. Morrian slowly began to curl her fingers into a fist, and I saw Rhodri start to struggle for breath. She was strangling him with magic. I started singing again, quietly, this time focusing on a counter-melody to break the strangling spell. Lissa threw herself between Morrian and Rhodri. "Don't, I beg you. Please." Tears filled her eyes and dripped down her cheeks.

Morrian paused, and Rhodri gasped for breath. "But I must, little princess," she said in a coddling tone as if Lissa was three. "Everyone dies eventually, you know. By killing him now, I save you from having to watch him descend into old age. Wouldn't you rather savor memories of him as a young man, instead of watching him slowly lose his looks and his mind as age takes its inevitable toll?"

"No," Lissa said. "Take me instead. Spare him. Let him go back to his family. Please, do not kill him."

Morrian smiled at her indulgently. Preoccupied as she was with Lissa, she didn't seem to notice that I was nearly finished breaking her spell. Dynin moved from the castle entrance and started walking carefully and quietly toward her. She didn't seem to notice him, either. I looked at him quizzically. What was he doing? "Ah, the true sign of love: offering your life for your prince. How cliché. Unfortunately, my dear, such tactics do not work with me. In fact," she began closing her fingers again, "they make me all the more determined to kill him."

Abruptly she turned to me. "And do not think I have forgotten about you, either." She raised her other hand, and my voice literally stuck in my throat. No sound escaped my mouth. She created a fist with her hand, and though it didn't choke me, exactly, it squeezed my throat hard. I gasped, and my vision blurred for an instant. Then the pressure eased a bit, though it still felt like a rope was bound tightly around my throat. She smiled at me. "Try to end spells now, little Brenwyd." I tried to open my mouth and sing, but my voice wouldn't come, just hacking coughs. She turned back to Rhodri, and closed that hand into a fist. Rhodri's face went red, then became tinged with blue, and he collapsed.

"No!" Lissa screamed again, half sobbing. "Rhodri!" She collapsed at his side. I could see him still struggling to breathe, but it didn't matter, the spell was done now...but then the miracle happened.

A word to the wise.

Never forget about your horse.

While Morrian had been dealing with me, Dynin had walked up behind her. She either didn't see him, or merely dismissed him, to her folly. For at the moment Rhodri exhaled what I was sure was his final breath, Dynin reared up, neighing angrily. Morrian whirled, startled, and had just enough time to see Dynin's hooves waving over her head before they came down on her head, and she crashed to the ground. The invisible rope around my neck disappeared, and I heaved in grateful breaths. Rhodri gasped and his chest began rising and falling rapidly as he sucked in air. Dynin dropped back to the ground, looking enormously pleased with himself. Unbelievably, instead of falling to the ground unconscious, Morrian staggered back up for a brief second, raised a hand, shouted a word I didn't recognize – and disappeared. I supposed the blow from Dynin had injured her enough that she couldn't continue to fight us, but she still had enough strength to get herself away. I was amazed it hadn't killed her, or at the very least knocked her out cold, but for the moment, she was gone. We stared at the place the sorceress had been for several long seconds, silent.

Good boy, I said to Dynin finally, too tired to think of anything else. He whinnied in triumph and arched his neck, as if he were showing off for a mare.

"Oh, Rhodri." I heard Lissa say. "I thought I had lost you again."

"Sorry, Liss," Rhodri croaked. Dynin and I walked to them.

Lissa tried to smile at him. "Are you going to scare me like this often? Because I do not know how much more I can take."

Rhodri smiled in return, though the expression was streaked with pain. "It won't be intentional, I promise." He stood up with her supporting him and wrapped his right arm around her. His left dangled uselessly. Then he looked at me. "Are you alright?" I nodded, too tired to speak. I focused on his wrist. I needed to heal it before we went anywhere, but I didn't feel up to it at the moment. He released a gusty breath and kicked at the stone courtyard floor. "Grindles, this didn't go well. We came too late." His tone was bleak. I agreed with him. We had seriously underestimated our opponent.

"Well, you did wake me," Lissa said. "And I am grateful for that." Rhodri looked at her and his expression softened, but his eyes still held dismay. Lissa disengaged herself from him and came to embrace me. "Oh, Aislinn, Rhodri told me how you found him and brought him back. How can I ever thank you enough?"

I cleared my throat. It felt clogged, but there was also a strange hollow feeling in it that I couldn't place. Perhaps it was because of being almost magically strangled. "Don't give me too much thanks, Liss. You are the one who set me on the right path to him." At least, that's what I tried to say. I stopped halfway into it, panicked and confused, and saw similar expressions on Lissa and Rhodri's faces. I tried it again. And once more. Then I simply tried to scream. It was only then that I allowed myself to realize the awful truth.

My voice was gone.

Gone! Can there be anything more devastating to a Brenwyd? We depend on our voices for so much. We use them to fight and to heal. To soothe and to inspire. Without it...without it we are crippled. Of course, any normal person would be, but we are crippled far more, for without our voices, we are not able to do what we are meant to do. A mute warrior can still fight, a mute peasant can still farm, a mute king can still govern, but a mute Brenwyd cannot perform their duties. Despair rose up to engulf me, the blackness and completeness of it causing me to gasp, and my legs, already feeling weak from the encounter with Morrian, gave way so I collapsed to the ground in shock.

Lissa's hand had come up to cover her mouth. "Oh, Aislinn..." She stopped, as if scared that the sound of her voice with mine gone would offend me.

Dynin nosed me worriedly. *Girl? What happened?*

Morrian, I thought to him, still processing. *That spell...she didn't intend to strangle me, she wanted to cripple me. She...she took my voice.*

How will you get it back?

I don't know...another Brenwyd could break the spell. I looked at Rhodri. He was at a loss. This sort of problem was supposed to be in my list of things to do...but without my voice, I couldn't heal myself. And I couldn't heal his wrist, either. *Dynin, tell them that we need to leave. We can do nothing more here for the moment.* He relayed the message.

Rhodri nodded. "Of course. There's nothing to do now but go to my father. We need help." He looked towards me. "And surely someone will be able to break the spell for you, Aislinn." I nodded a response automatically, starting to feel the painful pressure of tears building in my eyes. I blinked rapidly to contain them, not wanting to lose control in front of Lissa and Rhodri, not when we still had a job to do. Rhodri was right; we would go to Darlesia, and one of the Brenwyds there would be able to heal my voice. I would not be voiceless for long. But my mind did not want to take comfort from the thought. Instead, it seemed to prefer dwelling on the fact that in my first real test against magic I had absolutely, utterly failed. *Abba, why?*

Lissa was looking around the courtyard, the sheen of tears appearing once more in her eyes as well. Though night had now fully fallen, the moon was full and shone brightly, illuminating the courtyard in its pale light and revealing the lumpy shadows of people collapsed in sleep. "I should have known better than to take a gift from someone I did not know. How many times have my parents warned me not to? And Boomer! He tried to warn me, I should have known he would not act so strangely without reason. How can I have ignored him?"

Rhodri moved so he stood in front of her. "Lissa, I told you: this is not your fault. It's likely that if you hadn't taken the rose yourself, she would have forced you to prick it. It still would have happened. Do not blame yourself."

I forced myself up from the courtyard's stones and joined them. I was not the only one hurting right now. I put a comforting hand on Lissa's arm, relaying my own words through Dynin. *Lissa, Rhodri is right. It's not your fault. Truly, Morrian should never have been able to reach you in the first place. One of the Brenwyds should have sensed the presence of someone with magic, and the guards should have been on high alert. But she bypassed us all. We weren't looking for her, so we weren't ready, as she intended. But we will break this curse. We have a month. With Abba's help, we will break this curse. I promise.*

Lissa sighed. "But why didn't any Brenwyds sense her? How is it possible? Where did she come from? Why didn't Abba warn us?"

Her questions echoed my doubts from earlier, doubts that were starting to return. I had really thought that I would be able to bring Rhodri home in time to break the curse. I had thought that Abba meant it to work. But now.... *I don't know,* I answered finally. *I truly don't. But,* I continued slowly, *I...I am choosing to believe and trust that what I have been taught, and have learned, all my life about Abba, that He is in control, and that He is good. He already has a plan in place to defeat this evil, and we just have to believe, Lissa. You must believe. I know it's hard. I've already yelled at Him today about it. Right now, I'm not feeling very happy, either. But I have decided that, despite my emotions, I will trust Him. I will.* I felt my mind settling a little as I reasoned through the decision. I was still upset and hurt, but I would keep trusting. I would. Part of having faith was maintaining belief despite hardship. Otherwise, it wasn't really faith. *Be strong and courageous,* I remembered the reminder from earlier. I would just have to keep being strong and courageous a little longer.

Once Dynin had relayed my words, Rhodri added, "She's right, Lissa. The first couple of months I was stuck on Earth, I was mad at Abba. I wanted to come home so badly, but I couldn't. I resented it. I became angry in general. But then I realized I didn't want to live angry. I didn't like myself that way. So I decided that, despite my circumstances, I would trust that Abba is all the Word tells us He is, and that somehow, someday, He would open the way back home to you. And here I am." He smiled at her and tilted her head up slightly to look into his face. She sighed again and leaned into him – which jarred his injured arm and caused him to release a sudden cry of pain, startling me and Lissa.

"Oh, your arm! I am so sorry, I forgot," Lissa cried out.

I could see Rhodri's jaw clench as he bit back more pain. *Alright, before we do anything else, I'm splinting that arm. It needs to be immobile if you want to keep it from further damage*, I said. I didn't wait for Dynin to finish repeating the words before I walked off toward the stable in search of medical supplies. Because of all the horses cared for in the royal stables, there was a whole room dedicated to medicinal purposes and equipment, despite the fact that Brenwyds were readily available to heal injuries.

I returned to the courtyard with several rolls of linen bandages and two boards of wood to make a splint. I motioned to Rhodri to sit down and hold his arm up. He did as I bid and I settled to the task. Father had made me learn how to tend wounds without singing, so that I would understand better what I was healing with my voice. At the time I had thought it mostly unnecessary since I had already learned human and animal anatomy, but now I blessed the training and resolved to apologize to my father for putting up a fuss. Rhodri grunted and groaned several times, biting his lip to stifle them, the loudest occurring when I actually set the bone back into place.

Once the splint was done, I created a sling for Rhodri's arm to rest in until we got to Darlesia. "Thank you, Aislinn," he said gratefully. I nodded, and we stood. "We had best leave now. That witch might come back at any moment, despite the blow Dynin dealt. And if I remember correctly, the longer a spell lasts, the stronger it becomes, yes?" I nodded confirmation. "Then we should still move quickly." He looked to Lissa. "Is there anything in the castle you'd like to bring?"

Lissa looked up at her home. "Nothing urgent that I cannot get at your father's castle," she said finally. "Let us go." Rhodri took her hand and we started walking down through the city. "Aislinn,"

Lissa said as we passed through the castle gates, "How do you think the spell will be broken now?"

I had been pondering that very question. For the last couple of hours my only thoughts had been of getting Rhodri to Lissa so he could kiss her and break the spell at its starting point. But we had arrived too late for that. So now what? I listened to the spell and found that it did still all connect to one beginning point as I had heard earlier, but now that point was not Lissa. So, what was it? I shrugged my shoulders. *We'll find a way*, I finally answered. *No spell is unbreakable. She's been defeated before; she'll be defeated again.*

"Who is she? Do you know? You still haven't answered that question."

The remainder of the walk through the dark city was taken up by explaining to Lissa in detail what had occurred that day and my thoughts on Morrian's identity. Once I said who I thought she was, I was gratified that Lissa didn't think it silly. In fact, she supported it. "Of course," she said in response. "I knew that name sounded familiar. Morrian was – is – the name of Nivea's stepmother. I've read it in the records."

"Are you sure?" Rhodri asked.

"Yes," she answered. "Most recordings of her name were blacked out after the Battle of Kheprah, because people wanted to forget, but it was preserved in a few places so not everyone would. It has been some time, but that was her name in the records, I am sure of it."

"Couldn't it be someone who simply took her name because of its history, to seem more powerful?"

I frowned at Rhodri. *No, it is her. Why are you so doubtful?*

He sighed with a rueful half-grin. "Sorry. I suppose I've spent too long in a world where the only magic is found in movies."

"What?" Lissa and I asked at the same time, though of course only her voice could be heard.

He chuckled. "I'll explain later."

By the end of the conversation, we had reached the city gates and passed them. I mounted Dynin and began trotting him around in a large circle at an easy pace to warm up his muscles properly before leaping into a transfer gallop. "You mentioned that there is a barrier of fog and thorns around the borders? Will that be a problem?" Lissa asked as I circled around her and Rhodri.

I shook my head. "I shouldn't think so," Rhodri agreed verbally. "Brenwyd horses can transfer right past it."

"But would she not have thought of that?" Lissa wondered. "She is so powerful, it would seem she has considered everything."

"No one can think of everything," Rhodri said. "Besides, how could she block the transfer ability, even with magic? It doesn't make sense."

Lissa sighed. "No, but little about this day makes sense."

Just as I was urging Dynin to pick up speed for the transfer and was beginning to picture the field behind Rhodri's father's castle specifically kept clear for transfers, I sensed a ripple of magic scrape across my song sense. It was subtle, but there, and I slowed Dynin to a halt, frowning as I looked around.

"What is it, Aislinn?" Rhodri asked, also starting to look around. I listened more closely with my song sense, but heard nothing more. Morrian didn't seem to be returning, and none of us had fallen asleep, so what had the magic been for? "Aislinn?"

Mystified, I simply shrugged my shoulders and gave them what I hoped was a reassuring smile. Since there didn't seem to be any imminent danger, I didn't want to worry them. Perhaps it was still from the main spell that had been enacted earlier. I urged Dynin on again, and my surroundings began to blur in the familiar way.

I started to relax slightly at the thought of enlisting the aid of more experienced hands and minds to help Ecclesia, but then a sudden jolt jerked me off balance and Dynin snorted angrily. The next moment I felt his hindquarters sink and he slid to a stop, which threw what was left of my balance to the winds and I tumbled off.

I landed hard on my back and my head thumped painfully into the ground. I gasped, trying to force air back into lungs that felt crumpled, and spots appeared in my vision. I shut my eyes to stave off dizziness and focused on taking slow, deep breaths. Fortunately, it seemed I had landed on a relatively soft area of ground, and once I got enough air back in me, I didn't think I had been injured beyond some bruises. *Dynin?* I asked, still keeping my eyes shut. *Are you alright? What happened?*

I think I am fine, he said. I felt his muzzle nudge my head. *Are you alright? I am sorry. I did not mean to.* He was genuinely distressed. Unless a horse had a malicious streak or a rider was truly abusive or incompetent, horses tended to be very embarrassed when they lost their riders, Brenwyd horses especially.

I slowly sat up, keeping my eyes closed until the initial lightheadedness of changing positions passed. *It's alright. I think I'm fine.* I opened my eyes cautiously. There were a few black dots, but they passed quickly and my vision returned to normal. Dynin was standing directly in front of me, and he was anxiously sniffing me all over. *What happened?* I repeated.

I do not know. He sounded annoyed and angry. *There was suddenly a...a wall, or some such thing, blocking the way, and I could not get past it and I had to stop.*

What? How is that possible?

I do not know. I have never felt anything like it.

I started to look around at our surroundings, and I realized we were in the forest on the road to Darlesia. Or more specifically, just off the road. I had landed in a patch of grass and moss, thankfully missing any tree roots. I reached a hand around to feel the back of my head, and winced as I found the tender spot. But I didn't feel any broken skin, and when I brought my hand back around there was no blood spotting it. I'd have a headache for the rest of the day – or night, rather – but I didn't think there was lasting damage, which was fortunate since I couldn't heal myself.

I turned my attention to Dynin and ran my eyes over him. I saw no visible cuts but, given the jolt and sliding stop, I was worried he might have strained his tendons or sprained a ligament. *Go trot out for me,* I ordered him. He grumbled, but did as I said. I felt a wave of relief as I saw no indication that he was lame. When he returned to where I sat, I used him to help myself stand. Only a little bit of dizziness accompanied the movement. *Now, where exactly are we?*

We are near the barrier, Dynin said, looking behind me.

I turned and saw the wall of thorns and fog. My stomach dropped as I fully realized what it meant. No...it couldn't be. I shut my eyes and shook my head slightly, wanting to convince myself it was just a trick of my vision after my fall. But the thorns and fog stubbornly stayed put. And we were on the Ecclesian side of it. Somehow, Morrian had managed to frustrate Dynin's transfer ability. And if we couldn't transfer out...then no one else could transfer in.

I sank to the ground again, sliding down Dynin's side, and let the tears that I had suppressed earlier come in full force. Within a few moments I was completely overcome by silent sobs. Every time today I had seen a sliver of hope, it kept vanishing from sight. *Abba, I can't take this again. What are we supposed to do now? We are stuck here, and no one knows we're in trouble. We keep being stymied at every turn. I don't even have a voice to fight with anymore. Where are you? I know I said brave things earlier, but every time I keep making up my mind, something knocks me down again. Where are you? Where? Show me! I can't do this alone.*

My thoughts continued in this vein, though the force of my sobs gradually diminished until I simply rested against Dynin's legs with my eyes closed, feeling spent. He bent his head around and lipped at my hair in his comforting way. A tired calm quieted my thoughts.

And in the quiet, I began to See.

A vision appeared in my mind, a mountain valley surrounded by towering peaks. The mountains were painted in hues of slate, flint, ebony, and sable, broken up here and there by the dull sage of scrubby plants clinging to life in the rocks. The valley itself had a silvery cast in the moonlight, but there was the slightest shimmer of emerald in the tawny winter grass that indicated the approaching spring. There were clumps of evergreen trees and bushes in the valley, and a stream flowed through the length of it. It came from the mountains on the north side of the valley, and spilled into it via a long, narrow waterfall that fell into a small pool at the base of the mountain. In width I judged it to be less than a quarter mile across, and perhaps a mile and a half long. It was a pleasant scene, all told, and my fingers suddenly itched with the urge to capture it on canvas. As I watched, I saw a shape - a large, dark shape that reminded me of a bear yet wasn't one - move between the trees. I couldn't make it out well. *Here*, a small voice whispered. It resonated through my body and brought a strange peace to my mind. *Look here. Have courage. Trust me.*

What? I asked it, but it didn't answer and the vision dissolved. I blinked, coming back to myself in the forest.

What is it, girl? Dynin asked.

I Saw something...a valley in the mountains. I think...I think we're meant to go there. My hope began to return, and with it, a sense of awe. Abba had heard me. He had *answered* me...once I had taken the time to quiet myself and listen. In my haste and worry earlier, I had forgotten the importance, even in the midst of crisis, of taking the time to pray and really listen. Now, despite my lingering worry, I felt a renewed sense of purpose. I wasn't alone. Abba would guide us, as long as we trusted.

A small smile flitted across my face. I rose to my feet and climbed back on Dynin. *Come, Dynin. We must tell Lissa and Rhodri of the change of plans.*

❧✦❧

Lissa and Rhodri were surprised, alarmed, and upset to see me return on Dynin, especially when they heard why. But I tried to hush their dismay by explaining what I had Seen, and my conviction that it was where Abba was guiding us next. I'm not sure I convinced them, but they overlooked their doubts for the moment. We took a few minutes to go back into the city and quickly gather some supplies, since we would not be getting to Darlesia as expected. Lissa wrote out a list of everything we scavenged from merchant stalls so we could properly reimburse them later. Rhodri and I also took the opportunity to change back into Niclausian garb, since we were both still wearing Earth clothes. Once we each had a pack and loaded Dynin with more, I remounted him and, fixing the image of the valley firmly in my head and passing it to him, urged him into a gallop.

I felt a little trepidation about transferring, given our last experience, but this time it went smoothly, and we arrived in the valley from my vision. It looked just as I had seen, and the quiet rushing of the stream was a soothing sound to my ears. It was also colder than Kheprah, and after I dismounted Dynin and sent him back for his next passenger, I dug a heavier-weight cloak from my pack. Clearly, we were somewhere high in the mountains that lay on Ecclesia's northern border, and the air still contained the bite of winter's chill. I looked around me carefully, looking for the... thing...I had seen moving in my vision. I hadn't mentioned that bit to Lissa and Rhodri, not wanting to alarm them further. I saw no sign of whatever it had been, and decided not to worry about it. Fortunately, no one had seen a mountain ogre in decades, so I didn't have to worry about those fearsome creatures. Legend said they could tear a man limb from limb and enjoyed eating their victims. I wasn't sure I believed all the stories, but I was certain I didn't want to meet one. For a few moments I thought I sensed something with my mind, some sort of animal, but I couldn't identify it and it retreated quickly.

Dynin soon arrived back with Lissa, and we began gathering wood for a fire. We had decided prior to departing Kheprah that, assuming we found no danger in the valley, we would set up a camp and sleep the rest of the night. Though Lissa commented dryly that she had had enough sleep for one day, Rhodri and I were approaching exhaustion. We got a nice fire going, and once we decided there was enough wood for the night, Rhodri and I settled down to sleep, with Lissa keeping watch.

⊹⊱⊰⊹

He watched the group curiously. It had been a long time since anyone had come to his mountain valley. The young blond woman was on watch, and she sat close to the man with her hand entwined in his. He guessed that they were a couple. The other young woman, with auburn hair, slept on the other side of the fire. The horse stood near her like a large watchdog, nibbling at the grass. She had sensed him earlier, before he thought to guard himself. She was a Brenwyd. A Brenwyd, he thought with longing and no small amount of pain and regret. How long has it been...but no matter. He had sensed a great magic in the land earlier that day. It had rolled through with a storm, and it had a familiar taint. It had been over two centuries since he had sensed it last, but he recognized it easily enough, though he scarcely believed it. Morrian. He was sure of it. But how it could be so, he didn't know. And it scared him.

The Brenwyd stirred slightly. The firelight played off her features, fair as all Brenwyds were, yet, though he had seen such features many times before, hers strangely fascinated him. There was joy and laughter there, things he had not experienced in years. And indeed, it had also been years since he had seen such beauty, though he couldn't recall ever seeing a Brenwyd with freckles. They lent her an innocent air, like a small child. Curiously, though, he hadn't heard her say a word in all the time she and the other two had set up camp. The others had asked her questions, but she had either nodded, shaken her head, or glanced toward her horse. *Could she be mute?* he wondered. He'd never heard of a mute Brenwyd, not since...he growled at the memory. If Morrian really was somehow still alive and moving, he had no choice but to face her, but inwardly he trembled, knowing well the price he had paid the last time he'd done so.

An Unexpected Meeting

I woke early the next morning in the dim light of dawn. Before I had drawn two breaths the remembrance of everything that had occurred the previous day crashed over me, and before I could stop myself, I began to cry. I allowed myself the luxury for several minutes. Though my vision and the reminder of Abba's guidance and presence had bolstered my spirits last night, I was still upset. And given everything that had happened yesterday, I thought myself entitled to some tears.

After a time, though, I forced myself to stop crying. It was a relief for my emotions at the moment, but in the long run, crying wasn't helpful. I needed to start thinking of what in the Five Realms we were supposed to do next, and determine what it was in this valley that Abba wanted us to find. I took several long, slow, deep breaths. *It could be worse,* I thought determinedly. *I could be dead* (though upon reflection I decided that wouldn't be so bad, since once dead in this world I would travel to Abba's eternal paradise). *Lissa and Rhodri could be dead. Everyone in the kingdom could be dead. At least with this sleeping spell, we have a chance to save the kingdom, and we have a rather long time frame to do it in.* I took a deep breath, wiped the tear tracks from my face, and sat up, alerting Rhodri, who was on watch, that I was awake. Unfortunately, the movement also caused the muscles in my back and neck to start up a strenuous protest. I hissed in a surprised breath and winced.

"Are you alright?" Rhodri asked. I turned to him carefully, still wincing. I shrugged my shoulders. "Sore from the fall, are you?" I nodded. *Ouch.* Normally if I'd taken a fall my mother would insist on me taking a long, hot bath with salts, which did wonders for leeching the soreness from muscles. However, right now hot baths were clearly out of the question. "Are you sure your head is alright? No blurry or double vision or headaches or dizziness?" I raised an eyebrow as I considered him. I had never known Rhodri to take on the role of nurse. He shrugged and smiled a bit self-consciously. "Head injuries are taken very seriously on Earth. If you ever bump your head, you usually have to get checked over for a concussion. I only want to make sure you're alright."

I smiled and nodded in thanks for his concern. Dynin glanced my way from where he was standing with one of his hind legs half-cocked in a resting position. Judging by the large area of cropped grass around him, it seemed that he had made good use of the rest. *Morning, Dy,* I said.

Morning, he replied. *Did you sleep well?*

Well enough. I stood carefully and stretched my arms over my head. Despite my reluctance to move, I knew that it would do my muscles better to get moving than for me to stay in one place.

"Did you have any dreams?" Rhodri asked. I shook my head. I had actually been half-expecting dreams when I had gone to sleep, hoping Abba would relate more guidance through my Sight, but nothing had appeared to mar the blackness of deep sleep. I supposed it meant that Abba had decided we knew enough not to need guidance, or perhaps he would supply it later. I hoped the latter was the case. I had no idea what to do next beyond investigating the valley.

Rhodri and I lapsed into silence as the sky lightened. It took some time for the sun to rise high enough for its rays to peek into the mountain valley, but we could see the progress of the light by watching the eastern sky paint itself crimson, orange, and amber. "That sunrise is rather appropriate," Rhodri commented, breaking the silence. I knew what he meant. Across Niclausia it was widely held that a red dawn presaged trouble, whether it be of a natural or human nature. I nodded agreement with him.

"What?" Lissa's voice asked sleepily from behind us.

"Red sunrise," Rhodri answered.

"Oh." She got up and sat beside him.

He placed an arm around her shoulder and drew her close. "I know it likely doesn't feel like it, but happy birthday, Liss."

She sighed, but managed a small smile. "It does not, but thank you. Only yesterday everything was so normal...and now..." She took a deep breath that sounded suspiciously like she was fending off tears. "But at least you are here, Rhodri. I thank Abba for it. It makes things a little bit better."

"Only a little?" He assumed a wounded air. "Surely I should qualify as making things a medium bit better."

I shook my head at his teasing, but Lissa gave him a small laugh. "If you put it that way, then I suppose. But I cannot admit to you making things a large bit better. Remember, I know full well how you sing."

I began shaking with silent laughter as Rhodri continued his offended front. He knew as well as anyone that he was horribly tone-deaf. "What? You mean my serenades weren't what won me your hand? I was sure of it!"

Now Lissa started laughing genuinely. "What won you my hand was that you always know how to make me laugh. Even now, in the worst of circumstances, you are making me laugh. That is what I treasure about you."

Rhodri dropped the offended front and gave her a tender smile. "And you always know when to remind me to be serious." He leaned in to kiss her.

I cleared my throat and gave them a look. Having been roped into acting as chaperone for all of their courtship, I often turned my back and pretended I wasn't paying attention to what they were doing, but kissing directly in front of me was much harder to pretend to ignore.

Rhodri turned my way with a laugh. "Apologies, Aislinn, but do give me some liberty. I was gone for six months."

I shook my head and turned toward Dynin to have him relay my words. *You were supposed to be gone for six months in any event. You were merely supposed to be at your father's castle instead of another world.*

"Fair point, I suppose." He started to say something else, but my attention became fully distracted by watching Dynin walk. He had moved closer to us when I asked him to speak for me, and then began walking back to where he had been grazing. I knew his walk as well as I knew my own, and I could tell when something was off.

Dynin, are you feeling tenderness in your legs anywhere? I asked.

It is fine, he said in a brusque manner.

Then why are you moving so delicately? I rose and walked over to him, intending to fully examine him.

I am stepping carefully. I am just a little sore. I am fine, he insisted. Still, I ran my hand down his legs, searching for any bumps or heat. Given his abrupt sliding stop yesterday, it didn't surprise me that he was also feeling sore. Rather, I was more upset with myself for not thinking to make any poultice to apply to his legs before I slept last night. I had been trained to take care of my animals before myself, always, but I had been so tired when we finally set up camp last night that it had slipped my mind.

I felt a little bit of heat along the tendons of his hind legs, but they didn't seem too inflamed and he barely flinched when I pressed them gently to gauge his reaction. Listening to his song, I heard only a slight discordance to indicate the injury. He was right; it wasn't bad. I released a sigh of relief. *Well, I think you're out of being ridden for the next couple of days, but you should heal well.*

I told you, he said.

Yes, yes, but I had to check. I began rummaging in my medicine sack. It was full of useful herbs, bandages, and a few other medical supplies my mother always insisted I take with me on rides. I had mostly done it just to humor her, since I had never imagined a scenario when I wouldn't be able to heal an injury with my voice, but now I blessed her for it. I didn't have much in the way of supplies, but I should have enough that, if I used small quantities, I could make a poultice to calm the inflammation in his legs. The cold water from the stream would also be helpful in drawing out the heat.

"Is it bad?" Lissa asked, the corners of her mouth turned down. Even though we couldn't transfer out of Ecclesia, Dynin was still our main means of transport, and having him lame would only add to our difficulties. I smiled reassuringly and shook my head. Relief crossed both hers and Rhodri's faces. "Will it heal quickly?" I nodded again, taking out the proper herbs from my kit.

Dynin, go and stand in the stream. Let the water run over your legs.

But it is cold, he grumbled as he started to move.

That's the point. It will help. I busied myself with grinding up the herbs. Lissa came to help me.

Rhodri was looking around the valley. "You're sure this is the valley you Saw in your vision?" he asked. I looked up at him and frowned. Of course I was sure. He raised his uninjured hand in a gesture of surrender. "I'm only asking. We couldn't see it very well last night."

"It is pretty," Lissa said, swiveling her head to take it in. "But I do not understand why you Saw it, Aislinn." I shrugged. I didn't know, either.

Rhodri sighed. "Regardless of whatever we find here, we must figure out what we're to do next. The other kingdoms are closed to us, and they can't get to us, either. We need to figure out a way to let them know what's happened here." Lissa and I both nodded.

"Do you have any ideas of how to make that happen?" Lissa asked. "You mentioned yesterday that you tried to send a bird over the barrier and it was unable to do so."

Rhodri turned his gaze to me. "Aislinn, do you think you could reach someone on the outside with your Sight?"

I blinked and rocked back on my heels, thinking. I knew what he referred to. Those with Sight were sometimes able to communicate with each other over long distances through dreams, provided at least one of them was asleep. However, it generally worked best when the people communicating knew each other well, and most of my good friends with Sight were currently asleep. I shrugged my shoulders. "It's possible," I mouthed carefully. I began running through people in my head that I might contact. I turned toward where Dynin stood in the stream so he could relay my next words. *It could also be very possible that many Brenwyds outside Ecclesia have had visions and dreams about what happened. Morrian blocked physical travel to Ecclesia, yes, but she cannot stop Abba from communicating with us. Also,* I added as a thought occurred to me, *any Brenwyds near the Anianol Forest yesterday should have sensed the curse fall. It was a huge disturbance. Not to mention all the panic among the animals on both sides of the barrier. This cannot remain secret.* The more I thought on it, the more I realized it was true. Morrian may have taken measures to prevent interference, but even she couldn't curse a whole kingdom and keep it a secret for a month.

"Yes. I hadn't thought of that," Rhodri mused. "But surely she knows that as well."

"Maybe she assumes that the strength of the spell will keep it intact for the full month despite outside Brenwyd interference," Lissa suggested.

"Maybe." Rhodri turned his gaze to me suddenly. "Or maybe she has a plan to deal with any Brenwyds who come to destroy the barrier."

My eyes widened and I straightened as I caught his meaning. My hand flew to my throat.

Lissa caught the movement. "You think the way she took Aislinn's voice is a defensive measure."

"It's certainly effective."

"But what if there are a lot of Brenwyds? Several regiments worth?" Lissa wondered. She turned towards me. "Are there not limits to what any spellcaster can do?"

I nodded. I glanced toward the creek and told Dynin to come back over. *Yes. But normally, I would have thought that cursing a whole kingdom would be beyond the strength of one spellcaster. Yet she did, and was still strong enough to nearly kill us in the courtyard. It does not make sense. And there is something else.* While Lissa and Rhodri had been speaking, another piece of the conversation I'd overheard yesterday had returned to me. *She told her master that she intended to stir up trouble in the other kingdoms to keep them distracted. Something about waking monsters and activating servants.*

Lissa blinked. "Waking monsters? But monsters have not been seen in any of the kingdoms for almost a hundred years. Even if there are still some left in the wild places, surely there are not enough to prove a great threat." I shrugged and began applying the poultice to Dynin's legs.

The first of our ancestors to come to Niclausia had been nearly overwhelmed by the number of monsters freely roaming the continent. They had named them for monsters talked about in stories from the old world – Earth, rather – and the records spoke of sirens in rivers and on the coast, pooka and kelpies in bogs and swamps, chimeras and hydras lurking in the Anianol Forest and caves, ogres and goblins in the mountains, and many more. Not all were dangerous, though. Centaurs and satyrs had lived in grasslands, brownies in burrows, and dragons had ruled the skies. But whether friendly or not, in the last two hundred years they had all disappeared. Part of it was the Monsters' War of a hundred years ago, when some sort of madness infected the friendly monster species and turned many against us. The people then had had to fight back for their own survival. As for the others, most thought that the unfriendly monsters had finally been hunted to low enough numbers that their populations couldn't be maintained and so they died out naturally. I had always wondered if they were all truly gone, though. There were reports and stories every so often of hunters or foresters stumbling across a monster or two, but they could never be verified.

Rhodri's voice pulled me from my musings. "She said she had servants in the other kingdoms?" he asked. I nodded. "I suppose we should assume that they're magical servants. They could cause a lot of trouble."

"Yes, but again, there really has not been much magical activity in years," Lissa said. "So where could all these servants come from?" Silence fell as we pondered the problem. I finished applying the poultice and wrapped bandages carefully around Dynin's hind legs to hold it in place. A thought flitted through my mind as an explanation, and I frowned. *Surely not*, I told myself. *No one could have that much forethought.* So I kept it to myself.

Dynin startled us all out of our thoughts with a loud snort and stamp of his foot. *That is enough. You will not be able to help the kingdom by trying to theorize things that may not even happen. Focus on what is in front of you right now. Girl, you said the One gave you the vision of this valley. Should we not be trying to determine why?*

We all blinked and looked at each other. Dynin was right. We should focus on what was currently in front of us. I blessed his animal common sense.

Rhodri released a gusty sigh. "Yes, of course. One step at a time." He looked around. "Where should we start?"

I followed his lead and focused on really examining the valley. It was almost completely encircled by the mountains, but I made out a path leading out of the valley to the south. It looked fairly unused, more of an animal track than a human path. I pointed towards it. *We could start by following the path*, I suggested. *See where it leads.*

Rhodri looked to where I was pointing and squinted. "What path?" I sighed and started walking towards it, beckoning them to follow.

In a few minutes, we stumbled over it. I stopped and crouched, examining the track with curious eyes. I saw no familiar animal tracks, but there were large depressions pressed deeply into the ground. "What sort of tracks are those?" Lissa asked warily.

"It looks like some sort of large boot print," Rhodri commented, copying my pose. I nodded agreement, brow furrowed. Whoever had made the tracks walked on two legs and wore shoes, but the prints were much larger than any human tracks I had ever seen.

"You do not believe it could be...something nonhuman, do you?" Lissa asked anxiously. Given our recent conversation, the possibility of monsters loomed large in all of our minds. Rhodri and I exchanged glances and stood.

"Whatever it is, it's sleeping the same as everyone and everything else in the kingdom," Rhodri said in a reassuring tone. But I noticed that he dropped his right hand to touch the hilt of the sword hanging from his left hip. I could tell Lissa caught the movement as well by her raised eyebrows, but she decided not to comment.

I began walking along the path, and the other two and Dynin followed. It led over the stream at a ford that had stones placed in a manner that let us cross without getting wet...except for Dynin. I ordered him to stay on the other side of the stream to avoid getting his bandages wet. He protested, but I was firm.

Once on the other side we entered one of the small clumps of trees and bushes. Hollies were abundant, as were pines and junipers, along with aspens and birches and a surprising number of fruit trees whose buds were just beginning to open. As we walked through it, something about the trees began to bother me, but I couldn't figure out what. We left the trees and came once more into the open, and the path curved around another stand of trees. It seemed to be leading to the rock face at the north end of the valley. I strained to look ahead and examine the rock face. Did the path lead from the valley to somewhere?

"Aislinn, wait." Lissa's voice halted me. I turned to see her frowning at the trees we were passing, and she stepped closer to them. "Do these trees strike you as odd?"

So she had picked up on it as well. "How can the trees be odd?" Rhodri asked, puzzled. "They look normal to me."

"Yes, but—" Suddenly I gasped, cutting Lissa off midsentence, and looked at her with understanding. "So, you do see it?" she asked. I nodded.

"See what? They're trees." Rhodri still sounded baffled.

"Yes, but it is too tidy," Lissa explained. "If we were walking around someone's estate then I would expect this upkeep, but this is a wild valley in the mountains. There should be fallen limbs, old piles of leaves, overgrown bushes, but there is none of that. It is natural growth, but it is maintained. Not to mention I have never seen such clusters of apple, pear, and cherry trees occurring naturally, especially as high up as I suspect we are." She was right. Given we were exiting winter, there should be layers of leaves under the trees. But there weren't. There were some here and there, but mostly it was a clean carpet of grass.

"What does that mean? Someone lives here? Where?"

"I do not know about someone living here, but someone certainly tends this valley." Unease crossed Lissa's face.

Rhodri clearly saw it, too, as he said in a light tone, "Well, whoever it is, Liss, I should think you'd get on well with someone who enjoys gardening."

A reluctant smile crossed her face. "If we meet the gardener, I hope that is the case." She came back to the path, and he wrapped his arm around her, pressing a light kiss to her forehead. I turned to give them some privacy and started walking on again, returning to my study of the cliff face and trying to squelch the brief flash of envy that I felt. While I didn't have a desire to be married anytime soon, watching Lissa and Rhodri's relationship over the past years had caused the desire for such a relationship of my own to plant itself in my heart. I had been pursued a few times by interested men, both Brenwyd and non-Brenwyd, but the most feeling I had ever been able to muster towards any of them was that of friendship. I had decided to content myself with being patient. After all, my parents had not met until my mother was nearly twenty-two. I was only eighteen. I had time.

I shook my head to dismiss the thoughts and focused on the cliff face approaching. The narrow waterfall tumbling into the pool was to my far left, and the noise from it was starting to increase. Now that I had a clear view of it, I noticed what looked like thick briars on either side of the pool where it met the cliff, and an incongruous burst of color at the base. I changed my course so I walked towards it. The bursts of color were flowers, the early-blooming crocuses and daffodils that always first indicated the arrival of spring. Here was more evidence that someone with gardening tendencies frequented the valley.

As I got closer, I recognized the briars as rose vines. They were carefully pruned so they ran up the cliff face next to the waterfall, and I imagined that in early summer it was a lovely sight. "Why would anyone tend to roses up here and yet not live here?" Lissa wondered aloud from behind me. She passed me and hurried to examine the vines closely, though she didn't reach out a hand to do so. Given what had happened yesterday, I didn't blame her. "These are not wild vines. And look; I would judge that a pruning was done recently." She gestured to the evidence of snipped branches. I nodded agreement as Rhodri and I joined her, keeping a careful eye out. I wondered if the gardener was the presence I had sensed both in my vision and the night before. If it was the gardener, how had he or she escaped the curse? Or were we beyond Ecclesia's technical boundaries here, as I had been in the forest? Looking into the pool, I saw that the water was startlingly clear, so clear I could not tell if it was two inches or two feet deep. The rocks at the bottom were small, round stones with all the colors one might see in a rainbow.

I nudged Lissa and pointed out the multi-colored rocks. "That is curious," she said, her eyebrows raised. "Where does one find rainbow stones?"

"I've seen colored stones in ornamental gardens on Earth, but I never thought one could find them naturally," Rhodri commented. I shrugged. I had never seen colored stones anywhere, so I had no comments to offer, even if I could speak. I was starting to regret leaving Dynin across the stream. In leaving him, I had left my only means of speaking.

Not seeing anything of particular use to us by the pool, I began moving along the rock face, keeping alert for the presence from the night before. Rhodri followed me. As I moved, I began picking out odd details that from a distance had seemed part of the natural rock, but now did not. Several holes at irregular intervals dotted the grey rock, a tall promontory jutted out of the rest of the cliff, and there was a large boulder that seemed more regularly shaped than was natural, roughly the size and shape of a door. When we reached the area right before the boulder, Rhodri and I looked at it silently for several moments. The more I looked at it, the more it looked for all the realms like a door, and the holes looked like windows. Had someone chipped a dwelling out from the inside of the rock?

"I don't know what you see, Aislinn, but this doesn't strike me as entirely natural," Rhodri commented. Apparently, he was also seeing the resemblance to a house. "Do you think we should try to open this...door?" I shrugged and nodded. I supposed we might as well. "If we can determine how to open it, that is," Rhodri added under his breath as he started to do so.

As I watched him, a slight movement from up the cliff face to my right caught my eye. There was a gap with several large boulders, likely the result of a rock fall, and I thought I had seen something move between two of them. I fixed my gaze on the spot and extended my thoughts toward it. As I had suspected would happen, the presence brushed against my consciousness. Again, I puzzled over it. It was not completely animal, yet I did not have the gift of human mind-speaking as some Brenwyds did. So how was I sensing this presence?

Perhaps because I am sensing you in turn, a strange, masculine voice said in my head, making me jump with a slight gasp of surprise.

"Aislinn?" Rhodri was looking at me with raised eyebrows and a puzzled expression. "Are you alright? Did something bite you?" I frowned at him and shook my head. I waved a hand at him to continue his efforts. "Very well. Could you help me?" I motioned my hand for him to wait, then, with a thought, gestured back towards where Lissa was still examining the garden. "You want me to go back to Lissa?" I nodded. "Why?" I gave him a look. I couldn't exactly explain. He caught it and nodded ruefully. "Right. Sorry. Very well then. I'll go help Lissa..." he looked toward his fiancée, "check the roses for poison thorns and the pool for pond monsters." He walked over to her. I stared after him, shaking my head but smiling a bit at the statement. I had missed Rhodri's humor over the past six months.

I returned my attention to the rock fall, where I now observed a black shadow lurking. *Who are you?* I asked mentally.

No one you would know. The voice was pleasant and melodic, yet I heard an underlying sadness and stoicism that intrigued me.

If I knew, I would not be asking in the first place. Who are you, and why do you hide yourself?

A pause. *I am someone who likes to be alone. And so when people come, I observe them until they depart.*

You live here? Where?

In my castle. You are standing next to it. Your companion was just trying to enter it. The voice sounded irritated as it said the last sentence.

I turned to the curious rock formation. *You call that a castle?*

Any man's home is his castle, is it not? Now he sounded testy. Hmm. I would have to proceed carefully.

I suppose. Why won't you come down so we can talk face to face? Isn't it customary to greet guests?

I heard an annoyed "humph." *Guests are invited. You were not. Therefore, you are not guests and so I have no obligation to greet you.*

I frowned. He sounded like a grumpy old hermit. Perhaps he was. But...wouldn't such a person prefer to tell us off in person instead of waiting for us to move on? And he must have noticed us last night. *Were you the one I sensed last night?* I asked.

Yes. You are observant...You are an animal speaker, are you not?

Yes.

That would explain it, I suppose. His tone changed from irritated to sad.

But you're not an animal, I objected.

And how do you know this? You sensed me and are speaking to me. And I know Brenwyds are not both animal speakers and mind speakers. So I must be an animal. He sounded a little angry at the statement. His emotions seemed very changeable.

Your speech is much too human and refined for an animal. And you have not yet answered my questions. Who are you and why were you watching us?

As I said earlier, you are not guests, so you are trespassing in my home. Therefore, I do not think you are in a position to ask me questions. So, answer one of mine: why do you not speak? I have never heard of a naturally mute Brenwyd. I was momentarily floored, and now I felt irritation of my own flare. Yes, I supposed we were technically trespassing, but we had not known anyone lived here, and I had been polite in my queries. What right had he to ask me for answers when he gave me none? *None, I suppose,* his voice came to me, sounding almost sheepish now. *Forgive me. I have forgotten the niceties of conversation.*

Then perhaps we should start this conversation over, I said. *Now. My name is Aislinn. And you are?* Silence met my reply.

I jumped when Lissa's audible voice spoke from behind me. "Aislinn, what are you looking at?" I hadn't noticed that she and Rhodri had walked up behind me. Since I couldn't explain, I pointed towards the rockfall.

What are you doing? The voice sounded alarmed. *I did not say you could reveal me.*

Well, I cannot tell them what I'm doing, as you have observed, so I must answer as best I can.

"Aislinn, what are you pointing...what in Niclausia?" Rhodri was looking at the rockfall, and at that moment the figure moved. It stood slowly, revealing that it was well over six feet tall, easily large enough to have left the tracks on the path.

Lissa gasped and moved behind Rhodri, who put his good hand on his sword. I held up a hand and shook my head at his action. "You need not fear me, young prince. I mean you no harm. In fact, were it not for your friend here, I would have simply waited for you to leave before coming down." He sounded a little disgruntled at this last comment, but his voice startled me. Mentally it was smooth and musical, but his audible voice was quite rough, deep, and sounded as if he was speaking out of a growl. It was a bit of a challenge to make out his words.

His words didn't do much to reassure Rhodri, whose hand remained at his sword hilt. "A fascinating theory, since she cannot speak currently. Who are you? And what makes you think I am a prince?"

"Because you are, are you not? There is a royal crest on your tunic, and I doubt a mere servant would be wearing such rich fabric." He nimbly climbed down from the rockfall, jumping the last two yards and landing easily. Rhodri briefly glanced down at his tunic, which did bear his family's crest of an oak tree and crossed swords over an open book, and was made from damask. He usually wore something less elegant when out riding, or in general, but he had been wearing it the day he vanished since he had been taking a formal leave from the king and queen, and so it had been what he'd changed into before we left Kheprah.

"Fair enough," he said. "But who are you?"

"As I have told your friend here, since you are trespassing on my land, I do not think I am obliged to tell you anything." Rhodri frowned deeper, but the man went on. "However, as she has also reminded me of common courtesy, you may call me Mathghamhain."

"We may call you? Is that not your name?"

"It is my name. Originally, you are right, it was not, but it is now." He shifted his head to me. It was impossible to tell anything about him, other than his great height, for he was cloaked head to toe in black robes and a cowl completely obscured his face. "And now, shall you tell me yours?"

Rhodri and I glanced at each other. I nodded, trying to encourage him to. "Very well," he said. "As you have surmised, I am Prince Rhodri of Darlesia, and this," he stepped a little away from Lissa, who still hid behind his back, "is Crown Princess Calissa of Ecclesia."

"Ah." Mathghamhain directed his next words to Lissa. "Please, Your Highness. Do not be afraid. I mean you no harm. If I did, I would have driven you from the valley yesterday." He turned slightly towards me. "So you see, I have answered your question. Will you answer mine?"

I gazed at him steadily. *I am not much in the habit of speaking to people whose faces I cannot see. Will you not take your cowl off?*

"Aislinn, what's he talking about?" Rhodri muttered.

You would not wish me to.

Why? Do you consider yourself so ugly? Or is it that you think yourself too radiant for mere mortals to look upon?

It is not that I consider myself ugly; it is that I am, and I do not wish to frighten you. There was definitely sadness in those words, along with bitterness.

"Why do I get the feeling there's some conversation going on that I am not a part of?" Rhodri asked.

"Because there is," Mathghamhain replied. "I apologize. It has truly been a long time since I have interacted with people. I have the gift of mind speaking, and so have been talking with your friend here, since she seems unable to speak aloud."

"But I thought mind speaking was only a Brenwyd ability," Lissa said, a little timidly.

A pause. "You speak truly." For a moment, my heart leapt with hope.

The same hope sparked in Lissa's eyes as she took a step toward him. "Then you are a-"

"Once. No more." I wrinkled my brow in confusion. What could that mean? "I was asking your friend why she is unable to speak, because I have never heard of a Brenwyd being naturally mute, though I recollect a time when many were rendered dumb through the spells of a powerful sorceress, and yesterday I sensed a great magic roll throughout the land. I fear she may be moving again, though how I know not."

Now this was significant information. Lissa, Rhodri and I all looked at each other in surprise. I turned back to Mathghamhain. *Yes, it is true that a spell took my voice. It was cast by a woman called Morrian.*

"Morrian..." His voice was most definitely a growl on that word, but I thought I heard a slight tremble. He seemed to sink against the rocks. "As I suspected."

"Pardon me, but how do you know her?" Rhodri asked. "It is our impression that she is, somehow, the witch from Queen Nivea's time, over two hundred years ago."

A pause. "That is true."

"Are...are you claiming to be over two hundred years old?" Rhodri sounded very dubious.

"I have lost track of the years...but if you say it has been that long, then yes. I am."

"How?" The question burst from Lissa's lips, and she came out from behind Rhodri's back a little. I blinked and felt my jaw drop at the casual confession.

"Apparently, Abba has seen fit to extend my life." He sounded resentful of the fact, though maybe not. It was hard to judge his tone of voice through the growl.

"Forgive me if I sound skeptical," Rhodri said. "It's a rather fantastic thing to believe. How do we know you're not simply delusional?"

"You do not. However, I would think a prince who has traveled between worlds would be a bit more open-minded."

Rhodri's eyebrows shot up. "And how would you have come by that information?"

There was another pause, and I got the feeling Mathghamhain was considering us carefully. "I believe it would be easier to show you than explain. To see is to believe, is it not?"

"Sometimes," Rhodri answered.

Mathghamhain turned. "Come." He stalked away toward the pool.

"What do you think, Rhodri?" Lissa whispered.

"I don't know...it's an impossible thing to claim, and he's not exactly inspiring a lot of trust in me right now."

"He certainly has a frightful appearance. Perhaps he is one of the monsters that Morrian meant to wake. How could someone simply stop being a Brenwyd?" Lissa looked at me. "Aislinn? What do you think?"

I shook my head slowly and shrugged. I did not think he was a monster. I did not understand his statement about no longer being Brenwyd, either, but what I was sure of was that he hated Morrian. Could the reason Abba had led us here be to meet him?

"But let's go see what he wants to show us, all the same," Rhodri said. I nodded, and we followed our strange new acquaintance to the shores of the pool.

"Watch," he instructed us. Then his head bent toward the pool, and he reached a gloved hand into the water, then said as if by rote: "Abba, show your servants the events of the land." For a moment, the water remained clear. But then, it started to change.

The rainbow pebbles in the pool began to glow and the bottom became clouded. Then the colors merged and formed an image, blurry at first but quickly made clear, and we were looking at a forest track running through a clearing in the evening. It was so realistic I felt I could fall into the pool and emerge in the forest. Indeed, almost without realizing it my hand stretched toward the water. Mathghamhain caught it swiftly. "Do not touch the water." I reached my hand back, wondering at the feel of his hand through the glove. Somehow it hadn't felt quite...normal. But any musings on that vanished as riders appeared on the track and hoofbeats reached my ears.

"We will stop here for the night," a voice said, and I jumped, for it was Rhodri's. Lissa gasped. Yet he had said nothing from right beside me. I watched, fascinated, as I discerned that the lead rider of the company in the image was, in fact, Rhodri, and that it must have been before he fell through the portal to Earth, for his hair was long and brushed his shoulders.

"You do not wish to travel further tonight, Your Highness?" another man asked. I recognized him as Iwan, Rhodri's valet. He had been one of the riders to come back to Kheprah to tell us of Rhodri's disappearance.

"No. The light is leaving us, and I'll not risk the horses on this trail in the dark. Besides, we may not find another spot so suited to camping for miles."

"Very well, Your Highness." The riders went about making camp, and Mathghamhain dipped a finger into the pool and dissolved the image.

"What magic is this?" Rhodri, the real Rhodri, asked from beside me, his voice tense.

"No magic, Your Highness. It is a pool that Abba endowed for my use so that I may keep up with what goes on in the world, if I wish. You heard me petition him before the image appeared. I do not control what appears in the pool. Sometimes I ask, and no image forms. Other times I see things without asking. Abba shows me what he believes I need to see, nothing more and nothing less. In this way I have glimpsed each of you, but you must forgive me for not recognizing you immediately. I am not accustomed to those whom I see turning up at my castle."

"Castle?" Lissa asked. "What castle?"

"It is there," Mathghamhain pointed behind him. "I realize it does not look like much, but it suits my needs."

While this conversation had been going on, I stared at the pool in fascination, and I now saw another image forming. I tugged Rhodri's sleeve to get his attention, and then pointed at the pool. This time, a true castle we all knew formed in the pool, and I heard Rhodri draw in a sharp breath. It was his family's castle, where he had been going when Morrian had flung him into the other realm. The image then switched to the great hall of the castle, where Rhodri's father, Lord Prince Ceredon, Duke of Clunglasham, sat on his seat and listened to a man speaking to him urgently. Rhodri's mother, Lady Duchess Rhian, sat beside him, an anxious look on her face. Of Rhodri's two sisters and three brothers there was no sign. That was not surprising. They were all married, save for one of his brothers, and had their own lands and properties to manage. I recognized the Brenwyd man before Lord Prince Ceredon. It was my father's friend, Sir Eiwas.

"-And then I saw a great mist going out in every direction over Ecclesia, completely covering the landscape. As it reached the people and animals, they fell to the ground in sleep. It stopped at the borders, whereupon a great hedge of thorns sprang up as a barrier to anyone wishing to enter the kingdom. I was so troubled I rode to the border this morning, and found the mist and wall of thorns exactly as I had dreamed. There is some great magic at work in Ecclesia, your grace, and I beg leave of you to gather as many Brenwyds as possible to go try to tear down the wall."

"But Sir Eiwas, you implied that you had news of...of Rhodri," Lady Rhian said, her voice trembling as she spoke her missing son's name. She was an elegant woman, with thick burnt umber brown hair that had started to become streaked with gray, startlingly emerald eyes, and skin the same dark honey shade as Rhodri's. She was always perfectly dressed and composed with never a hair out of place. "What of that?" I glanced at Rhodri. He stared at the images of his parents with great longing and blinked rapidly. Lissa had put a hand around his waist and studied his face anxiously. Sir Eiwas's reply recaptured our attention.

"Your grace, I do indeed, though I know not quite what to make of it. After I saw the mist cover Ecclesia in sleep, my dream shifted to a particular part of the forest where I saw a young woman, and I identified her as the Lady Aislinn, Princess Calissa's particular friend." I raised an eyebrow in surprise. "The mist rushed upon her, but several yards short of her, it stopped. I know not why. She then turned her back to the mist and began to sing, and a strange doorway appeared in front of her. It was not a true doorway, but I glimpsed through it things I do not understand and do not fit with the Anianol. She passed through this gateway. After a short time, she stepped back, and with her I saw Prince Rhodri." Lady Rhian pressed a hand to her heart, as if the longed-for news were too much for her to take after so many months.

"Did he look well? Uninjured?" Duke Ceredon interrupted. I noticed that his face looked more lined than the last time I had seen him six months ago.

"He looked quite well, my lord. But my dream was not yet finished. After they stepped back through the gateway, they entered the mist, but did not sleep. They traveled to Khephrah, and I watched Prince Rhodri go through the palace to where the Princess Calissa lay, and he wakened her with a kiss. Lady Aislinn remained outside, and a woman, the sorceress who I assume cast the spell, appeared to her. They did battle, and while Lady Aislinn, Prince Rhodri, and Princess Calissa managed to drive her away, I sensed she was not defeated. Not at all. My dream ended there, with the three of them standing in the courtyard."

"But Rhodri remained unharmed?" Lady Rhian asked.

"So it appeared to my Sight, my lady. But I know not what they did next."

Duke Ceredon stood. "We must send a battalion into Ecclesia immediately. Whatever mischief has been loosed there, it must be defeated and Rhodri brought home."

"But that is the trouble, your grace. I tried to travel inside Ecclesia's borders to observe things for myself, but I was unable to enter. When I tried cutting my way through the thorns, they regrew faster than I could cut, and when I tried to transfer in, something rebuffed my horse and he was unable to transfer. He said there is some magic barrier preventing him."

"You mean Rhodri is trapped there?" Lady Rhian said, clasping her hands together in a worried way.

"It appears so."

"Nonsense," Duke Ceredon said. "If you gather the Brenwyds of the province, I am sure you shall be able to break through any such barriers, Sir Eiwas. And when you do, finding Prince Rhodri, Princess Calissa, and Lady Aislinn and getting them here to safety is your primary mission."

"Of course, your grace, but I have never sensed a spell so powerful. It may take us some time," Sir Eiwas warned. "I had never even dreamed of such power being manifested in a mortal."

"Nevertheless, Sir Eiwas, I command you to go and gather such men as you need immediately. And I shall ride with you myself."

"Ceredon!" Lady Rhian objected. Her husband looked at her.

"He is our son, Rhian," Ceredon said. "And I swear to you I will bring him home. Rhys will oversee the province while I am gone. It will be good for him." Rhys was Rhodri's oldest brother and the heir to his father's lands in Darlesia. "But such a powerful sorceress, your grace," Sir Eiwas said, clearly distressed. "I would prefer taking only Brenwyds."

"You will have to endure my presence, Eiwas, for I shall be accompanying you. Besides, our eastern border abuts Ecclesia's. It is also in the interest of the security of the duchy that I go, and how could I send men to a place I was unwilling to go myself? I trust you and the Brenwyds completely. Now go and raise as many men and women as you think necessary. I shall follow you shortly."

"Your grace." Eiwas bowed to Ceredon and then Rhian in a formal leave-taking. "My lady duchess." He turned and hurried out of the room. Once he had gone, Ceredon took his wife's hands.

"Do not fret for me, Rhian. I promise I will come back to you."

"But the forest...it already took Rhodri..." I had never heard Rhodri's mother sound so unsure. She was always a steady, reliable presence. I found it very unsettling. I could only imagine how Rhodri felt to hear his mother so upset about him.

"And out of it I will bring him to you. I need you to be strong while I am gone. For the children. For the province. And for me."

She nodded wearily, tears sparkling in her eyes. "I will do my best, Ceredon."

"I know you will, my jewel." He kissed her, and then walked out of the room, calling for his valet to bring his armor. The image dissolved. Rhodri, Lissa, and I looked at each other with wide eyes, and something like hope. Other people knew our plight. Help would be coming, even if we could not leave to raise it. We had been right in our discussion earlier.

"Your parents, I assume, Prince Rhodri?" Mathghamhain's growly voice asked.

Rhodri nodded. "Yes." His voice was tight. After six months away, even a glimpse of his parents through a pool was nearly overwhelming.

Lissa put comforting arms around him. "Help is coming for us. It will be alright." She sounded rather relieved. I, on the other hand, was not quite so sure, remembering the other parts of our discussion this morning. I looked to Mathghamhain. It truly did irk me that I could not see his facial expressions. I had half a mind to go and yank his hood off. He couldn't be that ugly.

I would not recommend that, he said darkly in his mind. *For that would greatly irk me.*

I was taught that it was rude for mind speakers to read others' minds uninvited, I retorted.

There was a silence before he answered. *That is true. Forgive me.* I was struck again by the fact that his mental voice sounded so different from his vocal one.

Why do you feel the need to cover up so? I asked.

I...was the victim of an...accident not unlike what you have suffered. But no more of that. You are right to doubt the ability of help to come. It took a great force of Brenwyds to cast Morrian down the first time, and she has only grown stronger since then, if she is able to have cast a spell of this magnitude and not die. And...she often has a spell within a spell to attack those who try to break it.

"What do we do until they are able to break down the barrier?" Rhodri asked, drawing my attention away from the mental conversation. A deep frown was on his face. "It could take some time, especially if we are right in our suppositions from earlier."

"Oh...I had forgotten," Lissa admitted, worry clouding her face again. "But surely if a large enough host is mustered, they will be able to break through, even with interference. No matter how powerful, she is only one witch."

"Ah, but she is often upheld directly by the power of the Shadow Angel and his minions," Mathghamhain said darkly. "And so she can endure more than one can think possible. Do not underestimate her. Even when her spells fail, there is often a hidden backlash against the one who dismantled it. She cannot be defeated without creating some irreparable damage. Without any idea of what they are combating, I doubt the success of the initial attempt at breaking this spell."

Rhodri frowned at Mathghamhain. "You certainly paint a cheery picture. Have you no belief in hope or the power of Light over Dark?"

"I am merely trying to prepare you for what may be required to defeat her."

"If, as you claim, you truly were alive at the time of Morrian's defeat two hundred and fifty years ago, I think your words would be better spent telling us how that was achieved than casting down our hopes."

"And it is because I know of what it took to defeat her that I am giving you such stern warnings now. You do not know her as I do."

"Then share your story and help us know her," Rhodri said. "Then Aislinn may be able to relay the knowledge to the Brenwyds on the outside through her Sight. And perhaps this time we really will kill her." At this he went silent. "Well?" Rhodri said impatiently.

"If only you knew what you ask," Mathghamhain said at length, and I caught the nuances of a deep pain in his voice, growly and gruff though it was.

Rhodri, however, didn't seem to hear it. "It is because I don't know that I am asking. Tell us your tale."

"Perhaps you should first tell me yours. After all, you are in my valley. I heard what the man said as well as you, but there were many details lacking."

"You mean your pool did not show you?"

"As I said," Mathghamhain said slowly, seeming to grow irritated with Rhodri's needling, "Abba is the one who controls what images I see through it. I saw nothing yesterday, and only knew of the spell because I sensed the magic spread across the land."

I could tell Rhodri was about to make some reply that would not help Mathghamhain's mood, but fortunately Lissa interrupted. "Pray, excuse us for a minute, Mathghamhain. Your story and claims are much to take in after yesterday. Let us discuss things for a few minutes, and then we shall tell you our tale." Though she spoke to Mathghamhain, her gaze was trained on Rhodri and her tone of voice had steel in it. I had a feeling Rhodri was in trouble.

"Very well." Mathghamhain left the pool and walked toward his "castle."

"What has gotten into you?" Lissa whispered to Rhodri harshly. "Why were you needling him like that with questions?"

"He's claiming impossibilities, Lissa," Rhodri answered in the same tone. "And I don't like how he's cloaked. It makes me distrust him."

"He does have a point about us trespassing on his mountain. We must treat him with courtesy. He could be a very valuable asset. Perhaps he is the reason Abba sent Aislinn the vision of the valley."

"You believe his story?"

"The pain I hear in his voice as he speaks of Morrian does not sound like the sound of someone who is lying."

"You can hear a tone beyond the growl? His voice makes me almost agree with you about monsters. Perhaps he is a werewolf or something of that nature."

I tugged Rhodri's sleeve and shook my head at his remark. "I was only being facetious, Aislinn. Partly, anyway. How do you feel about him? Do you think he's telling the truth?" I nodded.

"Why?" I gave him a look. I couldn't very well explain. "Ah, yes, bad question. Sorry." I shrugged. "Do you trust him based off your mental conversations with him?" I nodded. While I thought his manners could use some improvement, he did not come across as a liar. Rhodri mulled that over, and sighed. "Very well. Let's exchange tales with him. I suppose I should be more diplomatic, but I don't feel particularly diplomatic at the moment with him disparaging Father's forces."

"Then it is a good thing that I am," Lissa said, smiling briefly. I turned and reached out to Mathghamhain, indicating my wish to communicate for him to pick up on. I could not initiate a mind conversation otherwise. He caught it and came back.

"You have decided?" he said.

"Yes," Rhodri asked.

Mathghamhain inclined his head. "Good. I am anxious to hear it." With that, Rhodri began a bare-bones narration of our dealings with Morrian, starting with his fall through the portal and ending with my vision of the valley and our decision to come here.

"And so," Rhodri concluded, "we believe that Abba led us here for a purpose, and maybe it is to seek help from you."

"I see..." He sounded thoughtful. "You have truly been to the other realm?"

"Yes."

"Even in my time, there were tales that the gateways remained accessible, but from what you have said I believe they were more common. Did you like it there?"

Rhodri thought for a moment. "I didn't dislike it," he said slowly. "Many of the innovations and conveniences there were amazing – like the running water in pipes, the flying conveyances they have called planes that can traverse great distances in mere hours – but the spiritual element of life there was missing. Many do not even believe in Abba – or God, as he is called there – at all. Consequently, despite all their comforts, many people are unhappy.

There are also no Brenwyds, and I think that's part of why that world is so spiritually dark. From what I learned of its history, I can understand why our ancestors wanted to leave."

Mathghamhain nodded slowly. "I see. I know not if this history has survived, but I learned that part of the reason the gateways were opened to the Brenwyds to begin with was as an escape from persecution in that world from people who thought them witches and wizards."

"Yes, that is what we learned as well, but I never understood how that could be so," Lissa responded. "Nothing could be further from the truth."

"Much like you mistook the power of the pool for magic because you did not understand, so they mistook Brenwyd abilities for magic, or so the records said." He shook his head slowly. "But you do not want to hear a history lesson from me. You want to hear my story. And so you shall." His head lifted upward, where the sun was approaching noon. "But let me gather some food first. You must be hungry, and one thing I do remember of hospitality is that the host should never let his guests go hungry." Now that he mentioned it, I became all too aware of hunger gnawing away at my stomach, and I heard it growl. I felt a blush of embarrassment rise to my face at the noise. "And it seems Aislinn's stomach agrees with me," Mathghamhain continued, with something almost like amusement flavoring his voice.

Rhodri looked like he wanted to protest the interruption, but Lissa intervened. "Thank you, Mathghamhain, we are rather hungry. Would you like us to help you prepare?"

"No, Your Highness, that is not necessary. I gather my food from the mountain, in places I doubt you could reach." He stood. "I will return within one hour. In the meantime, feel at liberty to explore my castle. Its nooks and crannies may surprise you." And with that, he turned, ran to the rockfall, sprang up among the rocks, and was gone.

Morrian's History

"Well," Rhodri said. "He certainly climbs like a mountain goat. Perhaps he's an oversized satyr, you know, the ones that are half man and half goat."

"Rhodri!" Lissa sent him a reproving look.

"What? He's clearly not human. Not entirely, anyway. Aren't you curious about what lies beneath his cloak?"

"Well, yes, but...oh, never mind." She looked at me. "I suppose we have to wait for Dynin before you can tell us what you talked about mentally." I nodded, sighing. She put a hand on my shoulder. "We will get your voice back, Aislinn. Somehow, we will. We must."

Rhodri turned his gaze out over the valley and the mountains beyond. "I wonder if the scene we saw with my parents was just then taking place, or if it already had."

"But at least we know they are coming," Lissa said brightly. "Though we are trapped, they know and are coming. I refuse to let Mathghamhain's dire mutterings cloud my hope. I simply cannot believe one person's spells could stand up to a whole battalion of Brenwyds." I, on the other hand, could, though I didn't want to. I had listened to those melodies. It was a small miracle that I had been able to dissolve the thorns around Kheprah by myself. To dissolve the thorns around the whole kingdom? That would take many, many Brenwyds. Then again, across Niclausia were many, many Brenwyds. If Sir Eiwas's initial regiment was unsuccessful, they could spread the word to other communities. *No spell is unbreakable*, I reminded myself.

Resolved to adopt Lissa's own determined optimism, I rose and indicated we should go investigate Mathghamhain's "castle," and the others agreed. I let them walk ahead a few minutes and cast my mind out to Dynin to instruct him to find a way across the creek that avoided getting his bandages wet so he could join us.

When I caught up to Lissa and Rhodri, Rhodri was once again trying to open the door. This time, after a few tries he was successful. Inside was a dark, unlit hallway that even my eyes could barely make out. "Hmm. I think I can fix this," Rhodri said. He reached into his bag and pulled something out. It was a solid metal tube that I had never seen the like of before. One side had a shape reminiscent of spring-flower bulbs with clear glass over it.

"What is that?" Lissa asked, echoing my own unspoken question.

"This is what's called an electric torch, and it provides light without having to use fire." He pressed a button on one side and instantly a bright beam of light shot out the end with the glass. I scrutinized it even more carefully with interest. It was some sort of light source from Earth, I guessed.

Lissa gasped in delight. "But how does it work?"

"It has small objects called batteries inside, and they power the light. Here, take a look."

Lissa took it and examined it curiously. "If this other realm has such inventions, no wonder you did not dislike it. Do you think we could replicate it? These would be much safer than torches around the castle."

"Hmm, perhaps, but I have no idea how these things are made. Besides, if we wanted to light the castle with similar technology we would have to figure out how to create electricity here."

"Electricity? What is that?" They began to have a detailed conversation about Earth inventions. Though I was also keenly interested in the topic, at the moment the lure of exploring the castle pulled on me more. Seeing an unlit torch several feet down the hallway, I removed it from its hanging, lit it, and left them to their discussion.

It wasn't a castle like any I was accustomed to, with fine stonework and lavish furnishings. Instead, the hallways and chambers bore the marks of pickaxes and looked like they had been chiseled directly out of the mountain. I rather suspected they had. I found a kitchen, a pantry, what I took to be a parlor, one definite bedroom, and several other rooms that seemed to serve no one function. Furniture was scarce, but I was surprised at the skill evident in the finished product. I supposed that if Mathghamhain was the maker, and he really was as old as he said, he had had plenty of time to perfect his skills.

The most surprising discovery I made was that of a very well-stocked and – in comparison to the other rooms – well-furnished library. All the chairs in here were cushioned, and several very old-looking tapestries hung from one of the walls. In the middle of the room was an enormous table with books and scrolls lying across it, neatly organized. The other walls had wooden shelves from floor to ceiling, and each was covered with scrolls, parchment manuscripts, ancient vellum volumes and, surprisingly I thought for a person who claimed to be two hundred and fifty years old, many printed books with paper. These were a rather new invention in Niclausia, having been invented about seventy-five years ago, but they were very popular because they were inexpensive compared to traditional hand-written tomes. I browsed the shelves, noting famous authors, historians, or scribes here and there, but I was more interested in the artwork decorating the ancient volumes than the contents of the books themselves. Given my disability, books and I had a rocky relationship, but the artwork and calligraphy on some of the ancient books and scrolls was something I could fully appreciate. It was rare to find such tomes nowadays, and these were in very good condition. The books on the table were some of the finest examples I had ever seen, though I did have to stretch a bit to examine them. Of course, all the furniture in the castle was built to someone of Mathghamhain's proportions.

The hour was up before I realized it. I was outside when Mathghamhain returned. Dynin, despite my warnings to the contrary, had not bothered to find a way across the stream without getting his bandages wet, so I was reapplying the poultice and giving him a scolding. *I told you to find a way across without getting your bandages wet. Was it really so hard to do? I do not have unlimited supplies of these herbs, Dy, and I need them, with my voice gone. I cannot be constantly remaking this poultice for you.*

I am sorry. At least he sounded sheepish. *It was easiest to simply cross the water.*

I know. But there was no rush for you to come to this side. You had time to find another way across. Suddenly Dynin's head came up, nostrils flaring, and he snorted worriedly. I looked up to see what had alarmed him, reaching for my sword, but relaxed as I saw Mathghamhain's huge form climbing down the rock face, holding a package. I got up and laid a comforting hand on Dynin's neck. *Easy, boy,* I said soothingly. *It's just Mathghamhain. He won't hurt you.*

He smells of wolf and bear and predator, Dynin said, his eyes rolling so the whites showed. *Dangerous.*

I raised my eyebrows slightly. *Yes, his size is intimidating, but he will not hurt you. He said he would help us.* Dynin made no response, but continued his worried snorting. Every muscle in his body was tense. Though Brenwyd horses tended to be bolder than regular horses, they still retained a fear of predators. But why would Dynin sense such things about Mathghamhain? Rhodri's words came back to me: *He is clearly not human.* So what was he? Were we right or wrong to trust him?

You may assure your horse that I will come no closer to him. I should have warned you that animals find my presence alarming, Mathghamhain's voice entered my mind.

It's alright. I've already told him. Let him grow accustomed to you.

Hmm. Where are the prince and princess?

In the castle. They are investigating your library. I went back to packing Dynin's foot with the herb poultice. *I must confess, I was surprised to find such a place.*

I told you the castle might surprise you. Did you enjoy it? I definitely heard a hint of smugness in his voice.

I liked the illuminations and calligraphy. The art is beautiful. But I'm not much of a reader, I'm afraid.

What? He sounded so shocked and horrified that I had to smile. *You do not read?*

Not much. I prefer to paint. And garden.

But why?

I sighed. Despite now knowing that my disability was known on Earth, I still had to contend with the ignorance of people in my own world and I didn't feel like convincing him of its existence at the moment. *It has no interest for me,* I replied shortly, straightening.

No interest? How could it not? He seemed genuinely puzzled. *Especially with all the new stories that have been written since the printing press's advent?*

I like hearing the stories. I simply don't much like reading them. Anxious to change the subject, I turned and gestured toward the pool and its flowers. *Besides, you seem a poor choice for criticizing gardening. The condition of this valley seems to point to your own interest in the subject.*

True. I do enjoy caring for the earth, he admitted. *One of my few pleasures.*

I turned back towards him and let my gaze drop to his bundle. *What have you there? Surely you did not go hunting with all the animals asleep and defenseless.* The thought had occurred to me in the last hour, and I let my disapproval come through.

Of course not, he snapped. *I am not a b-* He stopped abruptly. Guilt filled me at the vehemence of his response. Maybe the strength of my disapproval had been a bit much. I had a feeling that he picked up on my apologetic feelings, because when he spoke again he was much calmer. *I have a storehouse a little ways from here where I store meat, vegetables, and fruit preserves.*

Oh. Now I felt very sorry. *I do apologize. What did you bring?*

Wild tomatoes and maize preserves, some dried apples, and dried mountain deer meat. It is not much, and likely much poorer fare than you are accustomed to, but I am nearly to the end of my winter stores, and food up here is scarce to begin with.

I shrugged. *It sounds enough like a feast to me. We mostly have bread and cheese. Do you grow any crops up here for yourself or do you only gather what you can find?*

A combination of both. I have a vegetable garden hidden in one of the tree stands there, he indicated with an outstretched arm, *and in the warmer months I make foraging trips to the lower elevations. I do mostly eat meat, however. Mountain deer and the like are very plentiful up here.*

Ah. Given that tidbit of information, I was glad he had brought more than just meat because I did not eat meat. Being able to communicate with animals, I simply could not make myself, though I knew animal speakers who did and some animals themselves were surprised by animal speakers who did not. They knew that predators eating prey was a natural part of life and accepted it, and humans were the most dangerous predators of all.

During our conversation, Dynin had stood directly behind me as if trying to hide, and now he poked his heard around my side cautiously. He extended his muzzle toward Mathghamhain slowly, then jerked it back and huffed nervously. *What is it?* I asked him.

I have never smelled anything like him. I smell wolf, bear, panther... and yet there is an underlying scent of man. I do not like it.

I stored that comment away for further pondering. *Shall we call Rhodri and Lissa, then?* I asked Mathghamhain.

No. We will go to them. I thought making a stew would be best to stretch the stores to all of us.

At the suggestion, I made a face. *Then I hope you can cook halfway well. The kitchen is not one of my strengths.*

Well, I am not the most skilled, perhaps, but what I can make is good.

⁊ᎶᏚᎶᏕ

"You are a better cook than I would have imagined for someone living all alone in the mountains, Mathghamhain," Lissa said as she tasted the stew beginning to bubble in the pot.

"Thank you, Your Highness, but it is because I live alone in the mountains that I can cook well. There is no one else to cook for me, and so if I wish good food, I must make it myself," Mathghamhain answered.

Lissa smiled. "I suppose I should have thought of that. And please, call me Lissa. This is not a court."

"But it is my castle, and thus, formality is required, at least while we are still getting acquainted." He turned toward me. "You are sure you have enough to eat?" I nodded. Upon discovering my vegetarian tastes after adding the meat to the pot, he had felt deeply embarrassed. Ever since, I had been trying to convince him that what was left of the vegetables he had brought, along with our own supplies, was plenty for me. "So, Mathghamhain," Rhodri said. "Since the stew is now set to bubble for the next hour or so, perhaps now will you tell us your tale?"

There was a heavy silence for several minutes. Mathghamhain drew in and breathed out a very audible sigh. "Yes. So we come to it at last. Please forgive my reluctance, Prince Rhodri, but I have never shared the tale with anyone in full before, and it is painful to recall. But I shall do my best to relate it in a concise manner."

Lissa reached out a hand and placed it lightly on Mathghamhain's arm. He flinched slightly as he felt the touch. "It is perfectly alright,

Mathghamhain. And please, if there is a part that is too painful, you may relate it to us at a later time."

"You are kind, Princess Calissa, but no. I must tell you all, for I need you to understand fully the power you are up against." His voice became more vigorous. "Very well. I begin. I know not what you have learned of your history, but in the third year of the reign of King Llewellyn his wife gave birth to a daughter, whom she named Nivea. However, the birth was hard and she was a delicate woman, and so soon after the birth, she died. The king had loved his wife dearly, as had his kingdom. The whole kingdom was in mourning for a year and the king swore he would never remarry. But when Nivea was ten, she and her father traveled to Lamasia for the crowning of its next king, and there he met a beautiful young woman named Morrian."

He continued the tale from there, describing how the king seemingly fell deeply in love with her, despite his vow, and so determined to marry her within a month. Of course, Lissa, Rhodri, and I knew the story well, but it was good to hear it again, and Mathghamhain added many details our history teachers had left out. Many of the king's royal advisors, having counseled him to remarry to leave a son (until that point no woman had inherited the throne, and our only ruling queens had occurred when their husbands had died and their sons were still too young to rule), approved the match, though the king's greatest friend, a Brenwyd, had a horrible dream warning the king not to marry her. It became a great quarrel between the two men, and the Brenwyd left the court. But when the king married, his queen seemed sweet, subservient, and kind, and so many soon came to greatly admire her. In hindsight, people could see how she slowly began inserting herself into all matters and building a loyal core of support away from the king, but she moved so slowly that not even Brenwyds closest to the crown realized what she was until it was too late.

Three years after his marriage, Llewellyn had a seizure and collapsed, and he was never the same. He could not walk or move his arms, and at times he was not in his right mind. Morrian nursed him day and night, helping him with his advisors and running the kingdom, and at first no one remarked greatly on this, for it was her role as wife and queen. However, she slowly poisoned his mind against Brenwyds, for try as they might they could not heal the king of his affliction. There began to be natural disasters, like famine, flood, and rumors of witches as well as a sudden increase in monsters that swept the land and cast Brenwyds in an ill light, though they tried as hard as they might to avert and alleviate the disasters. And so, nearly two years after the king's collapse, he signed the fateful order for all Brenwyds to leave the kingdom and never return, on pain of imprisonment. The populace was shocked, but not so unwilling as to disobey the order. The Brenwyds by this time knew there was some magic at work in the land, but the idea that the queen was behind it was only the faintest whisper in the back of anyone's mind, for Morrian had reportedly pleaded with her husband to desist from his path and promised the court Brenwyds she would try to sway his mind to rescind the order. She was cunning and clever in laying a foundation of professed love for Brenwyds. (At that point Mathghamhain paused, seemingly thinking, before saying slowly, "And also, her father had married a Brenwyd woman after her mother died of sickness and she had a Brenwyd half-brother whom it was understood she loved greatly." Rhodri, Lissa and I looked at each other in surprise, not having heard that before. Mathghamhain briskly took up the main thread of his story again.) So, she stayed above suspicion. For a time. The Brenwyds left Ecclesia, content to watch and wait, sometimes slipping back over the border to try and locate the source of the magic, but as a year slipped by, and another began passing rapidly, some began to wonder at the queen's lack of success. And then, the year Nivea was eighteen – she loved her father dearly, but had been kept as tightly as a prisoner, watched by her stepmother's servants – King Llewellyn died. In that same year, Morrian revealed herself for what she truly was. After the king's funeral, a Brenwyd delegation went to her and asked to be relieved of their exile. Morrian refused. Indeed, she had them arrested on charges of treason and accused them of poisoning the king so that they could take over the kingdom through Nivea. Before word of her actions reached the Brenwyds in exile, she had the emissaries executed as an example.

While her stepmother had been growing high in the king's favor, Nivea had been growing up. Though in her childhood she had been the apple of her father's eye, after his marriage Morrian gradually replaced her in his affections. And so she became rather solitary, wandering around the castle, helping the servants in their chores for something to do and sneaking into the city to talk with the citizens. She wanted to know her people. When her father died, she was devastated, but in no way prepared for what came next. After Morrian executed the Brenwyd delegation, she gave all soldiers the go-ahead to use force to keep Brenwyds out of Ecclesia. The Brenwyds had been gone long enough and were in such disfavor that many of the younger soldiers were suspicious of them, and whispers ran throughout the kingdom accusing Brenwyds of the very magic they were made to prevent, and so the soldiers followed these orders with few qualms. When her half-brother, the only Brenwyd to have been legally allowed in Ecclesia, tried to reason with her, Morrian showed him her true colors as a witch and had him thrown into the darkest dungeon. But this she did in secret. The people were startled and alarmed by her actions, but at that time a great storm devastated the province of Eredwan and she sent them great help, even going herself and working with the peasants to help them rebuild, and so the people were somewhat reassured.

It was Nivea who forced her next move. At eighteen, she was old enough to be included in the government as she would become the ruler on her twentieth birthday. Yet Morrian knew that to bring her into councils would derail her plans. So she planned for a riding accident to befall her. She called her huntsman, and instructed him on one of Nivea's frequent rides to lead her deep into the Anianol Forest and kill her, and then to claim one of the monsters had done so.

This very nearly worked, but the scheme went awry when an actual monster, a chimera, came upon them. The huntsman was badly wounded but managed to survive long enough to make it back to Kheprah and tell the queen it was done, for he assumed Nivea had met her end at the monster's maw, something his own death supported.

Yet Nivea lived, for in the middle of her struggle to escape, a monster hunter and several of his seven sons happened upon her. They killed the beast, but she had already been badly wounded and fell unconscious. Not knowing who she was, the man and his sons took her back with them to their home to tend her injuries. She recovered well physically, but when she woke she could not remember who she was or anything of her past. Thus she remained with the family as she regained her full health, for she knew nowhere else to go. A year passed, during which time she and one of the middle sons of the house fell in love and began making plans to marry.

By the end of the same year, evil things began to stir quickly and openly in Ecclesia. Morrian's half-brother, whom she had kept alive for her own pleasure to torture, escaped and fled to a Brenwyd settlement just outside the country and told them of Morrian. The Brenwyds, who had begun suspecting Morrian was a witch, took his arrival as a sign to begin amassing against her. They organized into an army, bearing flamestone weapons made for battling witchcraft, and swore to fight in Nivea's name. During this time, the half-brother went to the monster hunter's cottage to seek his help, for he was also a woodsman and forester who knew many secret ways in the Anianol. When he arrived at the house he found Nivea, whom he recognized instantly. He was able to restore her memory, and then he asked her to lead them, as the true heir to the throne. She agreed, and she and her adopted family journeyed to the Brenwyds' camp. The news that she was alive was impossible to conceal, and spread fast as dragonflight over the land.

This news brought Morrian fully out of hiding at last. Now she openly ruled with her army, imposing her will on the kingdom and forcing the lords to swear fealty to her. To ensure their loyalties, she bound them with strong magics they were helpless to resist. She also sent out men to find the best and fittest of the youth to form into the core of her personal army.

Terrified, those who could fled to the Brenwyds and Nivea. Brenwyds and soldiers from the other realms continued to pour into the army, until at last the two sides met in the fields before the very gates of Kheprah. At last, Nivea, Morrian's half-brother, and a few others managed to fight through and actually face Morrian. Her protection was strong, with so many counter-spells that it would have taken days to analyze and break them all. Even with the flamestone blades, the small company could not match her for longer than a few minutes before she overwhelmed them with her magic. But at the point she would have slain them, one threw all caution to the winds and leapt on her, pinning her to the ground, distracting her long enough for the other Brenwyds to break her magic. But he paid the price, and did not leave the field.

At that point Mathghamhain paused, as if lost in remembrance. "The breaking of her magic was so potent that everyone across the field was cast down to the ground... She flung her attacker off her, and so she was able to run to the Hellwyl. She jumped into the current, and it was so strong and deep there that, without her magic, we assumed she had perished. We searched the banks for days, but her body never appeared. That should have told us she still lurked. But in our weariness, we decided the river meant to keep her.

"Nivea was crowned queen the next day, to give the citizens something to hope in. Once the cleanup from the battle and Morrian's damage was done, she wed her love, Chiaran, and everyone conveniently forgot his status as the son of a woodsman. Those who chose to gripe about it were quickly silenced by reminders that the line of kings themselves had originated in woodcutter stock.

"Thus the kingdom looked forward eagerly to the future and strove to forget the past. Nivea's deeds entered the realm of folklore, and so the kingdom has gone on these many years. Until now. Morrian chose her time wisely. No one was looking for trouble. And it also suited her nature, for you, Princess Calissa, are the only first-born princess to have been born since Nivea herself." He finished, and we sat silently for several long moments. I was lost in my thoughts. Yes, everyone in the kingdom knew the story of Nivea, but it had been so long ago that many of the elements were considered more myth than reality. Mathghamhain took the opportunity to check the stew, and he began ladling it into large wooden serving bowls.

"What of the sleeping curse?" Lissa asked at length as she accepted her bowl. "Is that not true?"

"Oh, yes, quite," Mathghamhain answered. "Forgive me for not mentioning it. In truth, it is rather a small aspect of the tale, considering all else that was occurring. Three days before the battle, an agent of Morrian's managed to slip into the camp and poisoned an apple with the sleeping curse potion, which he made sure Nivea ate. Since it was a potion rather than a spoken spell, the Brenwyds were helpless to wake her. It was quite by accident that we discovered the cure at all. Chiaran had been alone with her and gave her what he thought was a last kiss of parting. She woke, which startled him greatly. He shouted so loudly I thought the attack had begun."

"So you were part of the army?" Rhodri asked.

"Yes."

"I still don't understand how you are still alive. Your voice sounds truthful enough, and the personal notes your story contained make me inclined to believe your claim, but forgive me for still being skeptical."

"Of course, Your Highness, I give you no blame. I would not believe myself." He fell silent for a few minutes. "As you have likely already surmised, I am not...not...entirely human in form, though I have endeavored to remain human in mind. You can tell me whether I have succeeded in that or not." There was a certain dry humor in his voice, though I thought it was to conceal a gruffness I interpreted as pain. I recognized it cost him to admit his condition to us. "This...change of form...came about on the battlefield. I attacked a spell head on, a rather powerful and important one, that had a backlash woven in against anyone who broke it..." His voice trailed off, but he didn't need to finish. We were well able to conjecture what happened.

Lissa's blue eyes widened. "This is the backlash you spoke of earlier?"

"Indeed." The word was hardly decipherable, getting lost in the midst of a guttural growl.

"And no Brenwyd could-"

"No," he barked abruptly, making us all start. He noticed. "I apologize. There were many attempts after it occurred. None were successful. It...puts me in rather a bad humor to speak of it." He sighed and turned away. "It is this spell to which I attribute my long years."

Will you not show us your form? I asked, curious, though I had a feeling he wouldn't.

No! he replied quickly, confirming my guess. *It is hard enough to speak to you of it. Do not push me beyond what I am comfortable to reveal.* There was a slightly dangerous note in his voice that made me decide to heed him. For now.

"So what do you suggest we do now?" Rhodri asked. "We saw in your pool that Sir Eiwas is leading Brenwyds to the border, but they're unaware of the true nature of the threat they're trying to fight. We need to find a way to tell them before they try to break the barrier." He turned toward me. "Do you think the animals still awake in the forest on this side of the barrier might be able to reach animal-speaking Brenwyds on the other side?" I nodded. "That will be our best option, then, most likely."

"Except we are nowhere near the forest," Lissa pointed out. "And given Dynin's soreness today, I doubt Aislinn wants him to try transferring for a day or two, yes?" She asked, glancing toward me.

Reluctantly, I nodded. Rhodri's suggestion was a good one, but I was afraid that if we pushed Dynin to make a transfer today it might result in him going fully lame instead of simply sore. If that happened, I couldn't heal him, and if the other Brenwyds failed to break the barrier on the first try, we would be stuck in the forest, most likely with Morrian breathing down our necks. I was actually rather surprised she hadn't magically tracked us and made an appearance today.

Mathghamhain tilted his head. "There are still some animals awake?"

"Yes, there is a small area between where the curse stopped and where the thorn wall is where some animals are still awake, where Aislinn was when the curse struck," Rhodri explained.

"Hmm. I agree, that could be useful, but I would not risk the horse going lame and becoming stranded in the forest. As you found in the castle, any attempt to break this spell will draw Morrian upon you, and without Aislinn's voice you are all too vulnerable. Tell me, why do you not carry flamestone weapons?

I would have thought you would think to carry them. You need them if you want any hope of defeating Morrian and her magic."

Rhodri, Lissa and I exchanged glances. "We do not carry any because we have none," Lissa answered him. "After the Monsters' War a hundred years ago, they began to be stolen from their owners. As a safeguard against further theft until the thieves could be found, it was decided to gather and hide them somewhere in these mountains. But the people who went to hide them never returned, and so it is unknown whether they were successful or if they were attacked by the thieves themselves. Even if they did succeed in hiding them, we still don't know where they are. None of the ones that were stolen were ever recovered, either."

There was a silence. "There are none left?" He sounded in complete disbelief.

"None that we know of – or I know of, at least," Lissa said. "Aislinn, do you know of any?" I shook my head.

Mathghamhain leaned heavily against the back of his chair. "That is a heavy blow, and it is terrible for us, for without them we stand no chance against Morrian." He sounded terribly downcast and defeated.

"We faced her in the courtyard with no-" Rhodri began.

"And your Brenwyd cannot speak." I scowled at the callous reference, but if he saw, he took no notice. "Flamestone is imbued with fire from the heavens and all are blessed by Abba so they have the ability to protect the bearer from spells, up to a point. Without them we would have fallen to Morrian as surely as the sun sets and rises." He paused. "You think I exaggerate? I do not. You escaped Morrian on luck, nothing more. Do you think you could have truly defeated her in that courtyard?" He waited. Our silence spoke volumes. We knew it was only by Abba's grace that we hadn't been killed. But still...

Rhodri stood abruptly. "You have pointed out more than adequately our weakness against Morrian. But unless you have an actual suggestion besides casting down our hopes, then we must face her as best we can as we are and trust Abba to make up the deficit. Do you, who stood by Nivea's side, lack such faith in His power?"

"...No. But I still do not believe you realize-"

"What we really face? No, you're right. We don't. But perhaps it is better this way, for it causes us to place even more faith and trust in Abba, and the priests and Brenwyds teach us that is our best weapon against evil, is it not?" His words were sharp and biting.

"Rhodri," Lissa said quietly, rising to put a hand on his arm. "Enough." Slowly, he sat again. Mathghamhain sat silently.

Is she truly so terrible? I asked gently.

Yes, he answered. His tone reminded me of Aiden when he came and sat with me during the furious thunderstorms that shook Kheprah during the summer.

How well did you know her?

I sensed surprise from him. *What makes you think that I did?*

How you speak of her...It seems to suggest knowledge of her beyond the average Brenwyd soldier.

In that, you are correct. I was...imprisoned in her dungeons for a time.

Oh. I am sorry. That must have been awful. I paused. *But I believe you are letting your fear speak instead of your faith.*

Faith? The word seemed to hold a hollow, bitter ring. *I have faith. I believe in Abba. What more is there?*

A lot more, and if you truly were a Brenwyd, you know better than that.

I could tell his body stiffened under his coverings, but he made no response. Instead, he shifted his position and said, "Very well. You've made your point, Your Highness. I apologize. I merely point out that you are at a severe disadvantage to battle Morrian." He raised a covered hand as Rhodri opened his mouth, presumably to protest again. "But perhaps there is something else. What of travel by sea? Even Morrian could not make a wall of briars grow in the middle of the ocean."

At the suggestion, we all looked at each other in surprise. It was a good suggestion. After all, Ecclesia did have an extensive coastline. "I hadn't considered that," Rhodri said thoughtfully. "But it would take at least a week to make the voyage to the nearest Darlesian port, and I know nothing of boats and sailing."

"But surely there would be some sort of magical defense," Lissa said, frowning. "I doubt Morrian would have forgotten the seas. She originally came from Lamasia, as you just reminded us."

"Of course, there is some sort of barrier, but if you could get at least as far as the leviathans' islands, you could enlist their help. Their fire could help break through the barrier. Indeed, I should think that, assuming they escaped the spell, they've already sent out scouts to investigate the magic."

"Whose islands?" Rhodri asked, puzzled.

"Leviathans? Do you mean changeling dragons?" Lissa asked. "The ones that can change the color of their scales? Leviathan is an old name for them."

"Yes, of course. They have always been powerful allies against evil." Seeing the looks on our faces, after a moment he added, "There is still an alliance between Ecclesia and the leviathans, is there not?"

"There is not," Lissa said, shaking her head. "Have you not heard of the Monsters' War?"

"Bits and pieces. I gather that something happened with many monster species that caused them to attack settlements en masse, and that they were nearly wiped out in response, but not much beyond that."

"You didn't see it through your pool?" Rhodri asked.

"It doesn't show me everything. And...to be truthful, I do not always pay strict attention to what it does show. If I remember correctly...many of the scenes from that time were bloody and full of carnage. I did not wish to watch too much."

"Well, that's understandable," Rhodri conceded. He went on to briefly narrate the War and its outcomes – specifically, that the leviathans, or changeling dragons, had agreed to withdraw completely to isolated sea islands so far out that the only way they could again have contact with humans was if a storm blew a trading ship extremely off course. Mathghamhain had a hard time believing it.

"It makes no sense," he said, sounding distressed. "No sense in the slightest. The leviathans were always allies, and the other species you speak of generally friendly. Why would they suddenly attack? It makes no sense."

"The records from the time are also at a loss to explain it," Lissa said. "I've read in the treaty with the leviathans that part of the reason they agreed to move so far out was at the behest of their own leaders, in case such a thing should happen again. The remnants of several other races went with them as well."

Mathghamhain stood abruptly and walked toward the door. He paused at the frame. "Pardon me, but I must think. It has been long since I have been in company with others, and the information you have brought is somewhat...overwhelming. Please, choose whichever bedchambers you like. Dusk comes quickly in the mountains." With that, he left.

"Well," Lissa stated after he disappeared. "That was interesting."

"Interesting?" Rhodri got up and started pacing agitatedly. "Will he help us or not? It appeared to me that he's scared of Morrian and would advise we all crawl into caves and never come out again rather than face her."

"He went through a very traumatic experience at her hands," Lissa said. "It is understandable that he wants us to fully comprehend the danger we are proposing to face."

"There is a difference between informing us of the danger and advising cowardice! We cannot go anywhere today, I'll grant, but tomorrow we must travel to the border and try to get a message through with or without him...what are you writing, Aislinn?" he asked as he turned toward me.

Indeed, I had been writing furiously for the past several minutes while he had been grousing. While in the library earlier, I had taken the liberty of procuring a blank book I had found, as well as a pen and ink so I could communicate. Despite my bad spelling, it was the best way I had to communicate without Dynin. *Abba guided us here with my Sight for a reason,* I wrote (or attempted to, rather. Fortunately, both Lissa and Rhodri were used to deciphering my spelling). *He is to help us, and I believe we are to help him. We cannot leave yet. I will try this evening to communicate with Sir Eiwas through Sight. I pray Abba they will not have set out yet.*

Lissa and Rhodri read the words silently. "Very well, Aislinn. But you had best try sooner than later. If I know my father, he'll be hurrying up the process as much as possible," Rhodri warned. I nodded. I also expected such a thing.

"How do you think we are to help Mathghamhain?" Lissa asked.

I bent over the book again. *I don't know. Encouraging him off this mountain would be a good start, I think. We'll talk with him again in the morning. Right now, I think it is best to respect his wishes and let him think through all we've told him.*

"She is making sense, Rhodri," Lissa said, putting her arms around him and resting her chin on his shoulder. "I, for one, would feel rather overwhelmed with all the information we told him today if I was unused to company. And he seemed genuinely upset about the leviathans and the flamestone weapons. You did not help with that." She frowned at him.

He sighed. "I know. I think part of why I was so sharp is because I know that, to a point, he was right to bring up such concerns, and it was playing on my own fear. I wish we had even a clue as to where the weapons were." He looked at me. "Maybe you could try to Search them out, too."

I sighed and smiled, raising helpless hands, then scribbled, *I'll See what I can. I'm going to go check on Dynin, then I'll find a quiet place to try and See.* The odor of the cooking stew began wafting toward us, and my stomach rumbled. I quickly added: *After we eat something, that is.*

Nocturnal Conversation

$\mathcal{U}$nfortunately, I was not able to contact Sir Eiwas through my Sight. Instead, I Saw him and Rhodri's father mustering a company and setting out towards the forest. As Mathghamhain had said, the remaining hours of daylight passed quickly. We did not see him again that day, though we left extra food in the kitchen for him. Lissa and I selected a chamber to share and set up a small nest of blankets and what pillows we could scrounge, since Mathgham- hain didn't seem to have extra mattresses lying around. Lissa fell asleep fairly quickly, but I found it more difficult. The information I'd learned and the problems facing us kept running around in my head and refused to be calmed. And even when I did manage to fall asleep, my thoughts continued to churn, for I dreamed.

I saw a military camp with hundreds of people – Brenwyds mostly – and my Sight centered on what I assumed was the command tent. There I saw a girl, about my age, studying a series of maps with furrowed brows. She was dressed for war, in chain mail, leather jerkin, some plate armor, a sword, and a bow and quiver. She was startlingly beautiful, though not Brenwyd. Her hair, just long enough to brush her shoulders, fell in ebony curls, her eyes were sapphire blue, her skin was pale ivory, and her lips more red than pink.

"How are you feeling?" a voice asked. The girl looked up and smiled at the speaker, whom I could not yet see.

"I'm fine, Steffyn. I only slept. There was no harm."

"You're certain?" The speaker had advanced, and I now saw his back. His voice sounded strangely familiar, but I couldn't place it.

"Absolutely." The girl looked back down at the battle plans and sighed. "I was only trying to refresh my memory."

"Hmm." Steffyn walked to her side of the table and joined her in studying the plans. He was Brenwyd, with pale blond hair and icy grey eyes. "You know the best battle plans in the world will not matter tomorrow."

"I know. Abba does." The girl turned around. "How did it come to this, Steffyn? Why?"

"I do not know." Steffyn continued staring down at the sheets of parchment. "I should have seen it before anyone else. I know her best."

"It's not your fault," the girl answered, turning back to him. "It's because of you that we fight her tomorrow." I never heard Steffyn's reply, for then the scene changed.

I Saw a small group of people wrapped in dark cloaks, leading horses with long bundles attached to their saddles, and several leading small carts holding more wrapped packages. They traveled for some time, always on an upward slope, twisting and winding their way up a mountain. At last, the leader held up a hand and the group came to a stop. A boulder as large as he was blocked the trail and he and several other men threw their weight against it and moved it. A pockmarked rock face was revealed. The man knelt and picked up a rock about the size of his fist and closely examined a line of holes in the rock. Apparently making up his mind, he placed it in the third from the top, pressed down on it, and then leaned his weight against the rock. He was rewarded by a door chiseled out of the very side of the mountain itself swinging inward silently, revealing nothing but blackness beyond.

"Come. We must be back to Kheprah by sunrise, and once we place the weapons inside, we must seal the entrance."

"It still seems unnecessary to go to these measures to secure them," one of the others, a woman, said. "Surely the royal vault would be safe enough until the thieves are caught. And easier to get to."

"The thieves would know to expect such a thing. They have shown themselves to be unusually cunning. Besides, it will only be temporary." The man drew the sword from his side, and white flames appeared, running up and down the length of the blade. They lit up the interior of the cavity the man had opened. "Though I confess I do not fully understand it either." The group began passing into the mountain, and again the scene changed.

This time I recognized those who appeared in my mind's eye. It was Sir Eiwas and Rhodri's father, with a large company of Brenwyds spread out behind them. I had Seen them earlier as they prepared to set out, but now they were at the thorn barrier, looking up at it. "I see you did not exaggerate, Eiwas," Duke Ceredon said. "It is indeed formidable. Do you believe you and this company can take it down?"

"We should be able to. I gathered more than I thought strictly necessary as a precaution. Once we begin our assault, whoever cast it will likely know it and come to investigate so we must be prepared for that."

"Of course," Duke Ceredon said. "Abba be with us. Begin whenever you are ready."

"Of course, your grace." Sir Eiwas turned his horse and went to confer with his other commanders. Lord Ceredon remained where he was, staring at the wall as if to bring it down with his own willpower (which to my mind was not entirely out of the question, as Rhodri's father was one of the most strong-willed people I knew). After a few minutes, a song began to fill the air. Strong, hard, with varying melodies ranging from soprano to bass parts, the wall of thorns began to tremble before it. I became dimly aware that I could sense it physically and not just through my dream, the song and spell were so powerful. Even watching through a dream, I could feel excitement begin to course through me as it seemed the barrier was about to fall. But before it could, disaster struck.

Duke Ceredon seemed to hear something and wheeled his horse around. I could not see what he saw, but he loosed a cry of warning as he drew his sword. The next moment, something animal in form leaped on him from above, knocking him from his horse. I heard the song break off and be replaced by others' cries as apparently more of the creatures attacked. I could not see them except for dark shadows that appeared canine in origin, and unearthly howls split the air. The whole company fell into confusion. I could not see what happened to Rhodri's father. My perspective of the picture changed slightly so I viewed it from the surrounding trees, and I saw several human figures in a loose ring around the company, chanting strange words. I could not understand them, but they sounded foul and I could sense the magic. The mist that had been clinging to the thorn wall suddenly descended on the mass of men and beasts, and within several heartbeats the noise died down. The mist rolled back, and with it went the creatures, vanishing into the trees. Where the company had been standing strong moments before, now all were collapsed on the ground. I saw wounds here and there, but I knew they were asleep.

The human figures came out from the trees onto the path. "Lady Morrian will be pleased," one said, a man with a nasal voice. "More Brenwyds to drain power from and so feed the spell."

"Aye," another man said. "Pleased, indeed. But remember, you're responsible for taking them to the fortress. My people and I must stay to watch the border and begin the next phase of the plan."

The other one waved his hand dismissively and answered in a bored tone. "Yes, yes, you've made that quite clear. You and your people can leave now, as a matter of fact." Then, my dreams dissolved to nothingness.

I woke, shivering, shaken by what I had seen. *So much for being able to warn them, I thought. What do I tell Rhodri? How can I tell him his father has fallen under the same spell that grips Ecclesia just hours after he had seen him for the first time in months, well and strong? Abba, what do we do? We are only three. Well, four if you count Mathghamhain, but I'm not sure I should. Abba, please help us.* I continued to pray, but Abba seemed content to be silent. Restless and not wanting to disturb Lissa with my movements, I cast aside the blankets and left the room. I wandered through the corridor, turning my thoughts over in my head. I found myself back before the library's door, and I went in. A single candle was burning, providing enough illumination for my Brenwyd eyes to see the room clearly enough. I was drawn back to the illuminated works I had seen earlier, and so pulled one off the shelf, allowing my finger to trace the intricate swirls of the border around the title page. It soothed my thoughts, though having my own brush in hand would have helped more.

I thought you were not much for reading. Mathghamhain's voice entered my head unexpectedly, startling me.

I jumped, let out an involuntary gasp, and looked up. Apparently, one candle and my Brenwyd eyes weren't good enough to notice his cloak-shrouded figure in the corner. *Do you enjoy startling people half out of their wits?* I rejoined.

I do not have enough visitors to answer that, he answered. *But can you not answer mine?*

I looked back down at the book. *As I said earlier, I enjoy looking at the pictures. I...I happen to be a bit of an artist.*

That is a valuable gift. He paused, then began again uncertainly. *Is it true, what they say, that artists have the vision to see beauty where others do not?*

I glanced toward him, considering the question. *Perhaps,* I said finally. *When I look for things to paint, I look for things that interest me, whether others consider them pleasing to look at or not. When looked at the right way, most things have beauty.*

Interesting, he repeated. *Is that how you see it?*

It is. I could tell he was brooding on that. An awkward silence ensued. I closed the book and returned it to the shelf.

Do dreams also disturb your sleep? I asked finally. I wanted to question him about how he had spent his afternoon, but decided to try and get him to begin discussing it naturally.

Dreams? No. Memories, never dreams. But you? What have you Seen?

I don't know quite what. I hesitated, and then continued. He might want to scale back fighting Morrian, but I wasn't about to back out of having him help us without a fight. He was the only one in the Five Realms who might have even the slightest inkling of a weakness we could use against her. *There were three. The first, I do not understand at all. The second, I have an idea. The third was all too clear.*

Would you...would you care to share them?

Of course. In the first, there was a great Brenwyd army camp. I have never seen such a gathering before. It focused on a girl, a human, in the command tent, studying maps. I remembered her image. I could tell Mathghamhain could see it in my mind, for I sensed a great wave of agitation I couldn't quite interpret. *Did you know her?* I asked.

Once. That is Nivea.

I nodded thoughtfully. It made sense. *Then a young man came up to her, a Brenwyd. He asked after her, and they exchanged a few brief words about the coming battle, nothing of significance. Then that scene ended.* I called up the image of the man in my mind, and that sent him into even greater agitation.

Did you hear his name? Mathghamhain demanded.

I was somewhat taken aback by his vehemence. *She called him Steffyn.* As I repeated the information, I realized the significance of the name.

You recognize the name? Mathghamhain sounded startled.

If it is the same. Steffyn was the name of a great warrior who was Nivea's champion against Morrian. The legends say that it was his support that propelled her to battle, and that he led the final devastating charge, even engaging Morrian herself and bringing her down. But he died on the battlefield.

This is the legacy he has in the legends? Mathghamhain sounded disbelieving.

Even so. Did you know him well?

I sensed a grim amusement from him. *Oh, well enough. He was a good warrior and certainly supported Nivea in everything. If this is how he is remembered...then history has been kind. Very kind. But the rest of your visions? What did they reveal?*

I sighed, remembering my glimpse of Sir Eiwas and Duke Ceredon. *That help is not coming. Lord Ceredon and his company were attacked by strange creatures and a magical mist, and I believe they now lie under the same sleeping curse as Ecclesia. And I think other, lesser magicians are helping Morrian. She mentioned something of the sort when I spied on her.* I remembered the scene, letting him view it.

I think you assume correctly, he said grimly. *Has there been an uptick in magic of late?*

No, not at all. In fact, Lissa, Rhodri and I were trying to determine what her words meant exactly because there have been no real magic users of any consequence for some time. The last major magic mischief I know of happened nearly ten years ago, in Lamasia. A pair of brothers was experimenting in the dark arts. Fortunately, it was caught early enough that no real harm was done. Other than that, it has been just keeping an eye on certain herb men and women that they don't stray too far from their craft, and even if they do it is generally with good intentions and all it takes is a warning to get them to shy away from it. I paused a moment, remembering the suspicion I had formed earlier. I hadn't wanted to add to Lissa and Rhodri's worry unnecessarily, but it occurred to me that Mathghamhain might be just the person to ask about it. *She also mentioned waking monsters. When the three of us were discussing it this morning, before we met you, we could not puzzle it* *out, given the scarcity of magic users and the absence of monsters. But I begin to wonder...*I paused again, trying to determine the best way to word my concern. *Perhaps I am giving Morrian's power and forethought too much credit, but...*

You think that perhaps she is behind the decline in monsters and magic users, for the purpose of lulling Niclausia into a false sense of security to better cast her curse, he finished for me, gleaning what I was trying to say from my mind. He moved from the corner and sank slowly into one of the chairs. *I wish I could tell you that you do give her too much credit. But I fear you are right, for that thought also entered my mind this afternoon. What you told me of the Monsters' War...there must have been some magic mischief set loose among the species, for the ones you listed were always peaceable. The leviathans, in particular, I cannot believe of turning against humanity in the numbers you describe, for they live by a strict code of honor and pride. To turn on their allies tears that code to shreds. Morrian did use the more war-like monsters in her army and for her purposes, and she knows well how to control them. And she is used to playing the long hand; she was married to Llewelyn for several years before she poisoned him, and waited years more before she finished him, for she knew she needed the time to firmly establish herself. This time, it seems, she is being even more careful.* His voice was grim. *As for magic users, what she did before was seek out those who had a talent for magic and teach them herself, but kept them secret. Instead, she would bring them to one of her country estates to ostensibly offer them employment and a better life, but she used the locations as magic schools. I would suspect she has been doing something similar for some years leading to this. Using the power of other people to craft and then cast the spell would explain how she is able to do so and still remain so strong.*

I also sank into a chair, feeling overwhelmed at the idea of an adversary so cunning and careful that she began to set the stage for herself a hundred years before she finally struck. *But why? What is the end that she hopes to achieve? Surely it must be more than subduing one kingdom,* I wondered, keeping the thought guarded from

Mathghamhain. I didn't want his gloomy outlook affecting my ponderings. I thought back to the conversation I had heard between Morrian and her master. She had said something about merely preparing the way for him...I could feel a memory of something trying to stir in the back of my mind, something I had heard long ago that seemed to connect with the current situation...but what was it? I frowned and shook my head a bit as if to physically clear my mind. If it was truly important, then it would eventually come to me. For now, the best thing was to move on to a different topic. *So the other realms are now truly in danger from monsters and magicians?*

From what you heard, it seems likely.

I stood again and walked to the tapestries, letting my eyes work in the semi-darkness to make out the woven images. With my thoughts so busy, I could not simply sit still. *There must be a way to warn the other kingdoms. I shall have to try again with my Sight. They must know what they are facing. Although, I suppose they will know soon enough. At least Rhodri's mother knows, and she can spread the word. That is a good start,* I mused. At the thought of monsters once again running rampant, another question from my dream occurred to me. *Oh! I saw some sort of monster in my dream, I think. The things that attacked Duke Ceredon and his party. They were very dark and hard to make out, but I believe they looked something like a dog or a wolf. They moved with the mist, like...like shadows themselves. Do you know what they might be?*

It sounds like shadow wolves.

At that answer, I turned back to face him with raised eyebrows. *Shadow wolves? They truly exist?* Every child in Niclausia has had nightmares about shadow wolves at least once. They are the demons that hover around ghost stories told after dark when the family is gathered around the fire. Made of mist and darkness, they steal through villages in the dark of the moon and steal naughty children from their beds, biting them to make them as they are. As one grows older, one realizes they are just a fairy tale meant to make children behave. At least, so I had thought until that moment.

Aye. They have a limited magical ability of their own and possess cunning intelligence, so they make use of darkness and mist to make their victims cower before them, but they are flesh-and-blood creatures. As it happens, they were one of Morrian's favorite monsters, but in the early years of her reign Nivea had hunters exterminate them, or so we thought. It is probable that a few mating pairs survived and found refuge with Morrian. Their only fear is fire, for it takes away their principal weapon of fear by burning through their darkness. With the mist Morrian has in the thorns...she must have commissioned shadow wolves in addition to her human followers to make sure no one got through to help.

I shivered involuntarily. *And so it is unlikely that we can expect help from outside, not as long as the borders are so guarded.*

I fear not. He sighed audibly. *I...I wish to apologize for my words and actions earlier. It was wrong of me. It is no small feat to escape from Morrian's grasp when caught unawares with no real idea of her character. You did as well as you could. Many did far worse on their first encounter with her magic.* Something about the tone of his mental voice made me think he had been one of them. Which, after a moment, I realized only made sense, given his current cursed state, though I didn't think he had been cursed the first time he approached her.

I went toward him and sat down in the chair next to him, placing a hand on his covered arm. The muscles underneath stiffened, in surprise, I imagined. *Apology accepted. So will you help us? If we can expect no outside help, then it is up to us to stop her, and I truly do believe we need your help. Abba led us here for a reason.*

He pulled away from my contact and stood, walking a few paces away to lean on the table. I waited for his answer, fighting the urge to swing my legs back and forth like a small child. I was tall for a woman, and it had been a long time since I'd sat in a chair where my feet did not touch the floor. Finally, with his back still to me Mathghamhain said: *Yes. I will help you, as I can.* He paused, then continued with sudden heat. *It is my...had those of us two hundred and fifty years ago made sure she was truly dead, you would not have to face her now. And...*His voice died away.

And? I asked.

And nothing. Suffice to say that some of my reasons I will keep to myself. He began walking around the table on silent feet. *You said there were three visions. You have only told me two.*

I had, in fact, forgotten my other vision in the midst of the conversation, and the sudden reminder of it made me straighten eagerly, for at last I believed I had good news to share. *The other you might find more hopeful, as I do myself. I believe it showed where the flamestone blades are hidden.*

He whirled around to face me then, a sudden movement with surprising grace for one so large. *What makes you think that?*

I saw a group of Brenwyds leading laden horses and carts along a mountain trail. They came to a rock face and stopped. The leader opened a hidden door and withdrew a sword from one of the packs. It had flames running up and down the surface.

That is a flamestone blade. Mathghamhain sounded eager. *Can you recall any distinguishing features of the rock face? I may know the place. Abba knows I've had more than sufficient time to explore the mountains.*

I...I thought for a minute. *I believe I can draw it. It will help me remember it firmly.*

Then do! He gestured toward the tabletop, where there were scattered pieces of parchment and paper, as well as quills and ink. Selecting a piece of paper and dipping a quill in an inkwell, I recalled the image and began to draw. I first drew the cliff face with the boulder in place, my eyes lidded half-shut as I imagined the image superimposed over the paper so that it seemed to me that I traced it from a pre-cut design. Then I drew it with the boulder removed. My artist's eye had subconsciously made note of all the pockmarks, and I drew them as accurately as I could. A quill was not the best drawing instrument, as it only allowed for bold straight lines and little shading, but it served for my present purpose. I finished and slid the drawings over to Mathghamhain for him to examine. He scrutinized them closely, saying nothing for several minutes.

Well? I asked finally. *Do you know the place?*

Perhaps, he said slowly. *There is a place, about three days' journey from here on foot, where there is a cliff with such markings. But I could not tell if any formed this particular pattern or not.* He set the paper back down on the table. *And even if I could, there are many boulders at its base. How could we tell which was right? The pockmarks are random, and it is hard to tell one such cliff from another with no specific markings.* His voice had taken on the despairing edge again that he seemed so fond of.

I cast an eye over my drawing, and frowned. I drew it closer. *What is it?* Mathghamhain asked.

There is a pattern here, I said, taking up the quill again. *Look.* I traced the regular outline my eye had discerned among the seemingly random holes. Mathghamhain bent over me to look, and I was very aware of his bulk looming at my shoulder. The connecting lines I drew formed an eight-pointed star, the symbol of my people. In times of need, we have ever looked skyward, and our oldest lore said that it was during a night with a bright, eight-pointed star that Abba had gifted us with our unique abilities. It was also such a star that had marked the birth of his emissary and son, Yeshua, on Earth. *This is how we will find the right place. They marked it so other Brenwyds could recognize it.*

Are you sure it is not merely a coincidence with your artistic mind? Do you recall noticing such a configuration in your vision? He sounded doubtful.

I looked up at him looming over me, irritated. *It is too clear to have occurred as a natural formation,* I said emphatically. *And artists in general may have a reputation for being fanciful, but I assure you I would never create a false image in my work. It must be how they marked it. Take me to this cliff you know. If it is there, I will find it.*

And then?

I took a deep, steadying breath. *Then we must face Morrian, no matter the danger...or the cost. She cannot go unchecked. Ecclesia – Niclausia, rather – stands to lose too much.* I gazed at him steadily.

I sensed that he returned my gaze, though I could not see his eyes. There was a very long silence. *We?* he finally said. *Are you sure?*

Yes. We. Abba led us here for a reason. I think he is calling you to leave the shadows. Two hundred and fifty years seems to me more than enough time to be alone.

I have already said I will help you.

I know. I only wanted to reinforce it.

Do I need it? The ghost of a laugh lay behind his words.

I think you do. So, we shall leave in the morning?

Unless the prince and princess have any objection.

They won't.

HIDDEN TREASURE

As a matter of fact, Rhodri did have a few objections. Not to the idea of the venture itself since he was as excited as I was by the possibility that we might find the long-lost flamestone weapons, but he was not yet ready to embrace Mathghamhain as a traveling companion. I understood his reservations after the confrontation between the two the day before, but we needed help, and Mathghamhain was the only help available.

Once we had established the journey plans, I told Rhodri, quietly, of what else I had Seen in my sleep. He took the news stoically, but I knew him well enough to read the subtle clues in his eyes and set jaw to know how much it was a blow. The last day and a half had been nothing like the homecoming he had been longing for. Lissa and I watched him anxiously, ready to offer support, but he merely thanked me for telling him and walked away to busy himself with readying the packs. After a moment, Lissa went after him, and I turned to tend to Dynin. Fortunately, the day of rest combined with the poultice and time spent soaking in the cold stream had almost completely cleared up his inflammation, and I was satisfied that he would be up to walking with us through the mountains, though I still wanted to bandage his legs with the poultice for another couple of days. I did not want to risk him trying to transfer until the inflammation was completely gone. Even if he could, Mathghamhain had said that there was no space to transfer to by the cliff he believed to be the one I had Seen. So, Dynin would walk behind us and carry some of our packs. Once we had the packs prepared and loaded onto Dynin, we followed Mathghamhain out of the valley and into the mountains to start our journey.

Nothing of significance occurred on the way, save that Rhodri lessened his suspicions toward Mathghamhain, and I became more intrigued by him. Mathghamhain was anxious to make up for his blunders, and insisted on doing all the cooking despite our offers of help. He also kept nearly all the night watches, despite our protestations that he share the duty with us. Still, it was a hard journey, up and down steep mountain paths, often with a disconcerting drop-off on one side or the other. When we stopped the first night, I took Lissa aside and helped her make some breeches out of her petticoats to wear under her outer skirt. Fortunately, when the curse struck, she had been wearing one of her plain, sturdy gardening dresses, but the several layers of petticoats underneath it were not optimal for hiking through the mountains. I had suggested that she simply borrow an extra pair of breeches from me and abandon the skirt altogether, but she didn't feel comfortable doing so. Given her mother's insistence on princesses always wearing skirts, I decided it was simply too ingrained with her, so we settled for making her undergarments more practical. The next day she moved markedly easier.

Throughout the journey I felt constantly on edge, and wondered if Morrian would make a sudden appearance, or send someone else after us. But that fear never materialized, and I wondered why. Surely she had some means of magically tracking us – the mirror I had seen her use in the throne room came to mind – but perhaps she knew we meant to face her again and was simply waiting for us to come to her.

Whatever the reason, I was glad when we finally reached the cliffs. Mathghamhain was walking ahead of us (by some feet, as his long strides covered nearly twice the ground ours could). He stopped suddenly and turned back. "We're here. Or, above it, rather. We need to get down to ground level before looking for the entrance."

"Ground level?" Rhodri asked. "What do you...oh." We had reached the place where Mathghamhain was standing, and discovered it was the ledge of a cliff. At the bottom, about fifty feet below us, there was a small valley with tufts of grass sticking up between the rocks. I immediately recognized it as the pockmarked cliff from my dream. This was the right place, I was sure. And yet...

But I saw them traveling along a rocky mountain path, I said to Mathghamhain. *Where is that?*

Gone, he said. *Remember, it has been many years. It was once all rock here, but the rocks at the bottom crumbled and grass grew up. This is it. You recognize the cliff, do you not?*

Yes...but what does that mean for the cave the weapons have been stored in?

I don't know. We'll see.

"So how are we getting down to ground level, exactly?" Rhodri asked. "I don't see a path."

"Yes, as I was just explaining to Aislinn, the path that was once here leading down has crumbled over time. Fortunately, I remembered that and brought a rope." He slung down his pack and produced a long length of rope from it.

Lissa looked warily from the rope to the drop. "You mean for us to descend this cliff with only a rope?"

"Do not worry, Your Highness. It's a safe method, frequently used by those in the mountains."

Lissa bit her lip nervously. "Perhaps...perhaps I will stay up here with Dynin. He cannot be lowered by rope."

Dynin snorted. *I should think not.*

Mathghamhain bowed slightly towards her. "As you wish, Your Highness."

"Very well, Liss. So, what do we attach the rope to?" Rhodri said, looking around. I followed his searching gaze, and realized there weren't any rock outcroppings or boulders to secure the rope to for our descent.

"Hmm. That I didn't think of," Mathghamhain said, sounding disgruntled.

"Well, when you have been here in the past, how do you get down?"

"Oh...well, I usually...jump." He sounded somewhat abashed and we could barely catch the words through his growly, gruff voice.

The three of us stared at him somewhat blankly. "Jump?" Rhodri said, voicing what I was thinking. "You can jump that far?"

"Well, I also...climb, and jump. It's a stop and go process." I looked back down over the cliff. Yes, there were certainly lots of handholds, but I wouldn't fancy climbing down it.

Rhodri seemed to have the same idea. "Well, since we mere mortals can't jump that far without breaking every bone in our bodies, and I can't exactly climb down with just one arm, what do you suggest?"

Mathghamhain's head turned towards Rhodri, then me. "I think I could lower you both down on the rope. You don't look too heavy."

Are you sure? I asked mentally at the same time Rhodri asked it aloud.

"Yes. I've lifted far heavier things than a lanky Brenwyd girl and soft Darlesian prince with a broken arm." At that, Rhodri and Lissa laughed, and I smiled. We had learned that despite his tendency toward gloominess, Mathghamhain did have a very dry wit and enjoyed using it.

"Very well, then. Aislinn, why don't you get lowered down first? That way you can look for the pattern while Mathghamhain and I are making our way down?"

Be careful, girl, Dynin said worriedly.

I will, I answered him as I nodded acquiescence. *Don't worry. While we're looking for the entrance, why don't you have Lissa start to rearrange your packs? We'll probably need you to carry some weapons.* Satisfied with having thought up a task to keep my horse and my friend busy, I went to tie the rope around my waist. Mathghamhain stopped me. "No, not like that. It'll cut off your breathing. Tie it like a harness, around your waist and upper legs, so it makes a seat of sorts."

Have you lowered people down like this before? I asked, following his instruction.

Yes. A long time ago. My makeshift harness secured, he directed me to the edge with my back to the empty space, and taking up the slack in the rope, carefully coached me to walk down the cliff. He kept feeding me rope as I went lower and lower. Finally, I reached bottom, untied myself, and told him to pull the rope up. While he got Rhodri situated, I began looking around the bottom for the star pattern. I closed my eyes, picturing the image of it in my brain, letting my Sight guide me. I put a hand on the rough, cool stone of the cliff and felt its roughness pull at the skin of my hand as I slowly walked along the cliff bottom.

"Find anything yet?" Rhodri's voice from behind startled me, and as I jumped, I stubbed my toe against a large boulder in front of me. I turned and scowled at him. I was getting quite tired of stubbing my toe on things. To his credit, there was a certain amount of chagrin in his expression, but I knew him well enough to pick out the amusement in his eyes. "Sorry."

I huffed, then was distracted by movement above us. It was Mathghamhain coming down the cliff, and he was indeed jumping after a fashion. His agility reminded me of the goats I had seen navigating the cliffs by Ecclesia's rugged coast, somehow finding footholds in what looked like bare rock. He reached the bottom in half the time it had taken him to lower Rhodri and me down. Rhodri raised his eyebrows. "Impressive."

Mathghamhain grunted. "Agility is one of the few things I appreciate about this form. Have you found it?" he asked, addressing me, obviously anxious to divert any questions about exactly what his form was. In the three days we had traveled with him, I had never seen Mathghamhain shed his dark, all-encompassing attire.

I shook my head in answer to his query, turning my eyes back to the boulder I had rammed my foot against. I started to go around, but a small mark nearly at the top caught my eye, and I leaned in for a closer look. One might say it was merely scratches left in the rock from standing out in the open for who knows how long. But to my eyes, it appeared to be the faint remains of an eight-pointed star that had been etched into the boulder at one point. I straightened and backed up, eyes glued to the cliff behind the boulder. "Aislinn? Do you see something?" Rhodri asked.

I held up a finger, signaling him to wait. I let my eyes rove over the cliff. I locked onto one pockmark, then another, and another. I smiled. This was it.

"Is this the boulder?" Mathghamhain's voice rumbled. I nodded. He promptly stepped up and pushed on the boulder, causing it to roll away with a grunt after just a minute. I raised my eyebrows at his display of strength. My keen eyes had caught the tensing of muscles under his clothing, muscles that were in places and of quantity that spoke to his nonhuman form. It reminded me of the muscles I would see tensed in a dog or cat right before it pounced on its prey.

"That doesn't look much like a door to me," Rhodri said, interrupting my thoughts. He was right. Moving the boulder had not revealed an opening into the mountain, but rather what simply looked like more of the cliff, though oddly smooth. I bent and picked up one of the small rocks that littered the ground, one about the size of my fist. My eyes traced the star pattern in the rocks and focused on the easternmost point of the star. That was the hole that was the key. I walked up, and just as I had seen the man do in my dream, I placed my rock in the hole and pressed my weight down upon it. I waited several seconds. Nothing happened. Then a few seconds more. Still nothing. Confused, I backed up a step, reviewing my calculations. This was the right hole, I was sure of it. So why didn't the door open?

"Would you like me to try?" Mathghamhain said. "It's possible that with the years the mechanism that works the door has grown rusty and more force is needed to open it."

"Are you certain this is the right place, Aislinn?" Rhodri added. I nodded sharply, and indicated for Mathghamhain to try. He placed his hand into the hole and leaned down on the pebble with all his weight. This time, I heard a slight creak and groan from a place inside the rock, and after several seconds, a piece of the cliff swung inward, revealing the door. I grinned, relieved that I had not made an error. "Well done," Rhodri said. He shrugged out of his pack and took the metal tube out of it that he had used at Mathghamhain's abode, what he had called an electric torch. "Shall we go in, then?"

"You and Aislinn," Mathghamhain said. "But I do not think I will fit." I stuck my head inside the opening and saw that he was right. It was barely tall enough for me and Rhodri.

I'm sorry, I said to him.

No matter. I will wait.

"Would you happen to be aware of any underground beasts we should be on the lookout for?" Rhodri asked, replacing his pack on his shoulder.

"Only snakes, mice, and spiders, though any of those would be sleeping like the rest of the country. I would watch for tunnel collapses. There have been many avalanches in the mountains, and they can collapse caves and natural passageways."

"You think we might be cut off from the weapons?"

"Perhaps. Be careful. Rock may look solid and stable, but it can be very fragile."

"Thanks for the warning." Rhodri turned to me. "Aislinn? Do you want to go first?" I shrugged. It didn't matter to me. I pointed at his torch, then him, then the tunnel. "I should go first because I have a light?" he guessed. I nodded, pleased he had picked up my meaning. He had gotten very good at reading my signs. "Makes sense, I suppose. Onward and downward, then." He entered the tunnel.

I looked at Mathghamhain. *You're sure you're alright with staying here?*

Oh yes. I have no wish to get stuck in a tunnel, believe me. Go. I turned to enter the tunnel. *Aislinn.* I turned back. *There is one thing...when you find the weapons...they choose their bearers. Don't be disappointed if the first one you pick up doesn't light for you.*

How do swords do that?

I know not. You would have to ask the smith who forged them. They were designed specifically for those who fought magic-wielders.

"Aislinn? Are you coming?" Rhodri's voice echoed from the tunnel. I turned back to the tunnel, and plunged into the darkness, guided by Rhodri's torch from ahead.

⋰⊱✿⊰⋱

I'm not sure how long we walked, but in the dark with nothing to judge by it seemed like hours. Rhodri and I said little to each other, content to explore our own thoughts. I wondered how in the Five Realms we were to defeat Morrian, even with flamestone blades, with not even one functioning Brenwyd. Without my voice, I couldn't fight spells. Yet I also remembered that the warrior Steffyn had done battle with her without magic, and wounded her, if the legends were to be believed. One of the first things I had learned from my father about battling magic-users is that wielding magic takes a toll on the person's strength, and that magic cannot guard against everything. I began reviewing every magic-fighting lesson I had ever had, something I had been doing multiple times over the past few days, trying to remember something – anything – that could give a hint as to how to best defeat her. Unfortunately, however, none of my lessons had ever covered how to fight an extremely powerful magic user when one had no voice.

"Aislinn," Rhodri said from in front of me. I looked up, and realized he had stopped. Looking beyond him, I saw why: the way was blocked by a large slab of stone. My heart sank. To have come so far, only to be stopped by a collapsed tunnel? I sighed. Every time we seemed to find something to give us hope, we ended up stymied. "There's writing here on the wall."

I turned where he was pointing with his light and indeed, runes were scratched into the wall. "It looks like a riddle," Rhodri said. "Maybe we have to answer it correctly to get past the block."

I looked at him with eyebrows raised. He shrugged. "On Earth, when people are looking for treasure troves in stories, often there are traps or tests they have to pass before they can reach the treasure." I looked more closely at the stone blocking our way, and I saw that it was fashioned into the likeness of a door. To the side, there was a round circle attached to the rock, and I saw that it was free to spin around. Different numbers were carved into the rock of the circle, and on the left side of it was a prominent notch. The numbers went from one to fifteen. I looked back at the words. Maybe Rhodri was right.

He voiced what I was thinking. "Maybe the words point to what numbers need to line up in this notch for the door to open. Like a combination lock." I frowned. What was a combination lock? Rhodri took note of my puzzled expression. "A combination lock is a lock that can only be opened by creating the right number combination," he explained. "It doesn't need a key. They're common on Earth." He shined his light over the riddle. "The question is, how do you translate words into numbers?"

I squinted at the words, but with the dim light and faded characters, it was near impossible for me to read. Fortunately, Rhodri read the words aloud for my benefit. The riddle read:

We fell through man's sin,

And a whole kingdom nearly dissolved.

The heir pulled us back from the brink,

Demonstrating Abba's love and forgiveness;

Now we begin again, hoping for peace.

I recognized the words. They were from a prominent ballad commemorating the triumph of Nivea over her stepmother – rather appropriate for our current situation. But why carve the verse beside a locked door in the mountains? I tapped my chin with my finger. Five lines...they likely corresponded to five numbers. And then, I realized I knew the answer to Rhodri's question: numbers have meanings, and so can be used to relay coded messages. Brenwyds learn them so that in emergencies when written words are too dangerous or revealing, they can write a series of numbers to get at least the bare bones of a message across. My father had been teaching me the numbers. While I had yet to memorize all of them – my brain mixed up numbers like it did letters and so it took me painstaking hours to memorize anything – I knew one through thirty-five. But how to match them up?

"Do you think if we just picked random combinations, it would work?" Rhodri asked. I shook my head. There were multiple different combination possibilities, and I didn't want to waste time with random guesses. I tapped my head to indicate I was thinking, then pointed to the riddle and then the wheel and nodded, hoping to indicate I knew the connection between them. "You think you can figure out the code?" Rhodri asked. I nodded. I then gestured for him to be silent. "Alright. I'll just sit here until you figure it out. Here, take the torch." He sat and leaned against the tunnel wall.

I considered the first line: *We fell through man's sin*. Well, knowing that this referred to Morrian and Nivea's battle, it was easy enough to guess the meaning of that. The number for man, his weakness and evil, was six. I turned the wheel so six lined up with the notch, and was rewarded with a very faint grinding sound, like something was turning a key in a very old lock. I smiled.

Now the next line: *And a whole kingdom nearly dissolved.* I decided the key words there were "kingdom" and "dissolved." A political entity unraveling would equal...disorder and chaos for the inhabitants, surely. Disorder! That was it. The number eleven represented disorder. Accordingly, I turned the wheel, and was rewarded with another grinding sound, this one slightly louder.

Now the third line: *The heir pulled us back from the brink.* Hmm. The heir was Nivea, as she saved the kingdom from Morrian, rescuing it from the chaos hinted at in the preceding line. Rescue... that word sparked a connection in my mind. Rescue was a synonym for saving, and saving was connected to salvation, which was represented by the number fourteen, which was on the number wheel. Another turn resulted in another grinding noise.

The fourth line: *Demonstrating Abba's love and forgiveness.* This one was trickier. There was a number that stood for love, but it was sixteen, which was not on the wheel. And there was the very specific pairing with forgiveness and connection to Abba. That meant I needed to determine a number that represented a specific divine concept. What did the two virtues combined mean? I ran over the meanings for numbers one through fifteen in my head. Aha! Abba's love and forgiveness were representative of his grace extended to us as his sinful creations. This line stood for the number five. The grinding sound after I turned the wheel proved my answer correct.

Apparently Rhodri heard it that time, too. "That sounds promising," he commented. "As long as it doesn't represent the mountain about to cave in on us, that is." I shot him a look that said, *not helpful.* He shrugged. "Just saying."

Now for the last line: *Now we begin again, hoping for peace.* Well, it couldn't be hinged on the word "hope," for the number representing hope was thirty-five, and the last one I knew so far. That left "begin again" and "peace" as the key words. While there was no number I knew of that stood for peace specifically, fifteen did represent the idea of rest, which peace certainly entails. But then why add the "begin again?" Perhaps it was only to throw people off, for when I considered those particular words, two numbers came to mind: seven, which stood for resurrection, certainly a way of beginning again, and eight, which literally stood for new beginnings. I decided to discount seven because the line specifically had "begin" in it. That left me with fifteen and eight. I decided to try both of them in numerical order, and hoped that nothing bad would happen if I selected the wrong one first.

Fortunately, I never had to find out. Spinning the wheel first to eight, I was rewarded with a very loud grinding sound, and the door swung inward with a groan. "You did it!" Rhodri said, springing up. I shrugged modestly, but threw him a cheeky grin over my shoulder. I shone his light into the revealed chamber, and saw what we had traveled to find: rows and rows of swords, spears, and arrows. Surprisingly there was no real dust, nor cobwebs covering the weapons, though after a moment's thought I decided that made sense since the chamber was so deeply sealed in the mountain.

"Are these all flamestone weapons?" Rhodri asked, sounding a little awed. I shrugged again, wondering as he was, for there were far more that I had imagined. Everything was arranged meticulously: swords leaned in sword racks, spears hung on the walls, and quivers full of arrows hung from the back wall of the chamber with unstrung bows next to them. Rhodri drew a sword from its scabbard. We both saw the tiny, whitish flames it reflected in the light of the torch, though they were not as bright as the ones I had seen on the sword the man in my vision had held, and I remembered what Mathghamhain had said about the swords choosing their bearers. I also noticed, relieved, that the blade showed no signs of rust, which I had been afraid of since the weapons had been stored here so long with no care. I supposed that their special properties preserved them from the usual ravages of time on weapons.

"That's flamestone, all right," Rhodri said. He touched the surface tentatively. "Amazing. I don't even feel the flames, though the metal feels warm. And it's so light." He held it out for me to feel. He was right; the metal was warm, like it was new off the smith's forge. It sent a burst of warmth running through my frame, and I felt hope rekindle in my breast. We had a chance against Morrian now. A small chance, perhaps, but more of a chance than we had before.

Rhodri resheathed the sword, bracing the sheath between his foot and the rack to keep it steady. "Now the question is, how do we transport these out?" We had discussed on the trail the necessity of bringing as many as each of us could comfortably carry, plus whatever we could load on Dynin, for we needed a bit of a stockpile ourselves, especially if by some miracle help finally made it past the barrier. I picked up several swords and held them lengthwise in my arms and turned to Rhodri, demonstrating my thoughts. He laughed briefly. "I suppose that's the only way," he acknowledged, and gathered his own load, though it was rather awkward with only one arm.

I went to the back of the chamber, intent on grabbing a couple of quivers, when a faint sparkle caught my eye to my right. I turned. There was another rack of swords, but one of them had a small diamond embedded in the pommel at the end of the hilt. It surprised me, for Brenwyds generally do not ornament their weapons, as it really adds nothing to the weapon except the likelihood of getting robbed for it. Still, it seemed to be tastefully done. Putting down my armful, I picked up the sword. Like Rhodri, I noticed the lightness of the blade, even sheathed, and I admired the beautiful gold and wood workmanship of the hilt and scabbard of the weapon. It had likely belonged to someone of high rank and had been a cherished possession. I also fancied it had been a woman's sword, for it seemed more elegant than the average knight's blade. I placed a hand on the hilt, and immediately the same warmth rushed through me, brightening my mood, but it was more intense. I drew it in a fluid motion, and saw that the flames on the blade burst into a brightness like they had not in the sword Rhodri had inspected. They added to the light of Rhodri's torch.

"Aislinn?" I heard him call. "What do you have there?" I thought that was plain enough, and I tightened my grip, intending to practice a few exercises to test the sword's balance. But before I could, the flames brightened tenfold and I became aware of a melody in the room that seemed to emanate from the sword itself, which was most curious. "Aislinn!" I heard Rhodri say again, sounding alarmed. I didn't really pay attention to it, though, because I could hear the sword's melody clashing against another one that seemed to come from...me. It was harsh, and discordant, and I winced to hear it. How could I have such a melody? I had never heard it about myself before. It wasn't me. It sounded like a spell, and I practiced no magic.

Suddenly I gasped, for I glimpsed the white fire spill up my arm and a flash of intense heat raced through my body, seeming to settle in my throat. I gasped again, coughed, and fell to my knees, dropping the sword with a clang on the stone floor. "Aislinn!" Rhodri was at my side, kneeling next to me. "Are you alright? What was that?"

I was drawing in great, heaving breaths, and I coughed and hacked a few more times. It felt like a ball of wool was stuck in my throat, and with every hack and cough it lessened until it was gone. I shrugged and looked down at the sword. It looked very normal now, lying on the floor, the merest hints of flame reflecting off the shiny surface. Cautiously, I picked it up again. The flames brightened, as they had before, but there was no burst of searing heat, or spreading of the flames. Hmm. Mathghamhain might have mentioned that the choosing process was a bit dramatic. For I assumed that was what had happened.

"Are you alright?" Rhodri repeated. I nodded and got up. He looked around the room. "Perhaps we should be more cautious in taking these back. We have no real knowledge of how to handle them. I don't fancy the idea of being burned by my own sword."

I frowned, looking down at my clothes and arm. "I'm not burned," I mouthed, looking up so he could see my lips. Or I thought I mouthed the words, anyway. My eyes went wide and I put an involuntary hand over my mouth. Rhodri stared.

"Did you just..." he started to ask.

"I think...I did!" I gasped. Aloud. My voice had returned. "I did! I did! I did!" I could talk! I started to laugh from elation.

"But...how?" Rhodri asked.

I looked down at the sword in my hand. "This," I said, showing him. "Remember what Mathghamhain said? Why flamestone blades are so important? They can shield the bearer from spells. Apparently, they can break them, too. When I picked it up, I heard a song I think came from the sword, and it rose up against one that seemed to come from me, and overwhelmed it! It must have been Morrian's spell...Oh! Praise Abba!" I had never so much enjoyed the sound of my own voice. I focused on his splint and reached for it. "Let me heal it." He allowed me to dismantle the splint, and I raised my voice in song to heal him. Oh! How good it felt to have my voice slide from note to note, rising and falling as needed along the tune of Rhodri's song. Never had I been more aware of the joy of singing. It wasn't nearly long enough for my tastes, though, as it healed within a minute. Rhodri tested it, flexing his muscles, closing and opening his hand.

"Praise Abba, indeed," he said, smiling. "I wonder if Mathghamhain knew this might happen."

"And not tell me?" I frowned. "That doesn't seem right."

Rhodri shrugged. "Well, as he's said himself, his manners are a bit rusty. At least now I won't have to listen to just one side of a conversation when you two talk." I laughed.

"There's that. Oh, Rhodri, this is so wonderful. We might really have a chance now." I sheathed the sword. "And I'm claiming this one."

"No argument there," he said. "But come on, we've been down here a while already; let's get back to Mathghamhain and tell him what we've found."

"Very well. But don't be surprised if I sing the whole way down the tunnel!" He laughed again, and we reentered the tunnel, and I fulfilled my promise of singing (nearly) the whole way. As we drew close to the entrance, however, I fell silent. I wanted to surprise Mathghamhain, and get back at him a little as well. I was certain he would have been aware of the possibility that the power imbued in the flamestone weapons could break Morrian's spell over me. Rhodri and I emerged into the sunlight. I squinted and blinked rapidly to adjust to the sudden, intense sunlight that was such a contrast to the dark tunnel.

"You have been successful in your venture, I see," Mathghamhain said from my right. I turned to see him rise from a rock where he had presumably been sitting. "Excellent. How many are there?"

"Far more than we can carry," Rhodri answered. "And quite the variety of weapons as well. Swords, spears, arrows, and I even saw a few pikes."

"Hmm, yes, many weapons were forged for the fight against Morrian to add to what we already had, which was sizeable as it was." Mathghamhain's cloaked head turned from Rhodri to me and back again. "And it seems that the power of a blade has also accomplished what I hoped: Aislinn has her voice back."

"How did you know?" I demanded, surprised. "I hadn't said anything. And why in the Five Realms did you not tell me of this possibility?"

"Because I was not sure it would happen and did not wish to raise false hopes. Their power cannot break every spell. I merely hoped the one Morrian cast on you was weak enough that it would." His head turned back to Rhodri. "And as for how I knew, it is rather obvious that the prince is no longer wearing his splint, meaning that you must have healed him, and to do that, you must have regained your voice."

"Oh." I should have thought of that. "Well, you still should have told me."

"And ruin the surprise?" He was definitely amused by my indignation. I opened my mouth to complain some more, but he spoke before I did. "I am glad it worked. You have a lovely speaking voice."

"Oh...thank you." I had never been told that before. In fact, the only comments I had garnered about my speaking voice was gentle teasing that I persisted in speaking with the accent of the Sarelind province, where my father's family was from and where I had spent a good deal of time as a child. It was considered rustic and a step below the precise, civilized accent of the capital. I personally liked the broad, lilting tones of the Sarelind accent. If other people couldn't understand it well, that was their problem.

"Which sword chose you?" Mathghamhain asked. I unfastened it from where I had hung it by my side and gave it to him. His posture tensed.

"Do you know whose it was?" I asked.

There was a long pause before he answered. He handed the sword back to me. "It was used by a young woman much like you." His voice seemed carefully controlled to me. I narrowed my eyes slightly.

"You...didn't get along?"

"No!" His denial was quite forceful. "Nothing like that. We were...good friends. Seeing this sword again brings back the memories, that is all." Hmm. Something more than just good friends, I thought, but let the topic drop. "And did any weapon claim you, Your Highness?" Mathghamhain asked Rhodri.

"No, but I didn't try many. I was more concerned with determining how many we could take. Is it necessary?"

"It is always best, but no. Not absolutely necessary." Mathghamhain glanced upward. Following his gaze, I saw Lissa and Dynin looking down at us. "We had best begin transporting these up the cliff and arranging them into our packs. I do not want to spend too much time here. It makes me uncomfortable being away from the pool so long. We have no way to know what Morrian is planning."

"I am certain that, were it anything we needed to act upon, Aislinn would have Seen something," Rhodri said. "But I do agree. It bothers me, in a way, that we've seen no sign of her trying to find us. We must find out what she is up to."

"Very well, then," I said, kneeling by my pack and beginning to disassemble it. "Let's begin."

11

$\mathcal{T}$ROUBLING $\mathcal{V}$ISIONS

$\mathcal{W}$e ended up using the rope to pull the weapons up to where Dynin and Lissa waited. As part of the process, I called up to her, and the expression of shock on her face made me laugh in a way I hadn't for days. Once we had the rope properly in place, it did not take long to load what weapons we could onto Dynin or in our packs, and then we started on our way. As darkness fell, we stopped and made camp. I went scavenging for what firewood I could find. We had stopped in a small valley so there were some scanty bushes with dropped branches we could use. I had wandered a little distance from the camp and was surprised when a large shadow fell over me. I looked up to see the dark form of Mathghamhain.

"Yes? Is something wrong?" I asked.

"No," he said. There was an awkward pause. I wondered why he had intercepted me. "Are you very upset I didn't tell you about the possibility of being healed?"

That's what he was worried about? "No. Slightly annoyed, yes. Upset, no."

"Good...I had no intention of doing so. It was merely that I was unsure myself and-"

"Easy," I said. "It's fine. It was a wonderful surprise. Why are you so concerned?"

Another pause. I had the ridiculous image of one of Lissa's former suitors, from before she and Rhodri were engaged. He was the son of one of Ecclesia's dukes, but he had a terribly nervous personality. One day, he had brought her a glass of water while a group of us young people were watching a joust, but had tripped and accidently doused her with it. The poor boy had looked like he wanted the ground to open up and swallow him. He stammered out apologies the rest of the day and Lissa finally claimed a headache to escape it. Despite not having much of a clue as to what Mathghamhain looked like, he seemed terribly upset with the thought that he might have made me upset.

"I would not want to be on bad terms with you."

I snorted. "It would take much more than that, believe me."

"Good. Are you an alto?"

I blinked at the sudden change of subject. "Yes, why?"

"I thought so. I have been thinking, and it has occurred to me that knowledge of how to battle a powerful sorceress may not be so common among Brenwyds nowadays. Is that assumption correct?"

I shrugged. "It depends. I would say, more accurately, that the knowledge has become more specialized. Every Brenwyd studies the theory and practices as best we can, but not everyone pursues all the details involved. At least," I sighed, "not until they already have some experience in petty magic users." I hesitated a moment, then added, "If Sir Eiwas and his forces had been able to get through, there would have been Brenwyds in the company who are familiar with the theory and techniques. As it is...I know all the folk songs and stories about powerful magic users defeated in the past, but I have not extensively studied the actual techniques. My best weapon against Morrian, on my own, is to sing the Creation song as powerfully as I can, but that is what I did last time and, well...you saw how that turned out." I lowered my eyes to the ground and returned to searching for sticks as I said the last sentences. Before he could say anything, I rushed on. "But now that we know more about her, we can better strategize next time. She was weakening as I sang the Creation song, just not quickly enough considering everything that was going on. Perhaps with a bigger, better distraction of some sort I will be successful next time. After all, if we only get her shield down, she should be able to be...killed easily." My voice hitched on the last few words. I knew the best way to stop Morrian was to kill her, but killing anyone was not something to take lightly.

"I see." I felt myself tensing slightly as I prepared to rebut whatever statement Mathghamhain was about to make about the direness of our chances; however, he surprised me. "Then perhaps you might welcome my assistance? I can no longer break spells myself, but I can help you practice the theory you've learned. It could be useful to you."

I turned and stared at him. "Could be...? Of course it would be useful! Are you trying to say you wish to show me some things that will help us defeat Morrian?"

"In plain language...yes."

"Then why not say so plainly? Do you think I would reject the offer?" I felt baffled as to why in Niclausia he would think that. Surely he had to know that any help or advice he could give about how to defeat Morrian would be eagerly accepted. We had already told him so when we accepted his help in the first place.

"No, not exactly..."

"Then what? Did you fear I would reject you as a teacher?" His silence told me I had guessed correctly. "Why?"

"I..." He gave me no answer.

I eyed him closely – as closely as I could without being able to see any true part of him. The thought gave me some sudden insight. "Is it because of the spell you're under? You think that if I knew what it truly is, I would – or I should – reject you?" Again, he made no answer, but I caught a quiet intake of breath that I took to mean I was correct. I stepped toward him and placed a hand on his cloaked arm. It felt thick, much thicker than a normal human arm, and muscled, but I could tell nothing more. I chose my next words carefully. "Mathghamhain, you must stop thinking of yourself so badly because of your appearance. Though I don't know what you look like or the particulars of your curse, what I know of you through our interactions over the past few days tells me you are someone who cares deeply about the world around him, who enjoys the company of others. But you have used your hurt as an excuse to withdraw from the world and to try to stop caring for anything but your own pain and loneliness. I say try, for you have not been successful. If you had, no amount of pleading would have roused you to help us. But you're still allowing your bitterness and shame to cloud your mind and interactions with us. You seem to think that you're not worthy of us. But we desperately need you. While you may not think highly of yourself, at least accept the fact that we think much of you."

He was perfectly still. "How much could you think of me? We barely know each other."

"Well, you may not think so, but I think it rather impressive that you are two hundred and fifty years old. And the fact that you have a sense of humor."

"Are those how you judge a person? Age and sense of humor?"

"Of course. Often they tell me all I need to know."

"There must be many people you think well of, then."

"Not necessarily." I gazed at him steadily. "But do you admit the truth of my words?"

He sighed. "Oh...for the most part. No one needs to tell me how low I think of myself. But you do not understand that it is correct. I have made grave mistakes and this...this is my punishment."

My eyes widened. "Surely you don't really believe that?"

"What else am I to think? Abba himself has not seen fit to remove this curse. And he does everything for a reason, isn't that what we are taught? You may have keen insight, but you still do not know the facts of my life. If you did, you would agree."

"Don't tell me what I would or would not do." I frowned at him. "It seems to me that your real problem is that you've lost hope that your curse could ever be broken. Perhaps it is that, more than anything, that keeps you trapped." I took a step back and scanned him head to toe. "And yes, Abba does have purposes for all that happens in our lives but everything happens in his timing, not ours. Maybe he has allowed your curse to continue because He knew that we need you now, as someone who has faced Morrian before. Because we do. And maybe now, a way will open to break your curse."

He made a dismissive noise and turned to walk away. "You do not understand," he repeated.

I marched around to be in front of him. "Then tell me! You said yourself, I don't know the facts of your life. Tell them to me, and perhaps I could help you break your curse. We could consider it practice for facing Morrian." As I spoke, I began to call on my Brenwyd listening sense to examine his curse.

"Aislinn. Stop." I saw his head shake back and forth. "Many have tried, with no effect. It is unbreakable."

"No spell is unbreakable. That is one of the first lessons taught in magic-fighting. And I am wonderfully stubborn."

"This one is. Leave it be, Aislinn. Save your energy for Morrian," he said roughly. "Go finish with the firewood. I'm sure we're all hungry." He stalked back to the campsite.

"Well," I said, looking after him. "That was enlightening...in a disturbing way." How could any Brenwyd, even a cursed one, lose such faith in hope, in Abba? What had happened to him? What did his curse do? There had to be more going on than a change of form. My eyes turned skyward. "Abba, how can I help him? What is your plan here?"

⁓⑤⅋⑨⁓

That night, I dreamed again. I saw a small island, dark save for some spots of flickering firelight in the windows of a large fortress. I viewed it from above. There was a tall, strong, rectangular wall with watchtowers at each corner. Within the wall was a circular keep, similar to the watchtowers, but bigger and taller. It was made of dark stone – an imposing edifice seemingly grown straight up from the rock below. I did not get too much time to examine the exterior, however, as my Sight tugged me indoors to a room. The room was furnished lavishly; thick woolen rugs dyed in patterns of lavender and silver with pops of amethyst covered the floor, except for a brashly vermilion carpet that slashed through the middle of the room and led to a large gilded throne, which was the only available seating in the room. Tall, gold candlesticks ran the length of the carpet, lighting the room with the aid of torches mounted around the walls. Between the torches were tapestries, expertly crafted, but the scenes were of magic and carnage that made me ill. Despite all the fabrics, however, the jet-black stone of the walls and floor still peeked through, giving everything a hard edge. A small door opened by the throne and a woman walked in. Morrian. Even in the dream, my breath stuck in my throat and I shivered. Her steps echoed through the bare space. Behind her came a man. I recognized him from my other dream. He had been the one with the nasal voice. "...are watching the border," he was saying as he came in. Morrian reached the throne and sat. The man stood before her. "And I have contacted our agent in the Darlesian court. Lady Duchess Rhian's messages will go unheeded, have no doubt."

"Make sure they do," Morrian said in a cool voice. "I want no more incursions at the border. Have you had any success in finding the prince, princess, and their Brenwyd companion?"

The man ducked his head. "Not yet, my lady, but I'm sure we will soon."

"Soon!" Morrian's sharp voice cracked in the room like a whip. "Soon. That is what you told me when you began searching three days ago. How much longer must I wait?"

"I will tell you as soon as we have anything, my lady, but with the loss of most of the others with the casting of the spell, and the dispersal of the rest across Niclausia for their tasks, we have reduced resources. We are doing our best."

"That is clearly not good enough."

The man began to look nervous. "But my lady, how much trouble can they be? You said you made the Brenwyd mute. They are no threat."

"Perhaps." Morrian's eyes were hard as volcanic stones. "But the fact that they have seemingly disappeared troubles me. I will take no chances." She paused, leveling her eyes at the man. "Send the alpha of the shadow wolves to me, with some of his pack. I wish to send them hunting."

The man bowed. "Of course, my lady." He exited the room.

Morrian remained on her throne, tapping her fingers on the armrest. She gazed unseeingly over the rest of the room. "Where are you, my little princess?" she asked in a hiss. "Where are you hiding?" She got up and walked out. My Sight followed her. She entered a hallway that I guessed went around the circumference of her circular castle. Many doors opened off of it, but she just kept going down, down, down.

Finally, she came to a door at the end of the staircase. She laid a hand on it, muttered a word, and it swung open soundlessly. The room she entered was in complete darkness. The rustling sounds of many people breathing reached my ears. Morrian snapped her fingers, and torches burst to life along the walls, revealing the room's occupants. It was full of sleeping people – Brenwyds, I noted. Morrian walked among them slowly, smiling satisfactorily. She turned from one row and went further into the room. Another door appeared, and this time she drew out a key and turned it in the lock to open the door. The room was already lit, and I saw two objects within. One looked like a white rose on a pedestal. The other was a white sphere hung seemingly in midair. Or rather, I could tell it was white. Mostly it was transparent, with a bit of white at the bottom like a thin film of milk. Morrian went to the sphere and put her hand on it as if caressing it and closed her eyes. The glow lit up her face. She smiled. "Now, that's coming along nicely." She withdrew her hand from the sphere and left the room, locking the door behind her. When she turned, the nasal-voiced man was there.

"I have sent the message to the alpha, my lady," he said. "He will be here at dawn.

"Excellent." She started walking away. The man glanced at the door she had locked before following her.

"Is the power drain going as intended, my lady?"

"Exactly so. Of course, there's hardly any power there yet. But it is coming. By the end of the month, we shall have more than enough power to open the gate and subjugate this land."

"And with the power of the very people meant to protect them," the man said, with an almost gleeful expression. "It is an ingenious plan, my lady. Infallible."

"No," Morrian corrected, turning on him suddenly. "Nothing is infallible. I learned that last time. Ever that cursed Abba seeks to thwart me, using the most unlikely, the most insulting of vessels. This is why we must find the princess and her companions. Do not forget that."

The man bowed his head. "Of course, my lady. I shall get right back to it."

"Good." He left. Morrian took one last round around the sleeping Brenwyds. She paused by the final man, studying him. "Well, who have we here?" she murmured, a smile curving her lips. "How fortunate. One more tool to use against the prince." She left, and I saw the man clearly. It was Rhodri's father.

I woke with a start, surprised out of the dream. It was infinitely disturbing. Rhodri's father and those with him were Morrian's prisoners. She was looking for us. She was calling the shadow wolves. And that sphere... "Aislinn? Is all well?" Mathghamhain's voice made me start again.

"No...no. I had a dream. Of Morrian."

"What happened?" his voice was instantly serious.

I got up and went to shake Rhodri. He woke grudgingly. He had never been a quick riser. "What is it, Aislinn?" he asked with a yawn. "Did something stir in the bushes that I need to investigate?"

"Not funny, Rhodri," I said, turning to shake Lissa awake. "It's about your father."

That brought him awake. "What about him?"

"Morrian has him."

"What?" I explained the whole dream to the three of them. Mathghamhain was extremely agitated.

"The fortress – you're sure it was circular? Black stone? On an island?"

"It looked jet-black, as if made of onyx. Do you know it?"

"Unfortunately." He got up and began to pace. "It is her old stronghold, off the northern coast. She would go there on retreat – or so everyone thought. She really went to practice her magic." Lissa, Rhodri, and I exchanged glances. If she was keeping herself cloistered there, as the dream seemed to indicate, then there was only one course of action to take, and we all recognized it.

"Can you guide us there?" Rhodri asked.

Mathghamhain stopped pacing. "You wish to battle her there?"

"Where else? If that's where she is, then that's where we must go. We have no other option. We're the only ones awake and inside Ecclesia, and so we are the only ones who can stop her."

Mathghamhain's covered head moved from side to side rapidly. "But you could face her anywhere else! She will be at her strongest there. It would be best to lure her elsewhere."

"How could we do that?" I asked. If we could do so, it would likely be best, as he said, but something was starting to stir in the back of my head, something from my magic lessons...

"I know not." I heard him let out a deep breath. "Forgive me my strong reaction. I...I have been there before, and hold no fond memories of the place."

"It's quite alright," I said. "My glimpse did not make me inclined to go visit, either. But..." The thought suddenly leaped into my head, and I straightened. "What if the spell anchor is there?"

"The what?" Lissa and Rhodri asked in tandem.

Mathghamhain turned his head to me, and I could feel his gaze. "Yes...that is possible. For such a large spell with such large effects, she would have to anchor it. I had not considered that." He began pacing again, but not so frenetically. It was a more thoughtful pace. "And therein could lie the weakness."

"What anchor?" Rhodri repeated.

"In my lessons on battling magic," I began, "I learned that some spells, especially large ones, actually need something physical they can be attached to in order for the spell to remain stable and not backfire on the caster. Some popular things are certain plants, generally poisonous ones, inanimate objects, things of that nature. A witch even used a cat as an anchor for a spell designed to spread disease. You recall, that was the cause of the Great Plague three hundred years ago."

"Exactly," Mathghamhain said. "For a spell of this scope, Morrian must have anchored the power to something. It could not exist otherwise."

"But what?" I wondered. I thought back to the lessons about spell anchors. "It would have to be something connected to the casting of the spell, the instrument through which..." My gaze landed on Lissa, and my heart lurched. No, no, it couldn't. It wasn't possible.

Lissa stared back at me, and she could read where my thoughts led. Her eyes widened. "You think I could be this anchor?"

I opened my mouth, closed it, and opened it again. "I suppose... perhaps technically, but it couldn't be. There has never been an account of a person being an anchor. It can't be you." I thought of something else, and my thoughts eased. "If you were, then surely the whole kingdom would have woken with you no matter how Morrian designed the spell."

"Perhaps," Mathghamhain said slowly, "but...Morrian is crafty and cruel. It would be just like her to have designed it thus, and if anyone could determine how to use a person as a spell anchor, she could. She knows we would know there would be only one way to end the spell then."

I glared at him. "But there can't be just one way! Assuming it is true, which it surely can't be."

"What would this one way be?" Lissa asked quietly. "If I am the anchor?" Rhodri took her hand in a comforting grip, and both looked to me for my answer.

I looked away from them. I knew my lessons. For a spell with an anchor, there was only one way to completely break it. I couldn't voice it, so Mathghamhain answered. "If you truly are the anchor, Your Highness...the only way to end the spell would be if you died."

Lissa's eyes widened, face paling, and her mouth parted slightly, though she made no response. Rhodri moved so his whole arm wrapped around her shoulders in a protective gesture, and his eyes went hard. "I refuse to accept that," he said in a sharp tone. "There must be some other way."

"None that I know of," Mathghamhain said, a tired note in his voice. "Your Highnesses, believe my words. If I was aware of any other way, any other idea, I would not have told you what I just did."

"Then perhaps we should be the ones to invent the new idea." There was a heavy silence.

Lissa took a deep breath. "If it is what is needed, Rhodri, then-"

"No! I won't believe it. Aislinn said anchors are inanimate, which you are not. It cannot be you."

"But what if it is?" She moved from his embrace to face him. "Rhodri, if it is me, then I cannot in good conscience let the spell continue. We have been taught to care for the protection and well-being of our people above all else. If this is the only way to do so, how can I refuse?" A heavy silence fell. I closed my eyes. This could not be, I repeated to myself. It cannot be. I must be missing something. There was something we were ignoring, something about the way the spell was cast...I thought back to my vision of the casting. Yes, Lissa had been the medium through which the spell spread, but even she had not simply just fallen asleep...

My eyes sprang open. "It's not Lissa."

Mathghamhain stirred. "What else could-?"

"The rose. The one Lissa pricked her finger on. It has to be. She fell asleep because she pricked her finger on the rose. The spell was in the rose already." Rhodri looked over at me with new hope.

"A rose," Mathghamhain mused. "Yes...I can see how that would work. Of course."

"So, if we could find this rose and destroy it," Rhodri said, "would that break the spell?"

"Quite possibly." Mathghamhain paused. "Yes. But there is still something about the princess's involvement that bothers me. True, I remember what you said of the rose, but-"

"But nothing," Rhodri said. "Aislinn said that anchors serve as the medium through which a spell is cast, yes?" He looked at me for confirmation. I nodded. "Lissa fell asleep because of the rose. Had she refused it, Morrian's plan would not have worked."

"She would have merely forced the princess to prick her finger," Mathghamhain said. "But I acknowledge your point."

"Then that's that. We have to find the rose and destroy it." Rhodri looked immensely relieved, as did Lissa. She leaned into his side, and I suspected it was a collapse from the release of tension.

"Would that only break the spell, or would it completely reverse it?" I wondered. "Remember, Morrian said she has designed the spell to sap Brenwyds of their abilities. Will destroying the anchor ensure that they wake with no effects from that?"

"I fear, Aislinn, that that is a question we shan't know the answer to until the spell is broken," Mathghamhain said solemnly. "I truly have no thoughts as to how Morrian could have designed such a curse, but you can be sure she had direct help from the Shadow Angel. Such a spell...it will be difficult to reverse the effects."

I pressed my lips in a thin line. There must be a way to ensure the rest of the Brenwyds in the kingdom woke with their abilities intact. I had no wish to become the only true Brenwyd in Ecclesia. Hadn't there been something else in the dream that had bearing on that? That strange sphere, maybe it was connected...I turned my eyes to the surrounding low bushes as I thought, watching their shadows on the rock bend and change in the wind and dance across Dynin's coat as he stood watching us.

"Shadows!" I blurted out suddenly, every other thought driven from my mind. "Grindles and spindles, shadows!"

"What about shadows?" Rhodri asked.

"I forgot...Morrian had her underling send for the alpha of the shadow wolves. I believe she means to send them after us."

"Shadow wolves?" Rhodri asked, sounding dubious. I could see Lissa's eyes widen in fear. She had always hated shadow wolf stories.

Shadow wolves? Dynin echoed Rhodri, sounding considerably more alarmed.

"And you forgot to mention this until now?" Mathghamhain said, his voice distorted in a growl.

"The talk of anchors distracted me." I stood and cast my eyes around our campsite. "I don't think we should sleep at night."

"Wait a moment, shadow wolves?" Rhodri repeated. "Those are myths."

"I'm afraid not, Your Highness," Mathghamhain said. "They are quite real. And extremely dangerous." His head moved as he presumably looked around as if he, too, now distrusted the night's shadows. "I think we had best do a hard march back to the castle. When shadow wolves go on the hunt, nothing stops them. At the castle we have a means of fortification against them, and we can gather more supplies for wherever we determine to go next."

We marched quickly for the rest of the night, nerves on edge, and far into the next morning before breaking for a rest. We then repeated the exercise, so that by morning on the second day we neared Mathghamhain's valley and – we hoped – relative safety. We hadn't spoken much on the march of what exactly our next steps should be and how to accomplish them after that first night. For one, we were pushing ourselves hard to move quickly, which didn't leave much breath for talking. For another, for myself at least, I didn't feel like addressing the issue again just yet. I took advantage of the time instead to mull things over in my mind and try to figure out a new idea or angle that could give us an advantage, and quiet Mathghamhain's fears of facing Morrian directly. Despite his opposition to the idea, I knew that, in the end, it was the only one open to us. To tell the truth, I liked the notion almost as little as he did, but I was not going to let fear stop me. Be strong and courageous, for the Lord your God is with you wherever you go. The verse echoed in the recesses of my mind whenever I began dwelling too much on my fear. I took it to heart. Abba was with us. He would show us the way...eventually.

As we drew to within an hour's walk of Mathghamhain's valley, by some unspoken consent we began to slow our pace. The silence that had characterized much of our return journey continued for a time, but eventually Rhodri broke it. "I don't think we should spend more than a day or two in the valley. We need to keep moving to try and catch Morrian by surprise. Moving will also hopefully keep those wolves off our trail."

Mathghamhain harrumphed from his position in the front and said, without turning, "So, you still have the idea that we should force a confrontation on her island."

"I do," Rhodri replied calmly. "If it helps, I don't much like the thought, either, but given all your talk of anchors and spells and such, I don't see we have much of a choice. Given we are cut off from the rest of the continent with Aislinn as our only Brenwyd, it seems to me our only chance to end the spell on our own is to destroy that anchor, at least as far as I understood it the other night."

I nodded. "Yes, when it comes down to it. I have been trying to contact someone on the outside through Sight each night, but as yet I haven't succeeded."

"I wondered if you were doing something of the kind," Lissa commented. "Your expression was too focused to be merely woolgathering."

"Hmm. The problem is, I think I'll have to fight through the spell itself to make even a small hole for the message to go through. Morrian was very thorough."

"She generally is." Mathghamhain slowed his pace so he was no longer several yards in front, but he continued facing forward. "But it is possible that, as an alto, you may have a slight advantage, Aislinn."

I blinked, surprised by the optimistic cast of the comment as well as its content. "How? Sopranos are the more powerful Brenwyds among women."

"Yes, and Morrian knows that, so she always bolsters her spells especially well in soprano, tenor, and baritone ranges. But in alto and bass ranges, there can sometimes be very slight gaps to take advantage of." His shrouded head turned toward me. "Next time you try, let me know, and I might be able to help you find them." Since our confrontation the night he initially offered to help me with his knowledge, he had avoided speaking with me, something our hard pace made fairly easy. I felt encouraged, and a little relieved, at this indication of his still being willing to work with me. I had worried, in hindsight, that my words had been too strong.

Rhodri startled us by clapping his hands together. "Bravo, Mathghamhain. That's the most hopeful thing I've heard you say so far. At this rate, you might even admit by this time next week that perhaps we might stand a chance after all."

"Do not be too hasty, Your Highness, that would rather take a year," Mathghamhain replied in the dry tone we had learned to associate with his humor.

I snorted inelegantly and rolled my eyes. "I rather think more than that, but that is not the point. I'm wondering why you didn't mention that earlier."

He hesitated. "I was going to, but after your news of the wolves, speed was more important than training for the moment. That was why I was asking you about your range and training the other night. Morrian expects the best to be facing her, so that is what she prepares for."

I raised an eyebrow at his figure ahead of me. "Should I be offended at that insinuation?" I wasn't, but I felt like teasing him.

The question stopped him in his tracks. "Oh...I apologize, I did not mean it in any way to be derogatory to you. I only meant that Morrian knows the usually most effective singers and knows how to thwart them, and makes it hard enough for them so they overcommit and either cannot fully lift her enchantment or die in the effort." I involuntarily shuddered. Many times my father had warned me against the dangers of overcommitting against a spell. The best one could hope for in such an event was to fall into a long sleep that would replenish one's strength. Often, however, such sleep lasted for weeks, or months, or even led to death. It was another reason why Brenwyds never went against magicians alone. "But she does not tend to expect only altos, and so there may be small areas in the spell that you could overpower right in your middle range."

"May be."

"Yes. We did use such gaps successfully against her the last time. This time she may well have thought to guard against them. But perhaps not."

"Perhaps." The word did not exactly inspire much confidence. Though Rhodri was right, he was speaking more hopefully than he had two days ago.

"I cannot be sure until I hear the melody for myself. You said you would welcome any help or knowledge I could give you in how to battle her. I am telling you this. Now who is being pessimistic?" He sounded amused as he asked the question. By this point we had positioned ourselves to face each other, and I was trying my best to look where I guessed his eyes to be.

I opened my mouth, then closed it, then smiled wryly. "You're correct. Far be it from me to be the voice of pessimism. Alright; I'll try to Search again in the valley, and I would most certainly welcome your help. As I said two nights ago, I stand by all my words." I looked steadily at him. After a moment, he turned and began walking again.

"We shall see," I heard him say quietly, so quietly I wasn't sure if he meant me to hear it or not. Certainly Lissa and Rhodri hadn't. I frowned at his back as he regained his usual distance in front. It had seemed that his prickly exterior may have been starting to soften, but clearly there was still much progress to be made. Maybe he truly did need more basic human interaction. Abba knows I would likely have gone mad living in isolation for two hundred and fifty years. Perhaps his pessimism and low expectations were a self-preservation mechanism.

"Are you planning on following him anytime soon or do you want the challenge of finding our own way back to his valley?" Rhodri's voice broke in on my musings, making me realize that he, Lissa, and Dynin were standing patiently behind me on the narrow trail waiting for me to start moving.

"Oh, I'm sorry. I was thinking."

"Clearly," Lissa said as we began to move again. "I think that you have been making good progress with him, Aislinn."

I looked at her in surprise, given my current musing on the lack of progress. "What do you mean?"

"His newfound hint of optimism, of course. I do not know what you've told him when you two have talked alone, but it certainly seems to have done him some good."

"What do you mean, when I've talked to him? We've all been talking to him. Which hasn't been much from anyone in the past couple of days."

"Yes, as a group, but out of all of us you have spoken with him alone most often over the entirety of the trip. He seeks you out." Her tone of voice was neutral. Too neutral.

I sent her a speculative glance. "Are you trying to imply something? He likely just feels more comfortable with me, as I'm Brenwyd and not royal."

"True." She sent a mock frown in Rhodri's direction. "Though I could name a certain person who has been acting decidedly non-royal enough recently to put anyone at their ease."

He grinned back at her. "Aw, go easy on me, Liss. I've just had a six-month vacation in a world where being royalty doesn't mean much of anything. It's all about equality. Rather nice most of the time, actually. Gave me a lot of ideas on how we can make some good changes here." He sobered. "After we defeat the spell, that is."

"Yes. That." Lissa sighed. "As much as I dislike his pessimism, Mathghamhain does often have a point in pointing out our weaknesses. We cannot go against Morrian again without a very good strategy."

"I know," I said. "But perhaps, if he can help me get through with my Sight, we may be able to call for reinforcements. If we could get even a few more Brenwyds, our chances would be much better."

Lissa nodded. "I know, but Aislinn, I do think that sometimes you unconsciously belittle yourself. You are extremely capable on your own. Your father has said so." She patted my arm in reassurance.

"Even so, Liss, I'm still just one."

"Depending on what else is going on in the continent, getting help might be trickier than we think, even if you can get a message through, Aislinn," Rhodri mused, his brow creasing. "Remember, you've reported that Morrian has planned distractions for the outside realms. It would have to be something big for Uncle Aelfwic to disregard a message from my mother. He would fear crossing my father else." Rhodri's uncle, King Aelfwic of Darlesia, and his father were mostly on good terms, but Aelfwic was always aware that Ceredon might well have become king had the elections been forced to a tie, as they nearly had been.

Two generations ago, the Darlesian merchant and peasant classes had risen in revolt against their king, who had been a tyrant, and removed him from the throne. In the ensuing chaos, the other nobles and Brenwyds had worked out a deal with them: they would allow the monarchy to return to the throne, but it would no longer be strictly hereditary. Instead, there would be an election after the reigning monarch died to choose whom from among his family would inherit. Further, if the monarch proved tyrannical or inept another election could be called and the monarch removed. Thus the throne could go to a child, a sibling, or a cousin of the previous ruler. In this way, there was a way to ensure that someone who would at least be a decent ruler came to the throne. The system was still fairly new, and so the balance of power was somewhat delicate in Darlesia. When Aelfwic and Ceredon's mother had died, it had been a close tie to determine who became king. Each had the qualities needed in a good ruler, but Aelfwic cared more than Ceredon about gaining the crown, and so had been able to take it. Still, the knowledge of the close election kept him ever mindful of the advice his brother gave. Or that of his brother's wife. Usually. (This system was also the reason Rhodri – and his siblings – had the courtesy titles of "prince" or "princess" despite their father being a duke, as theoretically they could all be eligible for the Darlesian throne in the next election. By marrying Lissa, however, Rhodri would lose that eligibility, which was a good thing as we Ecclesians are very proud of our independence from Darlesia despite being close allies with them.)

"Yes," I said grimly. "In my dream, Morrian's underling said he contacted an agent at the Darlesian court to counteract the reports your mother would send. But who could it be who would have that much sway with the king?" It was a troubling thought, especially since King Aelfwic was strong-minded like his brother. He listened to the counsel of others, but he rarely let it sway him from a set course.

"I don't know...his wife, perhaps, but I can't imagine Aunt Aellia doing anything like that," Rhodri said. "Besides, she and my mother are very close. She would believe her." He quickened his pace. "Mathghamhain!" Mathghamhain paused and waited for us to catch up with him. "Mathghamhain, could we use your pool upon our return to see what else is happening in Niclausia?"

"Of course. I already planned on it, given the information Aislinn has given us on what she has planned, since the pool's power is clearly unaffected by the curse."

Rhodri nodded. "Have you any idea how Morrian could insert a spy into the Darlesian court without being noticed? We've been discussing Aislinn's dream just now, and I know my uncle's court. He is not easily fooled, and there are Brenwyds constantly on guard against magic. It couldn't be anything overt."

"If Morrian has a follower at this court," Mathghamhain said, "you can be sure she has enabled him or her to be effective and persuasive. She was always especially good at the magic of suggestion. She knew how to control the power of her voice, how to use it in conjunction with her magic to get people to do as she wished. It is one of the easier magics both to learn and to teach, because everyone possesses some ability with words to be persuasive should they wish, and it is very subtle. Unless one is particularly looking for evidence of a persuasive spell, it would slip past most." He paused for a moment. "She is also good at spells of disinterest, which may be nearer the mark. Those spells can help make a person utterly unremarkable, which is usually the opposite of what magic does, and so they can also slip by guards. By the time one could begin to think that magic might be involved, the disinterest takes hold and one dismisses one's assumptions. Those two branches of magic are what kept Morrian cloaked for all those years, even from the people who should have known her best." His voice grew rougher with the last words. We all considered the information for a moment. I recognized the truth of the facts. In studying to fight magic, one also inevitably learned a bit about magic, and my father had taught me that persuasive magics were often the hardest to fight because they were meant to be unassuming by nature.

"How do you know so much of how she works?" Rhodri asked. "I know you fought her, and you mentioned that she kept you as a prisoner for a time. But knowing how she operates across so many spheres...forgive me, but that seems to indicate more than a general acquaintance." Lissa frowned slightly at him, indicating she thought the question too accusatory, but I could tell Rhodri was only genuinely curious. I was as well. Just what was Mathghamhain's connection to Morrian?

He was silent for several moments. "I believe I mentioned that Morrian's father remarried a Brenwyd woman after her own mother died," he said carefully. "She was eight years of age when that happened. I...grew up in the same town, and so had some dealings with her. Even in play, she was a master organizer. She had a natural aura of leadership and persuasion, and was able to influence the children who followed in her wake. Given the circumstances and my knowledge of what we discovered and theorized from before, I am well able to understand what strategies she is likely using."

"You knew her as a child?" Lissa asked, eyebrows raised. "What was she like?"

Another pause. "She was...different...When I have thought back on it, I can see the signs that she was leaning toward magic and sorcery. You also must understand, I am many years younger, so when I was a child, she was a young lady entering society."

"But being raised among Brenwyds," I said, "surely she must have known the evils of witchcraft."

"She knew. She did not care. She believed her father had betrayed her mother's memory by marrying again, and the fact it was a Brenwyd woman made it worse, I think. From what I understood, her mother was no great beauty, and of course the Brenwyd was. I believe she truly thought as a child that the Brenwyd had ensnared her father by magic. By learning magic herself, especially since it was expressly forbidden...I believe she felt it would draw her father back to her." I pondered the information. It certainly shed light on Morrian's motives. I felt a pang of sympathy for her, but I knew it was a useless emotion. She had chosen her path long ago, and such a path had consequences.

Lissa sighed. "Poor girl."

Rhodri glanced at her. "I know you have a tender heart, Liss, but pity will do us no good. That was a time long ago. We have to deal with who she is now."

"I know. But it seems terribly sad all the same."

"The prince is right, Your Highness. Pitying Morrian will get you nowhere, and she does not need it or deserve it. She knew full well the path she was traveling down, and she could have stopped if she truly wanted. She did not. Sometimes, evil is simply in a person's nature." Mathghamhain's voice deepened to nearly a growl, and he abruptly picked up his pace. "We are nearly there. Come. We should wait for any further planning until we can gather as much information as we can." He quickly left us behind.

"That seemed to strike a nerve," Rhodri said quietly.

"I cannot imagine his memories of her as a child can be very pleasant, knowing what she became," Lissa responded. "I think he may have been closer to her than he lets on."

"Oh? How close do you think?" Rhodri asked.

"I wonder...he said she is a good deal older than him, and that she had a half-brother, yes? Perhaps he was a good friend of her brother."

"That could explain a lot," I said thoughtfully. "He seemed to dwell on how the people closest to Morrian were just as fooled, and he was upset about it. Being close with the family, it would mean he feels guilty for not seeing it himself, and why he is conflicted about facing her." It made sense, and it would also explain, partly, why he thought so lowly of himself. If he blamed himself, at least partly, for Morrian's rise to power the first time, and then by extension the curse hanging over Ecclesia now, and he had lived with that guilt for all this time and his own physical curse...I couldn't imagine. His belief about his curse being a punishment that Abba had sanctioned began to make a bit more sense, given that perspective.

"Poor man," Lissa said. I grunted and lengthened my own stride to catch up with Mathghamhain.

It took me several minutes. He could move quickly when he wanted to. "You know, you shouldn't blame yourself for missing what Morrian was all those years ago."

"What makes you think I do?"

"Your tone of voice just now." I paused. "I...I don't need to know how close you were to her. It doesn't matter to me. But...I would think that two hundred and fifty years is more than enough time to feel guilty."

"You know nothing of it." His voice had returned to the near growl. I had a feeling that this was as far as I could push him for now.

"You're right. I don't. But...I do think that you shouldn't fear facing her so. Or at least, not let it affect you so much. I'm scared, too, you know. It was my first encounter with a magic-user of any kind, and I lost my voice." I had to stop for a moment as I remembered the moments of panic as I realized what Morrian had done to me. I took a deep breath and continued. "But it must be done. If we do not stop her before the month is up, we won't stop her at all. I know this, and it scares me, but...well, as my mother says, there's nothing for it."

We walked in silence for several long moments, then he sighed. "You...you are right. I do fear facing her. I have a...complicated past, and this whole situation brings it up to haunt me even more than usual."

I pondered what best to say in response to that. I wanted to encourage him, but I still barely knew him, and knew nothing of his past except my own guesses, something he had pointed out himself the other night. He had said nothing of his feelings of guilt, but I hadn't expected him to. Our friendship – if it could be properly called that – was too new for that. "My father says dwelling on the past too much is useless," I finally said. "It is past, and cannot be changed. But the future? That is always open to change. And Abba does not hold the past against us. So, neither should we." He made no response. "Mathghamhain? At least think about it, perhaps?"

Another long moment passed. Then, "Perhaps...I might try."

12

Monsters and Decisions

*D*ynin shook himself gratefully after the last strap was undone from the packs. *Can I go roll now?*

I smiled. *Of course. Come back when you're done so I can rub you down.* He trotted off in search of the perfect patch of dirt.

"So are we looking in the pool first or letting Aislinn Search?" Rhodri asked.

"Aislinn?" Mathghamhain said. "Do you feel rested enough for Searching?"

I considered the question. "Later, I think. It works best when the person is asleep, so I think I'll wait until dark. Besides, if I do manage to contact anyone, it would likely be better if I know myself what is going on outside of Ecclesia."

"That makes sense," Rhodri agreed. We walked over to the pool. Mathghamhain sat down and repeated the words he had said previously. The water remained clear. "Do you usually have to wait long?" Rhodri asked.

"Sometimes. All we can do is watch."

"Look!" Lissa's cry drew our attention to the pool. A scene had begun to form, the rainbow colors of the stones swirling together so that an image was revealed in the crystal-clear water. I recognized the place: a small room in Rhodri's father's castle that he used for everyday affairs, not the great receiving hall of before. Lady Duchess Rhian was seated in a chair, reading a message. Her eyebrows were slanted downward, her lips pulled down in a frown. She looked angry. Facing her, with only his back visible, was a man, and I recognized his profile as Rhodri's eldest brother Rhys.

She folded the message, and then abruptly crumpled it in her fist and threw it across the table. "I have never in my life felt so slighted," she exclaimed indignantly. "And on such a matter of importance!"

"Does he not believe the message you sent of what Sir Eiwas said?" Rhys asked. He sat beside his mother, so we were able to view him better. He looked very like Rhodri, with the same dark hair and high forehead, though his eyes were brown and blended well with his dark skin tone.

"No! He suggested that we wait until a message comes from Ecclesia telling of trouble before jumping to 'hasty conclusions' about witchcraft and spells. He said he regrets very much not being able to send a formal Brenwyd party at this time, but other magical matters have sprung up and must be dealt with first," she fumed. "As if any petty magic is more important than a whole country under a spell."

"Have you had any word from Father?" Rhys asked. "It has now been five days."

"No." The lines on Duchess Rhian's face turned from indignation to worry. "That, too, troubles me. Nor from Rhodri either. In my mind, it only confirms the danger. If there was a way, Rhodri would have contacted us as soon as he was able upon his return."

Rhys sighed. "I cannot speak for him, but Uncle Aelfwic may have a point with the magic he mentions. Not that I agree with his decision to ignore the Ecclesian problem, but in speaking with Delwyn this morning he told me that there is a sudden outbreak of magic appearing across our lands. He sorely misses those who went with Father and Sir Eiwas. The Brenwyds who remain are stretched thin."

"An outbreak of magic?" Duchess Rhian's eyebrows went upward in surprise. "What sort? There has not been a magical outbreak since you were a child."

"He said it was nothing too troublesome, but the sheer amount is worrisome. Fortune tellers. Healers with magical potions. Witches advertising curses and cures in the same breath. Elemental magic. He also told me that there have been many reports of ancient monsters such as minotaurs, sphinxes, and ogres being sighted in the woodlands, and sirens in the rivers."

"Monsters? I cannot believe it," Duchess Rhian said skeptically. "Not after the Monsters' War."

"I am not inclined to believe it either, Mother, but Delwyn said that since such monsters once roamed the lands, the Brenwyds cannot afford to take the chance if there are enough reports to substantiate so many rumors."

"And it is all happening now," a new voice said. Another of Rhodri's brothers, the one right before him, named Cerdic, strode into the room. Though most of Rhodri's siblings had inherited Duchess Rhian's dark coloring, Cerdic had fair hair and skin like his father. "Just days after Sir Eiwas's dream of trouble in Ecclesia. I think it no coincidence."

"You believe this is tied to what has happened there?" Duchess Rhian asked.

"I feel nearly certain of it."

"You have heard of the monster stories?" Rhys asked his brother.

"Oh, they are not mere stories, brother." Cerdic held an arm out to his mother. "Come to the stables, quickly. You must see what one of our hunters brought in this morning." Duchess Rhian took his arm and swept out with her skirts, Rhys following the pair. They quickly traversed the distance to the stables. The stables at Rhodri's family's castle were located on a courtyard off the back wall of the castle. The region was known for its horses, and so it was a large facility. Cerdic led his mother and brother around to the back of the stables, where a hunter stood next to something large in a wagon under a tarp. He had a frightened, uneasy expression on his face.

He bowed to the noble family. "My lady duchess, Your Highnesses."

"What is it you have hunted today, Edwulf?" Rhys asked him.

"Tell them how you came upon it, Edwulf," Cerdic instructed.

"As you wish, my lord." Edwulf was worrying a corner of his leather hunting jerkin. "I had gone out to hunt three days ago in the fringes of the Rimed hills," he said. "The cook said he needed more venison, and the best comes from there. I came upon a herd of deer, and readied myself to shoot, when..." He paused, and pure fear flashed across his face.

"Please, go on, Edwulf," Duchess Rhian said gently.

The hunter gulped. "Of course, your grace. I was about to shoot when...when it swooped down and picked up the very deer I had set my sights on."

"It?" Rhys queried.

"This," Cerdic said. He flung the tarp up to reveal what lay beneath. Duchess Rhian gasped and backed away, a hand over her mouth. Rhys's mouth dropped open slightly. I gasped myself. What Cerdic revealed was a creature I had only heard of in story. The head seemed like that of an eagle, but it gave way to the body and hind feet of a lion, with an eagle's wings and front feet. It was a beautiful creature. But also terrifying. It was... "A griffin," Cerdic supplied. "I assure you, brother, this is no trick. Edwulf in terror shot at the creature and brought it down. He brought it back because he thought no one would believe his tale otherwise. I came straight to you after I learned of it."

"Have you told or shown anyone else this?" Rhys asked the hunter.

He shook his head violently. "No, Your Highness. I thought it best you know first. What does it mean?"

Rhys stared down at the creature. "I do not know, Edwulf. I shall have to consult Abba." He turned his gaze to Cerdic. "Go and fetch Delwyn immediately. He must see this. If more ancient monsters truly are returning to our lands, we must send hunters to all the villages where the reports have come from. After you show him this, bring him to me and we will discuss how to deal with this...incursion." Cerdic nodded sharply and strode away. Rhys turned to Edwulf. "Show this to no one else. I will call a meeting of the guards and castle staff this evening and inform them of what has happened and our next steps."

"Yes, Your Highness." Edwulf replaced the tarp.

"Come, Mother," Rhys said, holding out his arm. "We must talk." They walked out of Edwulf's earshot. "What are we to do?"

"What you have said," she replied, her usual equilibrium apparently recovered from the sight of the griffin. "The idea of a meeting is a good one. We must not let the castle stew in rumors and doubt, especially with magic mischief loose in the land."

"But whose is it?" Rhys asked in a frustrated tone. "Mother, I cannot calm people's fears if I don't know the answers to their questions."

"Do as you said. Inquire of Abba. Talk with Delwyn. Have the Brenwyds who are Sighted bend all their will on the cause of this mischief." She paused and gazed into the distance. "I believe a visit to your uncle is in order."

Rhys looked at his mother in disbelief. "Now? When we know that monsters and magic are about? I forbid it."

Duchess Rhian looked at her son with restrained amusement. "You may be one and thirty years old, Rhys, but you do not command your mother. I take your suggestion and concern into account, but I think I must go. I intend to persuade Aelfwic that he must send an investigation to Ecclesia, and if I must wear his patience out to do it, I shall. But I cannot do that from here."

Rhys nodded slowly. "I see your point. But you will take no less than ten guards with you, and travel by carriage."

His mother smiled. "Again, your concern is noted. But for this mission, speed is essential. I shall ride. But I will take the ten guards, and I will ask Leofwine and his wife to accompany me. That gives me two Brenwyds." She patted his shoulder. "Fear not, my son. We all travel within the hand of Abba. He will not let us from his protection."

The scene changed, the colors swirling again as they formed a new image. Now, we viewed a night scene. Stars filled the sky, but they were quickly being swallowed up by dark clouds. Six people and two dogs appeared. One, a short woman with flaming red hair, stood as if in opposition to the other five, holding a dark-haired girl who looked oddly familiar with a knife at her throat. Opposite her were a boy with black hair, a girl with long, chestnut hair, and behind them and crouching were another boy with brown hair and a girl with red-gold hair. The girl on the ground had a hand pressed to her side as if stanching a wound, and as she looked toward the woman with desperation in her face I saw the pointed ears of a Brenwyd. They were dressed in clothes that reminded me of old-fashioned Niclausian garb: knee-length tunics, loose breeches, and soft boots. Two dogs were around the humans, one a large, brown dog with the look of the Brenwyd breed about him and the other smaller, with black and white fur, crouching by the red-haired woman. As Mathghamhain and I watched, the dark-haired girl forced the woman's hand up and behind her, then brought it down as she spun from her grip. I blinked as I saw the knife in the woman's hand slice through the girl's long, thick braid, leaving her hair about chin length.

"Clever," I heard Mathghamhain murmur. I agreed, given the circumstances, and I rather admired her for it. I don't know that the idea would have occurred to me in the same situation, and even if it did, I didn't know that I would have followed through on it.

I frowned and leaned closer to the scene. "You know, that girl looks familiar, and so does the boy with – oh!" Action from the scene in the pool cut me short. The smaller dog had lunged and grabbed the knife, which the woman had been forced to drop with a cry. She took it over to the girl on the ground and dropped it by her feet. The girl looked at her with a pained smile, then picked it up. White flames burst to life, highlighting an engraved star on the blade.

Mathghamhain gasped. "It cannot be..." He was cut short as the girl began to sing. Softly, her eyes trained on the woman. I realized that the woman must be a witch, for the storm was increasing with much more rapidity than was natural. As the others backed away, the girl lifted the knife and tightened her grip. White flames shot from the tip and raced toward the woman, only to stop short and begin spreading in a wide area above and to either side of her, reminding me of bubbles in river rapids. Or...

"It's a shield," I realized. "That knife is making the witch's shield visible. It's flamestone."

"Indeed." The girl kept singing, louder, and I saw when a section of the shield finally gave. The flames rushed in, covering the woman, and a shrill scream pierced the air. I winced.

The scene changed yet again. This time, I recognized the place. Morrian's fortress. It was daylight. The image shifted to the room I had seen at the end of my last dream, the one with the sleeping Brenwyds and Rhodri's father. A woman appeared in the room. Morrian. Her underling was following her. She did not look happy.

"Two days since I sent the wolves out," she said. "Two days. It should take mere hours for the wolves to find anyone, especially the only people left awake after the spell. Yet they remain unsuccessful!"

"Is it possible that they traveled outside Ecclesia in search of help?" the underling asked.

"No. If there was any such penetration in the barrier, I would have known it." She crossed the chamber and began climbing the stairs that led up to her throne room. She swept in and marched to the far wall. It was a shiny black, almost mirror-like. "Show me the princess," she hissed at the wall. Mist swirled on the wall's surface. It appeared to be trying to form an image, but it was vague and blurry. I became aware of the suppressed Creation song around me growing louder as the mist thickened in the image. After several minutes, the mist fled the wall, and the song faded from my sense. Morrian cursed. "It must be those do-gooder messengers of Abba. Only they could foil my wall." She spun and began pacing back and forth. "As if guarding the princess and her companions now will do them any good."

"Shall I begin the incantations that work against them, my lady?"

She paused. "No. Not yet. Let the wolves continue their hunt. The failure will only increase their desire to find them, and they will eventually. I won't waste power that can be put to other uses. How goes the waking of the monsters?"

The man's expression brightened. "Very well, my lady. Monsters now roam all the realms. We have woken griffins, elemental dragons, minotaurs, sirens, ogres, and the giant boar, and their awakening will lead to others. Our colleagues in those and the others of the Five Realms are causing plenty of petty trouble to keep the Brenwyds there too busy to bother with Ecclesia. And the message Lady Duchess Rhian sent to the king has been dismissed. All distractions outside the borders are proceeding apace and as planned. The land is being prepared for the opening of the gate."

"Yes...that, at least, is good news." Morrian smiled. "And the spell is working precisely as I intended in regard to the Brenwyds' power."

"How shall we use the power once it has all been collected?" the underling asked.

She smiled indulgently. "That, my dear Pelagius, is something you will discover once the month is up."

He bowed his head. "Of course, my lady."

She waved a hand in dismissal. "Go contact our agent in the Darlesian court. Tell her that she must cause a greater diversion for the king's attention. If Lady Duchess Rhian persists in her reports, he will eventually listen. We must make sure he has no opportunity to."

"Of course, my lady." He bowed and left the room, and the image shifted to another room, this one empty of human occupants. I recognized it as the small room I had seen in my dream. Clearly on display was the rose Morrian had used with Lissa. I had only glimpsed it in my dream, but now I could study it clearly. It was planted in a small pot and surrounded by familiar looking briars. I could just see the flower through the thorns, and it looked different from what I remembered. When Morrian had confronted Lissa in the garden, the rose had been all white. Now, though, it looked like the bottom on the flower had changed to deep crimson. Before I could fully ponder what it meant, the room dissolved and we were looking at the rainbow-hued rocks at the bottom of the pool.

No other image formed. The four of us turned to look at each other. "What does it all mean?" Lissa asked.

"That Morrian is doing a good job of keeping everyone else in Niclausia occupied," Mathghamhain growled.

"No, not that. I understood that. But what about the other images? The girl with the flamestone knife? The image of the rose?" Lissa looked at me. "Aislinn, perhaps I was imagining things, but it almost looked to me that the rose had turned partly red."

I shook my head. "No, I saw it too. What could that mean?"

Mathghamhain shook his head slowly. "I am not sure, but that knife...you saw the star?" I nodded. "There is only one knife I have ever heard of with such an engraving."

"Which one?" I asked.

"Do you know the tales of King Arthur and his cousin, Caelwyn?"

"Of course, everyone does," I answered. Then my eyebrows shot up as I realized the implication of his question. "You mean that that knife was Seren? It really existed?"

"Yes. I saw a drawing of it in an old manuscript once. It looked exactly like that."

"Then was that Caelwyn?" I felt awe at the idea that I may have just seen that famous woman. The stories of King Arthur's reign spoke of it as a golden age of Brenwyd and human relations in the old world, and much of that had been due to Caelwyn herself. And, like myself, she had only been half-Brenwyd, which was something I found very encouraging.

"I do not know. She seemed rather young, though I suppose it may have been an early adventure. In my time, the stories were seen as factual from Earth's history, but I do not know how they have changed over the years. I could not tell you how much of what you know is true."

"Oh, King Arthur was real," Rhodri interjected. "An archaeologist – we would probably say scholar – on Earth discovered his treasure hoard and city about a couple of years ago. It's still big news in England. There was a chronicle of his reign found with the artifacts, and it's provided verification for many of the stories about him."

"Truly?" Mathghamhain seemed fascinated. Then again, given his library, that wasn't very surprising. "Did you read any of it?"

"Sort of. I saw it in a museum."

"That is very interesting, but perhaps we could discuss it later?" Lissa said diplomatically. "I do not believe any of those stories will have much bearing on our current circumstances."

"If that scene with the knife was a representation of one of those events, it might," I said. "The way the girl used it to overwhelm the witch's shield...can we do that with Morrian? Perhaps that is why Abba showed it to us."

"It's possible. Quite possible. I have never heard of using them in such a way, but it would be worth attempting. At the very least it would distract her," Mathghamhain decided.

"Aislinn, did you say that the other girl looked familiar to you?" Lissa asked, a puzzled expression on her face.

"Yes, she did, and the boy with black hair." I thought about it for several moments. "I can't place them, though. They must just remind me of someone I know."

"Given that the Age of Arthur was about fifteen hundred years ago, that seems likely," Rhodri said. "Unless you've found some way to travel through time and have forgotten to mention it."

I snorted. "Not likely. Now, if you really want to hear Brenwyd folk stories that are just myth, I should tell you about the ones that do talk about time slips."

"What?"

I waved a hand. "Pay no mind. We are straying far off topic. The pertinent information is, Morrian is successfully distracting the rest of the continent with magic and monsters. There could be a way to defeat her shield with the flamestone weapons. And that rose is definitely at her fortress. I recognized that room. I saw it in my dream, though I mostly saw something else in the room with it. A strange looking ball. It was mostly translucent, with a white tint. It appeared to be floating in midair."

"*What?*" Mathghamhain's vehement query made us all jump. I repeated my description for him. "Why did you not say anything earlier?"

"I was going to, but then I remembered the shadow wolves, and we decided to move out. In light of that, it did not seem as important. Do you know what it is?"

"Possibly...I believe so." He got up and began pacing. The three of us got to our feet as well. "She has said that she intends to use the power she drains from the Brenwyds for something, yes?"

I nodded. "Yes." Then I stared at him. "You think this ball is how she's collecting it?"

"Your description sounds very similar to what I – that is, it sounds similar to a description I heard of her source of power at the Battle for Kheprah. Perhaps...perhaps if the sphere is for power collection purposes, then the rose...the rose might indicate the timeline. You said, Your Highness, that when you pricked your finger on it, the rose was all white?"

Lissa nodded. "Yes, it looked nearly pure white, which is a hard color to get."

"You think the change to red indicates the progression of the spell? That the farther along in the month it gets, the more of it will become red?" I guessed.

"I do. Magicians often need visual indicators on when their spells are ready, especially if they are preparing for a large one. Some spells require precise timing to perform correctly."

"What is Morrian's end game?" Rhodri asked suddenly.

We all turned to look at him. "End game?" Lissa asked.

"Sorry. It's an expression on Earth." He took a breath. "Look, it seems to me that there's something more here that she's planning than simply revenge on Ecclesia for what happened two hundred and fifty years ago. All these precautions she's taken – sending me to Earth, distracting the other countries, building in backlashes and briar hedges – these are all things that take time to prepare, and to be honest, seem a little much for mere revenge. I also find it highly suspicious that she seems to have been able to take advantage of so many of the events of the past few centuries. The Monsters' War. The disappearance of the flamestone weapons. The decline in magic users. I might be reaching with this, but in light of what's going on now, those events strike me more as moves in a very long-reaching strategy, and if they are, this has to be about more than sending just one country to sleep."

Lissa frowned. "Rhodri, are you saying that she directly caused those events?"

"I'm not sure. I know, Mathghamhain, you've mentioned that she could have been taking in magic users over the years and training them in secret, which makes sense, but could she have played a part in the other events as well?"

I glanced toward Mathghamhain. We had not shared with Lissa and Rhodri our suspicions about the Monsters' War. I hadn't wanted to worry them further unless needed. But I wasn't too surprised Rhodri had put the pieces together on his own.

"I believe it is possible, yes." Mathghamhain sat back down, looking a bit like a shadow collapsing in on itself. "I have done a lot of thinking over the past few days. I know you have accused me of rudeness and cowardice, but I have needed time to absorb and assimilate the information." Lissa began making protesting noises, but Mathghamhain put up a gloved hand to stop her. "No, Your Highness, do not deny it. I have not exactly been encouraging in my comments. The more I think about these events, in fact, the more certain I am that Morrian has engineered at least part of them, likely all of them. While it would not surprise me that the fierce monsters would rise up against humanity en masse, that the gentle monsters would do it, all at the same time, points to someone pushing them to do so. I believe that the main point of the Monsters' War was to break the alliance between the leviathans and the humans. The leviathans were instrumental in Morrian's defeat last time. Before she struck again, she would be sure to remove as many obstacles as she could. Thus, the same goes for the flamestone weapons. It would not surprise me to learn that she was the one who had them stolen in the first place."

"And if she figured out how to control the monsters during the war, it would explain how she can control where they are attacking now," I added.

Lissa frowned at me. "You knew of this?"

"We discussed it," I admitted. "But until there was more proof or it was necessary, I didn't want to add more worry onto your shoulders."

From the expression she sent me, I suspect that if Lissa had been one ounce less trained in etiquette she would have actually rolled her eyes at me. "Aislinn, I appreciate the noble sentiment, but I am the Crown Princess and will one day be queen. It is quite literally my job to have all the information possible about threats to Ecclesia and to worry about them. I can handle it. I have been trained for it. Please do not withhold information for such a reason again, or I may be forced to challenge you to a duel."

I had to laugh at that. "As you wish, Your Highness."

"I beg your pardon?" Mathghamhain said quizzically.

"Better not to ask, Mathghamhain," Rhodri answered him. "But my question still remains: what is Morrian really preparing for?"

We all thought for several minutes. Slowly, phrases I had heard from Morrian, from her master, from her underling, began to run together in my mind and trip a memory...a memory of a story I would much sooner have forgotten. Surely not, I thought. No one would be that bold. But... "Mathghamhain," I said at length, "much of what I have overheard from Morrian involves an invasion of some kind. She said...She told her master that when the month was up, his legions could come and conquer the land. That servant of hers mentioned a gate. Could it be possible...would she really... could she be trying for the Demon's Gate?" I stared in the direction of his face, wishing I could see it so I could read his expression. I very much wanted him to tell me I was wrong.

"Demon's Gate?" Lissa asked, dread in her voice. "Isn't that from the story of when Brenwyds were first gifted with their abilities?"

Though I couldn't see Mathghamhain's eyes, I could feel his stare and I presumed they met mine. "By all the realms...I hope you're wrong."

"But I could be right?"

"I would like to say no. But...now that I think of it, it seems an all too real possibility."

I pressed my lips down firmly over words that my father would have spanked me for, no matter that I had long outgrown that form of punishment. "Grindles and spindles. We desperately need help."

"Could you two explain?" Rhodri asked, a look of trepidation on his face.

I took a breath. "Yes, Lissa, you are partly correct. According to Brenwyd history, part of the reason that the original Brenwyds were granted their gifts was because Earth at the time was under attack from physical demons – fallen angels that followed the Shadow Angel. They had played a large part in precipitating the events around the flood of Noah, and for encouraging the Tower of Babel. If humanity was to survive on Earth without being completely destroyed by the evil, they needed guardians from it who could combat the twisted songs of the demons."

"Brenwyds," Lissa finished for me. "I know the story well. The Brenwyds defeated the demons, banishing them from physical form, and took it upon themselves to guard from their spiritual attacks ever since. But what is this gate?"

"The gate is the reason those first Brenwyds were victorious in the first place," Mathghamhain rumbled. "It was the entrance to earth that the demons had used to travel from their fallen realm. Its existence allowed them to have flesh and blood bodies. In the battle with the demons, the Brenwyds forced them back to it and destroyed the portal, preventing them from taking physical shape again. However, the oldest tales also come with warnings that one day someone might find a way to reopen it, and in doing so bring on the end of days."

Lissa and Rhodri listened with growing alarm on their faces. "You think Morrian is using this spell to drain the Brenwyds of their power so she can try and reopen this gate? For *demons*?" Rhodri asked.

"It could be a possibility," I admitted.

"But you said it was on Earth!"

"Yes, the original one, but there are passageways to Earth here, as we have so recently rediscovered. Perhaps there is another way to get to the gate from this realm. She has certainly had enough time to find it, if that is her goal." Heavy silence followed my last remark. Dynin even stopped his grazing to look at us nervously.

"Well, we simply cannot let that happen," Lissa said bravely. "Whether that is her true goal or not, we still have several weeks. We must travel to her fortress and destroy the rose to break the spell. If we stop the spell, from what you have said it seems to me that we stop her source of power to begin this invasion, and then we can deal with her." I had never heard Lissa speak in such a hard voice before. I applauded her for it. I knew many people in court underestimated her because of her generally soft-spoken demeanor, but she had a core of rock when it counted.

"Yes...we must stop her," Mathghamhain said. "But we must have a reliable means of reinforcement before we do." He turned in my direction. "Blame my pessimism if you wish, but it would be suicide to face her with no other support."

"I do agree," Rhodri spoke up unexpectedly. He sent a small smile in Mathghamhain's direction. "What I've really objected to when you've made similar statements before is that it seemed to be your immediate reaction and that you refused to consider other alternatives. But considering how we are speaking now, it is only common sense to have reinforcements. The question is, where to get them from? Even if Aislinn can make contact with someone through Sight, there's still a large barrier of thorns in their way."

I sighed. "I was hoping to be able to convince whoever I made contact with to raise a big enough force to break the barrier, but after hearing all the trouble being caused, I don't know how feasible that is."

"And, even if you did, Morrian would notice her spell being attacked and go to strengthen it. We would have to fight past her on the border to get to her fortress," Mathghamhain added.

I frowned at him. "Now that sounds like a return to too much pessimism."

"Wait," Lissa said, brow furrowed in thought. "What if that's exactly what we need?"

"What is, Liss?" Rhodri asked.

"A diversion to draw Morrian from her fortress." She looked around at all of us, her eyes finally resting on me. "Aislinn, you've Seen in your visions that we are being protected from Morrian's Sight. If you can make contact with the Brenwyds on the other side, they could cause a diversion for us by drawing Morrian out so we can safely enter her fortress and find the rose. By the time she realizes what has happened, it will be too late, and we should be able to get out before she could return."

We all stared at Lissa. We had been bemoaning the inability of help to come to us directly, but she had seen the one advantage it gave us. "Lissa, that's brilliant!" I cried out, jumping up in excitement.

"Yes..." Mathghamhain said. "But remember, the Darlesian force Aislinn already Saw did not have much luck."

I frowned at him. "That's only because they didn't know what they were walking into. If I can make contact, I can tell them, and they can be better prepared. It could work, I know it could."

"It could," Rhodri said. "Though Mathghamhain may have a point." I turned my stern gaze to Rhodri, rather surprised to find him agreeing with Mathghamhain again. He held up his hand in a gesture of surrender. "Easy, Aislinn. I do hate to admit it, but Morrian's forces at the border apparently took my father and Sir Eiwas's forces without much trouble, and without drawing her attention. To have an attack at the border that would draw her out for us...it would have to be huge. Multiple companies, perhaps as many as a regiment, from multiple provinces, and given the luck my mother seems to have had so far in drawing attention to our plight, the local nobility might choose the immediate danger to their own people over the hidden danger here."

"Perhaps, Prince Rhodri, I should be alarmed that you are agreeing with me twice within five minutes," Mathghamhain said.

"I'm a little alarmed myself, but there's nothing for it. We need a big distraction."

"Like what?" I asked.

"Leviathans!" Lissa burst out. Again, we all turned to look at her. "Mathghamhain, you said that the leviathans were instrumental in defeating Morrian the first time, and that she may have specifically targeted them in the Monsters' War?"

"The latter is still pure speculation, Your Highness, but yes."

"Well, we already discussed several days ago that sea travel may not be so impeded, so what if we made our way to the coast and went to their islands for help? Surely, they would be eager to help us, if all the old stories are true. They could try just burning down the barrier. That would get Morrian's personal attention, surely."

"It is a possibility, I suppose," Mathghamhain said in a rather unconvinced tone.

"What if they still have the madness that led to the Monsters' War?" Rhodri asked. "Wouldn't they have come back if they had figured out what had caused it and how to control it?"

"That could be a risk," Mathghamhain said slowly, "but given our options, this could be our best one."

"Not all the leviathans were infected with the madness," I said, remembering my history lessons. "Fire-breathing dragons would be a big distraction." I looked at Lissa with approval. "I didn't know you had such strange ideas in you. You've hidden it well."

She shrugged with a faint grin. "Or eighteen years of being your friend has finally worn off on me."

"Certainly took long enough. But how would we find the leviathans, exactly? The point of the treaty was their removal to such remote islands that people couldn't stumble across them." I sighed. "Why is it that with each solution we come up with, it presents more problems?"

"That, Aislinn, is the cost of strategy. Find one solution, and a dozen more problems rise up to be considered," Mathghamhain answered. "To win a battle – or a war – one must determine which strategy comes with the fewest risks and problems, try to mitigate them, and pray it all works. But I may actually have an answer for you for that one. I know my way well around boats. If we can get to the coast and find one, I can sail us in the right direction, and then, Aislinn, you can ask for directions from the sea life. They will know where the leviathans dwell."

"Oh. That does make sense."

"Although, the main problem with that," Mathghamhain continued, "is how much time it will take. We have some time, yes, but if it takes us a week or more to find the leviathans, that does not bode so well. And, the leviathans will need to follow a water source to the barrier in the forest. To attack it en masse, they will need a body of water nearby to cool down."

"Oh. I had forgotten about that." Lissa's expression dimmed. "There aren't any lakes or large rivers in the forest. Only streams. The Hellwyl does not go that far."

"What if they made an attempt on the barrier in the south? Somewhere near Tairport?" Rhodri suggested. "They could be next to the sea itself there."

"Perhaps," Mathghamhain mused. "I do not believe convincing them to help us will be a problem. They are always eager for a fight. We could ask them to send a large flight to the south, and then ask for a few to take us north to Morrian's fortress. This...this might work."

"Well, if you say so, Mathghamhain, it must be true," Rhodri said. "Where is Morrian's fortress, exactly?

"On a small island off the coast of the northernmost border of Ecclesia. It is at least a two-week trek from here on foot. Where could we find a boat to sail? If it helps, this valley is four days on foot from Eily." Eily was the name of the northernmost town in Ecclesia, though it was barely more than a hamlet and nowhere near the ocean.

Lissa's brow wrinkled as she thought. "The northernmost port with ships we could use for sea travel like that would be Helmond," she mused. "On foot, that's at least a week's journey if we move quickly. If it takes another week or more to find the leviathans... could they get us north and themselves south in time?"

"There is a reason for the expression 'quick as dragonflight,' Your Highness," Mathghamhain said. "If we can make contact with the leviathans within the next two to three weeks, we would still have time."

"Of course we can," I said. "We do have Dynin, and since he's now fully recovered, he can transfer us to Helmond. I've been there with my father."

I turned to Dynin, who had returned to his peaceful grazing after we left the disturbing subject of the Demon's Gate. He raised his head to look at me. *You three, yes, of course I could take*, he said as he chewed. *But he is too big. I could not get fast enough.* He was looking in Mathghamhain's direction.

I winced, for I knew Dynin had said it to everyone. In truth, I should have thought of it. And we needed Mathghamhain. He was the only one of us with ship knowledge, and he knew where Morrian's fortress was. "Do not worry yourself, Aislinn, he only speaks the truth," Mathghamhain said. "I am sorry for it, but it cannot be helped. I know a shortcut to Helmond through the mountains. We can make it in five days, assuming you do still want me along."

"Of course we do," Lissa said. "We need you. None of us know anything about sailing other than the wind propels the boat."

"And you know her island," I added. "Abba led us to you for a reason, remember. He knew you could help us." He shifted but made no response.

"So, we sound pretty decided. We're going to Helmond to look for dragons?" Rhodri said.

"It seems to be our best option," I said. "Especially with the luck I've had trying to contact people across the border." I looked up at the sky and closed my eyes. *Abba, give us wisdom,* I prayed. *Let us know your will in this matter. We go up against a powerful enemy, and without your help we will surely fail. Is this the course you have set for us, or should we take another?* A simple prayer, but all my heart went into it.

I was aware of the others talking back and forth, further discussing the idea, but I tuned out their words. We needed to seek Abba's will to be sure the plan would work. Whenever people in Abba's word embarked on a plan not blessed by him, things did not end well. A gentle breeze blew across the mountain plateau. I felt it play with the wisps of my hair that had escaped my braid and blow across my face with the gentleness of a father's caress, carrying with it a sweet, sweet smell of wildflowers and something else I could not name. I smiled, tilting my head slightly. As the wind swirled around me, a full course of action crept into my mind, almost as if whispered. I noticed that the sound of voices had ceased. I opened my eyes. The others were looking about them, a little wide-eyed, as the wind tugged at their clothes. Dynin turned his head into the wind and let out a whinny.

"Abba's Whisperer," Mathghamhain said as the breeze died. As usual, I could not see his face, but I could sense his awe, and something else. Remorse? Shame? It was a curious emotion. "I have not felt it...in I know not how long."

"I thought he only appeared in church services," Lissa said softly.

I shook my head. Abba's Whisperer was what we called his inspiring spirit, which whispered to any of his followers who earnestly sought it. It could also give gifts to his followers, Brenwyd or human, ranging from knowing different tongues to prophecy to healing. "It comes to any who earnestly seek it, or to any who need its direction. Which is what we needed."

"It spoke to you?" Mathghamhain asked. He sounded a little... envious, I decided. I definitely needed to talk to him later.

"In a manner of speaking. I believe we are on the right path. I remember...the verse from the book of the Romans in the Sacred Word, 'All things work together for the good of those who love him and-'"

"Are called according to his purpose," Mathghamhain finished softly. "Yes...I remember hearing that, once upon a time."

"Exactly. And we have been called to the purpose of ending this spell. So don't worry. There has also been, in my head since the curse struck, the verse from Joshua speaking of courage: 'Have I not commanded you? Be strong and courageous, for the Lord your God is with you wherever you go.'"

"I will try," he said earnestly. "But I hope you do not tire of reminding me."

I smiled at him. Perhaps he had not lost all his hope in Abba after all. "Of course not."

13

WOLF ATTACK

The remainder of the afternoon and evening passed in a flurry of preparations. Not only was there food to consider, but also water, and food for Dynin. Fortunately, he was content with the hard oatcakes that were customary fare for travelers in Ecclesia. Unfortunately for Lissa and me, it meant we had to make a lot of it, completely using up Mathghamhain's stored supplies. (Which really meant that I did most of the actual preparation and cooking while Lissa only stirred the mixture in the final step. Her lessons in childhood had, understandably, focused on politics and diplomacy, not cooking.) Rhodri went to work modifying our packs to be more comfortable for a long journey.

As the sun dipped toward evening, I found myself outside fiddling with Dynin's saddlebags to be sure they rested easily against his sides and wouldn't cause him discomfort. (And checking to make sure that Rhodri's adjustments actually accomplished their purpose. I had more faith in his ability to work with the leather and canvas, given his hands-on involvement with his province's horse industry, but again, he was nobility.) Dynin turned his head to look at me when I removed the packs from his back and began making minute adjustments for the fifth time. *They feel fine, I told you. Why do you keep doing that?*

I just want to be sure. He turned and thrust his nose against my chest, stilling my hands. He looked at me with knowing eyes. I sighed. He didn't even have to put it into words. *I know, I know. They are fine. I'm just...nervous.*

That seems perfectly natural to me, given what you have decided to do.

I know, but...I felt so brave and sure earlier, and I've been hard on Mathghamhain over his paralyzing fear of facing Morrian, yet...I'm a liar if I say I don't feel it, too. And that makes me feel like a hypocrite.

Dynin snorted into my tunic. *Of course you are afraid. As I said, it is natural to be afraid going up against her again. But will you let the fear stop you?*

No, of course not. I can't. Ecclesia...Mother, Father, and Aiden...they are all at stake. I have to try for them.

So there. You fear, but you are not letting it keep you from the right course. He just might, without your pushing. You are brave.

I smiled at him, wrapping my arms around his neck and pushing my face into his mane to inhale his distinctive, dusty horse smell. *You are wonderful, Dy, you know that?*

You tell me so often. Why should I not know that? His answer, colored with genuine puzzlement, made me laugh as I gave him an extra squeeze. A moment later, I sensed him shift into an alert mode. *He is here.* I released Dynin and looked over my shoulder. Sure enough, Mathghamhain stood multiple strides upstream from where Dynin and I had stationed ourselves. *I am going to graze,* Dynin announced and began walking away. He had grown used to Mathghamhain's presence over the past few days, but he still wasn't completely relaxed around him. I shook my head, but let him go without protest, turning myself to walk to where Mathghamhain stood.

"I did not mean to interrupt you," he said as I approached.

I shrugged. "You didn't, not really. I'm sorry, actually, that he is still wary. Normally he warms up to people quite quickly."

"I am not most people."

"But you are our companion. He will warm up to you, I promise."

Mathghamhain seemed to have his gaze fixed on Dynin's retreating form. "It would be nice..." His voice trailed off.

"What would?" I asked softly. For several moments, I thought he wouldn't answer.

He sighed. "It would be nice to...ride a horse again. Or at least spend time with one."

I stared at him, just realizing that his long years of isolation, and whatever his form was, had cut him off from more than human interaction. "Oh, Mathghamhain, I am even more sorry. I'll call him over and-"

"No, don't. It's alright."

I looked in Dynin's direction. Given how much we Brenwyds worked with our horses, and the fact that Brenwyd horses lived far longer than the usual span of horse years, we grew incredibly attached to them. I had chosen Dynin myself when he was a foal and I was ten, and I couldn't imagine living without him. Mathghamhain suffered a curse, indeed. "What was your horse like?" I asked.

He seemed to tense. "I would prefer not to talk about her, if you don't mind," he said sharply.

"Oh. Alright." I cast about for a different topic. "So...the way you were speaking earlier, it seemed to me like you might believe our plan could work."

He turned his head toward me and tilted it, as if considering me. "I think it is our best option, given the circumstances."

"Will the leviathans really help us after having no contact for so long?" I did feel uneasy about that point.

"I believe they will. It is hard to explain to someone who has never met one, but they hold Abba, honor, and courage very dear. A mission like this appeals to their code. No, I cannot imagine that they will turn us away, especially given we have the princess to speak to them. They held Nivea in extremely high regard, and should extend the same courtesy to her descendant."

I smiled at him. "When you put it that way, I have no doubt of it. I think we shall both need to be encouraging each other in the coming days."

"You want me to encourage you?" He sounded dubious.

"I need someone to," I said, sobering. "Do not forget, I am still green in my training. I cannot – I will not – let that stop me from facing Morrian, but I am aware of it."

Silence fell for a few minutes. "I believe you. You remind me, in some ways, of Nivea."

"Really?"

He nodded. "She, too, was very young, and at times unsure of herself, but she was determined to defeat Morrian for her people, and she never let her fear affect her actions." He paused. "I admired her for that. She had the chance to lead a normal life with Chiaran. Everyone thought she was dead. When she regained her memories...she was given the choice to remain where she was, incognito, or to come back and lead the army. She didn't hesitate."

I thought that over. I had never really considered what Nivea faced as a person. She was always a grand figure of history and story, the brave queen who won Ecclesia back. But hearing Mathghamhain speak of her so, I could empathize with a girl around my own age, suddenly remembering that she was the heir of a kingdom falling toward disaster and knowing that she had to step up to save it. It was a daunting prospect. She must have doubted herself very much. But she still stepped forward to do it. And she had won.

I smiled at Mathghamhain and reached out to pat his arm. "See? You have encouraged me already. You can do it. It is part of a Brenwyd's duty, after all. It comes naturally to us – even to one of a dour nature."

"Dour, am I?" He shook his head. "I suppose so. One doesn't usually tend to think of oneself in adjectives when one is alone."

"You're getting better." Sudden laughter interrupted us, and we looked toward the door of the castle. Lissa and Rhodri had walked out and were in conversation. They didn't notice us in the shadow of the trees. We were too far away to hear their words, but it was easy to see they touched on pleasant subjects. I smiled to see them still able to find joy in each other. Whatever harm this curse did, at least it had brought them together again. As we watched, Rhodri leaned down and stole a quick kiss from Lissa. He had been doing that often over the past few days, and my smile grew into a grin.

"It is good to see two people so in love," Mathghamhain's voice reached my ears. It was quiet and thoughtful.

"Well, it is a rare privilege to see their affection like this. It is normally reserved for completely private moments." I wondered then if he had had a love when his change had occurred...whatever it was. Had she stayed with him? Or had they decided to end it?

"How long have they been together?"

"Oh, forever it seems. Lissa and I first met Rhodri when she was ten and he accompanied his father on a state visit. Then, later, he spent several years at the Ecclesian court as a fosterling. It was about halfway into that stay that their relationship turned romantic. He asked for her hand a little over a year ago now."

"And...do you have a suitor or fiancé?"

I stared up at him in surprise. "Me? No."

"Any particular reason why?"

I cocked my head, both amused and bemused by the questioning. "Why so curious?"

"I..." He sounded abashed. "I simply...it has been a long time since...I was able to think and consider ordinary things of people. Forgive me, I did not mean to sound so prying."

I shrugged. "I don't mind. The simple reason is that, so far, I have not met whomever Abba has intended for me. I'm sure I will in time. I feel in no hurry. My parents did not meet until my mother was nearly twenty-two."

"Ah." He turned to look back downstream toward Dynin. "Do you need any help with those saddlebags?" He seemed eager to change the subject. Perhaps he worried I would use it as an excuse to query him. Given his response when I had tried to simply ask about his horse earlier, I was not about to ask him anything more personal at the moment, so I decided to humor him.

"You could help me take them back to the castle so we can pack them. Then...when night fully falls, will you sit with me while I try to See?"

"Of course. I do keep my promises." His head had turned back my way, and though I could not see his gaze, I could feel his eyes on me. For some reason, the idea of his hidden eyes latched onto mine made my heart beat a little faster, and I turned away first.

"I know."

✺

It was late by the time I retired to bed that night. I was tired. True to his word, Mathghamhain had sat with me before the kitchen fire, trying to help me break through the magical barrier separating us from the other realms. With his greater experience both of Morrian and magic in general, he could guide me through the spell better than I could navigate on my own. With his help, I was able to find several spots that did seem a bit weaker than the others, places where the counter-song to them fit comfortably in my range. Try as I did, however, I was again unsuccessful in my attempts to contact someone beyond the barrier. I tried for the better part of an hour before Mathghamhain called a stop to it.

"Enough, Aislinn. There is no need to exhaust yourself. Not tonight."

I shook myself from my state of intense concentration reluctantly, sighing heavily. "I did so hope I would be able to get through this time." It was a discouraging end to a day that had been rather hopeful. *Abba, why can I not get through? Help me! Send a message out, at least, if I cannot.*

The sudden awareness of a hand tentatively on my arm brought me out of my prayer, and I turned toward Mathghamhain in surprise. He had moved closer to me, and it was his hand I felt. "We can try again tomorrow. I don't know if you sensed this or not, but it did seem to me that the areas you were attacking and pressing against were beginning to give way a little."

I stared at him. "Really? Then why did you stop me?"

"Because I am not entirely sure, and because you are veering toward exhaustion. We will try again tomorrow, and see if the spell will give a little more. This could be better in the long run; Morrian may not notice what is happening until it is too late."

"Oh." I considered that for several minutes. He was right; I was very tired. Though today had not been especially strenuous, the hard activity from the past several had caught up with me.

"That makes sense to me," a new voice entered into the conversation, and I turned in surprise. Mathghamhain quickly removed his hand from my arm. Lissa was looking in the doorway.

I frowned at her. "I thought you were asleep."

She shrugged. "I wanted to wait for you, and I could do that more easily without falling asleep out here than in a bed."

"You have extremely good training in guarding your mind, Your Highness," Mathghamhain said. "I did not sense you."

She smiled. "Thank you. I have worked hard at it. But I do not think Aislinn is the only one who is tired here. You have also been concentrating hard tonight, Mathghamhain. I did not want to disturb either of you." She walked in and pulled me up to my feet. "Now I think we should all find our beds. Good night, Mathghamhain."

He inclined his head. "Good night, Your Highness. Aislinn."

"Good night," I said as Lissa pulled me gently from the kitchen and to our claimed bedroom.

"Were you really out there the whole time?" I asked as she closed the door behind us.

"I waited until I thought the two of you would be thoroughly engrossed in the attempt."

She glided from the door to her bed. "I was curious as to whether you would break through, and...it did not strike me as entirely right that the two of you should be completely alone."

I frowned. "What do you mean? We've been alone plenty of times. He's not going to harm me."

"Of course not. It was not the idea of him harming you that I meant. It was you and he alone at night with everyone else asleep. Forgive me, but my properly trained sensibilities could not allow it."

I blinked several times as the implication of what she was really saying worked through my mind. "Are you saying you were playing chaperone?"

"Bluntly, yes."

I stared at her. "Lissa, you have to know that is completely unnecessary. It's not as if Mathghamhain and I are...oh, you are ridiculous sometimes, do you know that?"

"Sometimes," she smiled. "But Aislinn, based on what I've seen over the past few days, it may not be so unwarranted. He actually went so far as to touch you of his own volition tonight."

I rolled my eyes. "He was reassuring me, Lissa. You are reading far too much into it. I barely know the man!"

"I know. But I can tell that there is some attraction between the two of you."

I snorted and lay down on my bed, looking up at the ceiling. "Really? What in the Five Realms makes you say that?"

"The way you converse. You have barely known each other a week, yet you speak with the ease of a long acquaintance. Your body language. You know I am good at reading people, Aislinn. I have had to learn because of my position. And what I am reading now is that there is an attraction between the two of you."

"As friends." I climbed beneath the blanket. "Lissa, this is not the court where one has to worry about every interaction with the opposite sex being misconstrued. We are two people thrown together by extraordinary circumstances and so have gotten to know each other somewhat well in a short period of time. And the fact we could converse only by mind speaking at first causes us to be a little more sensitive to each other's moods. It happens, you know. There is nothing more than that."

"So you say," Lissa said, her voice carefully neutral. "A month from now, I wager your feelings will be quite different."

I was tired enough that I didn't want to argue. "Liss, I so cannot even start to think of that that I shan't even argue with you about it right now. I'm going to sleep."

"Very well. But do not say I did not tell you so."

"Hmm." I turned to the wall. Leave it to Lissa to bring up such a subject in the middle of the worst crisis in Ecclesian history for two hundred and fifty years. Not that I necessarily objected to the discussion, but thinking about such things seemed rather unimportant, considering what we were facing. And besides, her claim was ridiculous. Any affection or feeling Mathghamhain felt toward me was no more than that of one comrade to another. If there was anything deeper, I was sure it was simply a result of having spent so long a time in solitude. I shook my head slightly to clear my mind and went to sleep.

⁂

It was a good thing I got plenty of rest that night, for we got precious little over the next week. We drove ourselves as hard as we could over the terrain. It was a difficult journey, most of it over the mountains, and though it was settling into true spring in the lowlands surrounding Kheprah, the mountain weather was not so convinced. Often the day started out with promising weather, but it became bad as the day went on, either because of falling temperatures or rain. The nights were always cold. Still, we had packed plenty of blankets at Mathghamhain's guidance, and were able to tolerate it. As we marched, Mathghamhain shared information and stories of Morrian from two hundred and fifty years ago that he deemed useful for us to know. In return, we told him more details of what had happened in the lands since then.

Additionally, Mathghamhain and I rehearsed how to battle Morrian with song. Or rather, I did. He was able to tell me of vocal exercises that would be the most useful for preparing myself. These often forced me into my lower range, since Mathghamhain believed that there would be the weak spots of her spells. When we stopped for rests, he would sit with me and help me try to find a way through Morrian's boundary spell with my Sight. It helped me learn how she structured spells, and I became more and more adept at navigating the chords on my own to find potential weak spots. Still, I had yet to achieve success in contacting someone on the outside. As the days went by, I tried to return again and again to the same areas of the spell to continue pressing at them, and I thought I was starting to make headway against it. I became hopeful that, given a few more days, I would be able to slip through.

As we traveled, I couldn't help but notice that though Mathghamhain freely shared stories of Morrian to help us, he never opened up and told us any personal stories, such as where he grew up, who his parents had been, or if he had had any siblings. He made stray comments here and there in the course of telling us other information that made me think he had been more closely involved with Nivea and her advisors in their fight against Morrian than he let on, but nothing concrete. And he never shed his dark, covering clothing. I had hoped that once he had spent some time with us, he would stop wearing at least his outer cloak. I became increasingly curious about just how terrible his change really was. When we sat together in the evenings trying to worm past Morrian's boundary, I began wishing more and more that I could at least see his eyes when we talked. It was disconcerting to be working so closely with someone whose face you could not read. Whenever

I tried to direct the conversation toward prompting him to reveal some of his personal past, he deftly brought it back to dealing with Morrian. I don't think Rhodri ever noticed such potential tangents, but Lissa caught several, as she gave me significant looks. She was also curious about our reclusive guide.

Everything changed halfway into the journey. For that was when the shadow wolves finally found us.

⁕⁕⁕

On the fifth day after we had set out from the valley, we began to emerge from the mountains and enter the foothills that lay just north of Helmond. We descended into an area of plateaus and steep hills, still rocky, but more grass- and dirt-covered. Dynin was especially happy for the change of scenery, for there was more grass available for him to eat. It was a choppy landscape, with large plateaus ending abruptly in sheer cliffs, and rocky hills jutting up at odd angles toward the sun. There were also some small trees and scraggly bushes. It had a desolated, lonely atmosphere I decided as we began to travel through it, the sun setting in front of us, causing me to squint ferociously. There was no clear path, but Mathghamhain led the way as if there was, suggesting to me that he had traveled this way somewhat often. When I remarked on the fact to him, he merely shrugged and said that two hundred and fifty years of relative isolation had caused him to know the mountains and surrounding environment as well as anyone knew their home village.

I was feeling rather tired. I knew I was in good physical condition, but we had been marching hard, long, and constantly, only stopping for rest in the early morning hours and from early to mid-afternoon. Mathghamhain didn't allow us to sleep at night for fear of the shadow wolves. As the sun continued its downward arc, he called a halt to light the lanterns. Unfortunately, Rhodri's wondrous electric torch wasn't quite enough for us to travel by at night, so Mathghamhain had secured two metal lanterns from his castle and two large pouches of oil to ensure we had enough illumination. He carried one and I carried the other.

I poured the oil into my lantern, careful not to spill it, and lit it with another wonderful item Rhodri had brought back with him from earth: a match. Lissa retrieved a water skin and passed it around. "Thank you," I said, taking several sips. "Mathghamhain, might we stop for even an hour and rest? We do need to keep up our strength."

"I know," he answered. He considered the setting sun. "We have been making good time, better than I had hoped."

"Then why don't we take a longer rest? We can light a fire and set up a watch in case anything happens."

His silence indicated to me that he was mulling it over. "Why do we not go a little way farther into the plateaus, and then rest for the remainder of the night?" he finally suggested.

"That sounds like an excellent idea," Rhodri said. "After all, we have seen no sign of these shadow wolves. Perhaps they have given up."

"Never think that, Your Highness," Mathghamhain said sternly. "They do not give up." Lissa looked between the two, but said nothing. Her face conveyed her fatigue, but she was too well-trained to speak of it. "Come; let us go. The farther we travel into the plateaus, the more fuel we will have for a fire."

I suppressed a sigh as I began to follow him. Or more accurately, Rhodri. Mathghamhain always went first, with Lissa behind him, then Rhodri, then me and Dynin. Dynin could not resist grumbling as we began the journey once more, as he had been in the process of hungrily devouring a patch of grass when Mathghamhain moved off. *All very well for him to say,* he complained. *He has not had to eat only tough mountain grasses for the past week.*

I haven't heard you complaining before now.

Why should I? It was all there was, so I had to make do. Now that there is better, he might at least let me eat. He does not have to carry all these bags. I turned my face so he couldn't see me smile. It was true, Dynin was not given to complaining when there was only one option available, whether it was food or locations or journeys or whatever. But whenever there were multiple options to choose from, he leaned toward indulgence over stringency.

Would you like me to carry a couple for you?

No. I am fully capable of handling it. I'm just saying that I should be able to eat a decent meal because of it. I scratched his neck affectionately. I loved the fact that, even though we were on a journey to save our kingdom and defeat an ancient, powerful sorceress, Dynin still focused on ordinary concerns like food enough to grumble about it good-naturedly.

Oh, Dy, I'm glad I have you to talk to. You help keep everything simple.

How? He sounded genuinely curious.

You just do. Never stop.

Alright. He sounded confused, but left it at that, nudging my side with his nose gently. I turned my attention to the sunset. It truly was glorious, with shades of yellows, oranges, and pinks gradually deepening to velvet-looking purples and blues that eventually surrendered to a night sky brilliantly studded with stars. The sky reminded me of the dress Queen Alyessa had commissioned for herself to wear for Lissa's wedding, a deep indigo with small diamonds about the collar, waist, and sleeves, as well as scattered about the skirt. My fingers itched for a brush and canvas, but I had to satisfy myself by firmly fixing the image in my mind and mentally musing on the proper color hues I would need to make up to capture it. *Thank you, Abba, for this,* I thought silently.

We continued in silence for nearly an hour, by my judgment, when I sensed that Dynin was growing uneasy. He was behind me, plodding along and snatching at grass, but he scooted forward next to me, his head up high as he looked around, ears twitching. *What is it?*

I do not know...but I have a bad sense. I frowned and looked around, holding my lantern high. My keen eyes didn't pick up anything unusual in the night, but as I halted to concentrate on my surroundings, I, too, became aware of an uneasy feeling that brushed across my mind, sending a sudden chill down my spine and causing the hair on the back of my neck to stand up, especially as I turned back to face the way we had come.

"What is it, Aislinn?" Rhodri's voice asked from behind me. I turned back around and found that the others had stopped.

"I don't know. Dynin says he has a bad sense." It was a rather vague term that animals used whenever they felt through their senses that something wasn't quite right with their surroundings. It was a general cue for any Brenwyd to listen carefully to the songs going on around them and...oh, yes. I should do that. I shook my head slightly to dispel the sleepiness that fogged my mind, and noticed that Mathghamhain, though stopped, had his head tilted back like he was looking up. I opened my mouth to ask what he was looking at, but he turned and asked an urgent query first.

"When was the last time anyone saw the moon?"

"The moon?" Lissa repeated, sounding surprised. "Why do you ask...?" Her voice trailed off as the rest of us looked up. Indeed, the moon that had been so full and bright less than half an hour ago was now covered by cloud and mist, as were many of the stars.

"Is a storm blowing in?" Rhodri wondered.

Dynin let out a nervous snort. *There is definitely something wrong.* I listened with my sense. There was the spell, of course, but other than that...

Suddenly a thin sound, very distant and far off, reached my ears. It caused goosebumps to rise on my skin and a new chill passed over me, this one far more deep-seated, and all fatigue left my body with the realization of danger. I looked at Mathghamhain. I could tell he was looking at me, and I sensed we both knew what was coming. "I am afraid not, Your Highness," Mathghamhain answered in a low, strained voice. "Quickly, go and gather as much wood for a fire as you can. We must build a bonfire."

"Why? What is it?" Lissa asked, alarm beginning to register on her face. I heard the sound again, and this time, I felt Dynin hear it as well. He trembled in the primal, ancient fear of a prey animal being stalked by a predator.

"The shadow wolves," I said. "They've found us."

"I'm afraid so." Mathghamhain began to cast about with his lantern for wood. "Now find wood, quickly. We have a little time, and fire is our best defense. The larger the blaze, the better."

Rhodri's face took on grim lines as he nodded. Lissa's eyes widened, fear crossing her face. "Shadow wolves?" Her voice trembled, but she managed to keep it from becoming a squeak. Mathghamhain gave a quick jerk of his head, then went to gather wood and grasses for fuel.

Aislinn, would you prepare a place for the fire? Near the cliff, he asked me mentally. We were in a small valley of sorts, very wide, almost like a plain, and to our right rose a rocky cliff. It was not completely sheer but sloped steeply upward. Looking up, I could see where it leveled off some distance above me.

Rhodri gently tugged at Lissa's arm. "Come on, Liss. Help us make the fire."

"But...wolves..."

"I know." His voice was low and even, reassuring. "But these are flesh and blood creatures. They can be defeated. That's why we have to make a fire."

She nodded slowly. "Yes. Right. Of course." Together they moved off, Rhodri's electric torch lighting the way before them. Dynin stayed with me, looking in the direction the wolves were approaching, head high, ears pricked, and every muscle taut. After a moment he began to walk back and forth in front of me, blowing hard through his nostrils and arching his neck, as if he were a stallion trying to warn a rival off his mares. A more distinct howl carried to us on the slight breeze, increasing Dynin's frenzy.

Save the bravado, Dynin, I told him as I worked as hastily as I could to clear a large area for a fire so we didn't set the whole plain alight. *I don't think it will scare them off.*

But it makes me feel better, he said in a small voice that made me regret my words. Wolves and horses are natural enemies. Dynin just barely tolerated it when I healed the normal, wild wolves who came to Brenwyds for healing. Magical, legendary wolves? Judging by his reaction so far, I would not be surprised if he chose flight over fight in the next few moments. Nor would I blame him.

Why don't you go after Mathghamhain and let him load some wood on your back? Then we'll really be able to make a big fire, I suggested.

Yes, girl. He went off quickly, the light of Mathghamhain's lantern making it easy to spot him. It also told me even more of the level of Dynin's fear. He was still rather suspicious of Mathghamhain, despite my efforts to have him let Mathghamhain help groom him when we unloaded the saddlebags at breaks. He claimed he smelled too much like a predator.

I finished clearing the area just as Lissa and Rhodri returned, each with as large an armload of branches as they could carry. Without a word, I began to arrange the wood as they placed it on the ground and hurried away to gather more. Within a few more moments, Mathghamhain and Dynin had arrived with their wood loads. The howls came again, more of them and much closer than I thought possible, given how far away they had been mere minutes earlier. Mathghamhain shifted to face the direction of the wolves. "Light the fire. They obviously know we are here. It has to be roaring before they get here."

"And then what?" I asked. "We cannot keep this going all night."

"Pray there are not very many...for we must kill them all." His tone forbade any more questions. He stepped several paces in front of me, brandishing the spear he had chosen from the firestone weapon cache in one hand, lantern in the other, and stood still, waiting.

I added his and Dynin's wood to the pile and reached for my flint from my pack. The howls increased, making me jittery and causing me to drop the flint. *Hurry, hurry,* Dynin urged.

I know. I am. I retrieved the flint and struck it, sending a shower of sparks over the wood. It didn't catch. I heard footsteps coming from behind me, and knew that Lissa and Rhodri must finally be able to hear the wolves. They dropped the wood they had managed to find, and then Rhodri drew the sword he had chosen from the weapons cache and joined Mathghamhain. Though the sword had not chosen him as mine had me, Mathghamhain assured us it was of no consequence to the sword's effectiveness as long as the wielder was a true follower of Abba, which Rhodri certainly was. Being chosen by a weapon simply increased the power and protective ability of the weapon for the bearer. Lissa helped me throw the remaining wood on the fire, and I again struck my flint. Again, the wood didn't light. More howls, even closer.

Lissa was trembling in fear, but she drew her bow from her quiver, strung it, and notched an arrow. Dynin remained close to me and Lissa. My hands were shaking slightly as I held the flint. My mouth was dry, and my heart hammered within my chest, each frantic beat a plea to Abba to extend his protection over and around us. A howl sounded so close it seemed to be right in my ear. Lissa gave a small cry from behind us, and I sensed that all of Dynin's instincts were screaming at him to bolt. Only his firm loyalty and love towards me kept him standing there. I sent him a wave of gratitude, and his fear diminished slightly.

"Easy," Mathghamhain said. "They'll wait to attack until they have us surrounded. Try not to think on your fear. Fear strengthens them. Aislinn, get that fire going!"

"I'm trying," I said, trying to keep my rising panic from my voice. I glanced toward him, noting his lantern. Lantern...I had a lantern. I had placed it on the ground when I knelt to arrange the fire. *Idiot, Aislinn,* I chided myself as I snatched it up. *You should have thought of that first!* I opened the glass door and grabbed a small branch, holding it within the flame. It lighted and I thrust it back into the wood pile. Within minutes, the rest of the wood began to burn. It blazed up into what was quite a large campfire blaze, but not quite as big as the inferno I sensed Mathghamhain wanted. "That's just going to have to – look out!" I shouted, looking toward where Mathghamhain and Rhodri stood at the blurred edge of the firelight where shadows flickered in the inconstant illumination.

Mathghamhain spun, striking with his spear, and the streak of black I had spotted lunging toward him faltered and I heard a wolf's cry of pain. They had reached us. The wolf retreated, but I sensed more, many more, just beyond the edge of the light.

"Lissa, stay near the fire and don't leave it, no matter what," Rhodri ordered his fiancée as he shrugged his shield from his back to his arm and took up an active defensive position. She nodded, even though he couldn't see it.

The wolf lunged at Mathghamhain again, almost faster than I could follow, but he anticipated its approach and struck it square in the throat, killing it. More howls immediately rose, almost deafening in their clamor, but not quite yet on us. I assumed the wolf had been a scout of some sort. I drew my sword and grabbed the lantern in my other hand, moving to join the men. When I reached them, I could see into the darkness, and I saw shifting forms, so black that I could distinguish their outlines in the night, milling back and forth as they considered the challenge in front of them. The wolves snarled at our defense and our fire. And unfortunately, I could hear their thoughts. They were bent on obeying the will of their alpha, and his orders were to capture the princess and her companions. Yet Mathghamhain's kill had made them wary, and our fire even more so. They even shied away from the light cast by the lanterns Mathghamhain and I held. I shuddered at the curses they hurled at us and the light.

"Good, Aislinn, you brought your lantern," Mathghamhain said. For some reason, I found his voice rather soothing, despite its roughness. Perhaps it was because of the fact that its roughness made it rather hard to tell what mood or emotion colored it, so it sounded calm and normal. I raised my lantern higher and gripped my sword more tightly, causing it to flame up as well, and I peered into the night. The wolves' outlines seemed undefined and blurred, so it was hard to tell for certain how big they were. Their eyes, however, were crystal clear: red as the embers of the fire they despised, almost glowing with hate for these people who tormented them with bright light. So far, they seemed content enough to watch. They knew we couldn't go anywhere.

"What do we do?" Rhodri asked, his voice also sounding calm and steady to me.

We wait here, Mathghamhain answered. *To venture beyond where the light reaches is almost certain death. We must wait for them to come to us. They hate the light, but they will. And then we must kill them all.* The howls had stopped, but the silence was more nerve-wracking. The wolves remained where they were, pacing back and forth and baring their teeth, which shone white against the darkness of their bodies. *Aislinn. Princess Calissa. Would you please start shooting your arrows? We cannot let this drag on indefinitely. The fire will not last.*

Are you trying to provoke a confrontation? I asked as I dropped behind him and Rhodri to do as he bid, sticking my torch into the ground and resheathing my sword so I could wield my bow. I glanced behind me and saw Lissa raising her bow in readiness. She noticed my look and nodded, her face pale but set in resolute lines. She might be terrified, but she would still fight.

Yes. We must get their numbers down. That will likely cause them to come within the light, but better now while the fire is still strong than when it's dying. With that, our arrows began to fly, and the plateau erupted into pandemonium as the wolves began howling and yelping anew. Several began charging toward us but stopped short of actually entering the light. Rhodri and Mathghamhain readied their weapons. Still, the wolves hung back, and actually retreated past where Lissa could see them. Even I had trouble making out their forms to shoot at, and so stopped. No sense in wasting arrows. A tense silence fell. Lissa and I looked at each other, wondering what would come next. Rhodri began shifting from leg to leg, clearly impatient. Dynin swiveled his head around, his ears moving in all directions. Only Mathghamhain remained still, his figure that of complete alertness and concentration. I was beginning to wish that the wolves would simply attack already, when they did.

From the corner of my eye, I caught movement from my right and turned in time to see a group of wolves charging toward us. I shouted and immediately shot several arrows. Three of the wolves went down. Lissa joined me in raining down arrows. As we countered the attack from our side, the men caught an attack at our front. Sending an arrow at the last wolf I saw/sensed from the side (and the last arrow I had immediately available), I turned to the front to see a wolf charge Mathghamhain, entering the firelight to do so, and I saw the creature clearly for the first time. It was the size of a normal wolf, perhaps a shade larger, but wrapped in a dark mist so it appeared much larger, especially when glimpsed in bad lighting. I registered all this in the few seconds it took for me to drop my bow and draw my sword.

Girl! Came Dynin's warning, and with the same motion that I drew my blade, I turned back toward my right, swinging the weapon deep into the neck of a wolf that had been intent on biting me. It yelped briefly in pain, but the flames from the sword quickly overwhelmed the beast and it dissolved into a mist.

"Mathghamhain?" I called, startled.

"It is normal," he called back, engaged in his own fight. I stabbed another wolf making a pass toward me, then had enough of a break to turn my attention to the front. I wondered if Mathghamhain's dark ensemble attracted the wolves to him, for he was currently engaged with three at once. Rhodri grunted as he jumped back toward me to escape the snapping of a wolf's jaws. I brought my sword up and dispatched it for him. From behind us, Lissa cried out. Several wolves were encroaching on her – no doubt, she had been the one Morrian had identified most clearly to them. Rhodri ran to her aid, while I narrowly missed being clawed. I heard Dynin whinny angrily, finally shocked out of his paralyzing fear, and he reared up, lashing out at the wolves around Lissa with his hooves, landing multiple solid hits.

Stop, I thought as hard as I could to the wolves. *Leave off this attack. Further aggression will only get you killed.* For a moment, it seemed to work. The wolves backed off into the darkness outside the firelight. But then the biggest wolf I had seen yet snarled and advanced partway into the light. It was the size of a small pony, and various scars crisscrossed its hide.

"Give us the princess," it said. I started as I realized it had actually spoken aloud. Its voice was half-snarl, half-growl, but decipherable. Oddly, it reminded me of Mathghamhain's spoken voice. "Give us the princess, and we will leave you in peace."

"Lies are as natural to your race as the darkness you shroud yourselves with," Mathghamhain answered him calmly. "Only a fool would believe you. But believe me when I say to you: continue to attack us, as I know you shall, and you will gain nothing but death for yourself and your followers."

The wolf snarled. "Who are you to threaten us? We are the ancient wolves, the terror of the night, rulers of the darkest forest dells. Once we roamed this land at will. When the month is out, we shall again teach the foolish humans what it truly means to fear the dark. You know not the great darkness that is coming. All not in service to the Dark Master will fall. You think your feeble threats cow us? Far better for you to be slain here by my wolves than to face the invasion that follows." More snarls met that remark – of agreement, so it seemed.

"I know that fire cows you," Mathghamhain answered. He held his lantern out towards the wolf. His ears went flat and he snarled again, baring his teeth, but to me it seemed a show of bravado versus actual bravery, though he did not move. "So I say to you once more: continue to attack us, and you will burn. Make your choice." His own voice nearly matched the growl of the wolf's.

Then, multiple things happened at once.

14

A Secret Revealed

A flicker of motion caught my attention, and I turned my head slightly to see it better. What I saw made my stomach drop in new fear. Two wolves had come around Mathghamhain while he was talking with the alpha wolf. Now they crouched in preparation to lunge, and they were within distance of landing on him easily. Mathghamhain must have sensed my sudden alarm, for he began to move even as the words "Look out!" began to leave my mouth. At the same time, Rhodri let out a yell from behind me, as if the attack on him and Lissa was being renewed, as it no doubt was. The blade in my hand suddenly blazed up, lighting the plain clearly. All the wolves howled. But more chilling to me than their eerie noise was the sight of the two wolves leaping on Mathghamhain, biting and clawing at him.

I began to run to his aid, but the cry of pain he sent out made everyone and everything on the plateau pause. He released a tremendous bellow, sounding a little like a canine yelp, a little like a bear's roar, and a little like a human scream. It was the most horrible sound I had ever heard, even more terrible than the wolves' almost unearthly cries because it had that undeniably human element. I stumbled back several steps from the force of it hitting my sensitive ears. I fell to my knees and instinctively dropped my sword and clamped my hands over my ears to block out the terrible noise. Adding to my auditory problems was the fact that the wolves howled yet again. Behind me, I sensed Dynin's similar distress at the awful, powerful noise. Mathghamhain loosed another bellow, this one more of a roar of rage, and lashed out at the attacking wolves with a ferocity that was astonishing and frightening.

He caught one wolf with his spear, the other with the torch, each dissolving almost instantly. The other wolves retreated – involuntarily, I thought. I remained on the ground, transfixed by the sight of Mathghamhain's rage. I sensed great waves of emotion from him: anger, desperation, and something I could only describe as very akin to relief. It was as if a dam built to hold back a river finally burst after years and years of holding the water in, and the river poured over the land with all the immense pent-up energy of the time it had spent in forced containment.

I watched open-mouthed as he tore into the remaining wolves, wielding his lantern and spear with such speed that he seemed surrounded by a constant small ring of fire. From the wolves, I sensed a new sensation: complete and utter fear. They feared this great thing that bore down upon them with fire, their most hated enemy; this thing that smelled like a man, and yet, to them, also like an animal. They began to waver, and then, amazingly, to retreat; not a false retreat, as had happened previously, but a true retreat.

The alpha, however, would have none of it. With an enraged howl, he recalled his wolves, and they obeyed. They began to mass around Mathghamhain, the rest of us forgotten.

I felt Dynin's breath tickle the back of my neck. I reached a hand out to his neck, and felt him trembling. Despite the anger he felt toward anything that dared to attack me, these wolves were still a lot for him to take. "We have to help him," I said, turning around to look at Rhodri.

He and Lissa had been watching the scene unfold with the same wide-eyed shock that I felt, but my words broke us all from our frozen states. "Of course," he agreed, readjusting his grip on his sword and bringing it up. Lissa swallowed visibly, but drew another arrow and placed it on her bow. Mathghamhain loosed another cry. I couldn't help but wonder how he made such sounds, since they really did not sound at all human. Lissa fired her arrow into the midst of the wolves, and Rhodri and I set to the pack with a will. My blade greatly increased the visibility, and the wolves near it whined in discomfort as they turned to assess the new threat moving in on them.

Suddenly, the wolves ceased their attack, sat on their haunches, and howled a keening, mournful howl of loss. I looked around to determine the cause of the commotion, dropping my sword as I clamped my hands over my ears again, wincing at yet another assault of sound. My gaze landed on Mathghamhain as he raised an arm up high and threw the lantern into the heart of the wolves. There was a tinkling sound of breaking glass and the grass, still dry from the winter, caught fire immediately, as did several wolves, whose howls of agony forced me back and nearly to my knees. Smoke entered my throat and made me start coughing, further driving me back towards our original fire.

Strong hands grabbed my shoulders and steadied me on my feet, helping me backward at the same time. "Come on, Aislinn. We have to get out of here before we get caught in it, too," Rhodri shouted above the crackling of the fire. "Lissa! Start climbing up the cliff. We have to get away from this level and as far as we can from the smoke." I saw her nod and turn to do as he said. I bent and snatched up my sword from where it had fallen.

The fire was spreading rapidly among the wolves and began to spread beyond them. I turned toward the rock face, intending to make my way up it as Rhodri and Lissa were doing, but a thought made me turn back to make sure Mathghamhain was also making his way to safety. He was not. The smoke made it hard to see, but I could make out his figure. He had dropped to his knees and was clutching at his left arm as if it was wounded. It was the side the wolves had attacked.

"Mathghamhain!" I shouted. "Come! The fire! We must go!" He moved his head toward me slightly. I blinked and squinted, my eyes watering so much anyone might have supposed I was crying. He lurched uncertainly to his feet, favoring a leg. Then he collapsed once more.

I can't, his mental voice came to me. Even that sounded weak. *I have not the strength. Go on, save yourselves.*

Are you jesting? We need you! You must come! He made no response. The wolves had all either been killed or fled and, deprived of such fuel, the flames began crawling even more resolutely along the ground. Mathghamhain was in very great danger of being burned. I whirled. *Dynin! Come!* He had been helping Lissa get her footing as she began her way up the rock hill, clutching her tattered skirts in one hand, and was just about to begin negotiating the slope himself. My call brought him back towards me reluctantly.

We have to leave, he said as he trotted over. *It is not safe.*

I know, but we can't leave Mathghamhain. He's hurt. You have to help me support him; I can't do it by myself. He snorted in dislike, but he followed me as I dashed toward Mathghamhain. The wind had changed direction during the battle, so it spread the flames and smoke away from us, but that did not give us a large window, and there was our own original fire to consider.

I reached Mathghamhain and picked up his uninjured arm, standing up under it and forcing him to his feet. His arm lay heavily across my shoulders, and it felt very wide and not quite normal, but I didn't take the time to fully consider it. *You should not be here*, he said sluggishly.

Neither should you. Come on! Dynin will support your injured side, but you must help us some. You're too big for us to completely carry you. Dynin took his place on Mathghamhain's other side, allowing him to rest his weight on his back. I sensed a vague grumbling from

Dynin about the weight, but mostly he was focused on getting us humans away from danger. Slowly, we began to move. I kept up a mental stream of encouragement toward Mathghamhain, urging him to keep going. He was very, very heavy. As we approached the cliff, I became aware of Rhodri running toward us.

"I'll take him," he said, breathing through a corner of his cloak. "You go on."

"But-"

"Aislinn, go! He'll move faster if I help him. I need both you and Lissa at the top to help him over." I argued with him no further and relinquished my burden. I glanced behind me to check on the fire. It was spreading quickly horizontally, but the strengthening wind was keeping it from moving too far in our direction, and also pulled the smoke away from us. *Thank you, Abba*, I praised as I ran to the rocky slope and began climbing my way upward. It was filled with small rocks and pebbles that caused me to slip and slide my way up. I worried for Dynin with his hooves.

I can do it, he assured me, obviously picking up on my concern. *Keep going.* As I reached the top, Lissa reached down a hand and helped pull me over the final lip of the hill. "Thank you," I grunted.

"Do you think they'll make it?" she asked me anxiously. I turned to check on the progress of the others. They had reached the slope and seemed to be renegotiating the arrangement. Rhodri moved to Mathghamhain's injured side, and Dynin dropped back. The two men began climbing up the slope – more like crawling, and Mathghamhain was forced to make his way on all fours. Dynin came behind them, carefully picking his way. I saw the wisdom of it. Because of all the loose rocks, it would be easy for Dynin to lose his balance and slip if he made one misstep, and if he remained Mathghamhain's support, he would bring all of them down with them if he fell. This way, he could concentrate entirely on his feet, but still be able to help push Mathghamhain up the slope if need be. I turned my gaze from their slow progress to the fire. It appeared that we still had a bit of a reprieve, but I could tell it would not last much longer. Added to that, on the higher ground we were safe from the flames, yes, but the smoke became even more of an issue. We would have to travel some distance from the rocky slope and the fire to escape being overcome by the smoke, and I did not think Mathghamhain would make it much farther than the top of the hill.

Come on, keep coming. You're nearly there, I thought to him. He sent me a sense of acknowledgment, but I was alarmed by how weak it felt. I could see no visible sign of the wounds, with all his clothing, though I could make out rips and tears. I would have to do a quick healing when he reached the top. And I would have to convince him to remove his outer cloak at least.

"Hurry," Lissa called down anxiously.

"We are," Rhodri grunted. "Be ready to help him over." Lissa and I knelt at the cliff edge, both of us coughing. I reached down and took ahold of the cloth at Mathghamhain's shoulder. He grunted, and I wondered if I was unknowingly clutching at a wound. There was no help for it, though. The fire was starting to reach the bottom of the hill, and though the rocks prevented it from climbing, the smoke was becoming even thicker in our eyes. I worried that the smoke would prevent me from singing. After a few more paces, I was able to get a better grip on Mathghamhain's upper arm, as was Lissa on his other side. He grunted and groaned again, and I knew I was pressing on wounds. I could feel the cuts under my hand and the wetness of the blood that was soaking his clothes. I shifted my grip slightly, and then put all my effort into hauling him over the lip of the slope. Rhodri climbed over and began aiding Lissa. Dynin helped from behind, and we got him over the edge. Dynin followed a moment later. We all lay there for a moment, catching our breaths – which set off another coughing fit.

Rhodri rose first. "We have to get away from here. Too much smoke in our lungs will kill us as surely as flames would."

"We have to wait just a minute," I said hoarsely, crawling over to Mathghamhain. "He can't go on like this. Mathghamhain?" I sent a tendril of thought toward him as well, hoping he was still conscious.

He gave out a low groan and struggled to a sitting position. Which meant he still towered above my head. *I hear you. I know. But I do not think that you will find it easy to find my song. I could keep going a little longer.*

Oh no you can't. You barely made it up here. I have to heal it at least a little. Could you take off your cloak so I can make a full assessment of your wounds?

No! It was very emphatic considering he was nearly unconscious from pain and blood loss.

Why not? I know you said you've been changed, but I'm sure I can handle it.

No. Just heal it as it is.

"Aislinn?" Rhodri asked, his voice urgent. The smoke was growing thicker. He had taken his water pouch from his pack and wet a corner of his cloak and Lissa's, which they were using to breathe through. I had no such protection and coughed again before answering him.

"I know. But I have to do this." I didn't have time to argue with him. So I just focused on healing him. I closed my eyes, both to concentrate and block out the smoke. As soon as I searched for his song, I understood what he meant about it being hard to find. I was overwhelmed by the discordance of a spell, of all things. I know he had said that he had run afoul of a spell from Morrian that had greatly affected him, but I had had no idea it was so vast.

I told you, his voice came to me, carrying a grim note. *Here. Let me show you.* He directed my attention to the song lying underneath the spell.

Thank you. I began singing. His usual song, too, had major discordance, and it meant he was rather badly injured. Unfortunately, the smoke had taken its toll on my throat, and I was unable to sing for longer than a few measures without my voice cracking horribly. I tried to keep going as long as I could, but the smoke continued to close up my throat until I was essentially as voiceless as I had been under Morrian's spell.

You can stop. That's enough, he said as he heard my voice struggling. *I can keep going for now.* His voice did sound stronger.

I nodded reluctantly. "Very well." It was all I could manage.

Mathghamhain struggled to his feet. Dynin moved himself to his wounded side, and Mathghamhain took the support gladly. "Let us go," he said with a little difficulty. "It does no good for any of us to linger here."

"Are you strong enough?" Lissa asked, her voice muffled by the cloak.

"I must be. Do not worry, Your Highness."

"He's right, Lissa, come on," Rhodri said. He led us across the plain with his electric torch lighting the path before him. I know he would have liked to run, but Mathghamhain couldn't manage it. So we settled for as fast a walk as he could manage. I kept a worried eye on him, trying to imagine what his wounds were. As we got away from the smoke, I could make out blood staining his clothes. And I knew that without being fully healed, and without him allowing me to fashion some sort of bandage, the wounds would continue to bleed. However, I could do nothing about it until we reached a safe place from the smoke.

I don't know how far we walked, but we were finally forced to stop when Mathghamhain collapsed. Fortunately, we were far enough from the smoke that it was only a faint odor in the air, though I could still just see its thick cloud in the distance. There was enough light from the moon and stars where we were for me to be able to see fairly easily, though Rhodri's torch was a great help. The two lanterns Mathghamhain and I had carried had been lost in the fight.

Dynin whinnied as Mathghamhain dropped to the ground beside him, and I was surprised that there was a note of pain in his voice. *He scratched me*, he said. *With claws.*

Oh, don't be silly, Dy, I said, rushing to Mathghamhain's side. *He can't have claws. And I'm sure he didn't mean it.*

"Is he unconscious?" Rhodri asked. He flashed his light over Mathghamhain's still body.

"Yes. It's just too much." He had fallen on his face, so I rolled him over onto his back. "I don't care what his protests are, I have to get all this extra clothing off him. I need to see what exactly his injuries are and how much blood he's lost." I began searching for the fastener to undo the cloak. It had to be around here somewhere. "Lissa, could you bring me some water? I need to clear some of the smoke from my throat."

"Do you think it's very bad?" she asked as she brought me the water pouch.

"Well, considering how big he is, it has to take quite a bit of blood loss to render him unconscious, and who knows what poison or infection might be carried in shadow wolf...wounds." My voice trailed off, for I discovered the fastener of his outer cloak, which was near his left hand. I reached to undo it, and my gaze drifted to his hand. He wore gloves, but one had been torn, and part of his hand was visible. At least...it should be his hand. I stared at it. Yes, Dynin had said he'd been scratched with claws, but I thought he had been exaggerating. Maybe I was simply seeing things in the dim light of the stars.

"What is it?" Rhodri asked.

"Rhodri, could you shine that light over here, please?"

"Of course." He did. Lissa looked over as well, and we all stared. Where his hand should be...it rather resembled more of an animal paw, and his nails were long and hard, and slightly yellow, reminding me a little bit of bear claws. The skin on his palm was black and tough looking, reminding me of the bottom of dog paws, the backs of his hands were covered in a dark fur. Dynin craned his neck to look and snorted triumphantly.

I told you.

"What in the Five Realms...?" Lissa breathed out.

"I don't know." I slowly undid the cloak's fastening and threw it back, finally revealing Mathghamhain's form. Rhodri played his light over it...and we all just stared.

"Grindles and spindles," I whispered. "No wonder he wears the cloak." I had a hard time processing what I was seeing. Mathghamhain had told us from the beginning that in the fight against Morrian two hundred and fifty years ago, he had disabled a spell with a severe backlash that had changed his form. I had imagined that it had scarred him severely, maybe damaged his limbs in an odd way. I had never really considered that it could have so completely changed his form into something that could not really be described as human.

His overall shape was humanoid – two legs, two arms, feet, hands, and head. But beyond that...it is hard to describe. His whole body was covered in dark fur – in the uncertain light I couldn't tell if it was dark brown or black – and his musculature was overall bearish at first glance. Upon further inspection, I could discern slightly human aspects to his muscle groups. Under his cloak he wore knee-length breeches and a loose shirt. His arms and legs were thick with muscle, but the most unnerving thing about his appearance was his head and face. From the shoulders up, there was a definite wolfish influence, and the fur on the top and the back of his head was lighter than the rest of him. His face...his eyes were closed, but he had a snout, rather flatter and less pronounced than the muzzle of a bear or a wolf, but yet it was those two things combined, and I caught a glimpse of rather large front teeth. I wondered how in the Five Realms he managed the spoken word through such a mouth, for animal mouths were not designed for talking. I did, however, understand full well how he had been able to release the bellows in his fight against the wolves. The only word I could think of that described the bear/wolf form with just enough human characteristics to make it almost horrific that I was looking at was... beast. It was a beast.

Dynin snorted and retreated several steps. *Did I not tell you he smelled of predator?* He asked. *Did I not tell you?*

This isn't his true form, Dynin, I responded to him, slowly and somewhat dazed. *Morrian...Morrian did this to him.*

He still clawed me.

I glanced at Dynin. I was able to make out some blood running down his side, but listening to his song, I sensed it was not serious. They were mere surface scratches. *I'm sure he didn't mean it.*

Lissa was clutching at Rhodri's arm. "Poor Mathghamhain...no wonder he was so hesitant to face Morrian again. To discourage us in facing her." She seemed to have difficulty in looking at him for a prolonged period, instead looking up at the sky. I didn't entirely blame her. I, too, had trouble gazing at Mathghamhain's strange beast face. Instead, I focused my eyes on his left arm. Here was where he was wounded, and the sight of the gouges brought me back into focus.

"Lissa, give me the water again, and find a clean cloth in a pack. I want to wash these wounds thoroughly before closing them. Oh, and could you grab my healing bag also?" I moved around so I was next to the wounds. They were rather awful looking. There were both claw and bite marks, every one of them going deep, and blood matted the fur all along his left side. They were still oozing. "Rhodri, can I have the torch, please?"

"Of...of course," he said, continuing to stare at the form. He handed it to me, and I shone it directly into the wounds. "I think I'm starting to understand just how lucky we were when we faced Morrian in the castle courtyard."

"Not lucky," Lissa said, kneeling beside me with the water, cloth, and bag I had asked for. "Protected by Abba."

"Thank you," I said. I rummaged through my bag, looking for a special wound-cleaning compound I had that had been pre-made for me by the castle apothecary. Once I had it, and a small bowl I kept in the bag, I poured some water into the bowl and mixed the compound in. While I waited the requisite five minutes for it to reach full potency, I examined Mathghamhain's leg as well. It, too, was covered in claw and bite marks. Using the torch to look at the wounds closely, I saw that my partial healing back at the rocky slope must have stopped all the major bleeding that had been occurring. His unconscious state was the work of the blood he had lost before then and the blood that had continued to ooze out while we fled the fire. Furthermore, I saw no sign that the bites were any different from those of a regular wolf. Encouraged, I began to scrub and rinse the wounds and immediately surrounding fur before finishing the healing. Even with Brenwyd healings, infection could still be a concern if wounds weren't cleaned properly before the new skin formed over them.

"Do you...do you think he'll be very angry?" Lissa asked as I went about my task.

"About what?" I asked.

"That we discovered his form in such a way."

"What way? Trying to save his life?"

"No; that we did it without his permission."

I shrugged. "In cases with severely wounded patients, the word of the healer overrides that of the patient. This is one of those times. And besides, we were bound to learn of what he was hiding sooner or later. If that upsets him, it's his problem. Not ours."

"Well, yes, but...he is rather ferocious-looking."

I sat back on my heels and looked at her. "Lissa, no matter what his outward form, this is still Mathghamhain. It is our perspective of him that has changed, not his character. Don't let this," I gestured at his body, "color your opinion of him. Rely on what we've learned on our travels. That he is a somewhat prickly, protective, eager-to-please loner who happens to also have lived a rather long time. In fact, this explains some of his character."

"Such as?" Rhodri asked.

"Why he can be so prickly about things. I'm sure I would, had I undergone such a change." I finished my task. "Rhodri, could you and Lissa set up a camp? I doubt that we'll travel any further tonight."

"Of course. Should I light a fire as well?" The question came reluctantly.

I sighed. "Well, I have definitely had my fill of fire for one night, but it may be best. Just a small one, though."

"Definitely." He and Lissa went to their task, while I began the second part of mine. Now that I had observed and examined the true nature of his wounds, it would be much easier to heal Mathghamhain. I took several more swallows of water, and then bent my mind to the matter. Having been guided to his true song earlier, this time I was able to bypass the spell that surrounded it. Out of curiosity, I took several minutes to consider it and try to find a weak spot, but it was rather overwhelming and so I switched my attention before it caused me to completely lose focus. Singing to heal the wounds was easy; however, as I sang, I became aware of the great melancholy and resigned despair that existed within it. It was so profound it nearly made me cry. Clearly, Mathghamhain had lost all hope that the terrible spell enacted against him could be undone, and he had lived with this belief for over two centuries. As for the strain of his song that indicated his belief of Abba, it was there, and it was true – but it was not vibrant and alive the way it was for all other Brenwyds whose songs I had listened to. It gave me a great insight into his character. He knew Abba's existence too well to ever doubt it, and he even accepted the stories of his miraculous works, but he no longer believed such things possible in his own life. He regarded his aid to us simply as something commanded by Abba, and so he was performing it out of a perfunctory sense of duty, not because of the burning love for Abba all Brenwyds are raised to embrace. His faith had become something distant to him. Considering his situation, I did not altogether blame him - but I resolved to try and lead him back to where his heart should be. Additionally, there were some passionate areas of the music, but of a nature that seemed to me to read more of hate and revenge than love. I supposed that would be towards Morrian.

It did not take me overly long to finish healing his wounds. New skin covered them, though there was no hair. I stopped and forced myself to consider his face closely enough to tell if there was any sign of his waking. He shifted slightly, and his features appeared to be more relaxed (it was rather hard to read anything out of them, though all my years healing animals and reading their body language was a great boon) but for now he seemed content to sleep. It did not worry me. After the fight and our subsequent flight across the higher plain, I was ready to sleep for a while myself.

"Have you finished?" Lissa's voice came from behind me.

I nodded. "Yes. He's sleeping."

"That sounds like an excellent idea," Rhodri said. He had just succeeded in lighting a small campfire and was rocked back on his heels. This fire let off a cheery light that brightened things considerably, though the smell of the smoke made my throat begin to ache again. "We should work out a watch schedule and rest for the remainder of the night. I doubt those wolves will be after us again anytime soon, if any even survived, but better safe than sorry."

"You think they were all killed?" Lissa asked, eyebrows raised in surprise.

"I think there's a good possibility. We had cut down their numbers significantly even before Mathghamhain lit the plain on fire, and that decimated them even more. Even if a few escaped, wolves are pack animals, right? They're not so likely to come after us in diminished numbers." He looked to me for affirmation.

I nodded again. "Yes, that is true." I glanced back where we had come from. I could still see the glow of the fire and the smudge of smoke, but the wind was still blowing away from us and the terrain was rocky enough I thought the fire should burn itself out before the end of the night. So I prayed, anyway. I felt uneasy at the thought of a wildfire burning through northern Ecclesia with the country asleep, but there was not much I could do about it. "I will take the first watch," I volunteered. I looked up at the sky, calculated how much longer we had left of the night. I reckoned it was roughly two hours until midnight, which meant there were about eight to eight and a half hours of darkness left. "I think three-hour shifts should get us to morning." Rhodri nodded agreement.

"Are you sure you want to take the first?"

I nodded and motioned to Mathghamhain. "I want to clean up his side as best I can, and I have a feeling it will be easier if he's sleeping."

"Very well. I'll make my bed over here, then." Rhodri pulled a blanket from his pack and set the pack itself on its side as a pillow.

"Then I shall sleep here," Lissa said, copying his motions next to me. "But what of eating something first? I feel rather hungry." At her words, I realized I was hungry as well. Famished, more like.

"That sounds like an excellent idea," I said. "Could you get the bread from my pack, please?"

"Of course." While Lissa rummaged around in my pack for my meager food supplies, Rhodri produced dried meat and bread from his pack for himself and Lissa. "Here."

"Thanks." I took the bread and began chewing on it as I returned my attention to Mathghamhain's side. I re-wet the cloth I had used to clean his wounds, taking a drink of water myself, and then set to cleaning up the rest of the blood dirtying him.

Dynin whickered to get my attention. *What about me? He scratched me.*

Ah. Yes. One moment. I had forgotten about Dynin's scratches, as they were nowhere near life-threatening. I stood to walk over to where Dynin chomped at grass on the other side of Mathghamhain. However, with the semi-darkness created by the stars, moon, and firelight, I accidentally tripped over Mathghamhain's legs and fell right onto his chest with a grunt. "Oof."

"Are you alright?" Lissa asked. There was a slight hint of amusement in her voice, and I was positive I heard a suppressed chuckle from Rhodri.

"Fine. Just a simple misstep." It was rather embarrassing to have fallen onto his chest. I was very glad he was unconscious. Unfortunately, my luck did not hold, for as I pushed myself up to get off him, he stirred in the way the waking do, and opened his eyes, staring directly into my (I'm sure) startled face. His eyes caught me completely off guard. Unlike the rest of him, they were entirely human, bright in the darkness, and colored a light silver grey.

A Beast's Story

At first he didn't seem completely aware of the situation, only rather puzzled to find me on top of him. I was mortified that he had caught me in the position, accidental though it was. "Aislinn? What...what are you doing?" His voice was thick and sleepy.

"Uh..." was all I answered, for I was completely fascinated by how his mouth moved. It formed words in a human enough fashion, but it was extremely odd to see a beast mouth make them. "I tripped..."

However, by that time, he was awake enough to realize that I could see his true form quite plainly. I saw the alarm and incredulity come into his face, and some irritation. He sat up, dislodging me, and I bumped to the ground in an ungraceful fashion. "What have you done?" He sounded completely aghast, and he stared down at himself as if trying to take in the fact that he was uncloaked in our presence. Dynin moved away as he sat up.

I frowned. I was not very happy with how he had dumped me on the ground, and feeling a little irritable myself. "I healed you. A simple thank you would suffice."

"But...you..."

"Removed the cloak? Yes. I needed to be able to see what I was healing."

"No, you did not. Do not lecture me on how Brenwyd healing works. I know all too well. You could have done it blind." He was now groping around him, no doubt trying to find the cloak. I happened to be sitting on it, but I did not feel like sharing the information with him at the moment. "It's easier when I can see what I'm healing. Not to mention I needed to clean the wounds Who knows what infection shadow wolf injuries might carry?" "Nothing I could not handle." His voice had grown very growly. Oh, yes, he was upset. It was rather alarming now that I was really seeing him (he had great canine teeth that reflected the light in an almost frightening way), but I refused to be intimidated. As I had told Lissa earlier, it was Mathghamhain. What he looked like should play no factor into the consideration of his character. "You deliberately went against my wishes merely to fulfill your curiosity. Are children not taught to have respect for others' privacy and requests anymore?"

I forced myself to meet his eyes squarely so he could see my own anger. They were the easiest part of his anatomy to focus on, anyhow, though I had to tip my head backward to do so. He was still seated, which was a mercy. I stood up in order to be completely level with him. I actually stood above him for a change. "Children? *Children?* I may not be as old as you are, but I am certainly no child. I know how to respect the privacy of others quite well, thank you very much, but you should also know that healers sometimes need to go against what a patient wishes to provide the best possible care. That is what I did. I won't deny, I was curious as to what you hid beneath the cloak, but that was not the reason I removed it. Not at all. If I was truly that curious, I could have undone the cloak while you slept any number of times on this journey before now. It is the very respect for privacy you doubt I possess that kept me from doing so, and seeing as I helped you escape fire, wolves, and healed your injuries, I think I deserve at least a thimbleful of gratitude rather than accusations and anger thrown in my face." My voice was very heated. It took him a little aback, I could tell. He blinked, and some bewilderment entered his eyes. The emotion lent his whole face a more human aspect. "Also, for someone who is trying to improve his behavior, this is very much not the right direction to go." He made no reply, but crossed his arms about himself, fingering the bare skin over his healed wounds. He seemed at a total loss, but still upset.

Lissa stepped up beside me. "Please, Mathghamhain, do not be angry. We were most concerned about you. You were wonderfully brave against the wolves. You saved us. Your outward appearance has no bearing on that." Then, in a move I applauded her for, she reached out and laid a hand on his bearish arm, a comforting, reassuring smile on her face.

That seemed to completely undo Mathghamhain. He blinked, and I saw his whole body sag slightly as the anger and defensiveness drained out of him. He hung his head and gently moved his arm away from Lissa's touch. She frowned slightly but did not protest. "I...I am sorry. It is merely...the few times in the past I tried to acquaint people with my...uncloaked form...it did not go well. And...I do not like looking at it myself." His voice was low. He raised his eyes to meet mine. He really did have lovely eyes, no matter what the rest of him looked like. And oddly...they seemed familiar. "I do thank you for the healing, Aislinn, and I beg your forgiveness for my reaction."

I smiled. "You are welcome. I was actually expecting some sort of reaction like that." He frowned, but Rhodri spoke before he could make a reply.

"So...this...is what Morrian's enchantment did to you?" he asked, having come round from the other side of the fire. He was frowning, too.

Mathghamhain breathed a deep sigh and gestured down at himself. "Yes...this is how I was changed. You understand why I was not exactly keen when you arrived to face her again."

"But I do not understand how no Brenwyd was able to undo this spell," Lissa said, puzzled. "Given enough time, they should be able to."

"Nor could any of us determine how we were unable to break it," Mathghamhain replied. "We tried. Many times. The spell...given how it affected me, it entwined with my song and interrupted it, creating a dizzying puzzle for anyone to unravel." He looked back to me. "You sensed this when you healed me." I nodded. "Overwhelming, is it not?" I nodded again. The boundary spell was intricate, but this was something else again.

"Is there a chance Morrian would have such a spell as affected you in place around her this time?" Rhodri asked. "You said it happened when you faced her directly."

"It did." He closed his eyes, remembering. I saw a shudder ripple through his body. "It was the final battle. We had clashed on the great plain before Kheprah, next to the Hellwyl. We knew that this would be the decisive conflict. We had been skirmishing with her forces for several months while we finished building and training the army. In addition to the Brenwyds, the rulers of the other realms sent soldiers from their own armies, for Morrian was a threat to them as well, especially if we were unable to stop her. I was with Nivea, as were a few others, and our task was to seek her out personally and kill her. The battle had been going on for some time, and still she had not shown herself. Her sorcery was on full display, but she had hidden herself from view, knowing that a force such as ours had been deployed. Finally...I found a way around to the back of the enemy forces. I went first, gripping my sword and shield with all the strength within me, searching for her. And I found her. She was in a small tent, watching the battle through her viewing glass, fortifying her troops with spells, as her other magicians were doing, for our force was easily winning the physical fight. Her soldiers fought out of fear of her and no other reason, while we fought for those who would die if Morrian was not stopped." His eyes opened, and he gazed into the fire. Lissa, Rhodri, and I listened as if in a trance. It was the first time Mathghamhain had told us a story from those long-ago days in which he used the word *I*. He seemed to forget we listened.

"I came upon her, from behind. She was so focused on her glass, she did not realize I was behind her. I raised my sword and struck at her, but the blade, though it was flamestone, bounced off her shield, shattering in my grip and injuring my wrist. She turned and saw me. Instead of being alarmed, she smiled.

'I was wondering when you would make an appearance,' she said to me. 'I knew you could not resist.' By then, my comrades had arrived. She looked at them all, her gaze settling on Nivea. Instead of glaring or shouting, her smile deepened. 'Why, Nivea, darling,' she exclaimed. 'It is true, you did escape the chimera. I'm so glad.'

"Nivea frowned at her. 'No thanks to your hunter,' she answered. 'Come, Morrian, the charade is over. Our troops are crushing yours. Surrender before more lives are lost.'

"Morrian laughed. 'But Nivea, you misunderstand me. I have never wanted this war. It is these Brenwyds who have pushed it on me, costing innocent lives.' Her voice became sympathetic. Her voice was and likely still is a potent weapon. We all stood there, slowly becoming ensnared in her spell. Her words were like honey, clogging our ears, slowing our minds and actions. 'All I want is peace,' she went on. 'I want to help the poor people of these realms, and magic is the way to do it. It is not evil, it is a mere tool, conforming to the wishes of the wielder. It is only the dogmatic rhetoric of the Brenwyds that has so maligned it. Come with me, Nivea. I have watched you grow up. You have the potential for great power, and you have a good heart. I can show you how to use magic for the good of all. Only dismiss these Brenwyd allies of yours. We can build the kingdom your father dreamed of, with no poverty, no hunger, no sickness. All these things magic can accomplish. Tell me, what is so evil about that?' Nivea made no reply, only looked at her, and I could see that while she was fighting the magic, it was hard. It was a pretty world Morrian painted a picture of. The other Brenwyds were likewise affected by the spell. They had not directly encountered Morrian and her wiles before.

"But I had. I was not fooled, and I knew to be on my guard. 'No such world can exist here in these physical realms, not with sin in the world' I said. 'Give up and surrender, Morrian, for you will lose.'

"She looked at me and laughed. 'Are you so sure?' She gestured toward my companions, frozen where they were, trying to fight off her enchantment. 'Is this the best you can do?'

"I stepped closer to her. 'I will not let you ruin any more families.'

"'How will you stop me?' she asked. "You cannot breach my shield. I have made it impervious to your little songs, and you have no other recourse to defeat me.'

"I stared at her. I knew part of what she said was true; her shield was extremely strong. But there was one way I might penetrate it. It was madness, but there was no other choice. 'Do I not?' I asked. Then I threw myself on her, pinning her beneath my body as I grappled for her throat. The shock of it disrupted her other spells, and my comrades came back to themselves. Nivea shouted at me to get off her, but I could not, not yet. The shield had to be disabled. Morrian grabbed my wounded wrist, and I cried out in pain. Any amusement was gone from her eyes.

"'I should have killed you when I first threw you in the dungeons,' she hissed.

"I made no reply. In my pain-induced haze, a bright, round orb caught my attention. It was a peculiar light, bright yet wreathed in darkness, and it seemed to come from her viewing glass. Morrian turned to deal with my comrades, who had begun to sing, and Nivea engaged her in combat, her sword completely engulfed in its flames. She slackened her grip, and I broke loose. She paid me no more attention. My vision returned to normal. I no longer saw the orb, but I knew it was there. I could sense it now. It was a spell anchor, and I realized that it was responsible for her impervious shield. I crawled over to her looking glass. It showed the battle. Though we now occupied Morrian's attention, she had other magicians working spells against our forces, and they were beginning to make headway against our offensive. It was a crucial point. I looked all around it for the orb I had seen. My hand brushed against the glass, and suddenly I understood. The glass was the source of her power. And glass was so very, very vulnerable. I raised my sword above my head, intending to strike it.

"Morrian finally saw what I was about. 'If you destroy that glass, you will call down on yourself a curse so terrible that you will wish you had not been born. You will be cast out with stones, and none shall give you companionship. You shall be forever alone, and it shall never be broken.' Though her words and tone were brave and gloating over the prospect of future suffering, I saw something in her eyes I had not seen before: fear. She had forced Nivea and the others back, and they were immobilized. Nivea stared at me, her eyes wide. I did not know what message she was trying to convey, but I could not let her sway me from my course.

"I stared at Morrian defiantly. 'Then so be it. I would gladly sacrifice myself to cast you down, Morrian.' And before she could make any more protest, or anyone else could, I smashed the hilt of my sword through the glass, shattering it into a thousand pieces. Morrian let out a piercing scream, and a great clap of thunder deafened me. I fell to my knees, pieces of mirror stabbing me in various places. I began to feel a great pain within my stomach, and collapsed over on my side, falling unconscious within a few seconds." He paused and blinked, as if recalling himself to the present. "I remained unconscious for the rest of the day. The others told me what happened after. When I shattered the mirror, I broke the source of Morrian's power, what she used to tether her spells to make them so hard to undo. Her shield collapsed round her, as did her spell restraining Nivea, who charged forward to put a final end to her, but Morrian dodged and drew her own sword. The loss of her power was a great wound, and she knew she was defeated. She ran from the tent, and the others pursued her to the river, where she threw herself in. They all assumed she preferred to drown herself than allow any one of us to have the final triumph of killing her. Obviously, now, she jumped into the river to escape and let us think that she was dead.

"Nivea and...and one other stayed with me in the tent. They told me I convulsed greatly as Morrian's spell took effect. The other was a Brenwyd, and..." He drew in a breath. "She told me later, with tears in her eyes, that she tried everything she could to prevent the enchantment from taking hold. But she could not, and so she and Nivea watched while I changed to what you see." He released the breath. "When the others returned, they decided to hold me in the tent and summon more Brenwyds to try and break the spell before I awoke. As you can see, it was unsuccessful. All the attempts were unsuccessful. And I understood devastatingly clearly what Morrian's last words to me had meant. I remained around the capital for a little while, living in an isolated cabin not far away, but...it was hard to remain so in the world. I could not go to the village or city openly. And so I finally decided to go to the mountains, where there was no one, and live out the rest of my days. Until I realized Morrian's spell must have included some sort of longevity element, for here I still am, two hundred and fifty years later." He fell silent, gazing into the flames.

I could sense how much it had cost him in emotional energy to tell us the tale, especially on top of his physical exhaustion still lingering from the wolf attack. I looked at him with compassion, pity, and sympathy. For his actions, he should have lived the rest of his life around the castle, perhaps on his own land, a great hero and recognized as such. Instead, he had been relegated to self-imposed exile because of Morrian's spell, and had endured it for over two centuries.

He closed his eyes for a moment, then opened them and refocused on the three of us. He looked haunted by his memories. "I...I make some forays into the lowlands, around villages. I have to at least a few times a year for certain things I need, such as cloth, rope, books, and the like. But the few times I have tried to make connections, those whom I tried to approach could not bear my appearance, or they have aged and died. So I stopped trying after a time. It was not worth it." He shifted his attention to Rhodri. "In answer to your question, she might very well have some sort of similar spell enwrapped round her anchor again. As such, I have been planning to be the one who destroyed the anchor. If she does have another such backlash...better me than any of you."

I frowned. "And when were you planning to tell us that? Right before you did it?"

"Something like that."

"And how did that sound like a good idea?"

He frowned, seeming puzzled. "If I simply took the initiative and did it, how would you stop me?"

It was a valid point, but that was not the point I was trying to make. "We have to work together to defeat her. That is abundantly clear. But we can't do so if one person makes plans of his own without telling the others. It rather defeats the purpose, as it happens. And if there is some sort of backlash spell contained within the anchor, and yet you had told us naught of the possibility, how well do you think we would have reacted to such a thing happening before our very eyes? Do you think we would simply be able to go on with the plan?" I didn't wait for him to answer the question. "If it's anything like the spell that caused your change of form, then the answer is most likely no. Indeed, I can very well imagine we would be frozen with shock and surprise long enough for someone to discover us and thwart our purpose. And then where would we be?" At that, I stopped and took a breath, waiting for his answer.

He was silent for several minutes, clearly pondering my words. Lissa, Rhodri and I all exchanged glances. I did have to admit it was rather noble of him to plan to take such a punishment upon himself a second time, but we needed him to stop holding things back if we were really going to be successful. "I had not considered things in those terms before," Mathghamhain said slowly. "I have long been alone on my mountain, companion to no one, keeping my own counsel. And even before this change came upon me, I was well used to dealing with problems by relying only on myself. I am a solitary person by nature." He looked around at the rest of us. I noticed that his ears drooped flat against his head, and his whole demeanor reminded me of a puppy caught in wrongdoing. The image almost made me smile. "I apologize." His gaze flicked to me in particular. "You accused me several days ago of letting my bitterness and pessimism cloud my thinking and said I needed to learn to open up to people again. You are correct. I will endeavor to do so from now on."

"Good," I said. "So, is there anything else we need to be aware of at this time regarding Morrian that you have been holding back?"

He sighed. "Ah, a few, but would you mind terribly if it waited until tomorrow? I own I am rather tired, and would like to sleep."

"Of course," Lissa was quick to say. I was more of the opinion that he could very well stay up a little longer and tell us everything he had left out, but Lissa sent a glance my direction that kept me from voicing my opinion. "I think it would be best for all of us to rest for the remainder of the night after that fight. After we eat, of course."

"Thank you, Your Highness," Mathghamhain said, though he darted a look at me that made me wonder if he sensed I would have rather kept questioning him. *I think, Aislinn, that you should take better care to guard your thoughts if you want to keep them private,* his voice came to me as the thought crossed my mind. *When I am tired, it becomes easier to read others' minds whether I will or no, as the guards I have around my mind begin to slip with my fatigue, so please do not be irritated. I cannot help it.*

Oh, of course. I knew that. And I did remember that, belatedly. I had friends and relatives who were mind speakers, and they tended to leave large gatherings earlier than most as they had no wish to hear others' thoughts as they began to tire.

Dynin snorted and stamped a hoof impatiently. *If you are done talking, girl, would you please see to my scratches? I have been waiting for some time now.*

Yes, Dynin.

⁘⊱⊰⁘

Fortunately, the rest of the night passed without incident. Or rather, without outward incident, to be precise. For when I turned the watch over to Rhodri and went wearily and happily to my bedroll, it was not the peaceful blackness of deep sleep that met the backs of my eyelids. Instead, I dreamed.

First my Sight took me to Morrian's dark island, to the receiving room of her fortress that I had viewed before. This time, however, she was not attended by her lackey. Several shadow wolves filled the chamber. They cowered before her, tails between their legs and ears flat against their heads, behavior quite different from what I had seen earlier that night.

"What do you mean, they escaped?" she asked in a cold, quiet voice. It was the sort of tone that got under one's skin and caused you to shiver involuntarily.

One of the wolves snarled, rather fearfully, but I made out words within the noise. "They escaped, lady. They built a great fire. They had the fire weapons. And there was a thing, a great creature I have never seen the like of before. It spoke and stood like a man, but it smelled and fought as a beast. It killed our alpha and most of the others, and then lit the plain on fire. Only we three escaped."

"And you chose to come to me." Morrian rose from the throne where she had been sitting and began to walk around them in a circle. "Why, I wonder? Why not chase them and avenge your alpha?"

"Too few," the wolf growled. "We are too few to go against them again. They had the fire weapons."

"Impossible," Morrian said simply. "I made sure all those weapons were lost. Those not in my storeroom are lost, moldering in the mountains."

"But they had them, I tell you. And the beast...I will not face him again, not without a full pack of wolves at my back."

Morrian paused in her circling to look at the wolf. "What is this? A wolf, admitting to cowardice?" Her tone was mocking.

All three snarled. "No!" the speaker howled. "Never that, my lady. But wisdom dictates one does not engage a foe stronger than yourself without enough reinforcements to be sure of victory."

Morrian surveyed the wolves and drew closer to the speaker, a slow smile spreading across her face, her voice still soft. "You wish for me to send you out again, after you have failed? This is what you expect me to do? You think I will be so upset with you for failing that I will charge you to gather the rest of the wolves and pursue the princess and her followers and kill them this time? Is that what you think I will do?" She began circling again. "Or perhaps you expect me to kill you. For call it what you will, you ran from your mission. You failed in your task. I do call your running cowardice. And cowardice is not tolerated in the pack, is it? Far easier to report to me, and for me to kill you, than to go and face the rest of the pack and say you failed. Is that what you thought?" The wolves said nothing. "Then I am afraid I will disappoint you. For I will not kill you. I am going to send you back to your pack and let you explain to them how you failed, and your alpha female can decide your punishment." At this the wolves looked even more fearful. "And additionally, you can tell her that as I have no use for things that have failed me, I will not send any more shadow wolves out after the princess. You say you encountered them on the plains and plateaus south of the mountains, headed towards the sea?" The wolves nodded. "I see...I will deal with them myself: the princess, her prince, the Brenwyd, and this beast you speak of. Properly. Do you understand?" The wolves nodded, looking more miserable and cowed than I have ever seen any wolf look. It almost made me feel sorry for them. Almost. "Now go, and report to your pack as I have said. And make sure the guard does not slip at the border." The wolves turned and hastened out of the room.

For a few heartbeats, Morrian stood where she was, alone. Then her lackey I had Seen before, Pelagius, came into the room. "You let them live?" he asked, clearly surprised.

"They will not live for long," Morrian said casually. "With the news they bring, the alpha female will have them forced to endure the sunlight, until all their magic is burned away, and then have them torn to shreds. It is far harsher than any punishment I could devise. And besides, they did bring some...interesting news as well. It seems that the princess and her friends are heading towards the sea."

"What do you think they are trying to do?"

Morrian tapped her finger against her chin as she thought. "They could be attempting to circumvent the barrier by traveling by sea...but if so, why come so far north first?"

"What do you wish to do now, my lady?"

Morrian frowned. "That, I am not sure of yet. The wolves spoke of a fourth accompanying them. A being who spoke and walked as a man, but smelled and fought as a beast. I wonder..." Her voice trailed off. After a moment, she resumed speaking. "I need more information before determining what to do. Since all my attempts to track them magically have been stymied, it seems I must send out more reliable scouts." A smile curved her lips upward. "Even supposed flamestone weapons cannot so easily frighten away the elementals. And then I can ask them what they were planning to do myself."

Pelagius smiled in return. "Of course, my lady." Before I could register alarm, my Sight shifted to another room in the fortress I had seen in my previous dreams. It was the room with the translucent sphere and rose within. But now the sphere was not so translucent. Instead, the bottom half of it was wholly white, as if filled with milk. The rose was nearly halfway red. Time was marching on against us.

I Saw a group of eleven riders making their way with great haste across a plain of tall grass. It reminded me of the central Darlesian plains, on the east end of which Rhodri's father made his home. Their wonderful horses were a result, in part, of the abundance of land available for grazing. As I watched, I realized the riders were none other than Duchess Rhian and her escort. I remembered that she had decided to travel to Feingeld, Darlesia's capital, and demand that King Aelfwic listen to her. But she should have been there some days ago. In becoming further involved in the scene, I realized that the riders were running from something.

I saw Duchess Rhian crouched low over her horse's neck, steely resolve written on her face. She glanced back, then returned her gaze forward and urged her horse on faster. I could tell the horse needed no urging. The riders were coming hard upon a wood, and something – several somethings – roared from behind them. However, before I could see what it was, the scene changed again.

No longer was I viewing riders on the Darlesian plains, but a great military camp at night, with many fires burning. It seemed somehow familiar. My dream drew me toward a hill, where a solitary figure stood, gazing into the distance. It was a man, a Brenwyd, in his early twenties from what I could tell. As my Sight drew me toward him, though, I noticed lines etched into his forehead, around his mouth, and around his eyes that aged him. At first, I thought his face merely reflected a set resolve to do whatever task was in front of him. But as I gazed longer at the unmoving figure, his eyes revealed much, much more: pain, anger, sadness, guilt. He roused my pity and I wanted to reach out and comfort him, for he seemed to be greatly conflicted and in agony about something. But what?

He turned, and for a moment I thought he sensed my presence. But then I became aware of a small rustling from the hillside and watched as another figure came out of the night to join the man on the hilltop. This one was a woman, about the same age; Brenwyd, fair-haired, and attired for battle. "So here you are," she said. "I've been looking for you for nearly an hour."

He grunted and turned back to look at the horizon. I still didn't know what he was looking at. Perhaps nothing. "I wish to be alone."

"I know. That's why I'm here. You've been alone too much. It's not healthy. Abba made us for companionship, not solitude."

"Some of us, mayhap," the man replied.

The woman sighed. "Steffyn, I know you are in pain. I know she put you through much, much more than anyone should have to endure-"

He cut her off abruptly, his tone short. "No, you do not. No one does. That is why I seek to be alone. No one can understand what I've been through. And when I try to explain, all I meet with is pity. I do not need *pity*."

"But Steffyn," the woman said, "we are your friends. We wish to help you. Yes, we feel pity, but we cannot help that. We simply want to help you become yourself again. Do not let her steal yourself from you. If you do, then no matter what happens tomorrow, she has won. Don't you understand that?" Her voice took on a desperate note, and the passion in her voice made me think she was more than a friend – or at least hoped to be.

At that, he turned to her. And I recognized him abruptly. He was the man I had seen with Nivea in my earlier dream. Steffyn, hero of the war against Morrian. But in no tale had I heard of him having feelings like this. And strangely, Mathghamhain had made no mention of him in his story...

His words brought me back to the dream. "Myself? You wish me to become myself again?" He laughed, but hollowly, with no amusement. "You are too late for that, Elfleda. Far too late. Don't *you* understand? I cannot be as I was. Not ever again. And your badgering is not helping matters."

The woman stared at him. "Then you could at least be courteous to those who are concerned for you."

"Courtesies matter nothing. Not until she is gone. Then we can all begin to breathe again. Live again. But until that is accomplished, what good is worrying over anything else?"

In the light provided by the moon and stars, I thought I could detect a sheen of tears in the woman's eyes. "Not even for me?" she asked softly.

Pain crossed the man's face. He turned away from her and shut his eyes. When he spoke again, the anger had gone out of his voice, but it was heavy with despair. "I'm sorry, Elfleda," he answered hoarsely. "But I cannot help it." There was a pause. "Perhaps it would be best for you to find another. Even if we triumph tomorrow, nothing can be as it was. Even between us."

"You don't know that. Only Abba knows what is to come. We cannot make such statements." She took his hand in one of hers and raised the other to his face, forcing him to look at her again. "I am willing to take the risk. I am not simple, Steffyn. I do know, and understand, that you cannot be who you were a year ago. But who among us can? Everyone constantly changes from who they were yesterday, last week, last month, last year. It is not something unique to yourself. But if you let yourself, I believe you can find a way to be truly happy again, and it will be a deeper happiness for the troubles you have overcome. Steffyn. Let the love of life back into your heart. Abba didn't make us for sorrow, but for joy. That is why the enemy chooses his weapons of fear, pain, and sorrow to conquer. It is why they are *her* weapons. But you belong to Abba. Let him fill your heart again with joy. It's there for the taking."

She looked at him earnestly, pleadingly. He looked back at her, an uncertain, tormented expression on his face. Tears seemed to be coming to his eyes. I felt certain that any moment he would relent and allow her in, allow her to comfort him from whatever it was that afflicted him.

But it did not happen. After several long moments of the two staring at each other, his eyes closed briefly. When they reopened, they had hardened, any sign of tears gone. He disentangled himself from her hands. Gently, but he pushed her away nonetheless. "I'm sorry, Elfleda," he said again. And I could hear the sorrow and deep pain in his tone. "But I simply can't." He turned and began to walk away.

Elfleda stayed where he left her, motionless, for several moments. Tears began streaming down her face, but they were silent. And when she spoke, though her voice was filled with pain, it was steady. Her eyes took on a faraway look I recognized. It was the look of a person about to give a prophecy. "Hear this one last thing at least, Steffyn," she said. He stopped, and turned back partly. "If you go into battle in this mindset, you will be vulnerable to the worst of Morrian's spells. No one will be able to help you, even if they try their hardest and give their all to do so. Yet, if you allow yourself to find the joy and love of life, and can once again soften yourself to the love of Abba, then all the effects will fall from you."

Steffyn's whole body posture tensed. "What do you mean by this?"

"I don't know." At this, Elfleda's voice broke. "I don't know. I only know that unless you allow your heart to change before you face her once more in the manner I just said, you will bring even more sorrow and hardship upon yourself. I See...I See a spell, a terrible, terrible curse..." She took a few steps toward him. "Steffyn, please-" But whatever she was about to say was lost, as he turned and walked away, never looking back.

16

A Candid Conversation

My dream faded to blackness. I opened my eyes slowly, trying to puzzle out what I had just Seen. My view of Morrian was alarming, but when considered candidly, it only made sense that any surviving wolves would report to her, and she would then learn of our direction. At least we knew she was sending more monsters after us. My glimpse of Lady Rhian was highly concerning, but it was my last dream that held my full attention. According to our history, Steffyn had been a great Brenwyd hero, staunchly supporting and upholding Nivea. And as a hero, he was brave, noble, and true, as well as an ardent follower of Abba. However, the man I had seen was one who seemed lost and tormented. And what of that prophecy Elfleda had given him? What spell had she been talking about? And now that I thought about it, why was it that Mathghamhain had given Steffyn no role in his narrative? Had he disliked him?

Suddenly my thoughts slowed. Mathghamhain's story. His moodiness. Steffyn's great conflicts. Elfleda's prophecy. *A terrible, terrible curse...* Surely what I was thinking could not be true...

I sat up and looked around. The fire had burned down to low coals. Lissa lay sleeping beside me. Above, the stars spread out across the sky, but from the color of the sky I thought it was near dawn. *Are you alright?* a voice asked in my head. It startled me. Not only because of its suddenness, but because of its familiarity.

I turned toward the coals. Sure enough, sitting by them as a great black shape was Mathghamhain. "I did not think you were sitting any watches tonight," I said quietly.

I saw the motion of his shrug. *I woke nearly an hour ago and observed the princess struggling to stay awake. I offered to relieve her, and she accepted. I do not need much sleep.*

"How are you feeling?" I asked, moving over to the fire. As I did so, I noticed he had replaced his cloak and hood on his body.

His head turned toward me. *Fine. You did a thorough job of healing. I do thank you. And I apologize once again for my less than gracious response earlier.*

I smiled. "Truth be told, I was rather expecting something of the kind. I believe I may have been disappointed else."

Do you have so little opinion of my manners, even now?

"I believe that you may suffer from something I do myself: speaking from emotion before fully thinking through a situation."

Hmm. Well, that is true enough, I suppose. But you still have not answered my question. Are you alright?

I sighed. "I am not sure I will be truly alright until this curse is broken. But as for the moment...I've had some dreams."

I thought so. Morrian?

"One of them. She knows we defeated the shadow wolves. Several survived to report to her. She knows our direction, and intends to send more scouts after us."

He tensed for a few moments, then relaxed again and sighed. *I suppose it was to be expected. I hoped that the fire would get them all, but it was a faint hope. Did she say what scouts she wants to send?*

"Elementals. Does that mean elemental dragons? Those are the ones who can control water, fire, air, and earth depending on the color of their scales, yes?"

He nodded. *Yes. They are a favorite of hers. Intelligent enough to do her bidding, feral enough to enjoy the destruction, and a natural counterforce to the leviathans.*

"Should we change our plan at all? We shall certainly have to move faster, though how I don't know."

He drummed his fingers on his leg. With his gloves in shreds and tatters, his hands were exposed for what they were. I glanced at them and then pointedly stared into the fire. *I...know not. Much of our success depends on the element of surprise...but we do have to face her. And for the sake of the kingdom, it must be before the month is out, and it is already half gone. I suppose we must go on. We shall have to discuss it with the prince and princess when they wake.* He sounded grimly determined.

I shot him a sideways glance. "Tell me. What is it you wish to gain from an encounter with Morrian?"

I sensed his surprise. *What makes you ask such a thing?*

"Well, she did curse you. Do you think that her death would free you?"

He made an annoyed sound like a growl in his throat. *I have long given up such a hope. There is some part of me that, yes, hopes that might be true, but I doubt it.*

"Why? It seems rather reasonable to me."

After two hundred and fifty years of attempts to break a curse, one learns not to trust much that such a thing can ever be done. His tone was dark.

I hesitated several moments before making my next statement. I would have to word it delicately. "Abba's timing is not ours, you know. I am sure He has a plan fully in place to repeal your curse. Or...perhaps one has been there all along, and you have simply refused to recognize it." I said the words in a bit of a carefree tone, as if just thinking of it, but had my senses tuned for any reaction from him.

He gave a surprised start. *What makes you say such a thing?* His tone was sharp, and vaguely suspicious. Oh, yes. I had definitely struck a nerve.

I turned to look at him levelly. "I'm not dense, Mathghamhain. I have noticed that when you speak of Abba, it is in a perfunctory way. I listened to your song. You seem to no longer view him as interested in you personally, when it is something Brenwyds are schooled in from infancy. I'm not saying that you have not – at least in worldly terms – a good reason for allowing such distance between yourself and Abba, but we Brenwyds are trained to expect hardship in this world and to trust Abba no matter what. You've ceased to do that. So it only made sense to me that you might be blind to whatever path he has laid to redeem you from this curse."

I felt his eyes on me. *You accuse me of not trusting Abba? What do you think this expedition is but a practice of trust in him?*

I shook my head. "Your words lack true conviction behind them. I believe that you are trusting Abba, as you say, to save the kingdom, for that is the greater good and something Abba would be concerned with. But as for you yourself, you have no trust, no faith, that Abba cares for you personally, and wants your good. You use your condition as a wall between you and him. Your thoughts are gloomy, downcast, depressed. If you truly had faith in Abba, no matter what the circumstances were, you would have a measure of his peace, of his joy, and you would never, never doubt his love." I paused, trying to gauge his reaction, but for all the response I could sense, I may as well have been talking to a boulder. I decided to add one last thing. "And I also believe that it would take more than simply the spell you suffer from to so harm your relationship with Abba. You admitted to knowing Morrian long ago. She imprisoned you in this fortress where we are going. What did she do to you there? Torture you?" Still he was silent, but at my last question he seemed to tense slightly.

A thought sprang to my mind, a horrible one, but I found myself asking it all the same. (I was not jesting when I said Mathghamhain was not the only one who spoke before thinking.) "Did she play with your mind?" With his mind-speaking ability, it seemed an all too likely possibility. I had heard stories of witches and wizards who encountered Brenwyds with mind-speaking abilities playing havoc with their minds and perceptions, making them see illusions as reality and the like. It was a nasty business. It could be done to non-mind-speakers as well, but mind-speakers were especially susceptible.

That seemed to hit the mark. Watching him, I was amazed (and horrified) to see him start to tremble. *Yes*, the answer came weakly to my mind. But the emotions accompanying it did not. The strength of his fear brought tears to my eyes. *Yes, she did. She made me see...terrible things. My worst fears. My most terrifying nightmares. The worst was, she made me think they were true. My friends dead. Myself alone in the world. Ostracized by those I knew.* A despairing humor rose behind the words. *I suppose those things came true enough, did they not?*

"Oh, Mathghamhain," I whispered. I moved over to him and took his furry hand in mine, squeezing it in compassion.

For some reason, however, the gesture made him upset, and he pulled his hand away. I frowned. *And this is why I never wanted to speak of it*, his voice growled in my mind. In that instant, my suspicions were confirmed. *I knew I would be smothered in pity.*

"Pity is not always a bad thing," I said.

I do not need it.

"We all need some pity from time to time," I retorted. "A compassionate ear, a shoulder to cry on. Only one blinded completely by foolish pride would make such a claim. Though I suppose I shouldn't expect you to accept pity from me, when you could not even do so from Elfleda."

At the name he went very, very still. Several heartbeats passed in silence. *How do you know that name?* he finally asked.

"I told you, I had a dream."

And what, exactly, did you See?

"I saw Morrian with the wolves. I saw Rhodri's mother and her guard fleeing from something on the Darlesian plains. And I saw a stubborn Brenwyd completely reject the offering of love from what seemed like a lovely girl because he would rather wallow in his own misery and pride than allow others in to help him heal." I stared at him.

And you assumed it was me?

"I know it was you...Steffyn."

He stared into the fire. Slowly, he raised his paw-hands as if examining them closely. Then he pushed his hood back and turned back toward me. I couldn't help catching my breath. The wrongness of such an appearance was nearly overwhelming. "I told you, I am Mathghamhain. Steffyn died a long time ago." This time, he spoke aloud.

"Oh, I'm not sure. Your personality seems not to have changed, from what I saw."

His pale grey eyes bored into me. "What you Saw...let me guess. The night before the battle?"

I shrugged. "I believe it was, though you would know better than me." I shifted, then asked in a quieter voice. "So, who was she? This Elfleda?" As I spoke the name, an uncomfortable feeling passed through me. I found, to my surprise, that I didn't like thinking about how this unknown girl had known Mathghamhain - Steffyn - so well. I found the feeling puzzling.

He turned from me and back to the fire, all the lines in his body sagging. "She was the best thing I had in my life. And, as you said, I pushed her away." He sighed, then continued in such a low voice I could barely make it out. "In the end, it was for the best."

"Were you...betrothed?"

"Not in so many words...but she and everyone else was certainly expecting it. For a long while, so did I." He stopped.

"Then Morrian happened?" I guessed. He turned back to me.

"You are very astute. And nosy."

I half-smiled. "Curiosity is a trait Brenwyds encourage." Then I turned serious again. "But you really are Steffyn...aren't you?"

A long pause. "I was."

"Why did you change your name?"

For a long time, I thought my question would go unanswered. In the east, the sky slowly lightened, signaling dawn's imminent approach. In truth, I was surprised he had answered so many of my questions already. "Do you know what Steffyn means?" he finally asked.

I frowned slightly as I thought. I knew the name was a variant of Stephen – an honored martyr from Abba's Word – but I had never heard a meaning given for it. "No."

"It means crown. My father gave me the name in the hope that it would always push me to be noble here on this earth, the best person I could be, so that I would be fully deserving of the crown I would receive when I reached Abba's paradise." He gave out a sharp sound then, one I took for humorless laughter. "If I did. How could I keep such a name when my very form reminded me each and every day how far I had fallen? Mathghamhain suited much better."

Now that I thought about it, I realized why that was so. "It means bear. How original." And how had I not picked up that hidden clue? I berated myself.

"I thought so."

"You truly think yourself beyond help and redemption."

"Two hundred and fifty years is a long time. I have fully reconciled myself to the fact that Abba has other priorities than one cursed Brenwyd." The words sounded wooden in my ears.

I shook my head. "No wonder your curse remains."

"And what does that mean?" He gave me a sharp look. "You are young. Not a child, as I so thoughtlessly accused earlier, but still very young. You cannot understand what it is like-"

"No, I can't," I said, my temper starting to flare. "I can't imagine what it is like to remain so long alone. What it is to be cursed. What horrors Morrian put you through. But I am old enough to know that Abba is personally invested in each and every one of our lives. And he always fulfills his promises. There are certainly enough stories to that effect in the Word, and many times the recipients of those promises waited for very long periods of time. Remember the story of Abram and his wife Sarai? God promised them a child, and he eventually gave them Isaac, but they were both very old before that happened. But they never lost faith. And so they were rewarded. Or what of Noah the ark builder? It took over a hundred years to build the ark, yet he still kept the faith. Tell me, isn't the length of your curse of your own doing? I heard the words Elfleda spoke to you, Steffyn. She said that this curse could be lifted, if you allowed the joy and love of Abba fully into your heart once again. Of course, at the time it wasn't clear what it meant, but surely you can see it now? There is hope, right in front of you. You have only to reach out and grasp it."

He stared at me, and his eyes grew veiled. He looked away, into the sky. "If such a thing were possible, I would." I opened my mouth again, but he forestalled me with a hand. "Aislinn, please. I know of what you speak. Her words have replayed in my mind every day for two hundred and fifty years. But it is too late. Perhaps, if I had turned back to her, my curse could have been averted. But I did not. Now the words taunt me, meaningless."

"They're not-"

"You truly think they still apply? I have tried, Aislinn. I have tried very much to make them come true. But I cannot."

I huffed. "Have you forgotten any lessons you received as a Brenwyd? We cannot force Abba's love at all, for we on our own do nothing to deserve it. It is so amazing because he offers it freely. And we have simply to open our hearts and take it. Is it really so difficult for you to surrender yourself to him again fully and truly?"

Steffyn made no answer. I heard noises indicating Lissa and Rhodri were beginning to stir. At the moment, I felt rather irritated with them for it. I wanted to talk with Steffyn until I could get him past all the stumbling blocks - his pride, pain, despair - that he had placed between himself and Abba's redemptive love. And I knew that he wouldn't cooperate with me at all with either of them awake. Steffyn noticed the noises as well. *Aislinn, please promise me this one thing,* he said finally, reverting to mind communication.

Why should I feel disposed to promise you anything? Inwardly I winced at how hard it sounded, but I was extremely upset with him and inclined to be peevish.

It is simple enough. Please do not tell the prince or princess who I truly am. I could not bear it. I am not the hero you say the stories make me.

I was inclined to make some sort of smarting retort, but I heard the earnestness, humbleness, in his voice as he made the request. And I also knew that a sharp tongue was not what he needed right now. And it was not of Abba. As my mother had often told me when my anger flared, harsh words never changed minds; loving ones did. So I subsided. *Very well.*

Thank you.

"Good morning," Lissa's sleepy voice came to us. "Mathghamhain, thank you so much for – oh!" She had focused on him, and his hood was still down. Now illuminated by the rising sun, I was struck anew by his imposing – and alarming – form. And I felt pity and understanding for him well up within me. For I did understand, I thought, at least a little, how after over two centuries of being stuck in such a form someone could conclude that Abba no longer truly cared for them. But that understanding did not mean I accepted his resignation and conclusion. Not at all. I determined to help him back to Abba, back to love – and hopefully, that would break his curse. *Abba, be with me and help me in this endeavor,* I prayed, and added with a mental sigh, *And help me keep my temper.*

"I am sorry for alarming you, Your Highness." Steffyn's voice jerked me back to the situation. He put a hand back to draw up his hood.

Lissa saw the motion as well. "Oh, please, do not draw your hood back up." Steffyn's hand stopped in surprise, and he blinked.

"I apologize for my reaction. But I wish to get used to your form, for it is you. And I can hardly do that if you continue to cover yourself from head to foot all the time."

Steffyn seemed truly taken aback by this request. "Are you certain?"

"Of course. Why would I not be?" She looked at him with her guileless blue eyes.

He bowed his head to her. "No one has ever asked such a thing of me before. I will do as you bid." At his words, a satisfied light entered Lissa's eyes.

"Good. Now that that's settled," Rhodri's voice said from the other side of the fire, "how about a bit of breakfast?" I started. I hadn't focused on the fact he had woken.

"That sounds like a good idea," Steffyn said. I glanced over to where Dynin was grazing. He had wandered a little bit away during the night, but was still well within sight. I sensed his deep contentment with the amount of grass available. I felt rather than saw Steffyn's eyes glance toward me and then away. "But I am afraid Aislinn has some bad news to share."

⁂

In the end, Rhodri and Lissa agreed with Steffyn's assessment that to move on was the only real choice we had. We were nearly to Helmond. We were committed to our course. Our best chance against elemental dragons would be to try to reach the leviathans first, and we prayed whatever protection from Abba that had shielded us from Morrian so far and had confused the shadow wolves on our trail would continue to hold. Hopefully Lissa and I could replenish our quivers from the port guards garrisoned at Helmond. Rhodri asked me if I could See anything more of his mother to determine her fate. I was, but what I Saw was not very enlightening. She and those with her were alive, but they were hiding in a cave that had an entrance covered by vines. Most everyone was sleeping with one person on watch, so there was not even any conversation going on that could help me understand what was happening. Still, to know they had escaped whatever was chasing them was reassuring. I briefly tried to contact through Sight the Brenwyds sleeping in her party, but though I definitely thought that this time I could sense the barrier weakening, I still couldn't get through. I decided to make a more concentrated attempt when we stopped for the night. If I could concentrate on it for a longer period, I thought I just might be able to make contact next time.

So, we set out. Though Steffyn said that we would reach Helmond today, there was still a long trek ahead. I suppressed a sigh as I trudged along, wishing Steffyn were smaller so he could ride Dynin. Then we would have no problem in reaching Helmond without being tracked down. But I wasn't about to suggest Dynin even try it at the moment. He was giving Steffyn a wide berth after last night. Last night. Was it really only last night that the shadow wolves attacked and Mathg – Steffyn – told us his story? It felt like longer.

I looked up and latched my eyes on Steffyn leading the way, a bit of a distance from where I walked with Dynin in the rear. I really felt quite irritated with him for his stubbornness. The way to break his curse had been told to him even before it struck, and yet, two hundred and fifty years later, he still refused to acknowledge it. "Men," I muttered under my breath. "Abba, why are they so stubborn? Why do they feel like they have to be so self-sufficient? It's perfectly fine to ask for help. But no, they must do everything themselves. Humph." I frowned slightly as I considered that and glanced upward. "But I suppose that's why all people do anything. We feel like we have to do everything, earn everything for ourselves." I sighed and looked downward once again. "But why is it men seem to feel that so much more?"

Why are you talking to yourself? Dynin asked me, a curious glint in his eye.

"Oh, no reason, really. Just fuming. Don't pay any attention to me."

Did he vex you?

I didn't have to ask who "he" was. "Yes, yes he did. Very much so."

How?

"He refuses to see what's right in front of him! Does that make any sense, I ask you?"

Dynin seemed to think this over for a few minutes. *No. But I have noticed most humans seem to do it. Why does it upset you coming from him?*

"Because no one deserves to live the rest of their life with such a horrible curse."

You mean there is a way to break it he refuses to consider?

"Exactly."

I see why you are upset.

"Thank you!"

But I also do not see how muttering to yourself about your frustration will help him. Should you not talk to him about it? Dynin could be infallibly logical sometimes.

I sighed. "I tried. This morning. Didn't you hear us?"

I was not paying attention. I was eating.

"Ah, of course. Well, I plan to try again soon. Mark my words, I intend to make him see it if I have to pound his head with a stone to do so."

How would that help? Would not it give him a headache and knock him unconscious? Dynin sounded genuinely baffled. Horses don't have much use for metaphors.

"It's a mere way of speaking, Dy, that means...well, I'll do whatever it takes to get him to acknowledge how to break his curse."

Then why not just say that?

I couldn't help it. I laughed, loud and clear. The others turned to look at me with inquiring gazes. I waved them off. "Talking with Dynin."

"If he made you laugh, I wouldn't mind talking with him," Rhodri muttered. "I can feel my sense of humor wasting away, given current events."

"Some people might call that a good thing, Rhodri," I said, straight-faced. Indeed, some of the older nobles and courtiers had been known to grumble about the jesting ways of Darlesia's youngest prince, saying that such an individual couldn't handle the serious responsibilities of running a kingdom.

"What? They obviously didn't grow up with five older siblings. A sense of humor was a necessity for survival."

Lissa took his hand and squeezed it, smiling slightly. "Indeed. I do not think I would have agreed to marry you else." He smiled back at her.

From his position at the front, Steffyn harrumphed. "Yes, all good and well, but if we are done discussing humor, might we press on? We have even more need of haste since Morrian has been alerted to our direction, and I believe that jokes and jests will be best appreciated after we have defeated her."

I frowned at him. "Don't you see? It is this mindset that still entraps you. On the contrary, now more than ever is the time for light-heartedness and joy, for doesn't it say in the book of Nehemiah that the joy of the Lord is ever our strength? Perhaps we should approach Morrian boldly singing the hymns and psalms of joy praising Abba, for doesn't the Word say such things cause the forces of darkness to tremble in fear? Joy and love are powerful weapons not to be dismissed or taken lightly."

He outright growled deep in his throat, then turned and began walking away abruptly, mumbling to himself. I could still make him out, and I wondered if he meant me to. "Women. Two hundred and fifty years and still they persist in badgering me."

"It's only because you need to be badgered! It's for your good!" I called after him. He deigned to ignore that, but strode even more rapidly away.

I scowled at his back. "Argh! Stubborn, prideful, arrogant, blind-!"

"Did I miss something?" Rhodri asked, a look of confusion on his face. "I was just trying to lighten the mood a little, not open the way to a deep philosophical point."

I transferred my scowl to Rhodri. "It's nothing to do with you. It's everything to do with him!" I pointed with exasperation toward Steffyn. Remembering my promise, I said nothing more, but began to follow after Steffyn's shrinking form, passing Rhodri and Lissa.

I heard Rhodri say, "Aislinn, wait, what–?"

But Lissa cut him off. "Rhodri, I would not worry about it, were I you. I believe it is a continuation of a discussion they were having when we woke."

"But what was–?"

"Rhodri." I didn't turn to look, but I imagined Lissa placing her hand on his arm in that gentle way of hers and smiling at him. Her voice lowered as if she didn't want me to overhear, but I could still hear her. "I think it is something they have to work out between themselves. Personally."

A few seconds of silence passed. "I still don't understand," I heard Rhodri say. "But you do have a better understanding of people than I do, and so I would be a fool to ignore your judgment."

At that, I stopped and whirled around. Lissa was in the middle of placing a light kiss on Rhodri's cheek, but I took no heed of that. "See? See? You understand that listening to others and following and believing what they say is sometimes the better course of wisdom. Why can't he?" I flung my arm behind me, gesturing toward Mathghamhain, then turned back around and continued walking, now throwing my hands up into the air. "Why? Why can't he see?" I paused, thinking. "Although, I suppose that if he's been thinking that way for two hundred and fifty years, I can't expect to change it in a single conversation. Oh, Abba, please work on his heart and soften it back to you." I thought for a moment, and then said grudgingly, "And help me approach him from the perspective of your love, because I know yelling and growing upset, no matter how warranted, won't help much at all."

HELMOND

*L*issa and Rhodri watched Aislinn storming up the path after Mathghamhain for a few minutes. With the flatness of the plateaus, there was no real danger of losing sight of either her or their guide. Rhodri stared after his Brenwyd friend with brow knitted in puzzlement. "Well, that was odd. I've never seen her act quite like that before. Is it something that happened while I was away?"

Lissa turned to him then with a knowing, secretive smile curving her lips. "You truly do not understand what it is, do you?"

Rhodri frowned. "What are you talking about?"

She laughed gently. He loved her laugh, the way her mouth parted and partially revealed her teeth, the way her eyes sparkled. He was so focused on taking her in that he nearly missed her words. "Aislinn is falling in love with Mathghamhain, of course. And unless I miss my guess, he feels rather attracted to her as well."

For a moment Rhodri thought he had misheard her. "Aislinn? Falling in love? With Mathghamhain? You must be joking."

"Why? It is a perfectly natural thing. She is the age for it. I was younger when I fell in love with you."

"Yes, but...she's Aislinn. She's never shown any serious interest in love or marriage." Indeed, the idea seemed almost unfathomable to Rhodri. While Lissa had captured his heart,

Aislinn had been like a little sister, always ready for an adventure, always laughing off romance, even as she grew older and began to attract admirers. She brushed them all off – tactfully and kindly, but she had dissuaded them all the same. Then again, he had been away for six months. Had her views begun to change? Lissa's words pulled him from his musings.

"No. But that has no bearing on it. I believe that Mathghamhain, precisely because of his rough manners and melancholy, has gotten himself into her heart. And I also have the feeling that she does not know it yet."

"How, exactly?"

"Because she still has enough perspective to be irritated with him. If she realized that her heart was warming toward him in love, she would be much more aloof from him, more awkward. Surely you remember how you felt around me before you worked up the courage to tell me you loved me?" Indeed, he did. He always felt completely guarded and awkward in her presence, constrained to hide his feelings from her if he wished to preserve their friendship. How relieved he had been the day he finally told her and then she'd told him she felt the same way. It had been the most freeing feeling he'd ever felt.

"Yes...I suppose I see your point. But after all, they've only just met. And there's the whole...curse issue."

Lissa nodded, sighing. "True. That is a problem. But there must be some way to break it, and I am sure Aislinn will find it. And I would say that being quickly thrown into life-and-death situations with a person leads to one getting to know them much more quickly than one usually would."

"Hmm. I would say that's reasonable." Rhodri smiled at her. "How did I ever end up with such a wise fiancée?"

She laughed again. "Wise? No. I simply know how to observe people. Anything else is a gift from Abba." She was utterly enchanting. As he leaned in to plant a kiss on her lips, he thanked Abba profusely for blessing him with such a woman.

However, the two were interrupted when Dynin suddenly snorted from behind them. *Excuse me*, he said in a humble tone. *I hate to interrupt, but we are being left behind. Ought we not to catch up?*

Lissa had jumped at the sound, placing a hand over her heart. "Oh. Yes. Quite right, Dynin. Come on, Rhodri."

"Yes, Liss. But just one more moment." He kissed her. Not for as long as he would have liked, but he was determined to get it in. He had gone without for far too long. "There. Now we can go."

Her blue eyes flashed like sapphires. "I do love you, Prince Rhodri."

"And I love you, Princess Calissa." At Dynin's impatient stamp of a forefoot, he took her arm and began hastening forward. "Now let's go, before this horse decides to trample us for being in his way."

⚜

The rest of that day was one long plod. In the mountains, at least the terrain varied so our minds were occupied with picking our way so as not to tumble down the mountainside. But on the plateaus and plains, instances where such care was needed came more rarely, and left the mind far too free to stew over unpleasant matters. I cannot speak for the others, but my mind alternated back and forth between worrying over how quickly we could reach the leviathans and avoid detection from the elemental dragons, and the whole problem of Steffyn. While I abided by his request and referred to him as Mathghamhain verbally, in my head I determined to call him by his true name. I also made sure to keep a strong guard about my thoughts, so that no whisper of them reached him. Fortunately, I'd had a lot of practice doing so, as Aiden was a mind speaker.

Clearly, Steffyn had to come to a place where he would abandon his stubborn pride. While he might not see himself as prideful, I believed that walls of pride and hurt were built up around his heart, built strong from his centuries of loneliness, belief that Abba didn't really care for him anymore, and belief that he could care for himself just fine. But I also believed that the root of the problem was whatever tortures Morrian had put him through all those years ago. And to be able to come to terms with what had happened to him and allow the healing process to begin, he had to talk about them. Therein lay the tricky part. If he could not even bring himself to tell his almost-betrothed the memories that haunted him, what chance did I have, who had only met him a little over a fortnight ago? *Abba, guide me*, I prayed. *Let your healing love show through me. Lead me to treat him as I must so that he comes back to your love again. Abba, he cannot go before Morrian again with this mindset still in control of him. He will surely fare worse. Your Holy Word tells us to constantly lift up our prayers to you and that you always hear us. I am lifting Steffyn to you, Abba God; fight against those self-made demons that hold him captive. Remove the planks from his eyes that block his vision. Let his curse fall.*

I had never spent so long at one time on prayer in my life. Yes, I prayed, but in little bits throughout the day, praising Abba when things fell into place, requesting things of him as my mind thought of it. But this was different. For many hours that day, I pleaded with Abba to break down Steffyn's walls. I beseeched him for protection against the force we were journeying to battle against. I recited verses from the Holy Word that I had memorized, verses of battle and power, of praise and victories, of promises and comfort. I knew how important such things were, and I realized that I – we all– had been neglecting to pray as we ought for what we were doing. Morrian received her great power directly from the Shadow Angel, the nemesis of Abba himself. If we had any hope of winning against her, we had to be cloaked in Abba's protection and clothed in his promises. My father had taught me that prayer was one of the most important weapons we had at our disposal when we went up against forces of evil, for prayer was our direct access to

Abba, and he was our only true hope of victory. I resolved to pray as much as possible the rest of the way to Morrian's fortress, and to alert the others to pray as well – including, and especially, Steffyn.

Midway through the afternoon, I was roused from my prayers and thoughts by a change in the air. The wind, which had been blowing gently from the southeast, began to pick up and shifted to blow from due east. It carried with it the tang of salt that signaled our approach to the coast. It gave me fresh energy, for it meant we were approaching Helmond, and shelter. Here on the plains, if the elemental dragons found us, we had no cover and precious little chance against them. In Helmond, we had the covering of buildings and the scent of other people and animals to hide ours.

Sure enough, within two more hours, I could see the outer wall of the small port city standing firm against the line of the horizon. We were still some distance from it, but the sight heartened me. "It's not much farther now," I said to encourage Lissa beside me. She had endured our hard march valiantly and without complaint, but of the four of us she was the one least accustomed to such continuous exercise.

She raised her eyes to where I pointed in the distance and squinted. "You can see it?"

"I can. We must be within an hour of the gates."

"Good." I called ahead to Rhodri, who was keeping pace with Steffyn, to let him know what I saw. He called back acknowledgment. Steffyn simply nodded his head and didn't even take a moment to slow at the news. Then again, he had likely seen the city outline before I had. I frowned at his back. He had been keeping a wide berth from me all day. "What is it that so consumes your thoughts?" Lissa's quiet voice broke in on my thoughts.

I met her tired eyes. "Hmm?"

"Aislinn, you have barely said two words to anyone all day, except when you shouted at Mathghamhain. It is clear something is bothering you."

"Isn't something bothering all of us?" I asked. She was not dissuaded.

"Of course, but that has not stopped you from being talkative before. Something new has come to your mind, something you have learned, and it worries you even more than Morrian, it would seem. I understand if you wish to continue keeping your feelings for Mathghamhain to yourself for the time being, but if you wish to talk, I am here. Was it hearing his story? Has it complicated things for you?"

I frowned at her, confused as to her meaning. "Feelings? You mean of frustration and fear?"

At that, she frowned. "Fear? Why would you fear him?"

"No, I don't fear *him*, Lissa, I fear *for* him. The man is proposing to go up against a powerful sorceress while refusing the protection of Abba over him! It could be disastrous!" The words came out a bit more heatedly than I intended.

For several seconds Lissa seemed nonplussed. "He's what?" Clearly that was not what she had expected me to say. The idea came to me at that moment that Lissa would be the perfect person to include in my efforts to bring Steffyn back to acknowledging Abba's love. Unlike me, she never (or at least, rarely) lost her temper with people when talking with them, and could manage to say the most critical things with words of kindness. It was part of why her father said she would make a good queen; when she made criticisms, the people she was talking to would never dream of taking offense because she said them in such a gentle yet firm manner.

I repeated myself, adding, "I tried to talk to him about it this morning, but he simply won't hear of it. He's convinced that Abba no longer cares for him."

Her eyes widened. "Oh, Aislinn, I am so sorry. I know he has a vein of cynicism running through him uncommon in most Brenwyds, but I never dreamed it went that far."

"Who would?" I stared off toward Helmond and unconsciously quickened my step. "And it scares me for what it might mean for him when we face Morrian. I know we will; when she senses the anchor being destroyed, she will come for us, and we must be ready. But if St-Mathghamhain keeps in this mindset...it can only end badly for him."

"And that would grieve you."

"Of course! He...he...he's simply being so stubborn! He doesn't seem to care, much, about his life." I stopped and swallowed at the sudden tightness that came to my throat. "You should speak with him. You put things more gently than I do. He would listen to you."

"If he is not listening to you, I do not think there is anything I could say that would help him."

I spun to her, surprised by the statement. "What do you mean? You excel in the art of gentle persuasion. And he respects you. Why shouldn't he listen to you?"

Lissa arched an eyebrow. "I am not the one he is attracted to."

I stared at her, and I remembered her words from the last night we had spent in Steffyn's valley. "Oh, Liss, you don't really still believe that he...that I...well, that we have those sorts of feelings for each other? I rather think I would know." I set my gaze determinedly forward, hoping the embarrassed heat I felt rising in my face wouldn't show as an obvious flush on my pale skin.

"On the contrary, I think sometimes we are the last to know our own feelings. Tell me this: have you seriously considered the question for yourself?"

"Of course not. It's silly, and the last thing I need to be thinking about for the moment. For Abba's sake, Lissa, love and courtship are not exactly important things right now. How can you persist in trying to see a relationship?" The words came out sharper than I intended, and I could tell from the silence that Lissa had been hurt. I winced. "I'm sorry, Liss, I didn't mean it like that."

I heard her take a breath that sounded suspiciously like a suppressed sob. "I know, Aislinn, but it hurts, all the same. I am not...I am not brave like you, you know. I will always act in the best interests of my kingdom and my people, but I have been trained to pursue those ends through diplomacy and negotiation, not direct action and fighting. I am scared, Aislinn. I am scared that in this crucial endeavor, I will fail Ecclesia. I know fighting and strategy, but I more trained in their theory than their execution. I cannot imagine being in your place right now, knowing that you have to go against Morrian directly after what happened last time. Aislinn, I am so scared for you. I am afraid that at any moment, when something goes wrong, I will become nothing more than a helpless pile of skirts and become even more of a burden than I already am, and that because of my inexperience we will fail. So...perhaps you are right, I am making too much of something that could just barely be there, but at least that something is familiar." She made a choking sound, and when I dared to look over at her, tears flowed freely down her cheeks.

"Oh, Liss..."

She held up a hand, forestalling my comment. "No, do not. I am sorry. This is not making you feel better-"

I ignored her upheld hand and gathered her into a tight embrace. After resisting for a moment, she relaxed against my shoulder as she cried. "Lissa, Lissa. Don't you dare keep on feeling inadequate for this. At least, if you do, know that I am scared, too. I'm rather terrified, actually, whenever I think directly about the prospect. I have actually been admiring you, in how you've been able to keep a brave face and rise to the challenge. Why, if someone had told me a month ago you would stand against a pack of shadow wolves and fight them off, I would have told them to go see a healer for mind fever. But you did, even though you were scared. Don't you see, Liss? That is your strength, and it's an incredible strength, and you are in no way a burden. I'm sorry for my harsh words; it's only

I'm so...I'm so upset with Mathghamhain, and I took it out on you, and that's not fair to you. Not at all."

"You've admired me?"

"Of course. How many people do you know who could face down a pack of wolves in a court dress without a scratch?"

She laughed, a little hiccup of a laugh, but it was a laugh. "This is hardly a court dress at this point. You may as well give me an extra pair of breeches to wear."

"Court dress makes a better story." I released her and looked her in the eye. Her tears were slowing. "I am sorry, Liss. If it really helps you feel better to...imagine something between Mathghamhain and me, then imagine away. I won't stop you. Just please don't be too upset if I do not contribute much to your theory."

Lissa began swiping at her cheeks to clear away the tear tracks. "I suppose that is the best concession I will get from you, so I will accept." Her hand found its way to a pocket in her skirt and produced a handkerchief, which she used to finish wiping her face. "You are sure I am no burden?"

"Absolutely not. Could you imagine Princess Etain enduring this journey as well as you have? She would have fainted before we even left Kheprah." I could tell Lissa struggled not to laugh at the comparison. In truth, the Walesian princess was a very nice person, but she had an incredibly nervous personality. That, plus the fact she had been completely coddled by her mother as the only girl in a family of seven boys, resulted in Etain often falling into a swoon when frightened or overwrought.

"Aislinn, you should not say such things. Etain is a good girl." Lissa was trying to sound prim and proper.

"I never said she wasn't. I only said that I can't imagine her enduring this journey as well as you."

"Well...thank you."

"You're welcome. Now, I don't want to hear any more nonsense about you being a burden or not a valuable member of this expedition. Contacting the leviathans was your idea, remember? We need you. You are certainly the smartest person amongst us."

"That is probably true," she admitted, straight-faced.

I looked at her in mock outrage. "You didn't have to agree so quickly, you know."

A small smile curved her lips. "I know."

He is coming. Dynin's voice entered my head. I looked ahead of us. Dynin had discreetly moved ahead of us to shield us somewhat from the gaze of the two men in front. Now, his warning told us that Rhodri and Steffyn had halted, and Rhodri was walking toward us.

When I met his gaze, he stopped. "Is everything alright?" he called, his worried gaze looking from me to Lissa, who had developed a sudden interest in smoothing her rumpled skirts as best she could.

I nodded. "Fine. Just women's talk."

"Oh." Having been raised with sisters, Rhodri knew when men's presence was unwanted. "Alright. If you're sure everything's fine."

"It is now."

He nodded. "Alright. Mathghamhain says we should be to Helmond within half an hour. We'll stay there for the night and start our sea voyage in the morning."

"Very well." After giving Lissa one last concerned look, he turned around to where Steffyn was waiting. I trained my eyes on his large, dark figure. He was looking toward us, and I met his eyes. I couldn't read the expression in them, and after a moment, he turned away and continued walking. I frowned. He couldn't keep walking away from me forever. I would try to talk to him again tonight, when Lissa and Rhodri were asleep. Somehow, some way, he had to come back to Abba.

❧ 🕸 ☙

Our arrival in Helmond, while encouraging in that it meant we could start on the next stage of our journey, ended up depressing our spirits. Of course, like the rest of the country, the people and animals of Helmond were asleep. Since the rest of our travels had been in places where there were no people, it was easier to bear the knowledge that not one of our countrymen was able to help us. With the knowledge thrust directly back into our faces, however, even Rhodri's jovial spirit was subdued.

As we passed through the gate and came upon the first of the sleepers, Steffyn paused and crouched down next to the oblivious guardsmen. "I never imagined the sleeping curse could be so powerful," he murmured. "She must have been just developing it when she used it on Nivea."

I sighed as I looked down the street. Helmond was tiny, only having a few dozen permanent families within its limits. Since it was the first port that ships sailing from Lamasia could anchor in, though, in the spring and summer months the population swelled to a little over two hundred depending on which traders and hunters were passing through. From the number of people in the street, it seemed that the seasonal hunters and trappers had begun to make their way into town to sell their winter loot to the trading ships for the start of the trading season. "We will have to move these people out of the way for Dynin. And I think we should check through the houses and be sure everyone is as comfortable as possible."

"Good idea," Lissa said. "We can at least do that for them." The task took us until dark had fully fallen. In the midst of it, Steffyn slipped down to the port to survey the available ships in the harbor. Most of the vessels native to Helmond were small fishing boats, but fortunately for our purposes, there were several deep-sea vessels in port as well. Most of the large trading ships from Lamasia anchored in a little farther south, in the city of Damyr, but there were always some smaller traders that stopped in Helmond first.

We set up camp for the night in one of the inns near the harbor. Despite its meager population, Helmond had a good number of inns and boardinghouses for sailors, trappers, hunters, and traders. I made Dynin comfortable in the stable out back, and he eagerly dug into the fresh hay. It was nice to have a real roof over our heads and real beds to sleep in again. Still, wanting to be cautious, we set up a watch rotation, and put the fire out once we had cooked dinner. Before any of us slept, however, I insisted on a group prayer. Lissa and Rhodri gladly agreed. Steffyn merely stayed silent as we praised Abba for his protection thus far, and prayed for it to continue. When I sang a few measures of the Creation song to refresh all our spirits, however, I sensed a response from him, a deep yearning to feel included in our worship. It quickly passed and I had no other thought but to curl up in my blanket and get some sleep before my next verbal battle with him.

Unfortunately, when Steffyn woke me, I felt that I hadn't gotten near enough. Still, it would suffice for now. *There is nothing to report,* he told me crisply through his mind speaking. After shaking me awake, he was quick to leave the room Lissa and I had chosen for ourselves and reenter the hall. I rolled out of my blanket and chased after him. "Wait," I said softly. "May we talk?"

He paused, his back to me. "Of what?"

"Can you not guess?"

"I've told you," he answered, a growl spicing his voice, "I've no wish to speak of it."

Abba, give me wisdom. "Alright. What do you want to talk about?"

The question seemed to surprise him, for he turned back to me. "You said *you* wished to talk."

"And I do. But you don't wish to talk about what I wish to. So, what do you wish to talk about?" Silence. "Steffyn-"

"Do not call me that," he snapped. Then, as an afterthought. "Please."

"Why?"

"Because I am not that person anymore. I told you that this morning."

"Would you like to be that person again?"

That question also seemed to surprise him. "Why ask that?"

"Curious."

He was silent for another few minutes. I had nearly decided he was going to end the conversation and continue to the room he and Rhodri were sharing when he did speak, and what he said was not what I was expecting. In a voice laden with sadness, he said, "What I would like to be has no bearing. I cannot be that person again, so there is no point in supposing I could be."

I remembered from my dream how he and Elfleda had discussed this very point, and it had not gone well. I changed tactics. "Very well, then, who would you like to be?"

He started, again surprised, and eyed me closely. "Why would you want to know?"

I smiled. "Curiosity again, I fear. Please. Tell me. Surely you have some idea."

"You think I am not happy with who I am now?"

"Your temperament certainly suggests otherwise."

His eyes flashed. "You have no idea what it is to be trapped in a form not your own."

I nodded thoughtfully. "You're right, I don't. But should that not spur you to be the best you can be, to belie your appearance?"

He shrugged. He seemed to resign himself to talking, because he followed me downstairs to the inn common room, where we had agreed to set the watch. "I've found one does not worry about that when one is alone most of the time."

"But?"

"But what?" He raised his silvery eyes to mine. Again, I was aware of a nagging familiarity about them. Somewhere, somehow, I had seen eyes very like that before I had seen him, and not just from seeing his human self in my dreams. But where? "Aislinn, why are you pushing me so hard? Can you not just leave me alone, and focus on Morrian? She is the danger. She must be stopped."

"I know." I lowered my gaze to the fire. "It will take Abba's strength to defeat her. You know that."

After a moment, he answered in a low voice. "I know. That is what you are for."

I moved so that I sat next to him. "Steffyn, if you harbor doubts about Abba and how he cares for you, it *will* affect our battle. Such a thing could be just what Morrian exploits to her advantage. Something my father always stressed in my lessons is that when a Brenwyd goes into battle against a magic user, he or she must have complete confidence in Abba's protection. Even an ounce of doubt works to weaken our voices and gives our Enemy a weakness to exploit."

"I know," he growled out. I could feel his tension. "You need not repeat these lessons to me. I learned them well. But you need not worry. I have faced her before. I know what I go up against. I can look after myself." His tone grew very defensive. "You just worry about destroying the anchor and countering any defensive spells Morrian has around it. You can use your sword for much of that; you could use the same strategy as the girl we saw in the pool with Seren. Then focus on getting out before she comes back."

I fought to keep my voice gentle. "And where is Abba in all of that?"

"There, of course. In the background, where he always is."

I sighed. "No, Steffyn. He must be in the foreground. For in truth this is not a battle between us and Morrian; it is simply one more battle between good and evil, Abba and the Shadow Angel. We're just vessels. We can't succeed without accepting his help and protection, especially if Morrian truly is trying to open the Demon's Gate. You need to open yourself back up to him."

He turned on me sharply. I was taken aback by the suddenness of the movement and the whiteness of his teeth against the darkness of the rest of him. "Do not continue pressing me in this, Aislinn," he growled. "I do not want to grow angry."

I raised my eyebrows. In truth, the fact he was growing upset was a good sign; it meant he was hearing me and that, deep down, perhaps so far down he didn't even realize it, my words were having an impact. "Why does it make you so angry?" He got up from the bench and began walking toward the stairs. I jumped up to follow him. "Steffyn, look. I am sorry that I yelled at you earlier this morning. That was wrong of me. But I am not sorry about confronting you about this doubt, these beliefs you harbor. They've harmed you greatly already the last time you battled Morrian; can't you see it is out of concern for you that I press you now?"

Without turning back, he said, so low I could barely hear him, "You need not concern yourself. Who are you to do so?"

Finally, my temper flared. I had been tamping it down, praying to Abba to help me control it because I knew harsh words would be no help, but Steffyn had a way of getting under my skin I had never encountered before. I stopped abruptly. "Alright then. Have it your way. Stay in your bubble of self-pity and angry pride. See how that helps you break your curse. I'm standing watch."

I could hear the hurt in my voice, and I marched away to a window, surprised by the tears that began cascading down my cheeks. In truth, though, it was a good question. Why did I care so deeply? I honestly barely knew him. I had only met him about a fortnight before. But had I really? Part of me wondered. Somehow it felt like I had known him for a long time. No wonder Lissa thought there was something between us. *Abba, help me*, I cried silently. *I don't know what to do. I don't know what to say. He's clearly not listening to me; I'm afraid for him, Father, so afraid. In the Holy Word of the Acts it tells of how you knocked your apostle Paul off his horse to get his attention. Could you do something similar here?*

Aislinn? Steffyn's voice came hesitantly into my mind. I stiffened and resolutely blocked my emotions. I heard him cross back towards me. *Are you...are you crying?*

Why would you care? I thought back hotly.

I'm sorry. He did sound very ashamed. *Forgive me. It was wrong of me. It has been a long time since...since I knew anybody well enough for them to be concerned for me. I suppose I have been in a bubble.*

Oh, really? I thought with a heavy dose of sarcasm.

I...I will think on what you said. Truly, I will. Just please...do not push me so hard. You can be...very intense.

I had a feeling that was the best response I could hope for. *Very well.*

And I am sorry. Again. I sensed his mental sigh. I heard him moving around the room. It sounded like he was rummaging around for something. *I do not think I have ever apologized to any one person more than I have to you. Apparently, I have a talent for offending you.* He sounded very abashed.

That actually cheered me up and made me giggle weakly, looking over my shoulder at him. *Do not worry about it. I wish everyone who offended me was so profuse in apology. It would make life much more pleasant.*

That many people offend you?

Annoy would be a better term, I think. But I do wish they apologized as you do.

Is that a compliment? He sounded somewhat bemused.

If you like.

Very well. He walked over to me and held out a hand. A square of white cloth lay in it, looking absurdly small in his large palm.

A handkerchief? Where did you find that?

I think it is really a napkin, but it should serve the purpose. I am not so completely lacking in manners, you know. I simply need...reminders.

Ah. Thank you. I took the handkerchief and wiped my face, feeling touched by his gesture, but also a bit silly from my behavior. I was not a crier. Then again, neither was Lissa, usually. Maybe it was just a symptom of the strain we were under. Men grew gruff and taciturn, women cried.

You're welcome. He turned toward the stairs again. *Good night, Aislinn.*

Good night, Steffyn. May Abba grant you pleasant dreams. It was a common saying among Brenwyds. He didn't answer that.

My watch was outwardly peaceful, though my mind was in turmoil. I knew, with a deep sense of knowing, that Steffyn could not go against Morrian this way and win. If he refused to change his mind and allow Abba back in, I would be better off facing Morrian alone. In the plan we had made, the idea was to leave the fortress after destroying the rose and before Morrian could return, using Dynin to escape. But something told me that was mere wishful thinking. Especially since...Steffyn could not ride Dynin. I stiffened at the realization. I should have seen it days ago, when Dynin had said so in the first place, but I had missed it. I doubted Steffyn had. Had he intentionally stayed quiet, intending to face her? In his spiritual state? I wondered if he truly had a death wish. My breath hitched at the thought, and I twisted the napkin tightly in my hands. No. I wouldn't allow it. He had suffered enough at Morrian's hands; I wouldn't let him meet death at them, too. And yet, I needed his help against her. He knew the traps she would try to spring, the pitfalls she would use. But could I fully trust him by my side without him trusting Abba? Morrian had certainly shaped her curse on him well.

Morrian...my thoughts paused on her. Before two weeks ago she had merely been a name from history lessons – no, not even that – yet she had changed everything. The morning of the day before Lissa's birthday, the world had seemed a bright, secure place (despite the mystery of Rhodri's disappearance) and I looked forward to a peaceful future. Mere hours later that belief had been shattered. As I considered events, I found it curious that I knew so little about Morrian, really. I knew she had been queen, that she came from Lamasia. I knew she was a powerful sorceress. But what had truly driven her to such lengths? How had her spirit been so corrupted that she sought to enslave a kingdom, a continent, in service to her dark master? Steffyn had said that her hatred toward Brenwyds had begun as jealousy when her father married a Brenwyd woman. I supposed I could – in a way – understand that. Children do not like to think of their mothers as replaceable, and do not always understand that a parent remarrying has no reflection on their love for their former spouse. Steffyn had also said that, even as a child, Morrian had possessed a domineering personality. But what had driven her to the brink? What had so driven her away from love?

As I pondered these things, I began really wondering how Steffyn knew so much about her. Yes, he had said he'd lived in the same village she had, but so much of his knowledge seemed to be on a much more personal basis than merely that of a younger child being aware of an older one. Of course, when he had fought against her all those years ago, he had probably done as I was now doing, thinking through his knowledge of her to try and find a reason for her actions. Yet something nagged at me, deep within, that there was something I was missing. Somehow, Steffyn had been connected to Morrian in a significant way...but how? Try as I might, no answer came to me.

The only thing I could think of was the theory Lissa, Rhodri, and I had already come up with, that he had been close with her half-brother, who had been killed in that final battle. They had both been imprisoned in Morrian's prisons. He had likely shared with Steffyn some of his half-sister's history. I felt a wave of pity for the man who had lived so long ago. To be imprisoned by your own sibling...I could not imagine it. Despite the age gap between us, Aiden and I were close, and I loved him fiercely. Dear, sweet

Aiden...I began to tear up again at the thought. I had resolutely not thought of my family often since the curse had struck. It was simply too painful. If we failed, they would wake with their abilities gone, and the realm would come under attack by whatever forces Morrian called on. More to the point, if we failed, I had a feeling Morrian would kill me before I saw any of my family again. Mother. Father. *Oh, Abba, please let me see them again.* I began to cry again.

This time, I received comfort. An unusual, all-consuming peace blossomed in my soul and spread throughout my body like a comforting wave of heat. My sorrow was still there, but it was assuaged by the knowledge that Abba grieved with me. I plunged my mind into Creation's song around me. Despite the discordant strains of the curse starting to taint it, the heart of it rang out in my mind pure and clear, bolstering my spirit. Again, I remembered, 'Have not I commanded you? Be strong and courageous; do not be afraid or discouraged: for the LORD your God is with you wherever you go.' I reached out and clung to the words, repeating them over and over in my mind, mentally grasping them as if my very survival depended on them. And well it might. *Thank you, Abba.* My mind calmed. I had my assurance. I would not be abandoned. I would not be forgotten. Abba would protect me. I turned my eyes upward, toward the room on the second floor where I knew Steffyn lay. Before we reached Morrian, I had to convince him of the truth of those phrases. *Abba, give me strength and wisdom in this matter, for it will not be easy.*

*B*REAKTHROUGH

My prayers took up most of my watch. The only outside inter-ruption I noted during this time was about an hour and a half in, when my ears detected a faint sound from outside. I tensed, care-fully opening the window to try and hear better. The noise was at the limit of even my hearing, but given the absolute silence of my surroundings there was no doubt it was there. It sounded like, as best I could tell, someone taking a piece of parchment and beating it up and down against the air or...very large birds' wings. My heart started pounding as I wondered if elemental dragons were about to descend on us. After a few minutes, though, the noise faded away, with something else that vaguely sounded like a cry. Try as I could, and extending my animal sense to the limit, I heard nothing else. When I checked with Dynin, I found that he had been sleeping and had heard nothing at all. It remained silent for the rest of my watch.

Rhodri had the next watch. I mentioned the sound I had heard in passing when I woke him, not wanting to worry him, but by the way his gaze sharpened I could tell he had the same thought I had. Because of it, when I burrowed back under my blanket, I was not feeling particularly sleepy. I stared overhead at the ceiling for a time, not wanting to toss and turn and wake Lissa, then I decided that I should try to make contact with my Sight again. I had neglected it the night before, which was understandable given the events, but I wanted to try again. The last time I had tried, I'd felt very close to making contact, but some part of the spell was still in the way.

I closed my eyes, and brought to mind how I remembered Delwyn, the Brenwyd that Sir Eiwas had seemed to leave in charge of the communities in Lord Duke Ceredon's province. I had met him a few times, but did not know him much beyond his face. I was fairly sure he had the Sight. I Searched for him, and Saw him asleep in bed next to his wife. This was the easy part. The spell did not interfere with my ability to See events and people as a silent observer; it was when I tried to contact him through dreams that it came up to block me. And again, when I tried to focus on getting his attention through various words (which began respectfully, but eventually degenerated to yelling anything I thought might get his attention), I heard the boundary spell rise up. I released an annoyed huff, and went Searching instead for the weaker areas as Steffyn had taught me. There!

I quietly slipped out of bed and out to the hallway, closing the door behind me so my quiet singing and humming wouldn't wake Lissa. The chords of the spell appeared before my mental eye almost as the briars they caused – thick and impenetrable. But even the thickest briars have small holes that one could sneak through, and the barely perceptible weaknesses were the holes I sought. I began humming a counter melody. When I had first started trying to break through the spell, I had worried that, should I be successful, and even if I wasn't, that Morrian would sense it and be able to track us down. Steffyn had assured me, however, that as I wasn't trying to literally bring the wall down and was only seeking a small opening, it should – hopefully – sneak past her. Regardless, on the off chance it did, he had told me that I should never try it alone, for he knew better how to listen in the spell for any sign that we had been detected. I didn't feel like waking him for the exercise at the moment, however. I wasn't exactly expecting success.

It came as a shock, then, when I suddenly sensed the chord I'd been pressing against give way. I gasped, and my vision took me to Delwyn directly. I lost all sensation of my immediate surroundings as I entered what we Brenwyds termed a living dream, those visions in which we actually make contact with the objects of our Searches.

I Saw Delwyn standing on a plain. I knew the plain. The same appeared to all Brenwyds who communicated through Sight, a meeting place in the spiritual realm where our Sight roamed and allowed us to make contact. If anyone were to come upon me now, it would seem as if I were frozen in sleep, but my mind was very active. Likewise, Delwyn would seem to be asleep as usual. But the conversation that took place on the plain was very real.

I felt like crying with relief and joy. "Thank Abba, it worked! It really worked!"

My exclamation drew his attention, and he turned to look at me. His eyes widened. "Lady Aislinn of Ecclesia?"

"The same," I said. "But you needn't bother with the title. I - we - desperately you're your help and any Brenwyd you can raise to follow you."

He still looked rather stunned. "You...you are well? Have you seen Sir Eiwas? He had a terrible dream about Ecclesia-"

"I know," I interrupted. "I know, and it's true. I've been trying to make contact with someone for days. I do not know how long I can keep this contact, so I will give you the short version..." I briefly narrated the events of the past couple of weeks, and ended with describing the course we were on now.

To Delwyn's credit, he only stared at me in shocked silence for half a minute before turning to the problem at hand. "So you and the prince and princess are about to make contact with the leviathans?"

"Yes. We set out tomorrow."

He shook his head. "Morrian...I can scarcely credit it, and yet it makes a certain sense. What is it you need?" His calm, accepting attitude was very soothing to my nerves.

"I'm not quite sure at the moment," I admitted. "But I think that, assuming the leviathans are able to break through the wall, there needs to be a Brenwyd force ready to enter Ecclesia to deal with Morrian. She cannot be defeated alone."

"Indeed not. Where will you ask the leviathans to make their attempt?"

I hesitated. "I'm not precisely sure yet. Somewhere in the south, likely near Tairport, wherever the barrier on the land is near the sea. Mathghamhain says that the leviathans need to be near a large body of water to engage in that sort of fighting." I had briefly mentioned Mathghamhain as an ally we had discovered who had had some dealings with Morrian, leaving out his curse and his age and instead implying he was a hermit scholar who specialized in the reign of Nivea. Which, when I said it, did not strike me as being false.

Delwyn nodded thoughtfully. "Yes, that would make sense. I have not had any messages from there in the last few weeks." Tairport was one of the largest port cities in Niclausia, and was unique in that it operated on some level of autonomy from the other kingdoms. It was located next to a very large natural harbor, very near where the boundaries of Ecclesia, Darlesia, and the southernmost kingdom, Sardesia, met. It had technically been founded by Sardesians, but it was the only port Darlesia had direct access to, and since the Anianol Forest petered out just above the city, it fell within Ecclesia's natural boundaries. Because of its immense wealth as a trading center where three nations met, there had been clashes over who controlled it politically, until the citizens of Tairport decided about a hundred and fifty years ago that they could govern themselves better than any of the larger nations and declared independence. I had a feeling that Morrian had included Tairport within Ecclesia's borders.

"Could you send someone to check – discreetly – the extent of the border to the south?" I asked. "It would be a help."

He thought for a moment. "I believe I can spare someone, considering the importance."

"Are the monster attacks very bad, then?"

"Bad enough, but it's all the petty magic that is truly causing problems. These magic users...it's as if they have Brenwyd horses, the way they move about so quickly and easily. All the nobles are focusing on protecting their own lands, and the Brenwyds in each province are so harried by all the calls for assistance that, though we know the importance of organizing a central response force, no one can spare the time. If the king would bestir himself from the capital, it would help, but Prince Rhys has had no response to any of the messages he's sent, and the messengers don't come back. Nor have we had luck in contacting Lady Duchess Rhian and her party." When I had shared what I had seen of Duchess Rhian, Delwyn had not been surprised. They had guessed something had befallen her and her escort, as they had had no word from them. Apparently, Rhys was barely sleeping between the stress he faced from the province's problems and the worry he had over the fates of his parents.

I winced at the report. "Morrian's plan is working then."

"Indeed." His face hardened in determination. "But now I know what is truly happening, I can organize those under me, at least, to fight against it. Lady Aislinn, you tell me where and when to have my forces, and I swear they will be there."

I felt like crying in relief, but managed to keep my emotions in check. "Thank you, thank you, sir. Now that I've broken through once, I should be able to do so more easily. I will contact you again when I have more detailed information, but in the meantime...

perhaps keep a watch on the south, in case I cannot reach you again? And pray Abba can coordinate us if we cannot directly do so."

He nodded. "Yes, that would be wise." He walked up to me and laid a comforting hand on my shoulder. Though it was only in a vision, it felt reassuringly solid. "Keep the faith, lass. It's a hard challenge you've been given, but you've acquitted yourself extremely well so far. Continue as you have begun, and I do believe there is every chance this witch will be beaten."

Those affirming words did bring tears to my eyes. I had felt lost and out of my league so many times in the past few weeks, that to hear someone in authority say I was doing well was a great confidence boost. "Truly?"

"Yes." He smiled at me. "Hold on, Aislinn. Abba will see you through. And when that barrier comes down, there will be as big a host as I can raise ready to support you."

"Sir, you do not know what that means," I said.

"I can imagine," he said quietly. He looked over his shoulder then, as if someone called him. "I must go. I can hear my wife calling me." Grim lines appeared on his face. "There must have been another attack."

"Of course. Go. I will contact you again as I can."

"I will be listening. Abba be with you."

"And with you." He nodded in response and walked away, seemingly vanishing from Sight as he woke. When he did, I felt myself released from the vision, and I opened my eyes, blinking blearily, suddenly aware that I was sitting on a very hard floor and leaning against a rough wall. Then I became aware that the hallway was full of morning's light, and I squinted against the unexpected brightness. The last thing I noticed, as my vision adjusted, were the three faces looking down at me with varying expressions. Rhodri and Lissa looked a mix between concerned and hopeful, while Steffyn looked mostly just inscrutable.

"Good morning," I said, feeling rather cheerful.

"Good morning," Lissa said. "So, you made contact with Delwyn?"

I grinned at her and got to my feet, feeling a little stiff. "I did. What gave it away?"

"Besides your complete nonreaction to anything we did to wake you?" Rhodri asked, a certain gleam in his eye that made me wonder exactly what he had tried to pull my attention from the internal to the external. He nodded toward Steffyn. "He told us. He could sense your mind was far away."

I slowly tipped my gaze up to meet Steffyn's eyes. "Mind reading without permission again?" I asked lightly.

"I only wanted to be sure you were alright. I did not listen in to your conversation," he answered. "I thought we agreed you would only try to make contact when I was on hand to listen for any hint of Morrian's presence."

I shrugged. "I know, but I couldn't sleep after my watch, so I decided to give it another try and didn't wish to wake you. I wasn't really expecting to break through."

"Hmm. Well, what did he say?"

At that moment, my stomach growled. I sheepishly laid a hand on it. "Well, why don't we break our fast, and I'll tell you?"

❧⚜☙

Lissa and Rhodri were much encouraged by what I had to report of my conversation with Delwyn. Even if I was unable to contact him again, someone on the outside knew what our plight truly was and stood ready to help us. Steffyn was harder to read. I thought he was genuinely pleased that I had finally succeeded in contacting Delwyn, but he seemed perturbed by it at the same time. Perhaps our quarrel was now shadowing everything I did in his mind.

Rhodri reported that he had heard nothing untoward in the night. Steffyn's eyes darkened when I reported the sound I thought I had heard, but he made no comment about it. He was being rather taciturn, even for him. I wondered if it meant he was still stewing over our conversations of the past day. I hoped he was, for it would mean some of my words had an impact. He could not run from Abba forever.

After eating, we made for the harbor. I let the others go ahead while I tended to Dynin. As I listened to him crunch down happily on the oats I had found for him in the stable's feed room, I gave him a good grooming. It was nice to have this familiar routine, still, in the midst of everything. I could almost imagine that I was back in the palace stables at the start of a normal day, with nothing more pressing on my time than the need to finish a painting.

Make sure you pick a big enough boat for me to come, Dynin instructed as I put away the brushes.

Outwardly I smiled, though inwardly I sighed. There was no guarantee we could. People could and did transport livestock, including horses, on ships all the time, but the idea of putting Dynin in a small stall aboard a floating box of wood made me uneasy. Then again, so did the idea of leaving him behind. "I'll make sure of it." I exited the stall, leaving the door open so Dynin could come and go as he pleased. There was no reason, in a sleeping town, to keep him locked up.

I was surprised to emerge and find Rhodri leaning against a wall of the stable, waiting for me. "What are you doing here? I thought you went to the harbor."

"I was, but decided that I should wait for you so no one was left alone."

I made a point of looking around at the sleeping people in the stable yard. "Because I clearly need protection from a horde of unconscious citizens?"

I meant the words as a joke, but for once Rhodri didn't smile. "Actually, I would really like to talk with you, alone."

"Oh? About what?"

"Lissa." We began walking toward the sea. It really was eerie how quiet it was. The quiet had been easier to dismiss in the countryside, where quiet was expected. In a coastal town, however, it was very different, and our voices echoed weirdly off the buildings around us. "What were you two talking about yesterday? She said it was unimportant, but I could tell she'd been crying."

I gave him a look. "You expect me to tell you when Lissa wouldn't? What sort of best friend do you take me for?"

He managed a wry smile. "No, I know better than that. What I would like, is for you to either confirm or deny my suspicions. Surely that isn't so disloyal."

"Hmm. Maybe. Go ahead, then."

"I think that Lissa was doubting her ability to continue through with this sort of mission. I think she is reaching her limits and thinks that she is more of a hindrance than a help."

His guess was on the mark, but I hedged in telling him that. Lissa had been speaking to me in confidence, after all. "Perhaps. What makes you think so?"

"I know I've been gone for the past six months, but I know her. She's most comfortable speaking diplomacy and politics over tea, not actually being out on the front lines fighting. But I also know that for Ecclesia's sake, she will push herself to do whatever she thinks she must, even if completely outside her comfort zone."

"Is that such a bad thing? I'm rather out of my comfort zone at the moment, yet I'm pushing on. What choice do I - do we - have?"

"I know. I wish you had a choice, because I'm worried for you, too, you know. But you have been trained for this - fighting magic and witches and such. Lissa has never trained for direct battle." He sighed. "I know she has a core of inner strength to draw upon, and I do not doubt her ability to rise to the challenge. But in this sort of situation, I know she does. I just want to know the best way to reassure her...even though, at the same time, I wish she was half a continent away and out of danger."

"You'd be a rather bad fiancé if you didn't wish that." I patted his arm. "Just keep telling her that she can do this, Rhodri. That's the best advice I can give you."

He nodded. "I know. I just wish there was something else I could do...maybe if there was a particular task she could do, something essential that caters more to her strengths."

"And takes her half a continent away from here at the same time?" I asked wryly. A rueful grin was my response. "I'll think on it. Certainly, she'll be needed to negotiate with the leviathans. She's very good at being diplomatic, no matter what the circumstances."

"And I'm not, is that it?"

I chuckled. "Given your first conversations with Mathghamhain, no, but you knew that already. Also, notice I didn't include myself in that distinction, either."

"Hmm." He looked at me in what I could only interpret as a cautious manner. "Speaking of Mathghamhain...what argument are you two in the middle of?"

I sighed and rolled my eyes. "It's...hard to explain. And part of it is confidential."

"Lissa thinks the two of you are falling in love." Rhodri could be nothing if not blunt at times.

I snorted. "Yes, so she's told me. And I've told her that she's imagining things."

"Ah. I don't see it, myself, if that helps. All I can tell is that you two seem to have a talent for riling each other. Then again, in many romantic stories from earth, the two people who start out arguing with each other all the time end up falling rather passionately in love by the end of things."

I stared at him. His expression was too straight-faced. "I'm not going to dignify that with a response." He cracked a smile. "I thought so." Then, I looked at him curiously. "How are you an expert on romantic stories from earth? I certainly don't recall you having a particular fondness for Niclausian ones."

"Uhh..." It was hard to tell with his dark complexion, but I was fairly sure he was blushing in embarrassment. "You remember Ian? His girlfriend really likes those stories, and so to humor her a lot he would watch them with her at our flat. I thought watching them would help me better understand Earth culture."

"Did they?"

"Not really, actually. I usually ended up more confused." We had reached the harbor at this point, and I saw Lissa and Steffyn standing far down the docks, where the larger ships were anchored in deep water. Helmond's harbor was a natural inlet of the coast, sheltered from storms off the ocean by a half-circle of cliffs. The docks were extensive, running from the cobblestone streets of Helmond along the base of the cliffs in both directions for half a mile, shorter docks stretching out perpendicular to the main one every so often so that ships could lower their gangplanks instead of having to send men to and from shore in small lifeboats. Lissa and Steffyn looked deep in conversation. I hoped that Lissa would keep in mind what I had told her yesterday, and that her gentler words would influence his mind more favorably. I was about to ask Rhodri exactly how one "watched" stories, when a faint sound came to my ears, seeming to come from the direction of the sea. Looking again toward Steffyn, I could tell by his change in posture that he also heard the noise.

"What is it?" Rhodri asked.

I frowned, straining to hear better. "I'm not sure. I think...I think I hear the same sound as I did during the night."

"Should we take shelter?"

"I don't know."

Aislinn, Steffyn's voice entered my head. *Do you hear that?*

Yes. It sounds like what I heard during my watch. Is it?

Dragon wings. Yes. He and Lissa began walking quickly back towards us. *Until we know if they are friend or foe, we should take refuge in a house so we are out of sight.*

Alright. I relayed the information to Rhodri, then made my way into the harbormaster's building while Rhodri waited for the other two. Fortunately, the door was unlocked. On opening it, I saw several men still within. I wrinkled my nose as the smell of stale alcohol hit me. Clearly, they had been enjoying a relaxing drink when the curse struck them.

I turned when the others entered behind me. Lissa looked nervous. "Is it the elemental dragons?" she asked.

"I don't know, Your Highness, but it is best to be cautious," Steffyn rumbled. He closed the door, then turned to close the shutters over the windows.

"What else could it be?" Rhodri asked, hand wrapped around his sword hilt.

"There are other monsters who travel by flight," Steffyn said reluctantly. "But whatever it is, as long as we stay quiet and out of sight, they may pass us by."

I reached out to Dynin, telling him to remain in his stall. When I told him why, he wanted to come to me, but I convinced him that we were all safer remaining where we were than risking being caught in the open, awake, in a kingdom that was supposed to be asleep. He was rather grumpy about it, though.

The sound of flapping wings was coming to me more clearly now. *Aislinn,* Steffyn called to me again mentally. I looked at him, questioning. *Could you, carefully, try to reach out and sense what sort of creatures are coming without alerting them of your presence?*

I can try, I answered. *But I'm not sure what I should be looking for.*

Only try to sense whether they are good or evil.

You think they may be good?

I think it possible that the leviathans may not have waited for any human ambassador to tell them of trouble. But I should like to be certain, either way, before they reach us. We should still have some time if we need to mount a defense.

Alright. I closed my eyes. It always seemed easier to concentrate on mental tasks with my eyes closed. I extended my animal sense. It was like a sixth sense to me, for I could extend it out nearly a mile when I pushed it in search of animals. I also used my song sense. That more than anything else would help me judge if the creatures that approached meant good or ill.

After a few moments, I sensed multiple creatures approaching. I had never sensed anything like them before. Their songs had light, airy notes, similar to a bird's, but there were fiercer strains underlying them speaking of strength with a fluidity to it all that reminded me of the songs of whales and dolphins. Interestingly, the melodies had complex harmonies, the sort I usually heard more in the songs of people than animals. My overall impression was of wildness and majesty, and I knew. These creatures were not evil. I heard no dark or dissonant chords to indicate such a thing. On the flip side, however, the wildness in the songs made me wonder if, even if they weren't evil, whether they were creatures to be safely approached.

I opened my eyes and looked at Steffyn. "I do not think they are evil, but...I'm not sure what they are, either." I reported my impressions of their songs.

His posture relaxed. "Ah. There is nothing to fear. They are leviathans."

"Are you sure?" I asked.

He nodded. "I can hear their songs, too. I remember."

"Should we go to greet them, then?" Lissa asked, excitement replacing her nervousness. Inwardly, I smiled to see it. She always had loved stories of dragons. I did too, for that matter. "It seems Abba has anticipated us."

Steffyn nodded toward me. "Perhaps Aislinn should make first contact and arrange a meeting place? They will not be able to fit comfortably in the confines of the town."

"Me?" I asked. "Couldn't you do it? You are familiar with the species, at least."

"You are the animal speaker. I cannot initiate mental contact unless they do so first."

"Oh." I looked toward the closed window, and imagined large, fire-breathing dragons flying toward us. "I suppose, then."

"Do not worry, it will be fine," Lissa encouraged. "They should respond well to a Brenwyd."

I tried to smile at her, then turned my attention back to the beasts that had grown much closer. I could sense five separate minds now, and they seemed curiously blocked. Usually, animal minds were open, with no barriers to communication, for they had no need of it. Only humans deliberately trained to guard their thoughts. Then again, these weren't exactly ordinary animals I was about to converse with.

I took a breath to steady my suddenly active nerves, then said, *Hello! Might I speak with you?*

The response took me by surprise. Usually, when I talk to animals, it is not as if I am "talking" to them. I understand them, and my mind converts the feelings and images I receive into sentences that I understand, and they likewise can glean images and feelings from my words so they can understand what I say. Animals that live around people do use quite a few real words in conversations, but wild animals almost never do. When the leviathans answered me, however, it was as if I were mind speaking with another Brenwyd.

I sensed a sudden flurry of excitement from the creatures, then: *Who calls to us from the land?* The voice was male, and rather dignified.

I do, I said. I sent a mental image of myself, and said, *My name is Aislinn. You are leviathans, yes?*

The excitement increased. *Indeed, we are. You are a Brenwyd?* That voice was female and seemed older than the previous one. Something about its cadence reminded me of my grandmother.

I am. And, if you would be willing, I – we – very much need your help.

You are truly a Brenwyd? You do not jest? A third voice broke in. A male, but different from the first one. Younger sounding in his enthusiasm.

Neriah, hush, the female voice said sternly before I could respond. *Contain your excitement. When a Brenwyd asks for help, it is a serious business.*

Yes, Elder. I apologize. He did sound rather abashed at the rebuke.

Now, what is it you need our help with? Does it involve the magic that rolled over the land some days ago? the old female asked me.

Indeed, it does, I said. *I travel with the princess of Ecclesia, her fiancé, and...another ally. We are the only ones in the kingdom who escaped a curse that put all the other inhabitants to sleep. We are seeking to break the spell and defeat the witch who cast it, but we need help. Would you be willing to meet us on top of the cliffs beside this town so we can discuss the threat further? It is of the utmost importance. If this witch is not stopped, all of Niclausia will suffer before the month is out.* I tried to remain respectful while doing my best to impress the importance and urgency of our mission on them.

The female remained silent for what felt like an age, though I could sense the barely suppressed enthusiasm of several of the others. They, clearly, wanted to help. The young male had called the older female Elder, so she must possess some rank in leviathan society and be the leader of the group. *We will meet you,* she said at last. *But tell me this first: what is the name of this witch?*

Her name is Morrian.

Instantly I sensed shock and loathing from all five creatures, as well as anger. *Aye, we will help you,* the elder said, her voice hissing through my head. I nearly gasped at the strength of her emotions. *For we have our own wrong to avenge on her. We will reach the cliffs in moments; we will await you there.* Then she withdrew the contact, and I really was left gasping by the suddenness of it.

"Are you alright?" Rhodri asked, a concerned look on his face.

I nodded. "Yes. They are simply...rather intense."

"Indeed," Steffyn agreed. "Did they agree to meet?"

I nodded again. "They will. They have no liking for Morrian either, apparently. We should hurry; she said they would be there within moments."

Conspiring with Dragons

We left the office and started walking toward the cliffs. I looked out over the sea eagerly for a first glimpse of the leviathans but was distracted by a demanding voice shouting in my head. *Girl. What happened? Where are you going?* Dynin, apparently, was not content with remaining quietly in the stable.

Everything's alright. The approaching dragons are friendly. They're leviathans! The very creatures we were going to seek!

So now we do not have to ride the boat? Ever practical, was Dynin.

No. I don't think so, anyway.

Can I come join you now? I do not want to stay here while you meet these...things.

I believe so, if you want.

They do not eat horses, do they? Dynin was certainly not enthused about our quickly approaching guests.

I don't think so. I can ask Stef...Mathghamhain if you want.

Why do you keep calling him by a different name?

Long story. Do you want me to ask?

A pause, then: *Please.*

I smiled and put the question to Steffyn. The query amused him. He actually met my eyes as he gave his answer. "No, they do not eat horses. They eat fish and other sea life, only resorting to wild land game if necessary. They do not like the taste of land animals, and besides that, they would never be so rude as to eat animals belonging to humans. Dynin has nothing to fear."

"Thank you." I relayed the information to Dynin, and he informed me he was on his way.

"Grindles, are those them?" Rhodri sounded aghast. I looked skyward once again, and I could hardly miss the five enormous dragons that were suddenly closing in on the cliffs. The dragons were dropping in altitude rapidly, and their size awed me. Lissa surreptitiously scooted close to Rhodri, her face reflecting a childlike awe.

"How in the Five Realms did they get so close without my noticing?" I asked, a little taken aback by how abruptly they appeared in the sky.

"They were camouflaged until a moment ago," Steffyn supplied. "Remember, they can shift the color of their scales."

"Oh. Yes, I remember that now." I'm sure my face looked the same as Lissa's as I studied the leviathans while they landed. We had just reached the bottom of the hill and still had to climb to the top, so I had ample time. Their bodies were all various shades of grey, from smoky to heather. Two of them tended toward darker hues of charcoal and iron, while the other three were at the lighter end of the spectrum. Their underbellies were ivory and cream, and the sun sparkled off their scales. As I watched, the scales on their legs and underbellies took on a slightly greenish-brown cast, matching the grass below them, while the scales on their backs reflected blue undertones. The lighter ones were smaller than the others, and their build overall seemed more delicate, so I decided that they must be the females. But when I said smaller, I meant only in comparison to the males; I estimated that from their noses to the tips of their tails they stretched to about forty feet, and the males were at least ten feet longer. Their wings spread out wide on either side of their bodies, and I estimated the span at roughly their body length. I could see a main wingbone connecting the wings to their bodies just above their forelegs, and the wing material itself was stretched over smaller bones. The sun shone right through it, giving it a translucent cast.

Dynin trotted up behind us, and I turned to welcome him, running my hand along his crest. I could feel him start to tremble under my fingertips as he took in the leviathans ahead of us. *You are sure they are not dangerous?*

Well, I'm sure they can be dangerous, Dy, but they don't mean us harm. It's alright. He didn't respond, but began to breathe heavily. Poor Dynin. I decided that once we finished with this venture I would spoil him immensely with treats for the rest of his life (not that I didn't already). He certainly deserved it, with all he had been asked to put up with. Dragons were definitely something far outside of his comfort zone. I sent soothing thoughts his way but didn't move my gaze from the creatures ahead.

Despite the distance still separating us from them, the wind from their wings as they landed was nearly enough to knock me over. Once landed, I could see that their backs were about ten feet high at the highest point, while their heads stretched on serpentine necks several feet higher. Their heads were sleek, with small rounded ears close to their heads that I could see they swiveled to catch sound. Their eyes were large in comparison to the rest of their face, almost catlike, and the irises were a startling cerulean blue. Their muzzles were rounded, and as one parted his mouth slightly, I glimpsed the sharp teeth within. I also noticed that their skin, while scaled, did not seem rough; rather, the scales appeared smoothed over, like a snake's. I was surprised to see that there was no line of spines on their backs, as I had so often heard in descriptions of dragons. There were some tiny ridges in a line, but they were little nubs in comparison with the rest of their body size. As the creatures pricked their ears toward us and walked closer, I noticed fine lines behind their ears that seemed to expose tissue, like the gills of a fish. I could well believe that they were creatures of the water just as much as the air, for the area between their talons was webbed, and their bodies had a streamlined look. I noticed that their forepaws differed from their hind paws. Their hind paws were rather what I had expected, shaped similarly to a dog's foot with great talons extending several inches out that dug deeply into the ground. Their forepaws, however, seemed nearly like a scaled human hand. There were five finger-like appendages, and the claws that extended from them seemed more like overly long, sharp fingernails. I wondered how much dexterity they had with them.

"They're huge," Lissa breathed out, unable to tear her eyes from the sight.

"I've seen some bigger," Steffyn answered. "Not by much, but this is the average size."

By this time the dragons had reached within several horse-lengths and paused. I couldn't help but feel some trepidation as I craned my neck to gaze up at them. One of the males lowered his head so he was eye level with us, and lay down on the grass. The other four copied him. "You are the Brenwyd who conversed with us just now?" He addressed me.

I was taken a little aback to hear him speak verbally. Yes, Steffyn had mentioned that they could communicate in such a way, but it was different to see and hear it for myself. His voice reminded me vaguely of Steffyn's, for it was low and growly, but there was also a slight hiss underlying his words, and it was rather breathy. I nodded, unable to speak for the moment.

One of the females moved her head to examine me more closely. Dynin shuddered and I could feel him ready to bolt. Surprisingly, I thought, she addressed him first. "Do not tremble so, creature. I mean not to harm you. I simply want to see you better. What are you?" She sounded curious, almost like a child. Her voice was higher in tone, confirming my guess that she was, in fact, female.

The question shook me from my awed silence. "You've never seen a horse before?"

She shook her head. "I have never left the islands before now. So, this is a horse? I have heard of such creatures. They truly are similar to centaurs. Can he really carry one of you humans? He seems so small."

At that, Dynin snorted, taking some affront. True, he certainly wasn't the largest horse around, but he was taller than most Brenwyd horses (a good thing, considering my height.) *I am perfectly sized for a horse, thank you very much,* he said. *It is you who are completely oversized.*

The female let out a sound that nearly sounded like a squeal. "Oh, he talks! I didn't know they talked." I had to smile at her enthusiasm. She reminded me of one of my young cousins squealing in delight over the discovery of a wildflower.

Of course I talk, Dynin answered, his indignation shaking him from his fear. *I am a Brenwyd horse. We were chosen just as they were by the Creator. Anyone knows that.*

"Forgive her, noble horse," the older male said, casting a stern glance at the female, though I thought I detected an amused gleam in his large blue eye. "As she said, this is the first time she has been to the mainland. Only a few of us come here at all since the sickness, and so the most all the rest know of land creatures is what we report. And we certainly do not know everything. Perhaps at some other time you can teach us more about Brenwyd horses, but now I believe there are more pressing matters at hand."

"Indeed," Steffyn spoke up. "May I be right in assuming that you sensed the spell from your islands and have come to investigate?" He had drawn his cloak and hood about himself once more so that his form was shielded from the dragons.

The dragon looked at him, head cocked slightly at a curious angle. I wondered why he was the one speaking when, on the flight in, one of the females had taken the primary speaking role. "You speak truly. In our stories, we have tales of other times when such magic has swept across the lands, and knew it was our duty to investigate, and to help as we could." He lowered his head by Steffyn and his nostrils twitched, taking in the scent of him. "Pardon me for such a question, but what are you? Your form seems human, yet your scent tells a more complicated story. I have not smelled it before." My eyes widened. Leviathans were certainly forthright creatures.

I could see Steffyn go rigid. "I...fell victim to a spell many years ago that changed my body. I am...human."

"Really? A spell?" The younger male spoke up for the first time. "Cannot the Brenwyd break it? All the stories say Brenwyds are magic-fighters." He looked at me intensely. "They also say Brenwyds are most fair to look upon. That seems to be correct." I blinked, and then blushed at the unexpected casual compliment.

"Yes, well...my curse is too...complicated to be broken, it would seem. But that is not the issue pressing us now," Steffyn said, changing the subject. "Our old enemy, Morrian, has risen again. It is she behind this curse that now ensnares Ecclesia. Our aim is to travel to her fortress to break it. Will you help us?"

I sensed the same emotions as before coursing through the leviathans. "To do any less would be an affront to our honor," one of the other females said. I recognized her voice. She was the one I had spoken with earlier. Her stature suggested to me that my earlier thought that she was an older leviathan was correct. She was the smallest of the group, and her eyes seemed more sunken into her skull. "We have been waiting for one such as she to surface." She sighed. "To my shame, we decided it was best to keep our suspicions to ourselves. We never imagined that the consequences for the humans would be so severe."

"Do you mean that you knew she was alive?" I asked, incredulous.

"Not exactly," she said. "But I believe we are telling the story out of order. Let us start at the beginning. My name is Bityah, elder of clan Arieh, member of the Council of Patriarchs and Matriarchs. These are Barak and Aliyah, leaders of clan Arieh." She nodded to the older male who had spoken first, and the female lying close to him. Then with a humorous note in her voice, she continued. "And these two impertinent younglings are Neriah and Kezia, warriors in training. They are young for such a mission as this one, but they represent the best of their peers. *When* they remember to stay silent and respect their elders and avoid asking silly questions."

The two younger ones dipped their heads in apparent chastisement, but the female, Kezia, cocked her head to consider the elder in a sideways glance. "But Elder, Barak has always taught us that the only silly question is the one left unasked," she said, curling her tail about her body.

Barak whipped his tail about to lightly tap her on the flank. "True, in training. But this is not training. Now is the time to listen instead of speak."

"Indeed," Bityah agreed. Despite the hard words, I had the feeling that the older leviathans tended to be indulgent toward the young ones. She returned her attention to us. "And you are?"

"I am Mathghamhain," Steffyn spoke up. He gestured to me. "This is the Lady Aislinn, of the Ecclesian court." I frowned at him. There was no need for them to know my technical title. He ignored it and moved on to Rhodri and Lissa. "And these are Prince Rhodri of Darlesia and his betrothed, the Crown Princess Calissa of Ecclesia."

"Royalty?" Bityah said, sounding impressed. She rose to her feet and dipped her head to the ground. "It is an honor to meet you, Your Highnesses." The others copied her motion.

Lissa curtsied in return. It looked a little odd with her tattered and stained skirts, but she still managed to make it look perfectly elegant. After a moment, Rhodri followed her lead with a bow. I simply dipped my head in acknowledgment. "Yes, but please, take no account of it for now. It does not matter for the moment," Lissa said.

"Truly?" Aliyah asked, speaking up for the first time. "In our stories of humans, being of royal or noble birth is of great importance."

"For other people and in other circumstances that is true," Rhodri said. "But Lissa and I don't stand much on our rank, and besides, for our current task it doesn't matter if we're royalty or peasants. Morrian must fall all the same."

"Indeed," Bityah agreed. "So please, tell us your tale so that we may understand fully the circumstances. You mentioned a sleeping curse, I believe. What exactly is it?"

"Aislinn?" Rhodri looked to me. "I believe you are best qualified to tell the story. You've been there for all of it, and have had the dreams."

I nodded. "Very well." So I narrated the whole of the story, beginning with the day before Lissa's birthday. It went rather longer than I thought it would, for Bityah and Aliyah interrupted every so often with questions about our customs or terminology. Bityah seemed more interested in our history, while Aliyah appeared to have an almost academic interest in human culture. Based on their fidgeting every so often, I had a feeling that Neriah and Kezia would have liked to ask questions, but they heeded the commands of their elders and remained quiet. In addition to explaining the story of the past few weeks, Bityah also had me explain fully the line of royal descent from Nivea to King Cayden with a brief overview of the major political events since the Monsters' War. From their questions, I gathered that the leviathans had kept a bit of an eye on humans since their retreat to their islands, but only enough to be aware of major events and to make sure no powerful magic rose up in the lands. Other than that, they had left us mainlanders in peace according to the treaty made after the Monsters' War.

When I finished, Barak rumbled low in his throat. "It is a great task you have set yourselves."

"We have no choice," Steffyn said. "Morrian must be killed this time."

"Yes," Bityah said. "The timeline you have outlined, Lady Aislinn, explains much. About a fortnight ago, I woke with a troubling dream of magic loose in the land. We were unsure of what to do, but confident that the Creator would reveal to us the proper action in due time. A week ago, I had another dream in which I saw that the ancient monsters were being loosed: elemental dragons, gryphons, minotaurs, sirens, ogres, and more. Additionally, Barak and the two younglings here ran across a sea serpent while out on a patrol, letting us know that, despite our distance from your continent, we were not safe. In ancient times, when such monsters were common and before the sickness, it was our task to help guard the human settlements from them. When the Brenwyds arrived in the Five Realms, they joined with us, and so we were able to drive the monsters nearly to extinction. In fact, some stories claim we did. But there were always a few that cautioned against such a belief, warning that one day the ancient monsters might rise again to trouble mankind and our services would be needed.

"Not all of us believe this, and so some," a low growl emanated from her throat, "doubted my veracity. It is true, I am very old, but I am as clear-minded as ever. My grandfather fought against Morrian, and I received my stories of her directly from him. But since not all believed me, it was decided to send out some small groups as scouting parties to see what was really afoot on the mainland and then make a firm decision about what to do. I believed so strongly in the truth of my dreams that I insisted on being part of a party myself. A most fortuitous happenstance, for given my position in our society I am able to negotiate with you and command our warriors without waiting for approval from the rest of the Council."

"Perhaps less happenstance, Elder, and more Abba's providence," Lissa said.

Bityah inclined her head towards her. "So I am inclined to think."

"There are others of you scouting throughout Ecclesia?" Rhodri asked.

"Indeed, Your Highness. Not many, but a few. We have only just arrived this morning."

"How long does it take you to fly from the mainland to your islands?" Rhodri continued.

"A good three days' and nights' swim for us with favorable currents. Five if we fly."

"I recall leviathans as being rather speedy in the air," Steffyn put in.

Bityah cast him what seemed a speculative glance. It was hard to interpret what her emotions were exactly. "We are, but it really is slow compared to our swimming capabilities." She paused. "I still do not understand the nature of this spell you say wrought such changes on you. It has truly lengthened your life?"

"I am still alive, am I not?" I could hear the defensiveness in his tone.

"To be sure...this is why you swathe yourself with these cloths?"

"It is."

"Can we see?" Kezia asked, finally letting her curiosity get the better of her restraint.

"Kezia!" Aliyah's voice cracked out strongly. "That is not appropriate."

"Why? I think it reasonable."

"If he were comfortable with showing his form, he would do so. It is impolite to force humans to perform things they feel uncomfortable doing."

I glanced toward Steffyn. He seemed tense, but of course with how he was covered I could tell nothing else. Suddenly, though, he drooped. "Oh, very well," he spoke, surprising me. "The others already know my form; if you are to help us, you may as well see it." With that, he threw back his hood and cloak, revealing his odd, beast-like body. Lissa, Rhodri, and I exchanged surprised glances. I would never have guessed that Steffyn would have voluntarily removed his covering for the leviathans. I wondered at it, and a small bloom of hope appeared in my heart.

The leviathans stared, though the older three clearly tried to avoid it. "Oh," Kezia said in a small voice. "That happened to you because of a spell this Morrian cast?"

"Yes."

"You were human before?" That was Neriah.

"Yes; a Brenwyd, to be precise."

"Oh!" Kezia sounded shocked. "I am so sorry; I see how thoughtless my question was now." She did sound rather abashed.

Steffyn shrugged. "It was a natural question. I know you meant no harm. Think nothing of it." I stared hard at him. Why was he being so seemingly carefree about his appearance now, when merely two days before he had kept it closely hidden?

"This sorceress truly is powerful," Barak said. He turned his head toward Bityah. "I believe we must call the other scouts to come here, and someone must be sent to the islands. The others must be told."

"Yes, that would be a good starting action, though the humans may have another plan," she agreed. She trained her gaze on Steffyn. "You know, the story of your curse seems familiar to me. My grandfather's name was Elazar. Did you know him?"

Steffyn gave a start of surprise. "I...I did, as it happens. He was one of a small number who...knew the truth of my case. He was a friend."

"Ah. I see. It is an honor to fight alongside you, then. What manner of help do you best need from us?" She turned her head to survey us as a whole.

The four of us exchanged glances, and I nodded to Lissa to indicate she should be our spokesperson. Rhodri had been right earlier; to stop doubting herself, she needed something to do that she was good at. And negotiations happened to be one of those things.

"What we have discussed amongst ourselves as a strategy, Elder Bityah, is the possibility of a diversionary attack on the thorn barrier big enough to draw Morrian's personal attention, so that we can then sneak into her fortress and destroy the spell anchor more safely," Lissa began. "As we have been, until just last night, cut off from communication with the outside realms, we have thought that, if you and your warriors should be willing, perhaps you could undertake such an assault on the barrier?" I felt my heart start to speed up a little as Lissa made the request. Yes, we had discussed it and agreed on it as our best option, but now that it came to asking the creatures it depended on, it dawned on me that if they refused, we would be severely disadvantaged, even with the fresh hope of help from Delwyn.

Bityah took several minutes to answer, a grave look in her eyes as she considered it. "I see. You would like us to draw the witch out to us so you can break the spell."

Lissa nodded. "Put bluntly, yes. We know it carries a significant amount of risk to your people, especially considering that our two species have not had formal relations since the Monsters' War, but I am asking you, as a direct descendant of Queen Nivea, to overlook the bad blood that caused the war and think instead of the friendship that once existed between us, and the many innocent lives that will be lost should Morrian not be stopped now. I am told that your people hold your honor to be of the utmost importance; to your honor, then, I make my appeal."

A toothy grin spread over Bityah's face. "You are clever in your words, Your Highness. Tell me this: once you are able to enter the sorceress's fortress and break the curse, how do you plan to flee before she returns? Surely, even if we give our all in creating your distraction, it will not hold her when she senses her entire spell give way."

Rhodri and I exchanged worried glances. That was the part we had not discussed in depth just yet. Lissa, however, didn't hesitate. "Again, you see the area in which we need your help. If you are willing, perhaps you could spare two or three of your warriors to help us enter and exit the fortress quickly. We know that we are asking much of you, and we cannot offer you much in return, but every person and creature on the side of good has a duty to stand against evil however they can, for if we do not, then the world is lost."

"Oh, Elder Bityah, can we not help them?" Kezia burst out. "I know you will say yes. We cannot stand by while such an evil person threatens innocents. Moreover, do we not owe it to the humans after the destruction the War caused them?"

Barak growled. "Kezia, your impertinence wears our patience thin."

"Peace, Barak," Bityah ordered. She turned her serious gaze on the younger female. "She speaks out of turn, perhaps, but what she speaks is the truth." She turned back to us. "We will help you, Princess. It has been too long since we leviathans have had a good fight. And do not worry about having nothing to offer us by human standards; what you do offer us is more than enough."

Lissa frowned. "What is that?"

"A chance to win back our honor among your kind." The old leviathan sighed heavily. "Kezia speaks truly in regard to the War. Those of us infected with the sickness wreaked havoc on your lands and villages, and in doing so tore our honor as a race to shreds. What you give us now is a chance to redeem it, both to humans and ourselves."

"If you don't mind my asking," Rhodri ventured, "did you ever figure out what caused the madness? From your words earlier, it seems that you suspected magical interference."

"We did." It was Aliyah who answered. "If, perhaps, only a handful of us had begun to turn against your race, we may have suspected nothing more than the seeds of rebellion that eventually bear fruit in any race. But for dozens of us to succumb to such madness...we knew there must be something behind it. The Brenwyds tried to help us, but the infected ones never let them get close enough, and the rulers of the time eventually lost patience with their attempts. Our removal from your society, with the remnants of the other peaceful races, was our only option to heal ourselves."

I felt myself perk up at that remark. "The remnants of the other races? Do you mean that there are other good species like yourselves on your islands?"

"Quite so. Besides our race, the centaurs, satyrs, intelligent griffins, brownies, and others of that sort agreed to the treaty and came with us into exile."

"Have you proof that the madness was magic-induced?" Steffyn queried.

"Perhaps not proof by human standards, but proof enough for us." Bityah resumed speaking. "When our races went into exile, we took the infected ones with us as we were able. Once we settled ourselves in the islands, they began to recover rapidly, and had virtually no memory of the time during which they were mad. They spoke of strange dreams that made them angry, an overpowering anger that overwhelmed all good sense and principles. What else could it be but magic? Once we decided that, it was evident that whoever could cast such a spell against all of us must be both cunning and powerful, yet there had been no such person of that capability in the Five Realms since Morrian. The stories said she was dead, yes; but as our Elders said, there was never a body recovered, and a servant of the Shadow Angel such as she might just be granted longer life by her master. We have had our suspicions, those of us who are older, but no hard proof. Not until now. Thus, when you told us her name, you confirmed our thoughts, and have made us all the more eager to aid in the fight against her however we may."

"But if your species and the others are no longer affected by the madness, why have you stayed away so long?" I asked. "Especially if you had suspicions about a powerful magic-user being abroad. Why didn't you send at least a few back to Niclausia to tell us your suspicions?" The question hung in the air, heavy like fabric.

Bityah sighed. "I wish I had a good answer for you, Lady Aislinn. But alas, I do not. In the generation affected by the War, they remembered too well the ferocity the humans unleashed against us when we unleashed ours against them, and feared to return to the mainland too soon after for fear of reprisal. Then, the fear became that, since we have so long been absent from your shores, our sudden arrival would again incite such fear and violence. It has taken our race nearly a hundred years to recover in numbers from the casualties we suffered during the war, and others of the races have still not recovered. No one wished to do anything to provoke such a catastrophe into happening again. So we stayed isolated, telling ourselves that surely the Brenwyds would realize what had happened and confront the magic-user responsible, then come to tell us it was safe to return. Now I see that we only deluded ourselves because of our fear, and that our silence has cost you greatly. For that, I am sorry." She closed her eyes and bowed her head. The others followed suit, though I thought the two young ones were rather shocked by the admission.

I was astonished at receiving the apology – the *apology* – of so noble a creature, and it seemed that Lissa and Rhodri were, too. It was Steffyn who broke the silence. "Do not blame yourselves for not giving a warning. Morrian is crafty, and likely if you had tried to return, she would have stirred up the madness again. What we must do now is move quickly, before she realizes what we are about. We already must be on guard, for Aislinn has Seen that, since the shadow wolves failed her, Morrian is now sending elemental dragons out against us."

"Oh, you need not worry about that," Barak said. "We defeated several last night, air elementals. We found it curious that they ventured so far out over the sea, for they know it is our domain. They were tracking you?"

"I knew I heard something!" I exclaimed. "In the early hours of morning, I was very sure I heard the sound of flapping wings. In fact, when we heard you approaching, we thought you might be the same."

"What? We are nothing of the sort," Neriah burst out indignantly. "They are too easily swayed by minds stronger than theirs."

"Peace, Neriah," Bityah said. "It is understandable. And remember, we are kin to them distantly. It is sad that they gave us no option but to kill them."

"You killed them?" Lissa asked, a startled look in her eyes.

"We had no choice," Barak said. "There has long been enmity between our two races. The elementals have enough intelligence to resent our greater intelligence and principles, and we disapprove of their eagerness for destruction. Still, there have been times in the past, according to our history, when we have cooperated."

"Alas, those times are few and far between," Bityah broke in. "We gave them the chance to surrender, but they wanted blood. I know that most humans find killing distasteful, but as long as we act honorably, we do not let ourselves be overly bothered by it. Now, how many of us do you need to assault the barrier?"

Our conversation about the subsequent details of our proposed plan continued at length. Now that we had the firm agreement of the leviathans, we could turn more toward figuring out details that until now we had avoided, or had not even realized we needed to figure out, such as how to contact all the other leviathan scouts quickly, before their presence was noted by Morrian or her own scouts and followers. We decided that, since the number of scouts came to twenty-five, there would be enough leviathans already in Ecclesia to successfully assault the barrier. I made my suggestion of launching the attack near Tairport because of its proximity to the sea, and the site was approved by the leviathans. We also decided that Barak, Neriah, and Kezia would help us get into and out of Morrian's fortress quickly while Aliyah and Bityah flew south to meet the others. That was when the problem of how to quickly contact the others came up. Steffyn, predictably, had been the one to point it out.

I frowned at him. "And you were doing so well in being at least halfway optimistic."

He frowned back at me. "I am not necessarily not being optimistic now. I merely point out the difficulty. It is all part of proper strategizing."

"Humph."

"Here is a situation in which I miss Earth technology," Rhodri commented, defusing the tension between us. "If we had some cell phones, there would be no problem in contacting people half a country away."

"They are not people, they are leviathans," I said. "Besides, for those things to work, don't both parties in question need one?" While we had been in London, he had given me a brief explanation of how cell phones worked.

"Good point."

"What is a cell phone?" Neriah asked, clearly puzzled.

"Nothing very relevant at the moment," I answered him. "What we need is a Niclausian answer to how to contact others as quickly as possible."

Dynin snorted, drawing everyone's attention. *You are thinking too hard about this. Where are these other...leviathans...going? Tell us, and the girl and I can transfer and tell them ourselves.*

I stared at him as he made the suggestion, feeling like one of the biggest idiots in the Five Realms. "Of course! Dynin and I have been almost everywhere in Ecclesia in training. I should have thought of that earlier. Dynin's right." I flashed a grin at Rhodri. "See? We do have a Niclausian equivalent to cell phones." He chuckled in response.

"I have heard of this ability of Brenwyd horses. Those stories are really true? You can travel anywhere within minutes?" Bityah asked, interested.

"As long as one or both of us know where we're going. We can also," I added as the thought occurred to me, "go to Tairport to see what the barrier is like there. If it is following our border exactly, it should be within a mile of the city walls."

"Are you sure it will be safe?" Lissa asked, concern in her voice. "I know that you say Morrian has been blocked from viewing us in her mirror, but if she has other scouts out looking for us, or followers near the barrier, they could catch you."

"It's a risk I'll have to take, Liss. We need to catch the other leviathans before they get too far overland, and we need to know exactly what the barrier is like at Tairport. I'm sure Abba will continue to watch over me."

"You should not go alone to Tairport at least," Steffyn spoke up. "It is possible Morrian may have extra defenses there as it is the only part of the barrier that lies outside the Anianol. Perhaps, Prince Rhodri, you could accompany her?"

"Of course," he agreed.

I frowned at them. "You do realize I would be very alone in the minutes it takes Dynin to transfer back here for Rhodri? And if there are followers of Morrian there, surely it would be better if they only captured one of us rather than two."

"If they do, that one should not be you," Steffyn said, his voice oddly urgent. "Forgive me if I seem to be callous toward your fate, Prince Rhodri, but Aislinn, if you are captured by Morrian's forces, our whole expedition comes apart. We...we *cannot* do it without you." The vehemence in his voice took me aback and stalled any immediate reply.

"He is right, Aislinn," Rhodri said, taking advantage of my silence. "Of the two of us right now, I am the more expendable one. In going with you, if we run into trouble, I could at least hold it off long enough for you to escape."

"But Rhodri, you just got back," Lissa said softly. "You are not so expendable to me."

He took her hand. "I know, Liss, but it is the bare truth at the moment. And this is only a possible scenario. It's far more likely that Aislinn and I go and encounter no trouble."

I sighed. "Oh, very well, if you feel you must. But only to Tairport; it would slow me down on the other trips." I turned back to the leviathans, who had been watching us curiously. I had a feeling they were as fascinated by how we looked and acted as we were about them. "Where are the other scouting groups heading for?"

It took some time for Bityah, Barak, and Aliyah to properly answer the question. Obviously, the leviathans didn't know the names of the towns along the coast, and so had decided to make for specific locations based on geography that they knew from previous scouting trips over the years. It turned into a bit of a guessing game, with them describing the landscapes to us, and we pooling our knowledge of the coast to determine the closest towns. Then we had to determine a central meeting point that all the other leviathans could aim for to meet up with Aliyah and Bityah before the attack. And, not least of all, we had to determine how long it would take them to meet and then travel to Tairport to know when to time our penetration of Morrian's fortress. I could then relay the information to Delwyn so he would know when to be in the vicinity with his Brenwyds. In this, Steffyn's knowledge of where Morrian's fortress was located was critical, for we could not risk lingering near the fortress long before the combined leviathan and Brenwyd attack started.

"It is a roughly two days' and one night's flight from here," he provided. "We will know when we get close, for there is an atmosphere of evil about the place one can sense from a good distance away. An uneasiness that creeps under one's skin...it is unmistakable."

"Two days...based on what you say of where Tairport is located, it will take nearly three full days and nights for us to travel there if we go along the coast as discussed," Bityah estimated. "The others will reach the rendezvous point before us, but they will wait."

"We can use the extra time to rest," Steffyn said. "We will need as much strength as we can muster if we are to be successful. Also, the attack, once you get there, should be launched no sooner than dawn. It is always best to fight spells and evil in the light, if possible."

Bityah bowed her head in agreement. "I see. Let us plan the attack for four dawns from now, then. We shall take the remainder of the day to rest, and set off at nightfall. We should arrive at the rendezvous sometime early in the fourth night from now, allowing us ample time to prepare ourselves for a dawn attack."

"I do not see why we must leave the north immediately after Lady Aislinn breaks the spell," Kezia commented after our murmurs of agreement had died down. "Would it not be better to wait for this sorceress to return and strike her down in her moment of weakness after the spell breaks, instead of leaving her to regather her strength?"

"Kezia," Barak growled warningly.

"I am only asking. It seems logical to me."

"Brenwyds have a better understanding of these things than we do. You would do best to listen to her counsel."

"It is...a reasonable question for one of your race," Steffyn admitted as we all exchanged glances at her words. I knew for myself that I wasn't especially happy with simply leaving Morrian be, but we had little choice with no Brenwyd reinforcements available. "But as we have said, Morrian is powerful, and Aislinn cannot defeat her without other Brenwyds supporting her."

"But are there not other Brenwyds coming to help us destroy this barrier?" Neriah asked, clearly thinking in agreement with his training partner. "Once the barrier is down, could they not use this transfer ability you speak of to join you in the north and so support you? Or will they not have many horses?"

"She also said that the Brenwyds and horses must have been to a location first before they can transfer there, youngling," Aliyah said. "It is a good thought, but none of them will have been to this fortress before, so they could not transfer there. At least, that is how I understand it. Is that correct, Lady Aislinn?" She turned her head toward me for my reply, but I could not give her one.

Neriah's question had hit me like a blow from a blacksmith's hammer. This whole time, I had been worrying about how I would handle it if Morrian returned before we could leave, how I could hold her off long enough for the others to leave, but now...now I thought I saw an answer so obvious I should have seen it long ago.

I turned to the others. "You know...that might just work." I met Steffyn's eyes. "Wouldn't it? With her spell broken like that, with enough Brenwyds for a company...couldn't it work?"

He gazed back at me with an inscrutable expression. "It is a moot point. What Aliyah asked is also true. They would not know where they are going, so they could not transfer to join us."

"But...what if someone, one of us, transferred south to Tairport, to be waiting when the barrier falls, who could then guide the other Brenwyds north?" I turned my eyes to Dynin, who was looking at me with an alert expression. "Dynin can't travel with us on the leviathans' backs." It was a fact I had been avoiding, not being very happy with it and knowing he wouldn't like it either, but now it had to be said. He snorted at it now and emanated displeasure. "But once we arrive close enough to the fortress, if we set down on the mainland first at a safe distance, I could call him. Then he can see where it is, and take one of us to Tairport to wait on the other Brenwyds and share with their horses where to go. It would also help us time the attack better, because then the leviathans in the south could be sure that we've reached the fortress."

"He can come to you, even if he has not been in a place before?" Aliyah asked.

I nodded. "Yes. It's because Brenwyds are closely bonded to our horses. We can call them from anywhere, and if the need is great enough, pressing enough, they'll come to us."

"Our need is certainly great enough," Rhodri said. "Aislinn...I think you may be right. That could work. Then, you would only need to deal with Morrian long enough for the other Brenwyds to join us, which they could do quickly if Barak, Neriah, and Kezia help them get to the island." He looked at Lissa. "Liss, you could be the one to go south. Aislinn and Mathghamhain can't, obviously, but you could."

She gave him a look. "And it would keep me safely out of harm's way, is that it?"

A sheepish grin crossed Rhodri's face. "Well, somewhat out of harm's way, yes. Can you blame me for looking out for your safety?"

"Hmm." She continued to look at him with a hard expression for several seconds, but then it softened, and I thought I saw relief enter her eyes. "Well, in this I will bow to your wishes. I will go on Dynin to wait for the barrier to fall and lead the others."

I was glad to hear her accept it, but I kept my gaze trained on Steffyn for his reaction. What we were proposing was a purposeful, face-to-face encounter with Morrian in her own castle – exactly what he had warned us against in the first place. I saw conflicting emotions cross his face. "Mathghamhain?"

He raised his eyes to mine, a resigned, blank look in them I didn't like. "I do not like it, but...to strike so closely on the end of her curse breaking would likely be the best time to defeat her."

"It seems a good plan to me," Bityah said, unaware of the undercurrents in the conversation. "It is a pity that we leviathans cannot also transfer and aid you, but certainly Abba will lead you to victory."

I turned toward her slightly, a grim smile tugging at my lips. "So we pray."

The Final Trek

The rest of the day passed quickly, for me at least. Dynin and I set off to intercept the other leviathan scouting parties, which took most of the afternoon. Abba was certainly watching over us, for on each trip Dynin and I were able to find our draconic allies within fifteen minutes at the most. At the sign of something awake in the area, they all swooped down on us speedily. What took the longest was explaining the circumstances to all of them. Leviathans, I decided, were an extremely curious species. Fortunately, all of them, whenever they let me finish explaining, eagerly agreed to the venture and set off toward the rendezvous to wait for Bityah and Aliyah. Once I saw the last scouting group off, I directed Dynin to take me to Tairport, then dutifully sent him back for Rhodri. As I waited for his return, I studied the port city. In size, it was second to Kheprah in Ecclesia, but Tairport seemed more of a sprawling affair to my eyes. Built of stone weathered and scarred from centuries of exposure to saltwater and storms, Tairport clung stubbornly to the shoreline, encircling the mile-wide natural harbor that made it famous continent-wide, like a mother jealously clutching her child. My musings on which shades of grey, white, and black I would use if I worked on a landscape of the city were interrupted by Rhodri and Dynin's arrival, and we proceeded to scout the city. Like everywhere else in Ecclesia, it was eerily silent, save for the waves slapping against the shore and docks.

The thorn barrier was clearly visible from the city. Seeing it outside of the forest gave me a whole new appreciation for the feat we had asked the leviathans to do. The thorns stretched upward for what seemed like miles. I couldn't tell exactly how far, because the barrier, like the section we had seen in the forest, was shrouded in mist and fog that swirled through the briars like a nest of snakes. It looked for all the realms like an impossibly high wall that eventually touched the sky.

"Do you really think they can do it?" Rhodri asked quietly.

I didn't turn to meet his gaze, for he knew me well enough to read my own uncertainty. "With Abba's help. It's the only way any of us stand a chance." After staring at the wall for another few minutes, we returned to Dynin, and he took us back to Helmond, where we made our report.

Bityah and Aliyah, true to their intentions, stayed long enough for the sun to dip behind the horizon, and then jumped back aloft and began winging their way south. Or, based on the muted splashes I heard some minutes after their departure, began swimming their way south.

The day's efforts had left me tired, and so, after again successfully contacting Delwyn and appraising him of our updated plans – he seemed a little unsure of going directly up against Morrian, but agreed it was necessary – I easily fell into a dreamless sleep in my bed at the inn.

⚬❀⚬

The next day passed slowly. We had decided it was best for us to leave partway through the second day after Aliyah and Bityah had left, so we were now in a waiting stage. After the nearly non-stop travel and actions of the last few weeks, the waiting began grating on me within the first few hours. I had a hard time keeping still.

First, I spent a long time giving Dynin a thorough grooming. Then I checked over all my weapons, making sure everything was clean and in good repair. Rhodri also seemed uneasy about the forced wait. Seeing me looking over my sword, he suggested a sparring match between the two of us.

I gladly agreed to it. We sparred from mid-morning until lunchtime. It was quickly apparent to me in the first few strokes that, though Rhodri knew the basic forms of defense and offense too well to ever forget them, he had grown very rusty on the finer elements of swordplay. So we practiced until the movements that he had trained in since a child once again came easily. Our sparring session was further prolonged by the curiosity of the leviathans. Apparently, while Dynin and I had been transferring here and there the day before, the leviathans had asked any and all questions they could think of about human history, culture, practices, and the like. Since warfare was one of their natural interests, their curiosity was increased tenfold. That part of the day was actually rather pleasant, for they had a very unique way of viewing events, and more than once I held back laughter. (I didn't want to offend them, after all, and I was still in awe of them.) Eventually, though, Rhodri and I tired and decided to stop.

Steffyn produced our next task, which was fashioning crude harnesses to fasten onto the leviathans that we could hang onto. To my surprise, the three creatures helped considerably with the exercise. I had noticed the day before that their front paws were shaped nearly like hands, and it turned out that they could use them as such. Barak said that they often used similar harnesses to transport things between the various islands. Once the harnesses were complete, Steffyn volunteered to test them out, as he had both ridden leviathans before and was the biggest member of the party. After several adjustments, we decided they were sturdy enough for the journey.

After that task was finished, I finally found myself at a loss as to what to do next. I wandered over to the edge of the cliffs and looked out over the sea, gradually turning until I found myself facing north – and our final destination. My fingers itched for a pencil and paper for sketching, but I had none with me. *Abba, are we – am I – truly ready for this?* I prayed. *I know you have told me over and over to be strong and courageous, but I don't know how much longer I can keep it up.*

At the soft sound of footsteps approaching, I looked over my shoulder. Steffyn. He paused when I saw him, an uncertain expression on his face – as best I could tell, anyway. *Am I interrupting?* he asked mentally.

I smiled and beckoned him over. "It's alright. We should probably talk."

We should. He came to stand beside me, also gazing into the north. *Are you sure you want to do this? We have no certain guarantee the wall will even come down.*

Normally, I would have snapped a response back to him about his doubt and pessimism, but because of the mental link between us he was supporting, I could sense that the query came more from worry than disbelief. I sighed and sat down. "I...I don't think it's a question of whether I want to or not. I have to do it. So I will. Praying for Abba's support every step of the way." After a moment, he sat down beside me. His seeking me out lifted my spirits a little. Perhaps he was starting to come around. He remained silent, so I continued. "I could use your prayers as well, you know."

That provoked a reaction. He looked at me, startled. A dark expression came over his face. "I doubt my prayers would help you."

"Why wouldn't they? Doesn't the Word say that Abba listens to everyone who cries out to him in need?" He stayed silent. "Well, it would comfort me at least to know I have your prayers. Even if you don't think Abba is really listening."

He gave me another startled look. "The idea of my prayers would comfort you?"

"Very much." In fact, I felt a little startled myself as I realized how much I wanted his prayers. "Every one helps, you know. And... perhaps, if you truly believe that Abba won't listen to you about yourself, you could convince yourself that he would listen to you for my sake?" He gazed at me steadily, as if trying to find my true motivations. Which, given his mind-speaking gift, he actually could if he really wanted to. I kept up my guard. Again, he didn't answer, and the silence began to weigh on me. Beginning to feel a little uncomfortable with his unblinking regard, I turned back to the sea. "It's only a thought."

"Why is it you feel so invested in my spirituality – or rather, lack of?" he asked finally.

"You asked me that two nights ago. I gave you my answer. You're my friend. Why shouldn't I care?" I turned back to him. "Why is that so hard to believe?" I let my eyes scan over his body for a moment, then returned them to his face. "Do you honestly think I'm scared off by your looks?"

He sighed. "It's...it's been a long time since anyone has shown such concern for me. I suppose I've simply gotten used to not having it, and now...it is strange." The admission hit me hard, and again I felt an upwelling of sorrow and sympathy for this man who had survived for so long without any form of friendship.

I closed the distance between us with a step and put a hand meant to comfort on his arm. I could feel the muscles tense under my touch. "Well, you may as well accustom yourself to it, for as long as I live, at least, you will have someone who cares for you."

Looking into his grey eyes, I could see indecision and longing. I noticed that my heart seemed to start beating faster. I found myself wondering which shades of grey would best bring out his emotions on a canvas, how to use light and dark in the eyes to show the very human aspect of his animalistic face... "Aislinn," he finally said, in the gentlest tone I had yet heard from his mouth, "your regard would be better used on someone else." He gently but firmly removed my hand from his arm, and turned as if to walk away.

Now I felt my anger flare, and I moved to keep up with him. "Why? Why do you consider yourself so unworthy of any regard? Mine, Abba's...why do you push everyone away?"

He tensed, and increased his speed. "Aislinn, please do not press me on this. Trust me."

"How can I trust you when you keep pushing me away?" I stopped, and sent a hard look at his retreating back. "Is it because you couldn't stop Morrian from coming to power in the first place? Because you couldn't save your friend, her half-brother, from her?" That was a wild shot on my part, but it proved effective. He stopped in mid-stride and turned back to me in an abrupt motion, eyes wide, an almost panicked look in them.

"What was that?"

I repeated the question, and added, "We've guessed that you knew him; it would only make sense, for it would explain how you are close enough to Morrian to feel so personally responsible for not stopping her. He died in that final conflict, didn't he? You couldn't save him."

This time, his stare was so hard it was as if he wanted to see clear to my bones. "You are right; I couldn't save him." His voice was rougher than usual, hollow. Haunted. "Such is the fate of my friends."

"But others survived because of your actions," I argued. "Steffyn, you may not think of yourself as the hero the legends make you. But then, who is? You are more of a hero than you give yourself credit for. You have value."

He turned away again. "Once, perhaps." He stalked away, and this time I let him, a helpless feeling overcoming me.

I kicked at the ground in frustration, angry tears leaking from my eyes. "Abba, why is he so thick? What is it that really happened to him? This...this feels like more than his physical curse. What do I do? What *can* I do?" It wasn't precisely meant as a genuine prayer on my part; I simply needed to vent. Abba, however, is not bound by our intentions. I became aware of a pressing in my mind, a gentle urging in my spirit: *Sing, child. Sing.*

My anger vanished in astonishment at such a prompt and direct answer. Sing. Of course. Singing was what Brenwyds did best, after all. When was the last time, I wondered, that Steffyn had listened to songs of worship?

In my memory, I reviewed the many hymns and songs of praise to Abba that I had learned since my childhood, many of which were found within Abba's word itself. There were songs of battle within my repertoire as well, but I sensed that a song speaking of Abba's faithfulness and goodness was what was needed now. Within a few minutes, I decided on one and began to sing, softly at first but gradually increasing my volume:

"Give thanks to the Lord, for he is good.
His love endures forever.
Give thanks to the God of gods,
His love endures forever.
Give thanks to the Lord of lords,
His love endures forever.
To him alone who does great wonders,
His love endures forever.
Who by his understanding made the heavens,
His love endures forever.
Who spread out the earth upon the waters,
His love endures forever.
Who made the great lights
His love endures forever.
The sun to govern the day
His love endures forever.
The moon and stars to govern the night,
His love endures forever.

As I sang, I became increasingly aware of Abba's presence all about and around me. I knew that if I kept singing, the others would begin to feel it, too, even at the distance they were, for such were the abilities of Brenwyds. Through song, we were able to bring the presence of Abba into greater focus for others, as well as soothe and calm distressed emotions and minds. So I kept singing, launching into another hymn, then another, and eventually dipping into the Creation song itself. Some time into my worship, I sensed rather than heard the others coming up behind me to listen. I was startled when, a few minutes later, a deep-throated humming joined in, creating harmonies around my melody line. I turned partway around, and realized it was the leviathans. They had formed a small semi-circle behind me, with Lissa and Rhodri sitting in front of them. I didn't see Steffyn, but I didn't let that break my worship. I smiled at them, then turned back to the sea.

When I finally finished, I felt at peace. Steffyn was, ultimately, in Abba's hands, and it was Abba who waged the final battle for his heart. It gave me pain to admit it, but I was not the one responsible for him. I could do my best to show him the way, but it was ultimately up to him. But that also meant that I was in Abba's hands, too, and he would lead me through the literal upcoming battle. Abba had promised to be with me – with us always, and I had to have faith that he would keep his promises. It would not be by my strength that I would battle Morrian. It would be by Abba's. And in his strength, I had the greatest confidence.

"Thank you, Aislinn," Lissa said softly from behind me. "I...we all needed that."

I turned to my audience with a smile. "I thought so."

"That was most beautiful," Barak rumbled. He lowered his head to mine. "I have heard stories of Brenwyds taking up such songs before battles and how it always settled and prepared the army for the conflict to come, but I never thought to experience it for myself. You have my utmost gratitude."

I inclined my head. "I thank you, but remember: my voice did nothing but make Abba's presence more tangible. It is always there; *he* is always there." I looked back up at him with a grin. "And thank you for the accompaniment. I didn't realize your race was musically inclined."

"We cannot sing like that," Neriah said. "But we chant as others hold the melody with humming. It is how we worship at Sabbath dusk and dawn."

"Really? I should like to hear that."

Movement caught the corner of my eye, and I saw Steffyn standing some feet away. He had – again – turned his back to me and was preparing to walk away. At least he had come back for the worship. *I know you say you have renounced many aspects of faith,* I thought toward him, deciding at least one more plea couldn't hurt, *but you know the truth of the songs. Please, accept it once again.*

I received no immediate answer, and so for a moment believed my words had gone unheard, but then: *You have given me much to think about. And...know that you do have my prayers, for what they are worth.*

⁓◦⬥◦⁓

After that, I found myself in conversation with the leviathans about types of music and worship until dark. It was harder for me to sleep that night, and I spent several hours tossing and turning. Eventually, though, my eyelids grew heavy and sleep claimed me. I had no sustained dreams, but I Saw glimpses of Aliyah and Bityah traveling south, apparently without trouble; I Saw the castle at Kheprah, its inhabitants still gripped in sleep; I Saw the animals trapped awake in the narrow strip of sleeplessness along the barrier in the forest, uncertain of what was to come; I Saw scenes from elsewhere across Niclausia, monsters attacking villages, magicians and Brenwyds fighting, Brenwyds everywhere being pushed to their limits to keep the realms in some semblance of safety in the chaos. When I woke with the colors of early dawn beginning to paint the sky over the water, it was with a renewed sense of purpose. It wasn't only for Ecclesia that we battled Morrian. It was so that the other innocent people living in the other realms wouldn't have to face her full powers and suffer for it.

We had agreed the day before to begin our journey north just past noon. The morning was spent in final preparations and fitting our packs to the harnesses we had made the day before. We decided that all three of the leviathans would wear harnesses, though only two would be carrying passengers at any particular time. Since the leviathans were unused to the practice, it would let them all share the burden of our combined weight without any of them becoming over-strained. To start, Lissa and Rhodri would ride Barak, and Steffyn and I would share Neriah, with Kezia acting as lookout.

I wondered what Steffyn really thought about riding with me, but he made no protest. He had been avoiding me most of the morning, except to ask questions pertinent to our imminent departure. I let him keep his silence. I would have him as a captive audience soon enough, if I felt so inclined.

As a final action before we took off, I gave Dynin another thorough grooming and removed any piece of tack or luggage from him so he wouldn't get rubbed in the couple of days he would be on his own. I stored his tack in the inn's stable. We had decided that Lissa would leave on Dynin with enough time for a quick stop in Helmond for her to tack him up before continuing to Tairport.

Are you sure you'll be alright? I couldn't help asking, feeling fretful now that the time had come to really leave him.

I will be fine. He nudged me with his muzzle. *I am staying on the ground. You are the one leaving it.* He seemed distrustful of the leviathans' flying abilities.

I smiled a little, but just a little. *I really don't like leaving you like this, Dy. Something could happen.*

We animals are also under the One's care, he reminded me in a gentle tone I'd never heard him use before. *Remember the words you sang and let them comfort you. I will be waiting for your call.*

I nodded, my throat suddenly tight with tears. I hugged him fiercely, took a deep breath to settle myself, and then walked over to mount Neriah. Lissa and Rhodri had already mounted Barak, and Kezia circled above us.

"Sit in front of me," Steffyn said as we were getting situated. "It will be the more secure position, since you are new to flying. If there is rough air, I will be able to keep you on securely."

I nodded, feeling a little apprehensive despite my excitement. "Alright. You...you won't mind the close quarters?" If I was in front, that meant he would be directly behind me, and possibly having to keep his arms around my waist. The idea made a strange, tingly feeling start in my stomach.

"It is a safety precaution." I sighed inwardly at the statement. A wistful thought crossed my mind, a wish that he would have a bit more emotion about the contact. Then I wondered at it. It did only make sense, after all. Even if most everyone at court would think it a scandal of the highest degree for me, an unmarried maiden, to have the arms of an unrelated man around my waist for a prolonged period...Now that I thought about it, I felt a little embarrassed and quickly turned my attention to securing myself so Steffyn would not notice the blush I was sure colored my cheeks. *Oh, for heaven's sake, Aislinn*, I scolded myself. *Now is hardly the time for such concerns. And that should not even be a concern for you. So why is it?* I asked myself. I couldn't figure out a correct answer. "Are you strapped in?" Steffyn's voice came again. He had settled himself behind me, and I could feel warmth at my back from his body heat.

"Hmm? Oh. Yes. All ready."

"Not to seem forward," he began in a hesitant tone of voice, "but take-off can be a bit rough, especially for a beginner, so if you allow, it may be best if I hold on to you, and you hold on to the straps in front of you."

"Oh. Yes, of course. It's perfectly alright." I kept my gaze resolutely forward as I felt the solid bulk of Steffyn's arms slipping around my waist. I could feel my face burning. I hoped fervently Steffyn wasn't sensing any of my embarrassment. I noticed that he was wearing his gloves again. Maybe to use as a padding between my skin and his sharp nails.

"Are you coming to join me or not?" Kezia called down from her place in the sky.

"In a moment, youngling, as soon as the humans are settled," Barak called up to her.

Neriah turned his head toward us. "Are you ready?" he asked. I nodded.

Steffyn said, "Yes."

Neriah then turned to Barak. "May I take off?"

"Yes," Barak said. "Mathghamhain, you are certain of the way?"

"I could not forget if I wanted to," he replied. I felt him stiffen as he did so.

"Then let us be off." With that, Neriah unfurled his wings all the way, crouched back on his hind legs, and then, with a mighty spring, catapulted into the air.

A gasp forced itself out of me as he climbed, and I felt like half of my stomach had been left on the ground, while the other half was digging into Neriah's back as if some force were trying to keep me on the ground. I felt my back being pressed against Steffyn's chest, but my embarrassment was lost in my concern with making sure I didn't fall off. Below, I saw Dynin raise his head to watch us depart. He reared and let out a piercing whinny in farewell.

Before long, Neriah leveled out where Kezia was hovering. Barak came alongside us. Lissa seemed to be gripping the ropes as tightly as I was, and Rhodri looked like he was gripping her hard as well.

"All good?" Barak asked.

"All good," Neriah replied. "The harness has settled and the weight is distributed properly."

Barak bobbed his head. "Very well. Good to continue?"

"Good to continue," Neriah and Kezia said in chorus.

Barak turned his head to face us humans. "Are you good to continue?"

Lissa nodded, while Rhodri agreed verbally. "We are good to continue," I called out to him.

"Good. Follow me, then. Mathghamhain, if you see we need direction, do not hesitate to let us know. Shall we start with a heading of due north?"

"Yes. We should be able to continue in that heading the rest of the day."

Barak bobbed his head again. "Arieh warriors, fly forward and well!" With that, we truly began the flight. After a few minutes, I became aware of how the ropes were beginning to dig into the skin of my palms. I relaxed my grip slightly, testing to see how my balance was affected as I really began to absorb the sensation of flight. Neriah seemed a very good flyer, with only a few bumps here and there from rough air. My ropes seemed properly secure. I peeked down, marveling at how far below the ground was. However, that view also began to make me slightly dizzy after a moment so I closed my eyes instead. It was a truly glorious feeling. It reminded me of when Dynin and I galloped flat-out and his hooves barely touched ground, except here we weren't touching the ground at all. The leviathan's wingbeats settled my mind in a steady, soothing rhythm. I found myself smiling in delight. I could get used to flying.

I take it you're enjoying yourself, then? Steffyn's voice entered my head. I opened my eyes and glanced back at him.

Oh, yes. Though I think it might be better if we had thought to bring heavier cloaks. Indeed, I was starting to feel just how chilly it was at this height and shivered, though I realized (though I would never tell him) that Steffyn's body heat and fur were doing a good job in helping me stay warm.

Yes, I had forgotten. He sounded rueful. *However, I have asked them to remain at a lower altitude than is their usual wont, so we should be alright.* I turned back to face the front. Since we had multiple hours of uninterrupted flight ahead of us, it was the perfect time for me to really corner him about Abba again. However, a whispering in my spirit bade me wait. So I said nothing, and waited.

⸙

Several hours passed. I was starting to feel quite sleepy – though not enough, yet, to brave falling asleep in midair – when Steffyn spoke, startling me. *Your songs.*

What about them? I asked.

It's been a very long time since I last listened to songs like that. And about...how we left things yesterday. I apologize-

Would you stop that? I interrupted, turning around as best I could to face him.

Confusion was written in his eyes. *Stop what?*

Apologizing! It's not necessary, you know, no matter what I said about liking being apologized to the other night. At this point, it's a bit absurd. I understand. You're a cranky, cursed Brenwyd who's been living on his own for over two centuries and has for some reason quite firmly decided his Creator is no longer interested in him, and that therefore no one else can be interested in him either. I understand when your statements or reactions are not according to formal protocol. I'm happy that you recognize your own rudeness, but really, you've certainly apologized to me in the last two weeks enough to last the rest of my lifetime, so don't worry about doing it anymore. You won't offend me. Just get on with what you really wanted to say that this apologizing is getting in the way of. By the end of my mental tirade, he was staring at me in astonishment, his mouth partly open (which, given his teeth, was a little alarming). I stared

TO WAKE A KINGDOM

back at him for several minutes. *Well?* I finally asked. *Haven't you anything else to say?*

His reaction, when it finally came, was the absolute last thing I expected. A curious expression crossed his face, he began to make a strange huffing and chuffing noise, and a merry light lit his eyes. Slowly, it dawned on me that he was *laughing.* Really laughing. *I'm glad you've finally found something amusing,* I said primly, feeling (despite my words) slightly offended. But mostly, I was glad that I had made him laugh. I was sure to guard that feeling, however.

It's been a very long time since anyone has spoken to me like that, he finally said, merriment coloring his mental voice. I decided I liked how it sounded with laughter. Much better than the solemn gravity he spoke with much of the time. *And I most certainly deserve it.* By then, he had regained himself and was once again serious. *Your accusations are rather accurate, though...it does pain me to hear it like that.*

Everyone needs a good dose of honesty every so often, my mother says, I answered. *You are most likely far overdue.*

Hmm. Likely, he admitted, though I heard the reluctance in his voice.

So. Now that's settled, you were saying something about the songs? I prompted. For now, I ignored his reference to yesterday's quarrel. I didn't think revisiting that topic would do either of us much good.

*Yes...I...I wish to...thank you. I...needed that. Much as it galls me to admit it. You...*His voice took on a rueful note. *You seem to have a way of shining light on things that I have long kept hidden, even from myself. It is not comfortable but...perhaps necessary.*

Hope flared up within me, bright and unquenchable. *Does that mean you-?*

No. His quiet refusal stopped me as surely as if he had shouted. *I mean...it evoked...many memories for me that I have long kept buried. I'm trying to...sort through them, and...* His voice trailed off.

And? I prompted.

He shrugged. *And...I do not know. There is a reason I have suppressed them for so long, and they do not seem to want to retreat. I am being forced to think about them.* He sounded a little angry at that.

I frowned. *So are you thanking me or blaming me?*

He let out a long breath. *Honestly...I don't know anymore. I only know that you poke and prod and make me think about and remember things I have tried my hardest to forget, ask questions of me that I would rather not answer.* I blinked, very confused as to what he was trying to say. *And yet...I cannot feel any – well, very little – resentment toward you for it, for I can see that you do believe you're acting with the intention of...helping me. You...you have convinced me of your sincerity. But... I do not want to face her with this turmoil. It will distract me.* That was delivered somewhat fiercely.

He seemed to be rambling. It was a far cry from his implacable attitude of yesterday. My songs must have struck a deep nerve. That, and...was Abba himself prompting this turmoil? *I sang only the truth,* I said. *Perhaps you need to make a final decision of whether to listen to it or fully turn away.*

I know better than to deny the truth, he said gruffly.

Do you? What have the last two and a half centuries been for you, but denying the truth of Abba's love and prolonging your own suffering?

At that, he quite definitely glared at me. *Oh, why did I decide to talk to you? It's much easier keeping my own counsel.* He fixed his gaze to stare over my head. *Put this conversation from your mind. We go to battle Morrian. That is all we must focus on. We must defeat her. Please, do not distract me anymore.*

I glared back at him. Did he really think I would let him end the conversation on that note? *No, it is not all we must focus on. To defeat her, we must know the truth, and focus on Abba. And it may be easier keeping your own counsel, but the fact you are so torn up and conflicted inside tells me that there is some part of you that recognizes how far you have come from the truth and wants you to embrace it once again. Don't let your foolish pride quash that impulse! You're right, we will battle*

Morrian soon. Very soon. Do you really want to face her again having forsaken the protection Abba extends to you freely?

He was sitting ramrod straight, hard tension in every muscle. *I can fend for myself,* he said with an icy note in his voice. *You just worry about doing your part.* Suddenly, for a reason I could not fathom, his tone reminded me of...something. Someone. *Morrian.* I caught my breath, chilled more thoroughly by that comparison than by the wind biting through my clothes.

Can you truly not see your own danger? I asked him, allowing a pleading tone to enter my thoughts. *If you face her like this...you could die!*

Something that is far overdue.

And where do you think your soul will go if you die in this state of rebellion against Abba? That question he didn't answer. I was all for pressing him further, but a quiet pause in my soul bade me be quiet. I had said all I could say and know he would listen. Again, I had to acknowledge that it was Abba who was ultimately responsible for Steffyn. So I bowed my head to pray that by the time we reached Morrian, Steffyn would once again be accepting of Abba's love and protection.

⁘

Steffyn maintained his rigid tension until he felt Aislinn relax and slump against him in sleep. Even then, he did not relax much. Besides the distraction of her body pressed against his, her words had produced a turmoil in his mind such as he had not felt since the eve before the last time he faced Morrian – and he acknowledged grimly the irony of once more having such turmoil plague his soul as a result of the words of a Sighted Brenwyd maiden. He didn't look, but he could picture Aislinn's face relaxed in rest, the worried furrow so often between her brows when awake gone, and her whole demeanor seemingly radiating peace with the world. It was something he had seen much of on their journey.

And yet...her words. Each flew straight to his heart, his mind, with devastating accuracy, with every argument they had. *You're a cranky, cursed Brenwyd who's been living on his own for over two centuries and who has for some reason quite firmly decided his Creator is no longer interested in him.* He could not deny the truth of the accusation. But it rankled deeply. Cranky, he could concede, though he believed the current circumstances excused crankiness. Although he was forced to acknowledge that his traveling companions had never allowed themselves to give into the gloom that had been his companion for many years, he had – up to this point – excused it as ignorance, since only he really knew Morrian. But Aislinn's songs the previous afternoon had provided another answer for their relative peace – Abba. He shut his eyes tightly at the remembrance, as if that would shut out the memory. He remembered a time when such singing had soothed his spirit instead of causing it to writhe in uncertainty. He knew he could not deny the truth of what she sang, the truth of what she said when she spoke of the danger of approaching Morrian without Abba's protection, and yet...and yet. He had faced Morrian on his own all those years ago. And lived. But with a terrible price. He opened his eyes and considered his gloved hands, which one could more properly call the paws of a beast, and noted the contrast between Aislinn's smooth, pale skin and his own arm covered in dark fur. A monster. Cursed. He looked once more past Neriah's head toward the horizon, where he knew Morrian's fortress lay, and was steadily growing nearer.

The fortress. Memories rushed in unbidden, forcing his eyes closed again. Memories of darkness. Pain. Humiliation. Torment. He remembered being chained, chains that burned as fire, and his wrists itched in remembrance. He remembered her, her sardonic smiles, her sadistic pleasure in singling him out. He remembered her forcing him to look into her eyes, eyes of madness, and the visions she forced on him, visions that left him screaming and pushed him to the brink of insanity. To the brink, but never over.

She knew her craft. Once she pushed him too far, he would no longer respond as she wanted. But she came so, so close. There had been days he wondered whether it would be better to allow himself to be pushed into insanity. At least then he would be somewhat free of her tortures. But always he had rallied, always he had determined to endure, by thinking of all those he loved who still knew not her real character, of all those she stood to hurt should he not survive and escape. Well, one person in particular, really. Elfleda.

The memory of her blue eyes, her blond hair, the way she laughed, the way she teased, her compassionate heart. That was what had kept him sane. But when he finally did escape, he found that those on the outside could not comfort him. He woke up, sweating, sometimes screaming, from nightmares. Eventually he decided to sleep as little as possible, but this had only made him more irritable, prone to angry outbursts. He had known they were worried about him. He saw the way Elfleda looked at him with concern clouding her face, but he could not speak of what she had done to him. What exactly she had made him see. And why those visions prevented him from seeking full solace and healing. He had been afraid that if he told, they would spurn him, for then they would know what he was capable of, the danger that lurked inside him. A danger he hardly admitted to himself, but of which he was so conscious that he pushed them all away. Including Aislinn. Including Abba.

Steffyn sighed, shuddering mentally and with effort pulling himself from his musings and memories. The past was past and could not be undone. This time, he would finish his duty. He would make sure, this time, that she died. *And then what?* he thought. *What will you do then, Steffyn? Spend another two hundred years on the mountain? Spend another two hundred years alone, with only the most meager human contact? Your curse will never be broken. She is too clever to allow her spells to lapse with her death.*

But is she? A small part of him wondered. Could her spells really survive her? Two hundred years had deadened his sense of hope, until it was nearly gone. But that voice was stronger than it had been.

He felt Aislinn shift her position slightly. He wondered if she was dreaming. He hoped not. Considering the challenge she was about to face, she needed this sleep, this rest. Worry for her sliced through him. Despite sending the princess to guide the others to them, Aislinn would still initially face Morrian on her own. She had some idea of what she was up against, which was good. And she was certain in Abba, which was also good. She would need it.

And what about you? a voice whispered in his head. A voice that sounded very like Aislinn. *Don't you also need that certainty?*

I'll be fine, he retorted. *I survived before.*

Survival is not living.

Who said I wanted to live this time?

You would be willing to die without reconciling yourself to Abba? You know what would become of your soul then. She had said nearly those exact words. He couldn't help wincing. He knew. His mother had made sure of it.

Abba has not showed himself so concerned with me, he thought heatedly.

Or have you merely determined not to be concerned with him?

Oh, go away, he thought grumpily. *This is ridiculous. I'm arguing with myself.* But that thought was closely followed by the thought that if he did not, somewhere deep within, recognize his lacking and his folly, he would not be having this argument with himself, and Aislinn's words wouldn't affect him so. Steadily, he pushed that thought away as well. He could wrestle with his theological concerns after Morrian was dead. Until then, nothing else mattered.

Truly? That errant part of him whispered. *You know the reason Brenwyds would take up songs of praise before battle, why they always prayed before engaging on the battlefield. It was so if they did die, they would die right-hearted before Abba. Do you really want to take a chance on your eternity?*

He growled. *Be silent. I have to concentrate.*

"Are you well?" Neriah asked. He had swiveled his head around to talk to Steffyn face-to-face. "Is the ride too jolting? I thought I heard a groan."

He shook his head. "No, the ride is fine. It is my own thoughts that are uncomfortable. Forgive me."

Neriah bared his teeth and a fierce glint lit the young leviathan's eye. "Have no fear. I am sure Barak, Kezia, and I can send fire on this sorceress before she has a chance to do much of anything."

Steffyn found his optimism ill-founded, but he couldn't begrudge it of him. Leviathans were a proud, confident race by nature. It was truly astonishing they so willingly bowed to Abba. He decided not to dampen his spirits. "I pray you are right."

"Neriah! Look where you are flying, youngling!" Barak called. "Or do you want to unbalance your passengers and have them fall to the ground?"

"I would catch them first," Neriah said, but he did as the older male said. Barak snorted, but did not otherwise reply.

Steffyn felt Aislinn stir, likely wakened by the words. "Has something happened?" she murmured, sounding sleepy. He glanced down at her. Her green eyes were still clouded with slumber.

"No. Not yet. Go back to sleep. You will need it."

"Alright." After several more minutes, he felt her mind slip back into slumber, and he was left to his thoughts, his traitorous, tormenting thoughts. He sighed and looked up into the sky.

He remembered his promise to her the day before. She had chosen her words well; certainly he believed, despite his estrangement from Abba, that Abba would care about someone as fervent and good as Aislinn. And so he found a prayer, his first in years – centuries, even – making its way from his mind: *Oh, Abba, I know I have no right to ask this, but if possible, protect Aislinn from any lasting harm from Morrian. She does not deserve it.* And he found his thoughts settling on a resolution he could make wholeheartedly:

to do his utmost to protect this girl from Morrian's wiles, and to make sure she would not have to experience the torment he had gone through at the sorceress's hands.

Morrian's Fortress

$\mathcal{O}$ur two days of travel at times passed agonizingly slowly for my tastes, and other times much too fast. We flew for so many hours that, despite our rest breaks every so often, I felt like the impression of leviathan scales was being permanently etched into my skin, and my eyes began to feel strained from squinting against the wind. So, I actually ended up sleeping most of the time. Lissa asked me, on our long break the second day of travel, how I managed it. I had no good answer for her. She looked disappointed, and I decided that she must have thought it would be more pleasant to pass the hours in oblivious slumber. In the hours when I was awake, I noticed that her expression never completely lost its edge of nervousness.

Despite my physical discomfort, I did find myself thoroughly enjoying flying. The views from above were incredible. I made a resolution in my mind that, assuming we all survived the coming confrontation, I would ask a leviathan to fly me over various aspects of the kingdom so I could make sketches from above. The idea presented tantalizing possibilities for the artist in me. And, it helped distract me from my growing unease as we flew further north. I believed in my words about Abba, and I believed in Abba, and I knew I had to face this witch. But that didn't preclude me from feeling fear all the same. Whenever my thoughts strayed too far in a fearful direction, I firmly set in my mind the images of my family. They were who I was fighting for. They were what was at stake. The exercise, along with prayer, served to firm up my determination again and again.

Those thoughts only occupied me when I was awake, however. When I was asleep, I alternated between true sleep and dreams. I didn't have what I would call proper dreams, but I saw various images and scenes that flicked from one to the other in no particular order, never seeing the same thing for more than a few seconds.

I saw Rhodri's mother and her party journeying through the night, the outriders looking tense with hands hovering over sword hilts. Duchess Rhian looked unusually grim and determined. I wondered what was hunting them. Then I watched Rhodri's brothers, Cerdic and Rhys, in council with men I recognized as captains of their guards and others I suspected were the headmen and headwomen of the villages within the province, obviously in serious discussion about something. I saw many scenes where I recognized neither the people nor the places, but I saw monsters – ogres, elemental dragons, and others – wreaking havoc on villages. Morrian was sowing her work well. Everyone was far too busy battling their own problems to take the time to trouble about Ecclesia, especially since it was on the other side of the Anianol Forest. Morrian appeared before my mind's eye, watching the scenes of havoc through her mirror wall, and obviously pleased with the view. The last thing I saw was the strange white sphere near the rose, and I saw that it was almost fully opaque. We were running out of time, though according to my calculation we should still have a week left before the curse finalized and Morrian enacted her true intentions.

It was in the midst of such half-dreams on the second night of our travel that I was jerked awake by Steffyn gently shaking my shoulder. "Aislinn, wake up."

I came fully alert with a start. "Are we there?" On our last stop some time previous, he had estimated that we would reach the mainland shore near Morrian's fortress before much longer.

"Nearly. I thought it was best to wake you now, so you can see as we fly in."

"Thank you." The night sky was clear, and with the light of the stars and moon I could see the terrain below. The northern mountains were now behind us, and the shoreline had changed from plunging cliffs to sloping dunes, like the beaches of the south. I hadn't realized the same held true this far north. Since looking down made me start to feel slightly dizzy, I fixed my gaze firmly on Kezia's gently bobbing head in front of me. I considered the tone of Steffyn's voice. Between my sleeping and the conversations we held with whichever leviathan we were riding when awake, Steffyn and I had not spoken candidly of serious matters again since the start of this final journey. I wondered if Steffyn would grow more agitated the closer we got to Morrian. If so, there was no hint of it in his voice at the moment. "And...how are you?" I knew he would understand what I was really asking with that question. I kept my voice low to keep Kezia from overhearing.

Several heartbeats passed before he answered. When he did, he answered mentally in a firm, decided tone. *I will be fine. Have no thought for me.*

Then you have-

No. His voice was calm. *No, Aislinn, please do not push me on this. I...I know you are concerned, but we must focus only on our tasks. If we allow anything to distract us from our purpose, we will fail. She will take the slightest inattention, the slightest distraction, and use it to gain the upper hand. Do not waste your energy in arguing and worrying about me.*

I released an exasperated sigh and turned to face him. *How can I not, when you insist on being so obstinate?*

Aislinn. I saw that his eyes were full of earnestness. Earnestness and...despair? *Please. Do not waste your worry on me. Remember, the whole kingdom, the continent, is at stake. If Morrian succeeds in opening the Demon's Gate, everyone will fall. We have to stop her now, and you cannot be distracted.* Behind his even tone was one of great sadness, and suddenly I was very frightened by what I thought I was seeing in his eyes.

But, Steffyn...

At that moment, Kezia unknowingly interrupted us, her head coming straight up and ears alert. "I can sense something in the air...a heaviness that does not seem natural. Are we nearly there?"

"Yes," Steffyn called to her, raising his voice. I felt him turn a bit so his words would carry to the other two leviathans, and Lissa and Rhodri on Barak. "Keep flying straight. It shan't be long now."

Barak drifted over closer. "Indeed. I can already begin to feel a great evil ahead." Now that he and Kezia had mentioned it, I realized that I, too, could sense something ahead, a great darkness that caused the hair on the back of my neck to stand up and goosebumps to rise on my arms, and it weighed on my mind with almost a physical weight. I looked to my right, and saw Lissa and Rhodri sitting up straight on Barak's back, postures tense. Rhodri's jaw was set in grim determination, while Lissa's brow furrowed in a worried expression. She turned her head and our eyes met for a few moments. In her eyes I saw fear, but that fear was overshadowed by a set resolve. Mine was probably similar. Lissa smiled then, a weak smile, but a smile nonetheless, and the sight of it inexplicably reassured me a great deal. I smiled back, a smile that I hope acknowledged how out of my depth I felt, but also the hope I had that we would succeed. I turned my gaze to look ahead of us, and sensed Steffyn lean forward against my back slightly as if he was searching for something specific up ahead. He was likely looking for the first glimpse of the fortress so he could tell the leviathans to land immediately on the mainland below to wait until dawn. The light contact between us made me frown as I once again considered his mindset.

A verse from the Holy Word threaded its way through my mind just then: *Let nothing trouble you, but instead bring everything with prayer, supplication, and thanksgiving to Abba...And the peace of Abba, which passes all understanding, shall cover you.* I knew it was no coincidence which caused that verse to come to mind just then; it was a reminder that, once again, I was ultimately not responsible for him. Abba was. Only Abba could change his heart, and that was if he let him. I had recognized that previously, but now I sensed something else, another meaning coming to me behind the verse. Deep in my soul, I sensed that Abba was telling me to let Steffyn go. I could do no more for him right now.

It was a hard command. I realized that I didn't want to give it up. I wanted to be the one able to change his heart and mind. Very, very much. I frowned a little more as I began to consider why, then decided not to go there, quieting the recollection of Lissa's suspicions about the relationship between myself and Steffyn. I didn't want anything like *that* on my mind at the moment. I released another sigh, this one a sigh of reluctant surrender.

"What?" Steffyn asked.

I blinked. "What? I said nothing."

"That was a rather heavy sigh."

"Oh. Nothing."

"Are you sure?"

"Now who's worrying?" He didn't answer that. I sighed again. I seemed rather fond of sighing. "Steffyn, look. I am worried for you, and I cannot help it. But I also know you are right in saying I must let nothing distract me. I...I will stop haranguing you. For now."

"For now?"

"At least until after we defeat Morrian."

"You sound confident."

"I'm trusting Abba. It does wonders for one's confidence."

"I thought you said you would stop that."

"I'm simply stating a fact." He was silent for long enough that I turned to look at him. He was staring at me, eyes thoughtful. "What?"

He shook his head slightly as if clearing it and shifted his gaze back to the sky ahead of us. "Nothing. You are right. We will talk more...after." A pause. *Aislinn?* This was to my mind, and it sounded very uncertain.

Yes?

There's...there's something I should probably tell you. He stopped.

Yes? I prompted.

About...Morrian. And me. You see, we didn't just-

"Is that it?" Neriah called back. As the current scout, he had been flying a bit ahead of us, and now came to a stop, hovering in place. He pointed with his left forearm. "I see an island up ahead, and there appears to be a man-made structure on it." I leaned forward, probing the darkness with my eyes for what he saw. After a few moments, I located it – barely. It was at the outer edge of my vision. I mainly made it out through the flashes of white that appeared on the otherwise ebony ocean as the waves met the rocks. This coastline, I could tell, was not like the gentle slopes of sand in the south. It was full of rocks, which the waves beat against mercilessly. A cold feeling snaked through my body. We were here. It was time.

"Yes, that is it," Steffyn answered the dragon. He turned his head so he was looking down. "We should land there, behind those rocks." I could see where he meant. Not directly on the coast, but close, and there was a large plain where there was plenty of room for the leviathans to land, and for Dynin (and other horses) to transfer. Kezia descended rather quickly, causing my stomach to feel like it flipped over itself and me to let out an involuntary squeak. I heard Steffyn grunt. When Kezia's talons dug into the ground several heartbeats later, Neriah landing next to her, it took a minute for me to get my bearings. Looking up, I saw Barak making a more decorous descent, coming down in ever-descending circles.

Steffyn undid his straps and dismounted down the leviathan's foreleg, which she held out for the purpose. Once he was down, he turned to me. "Coming?"

"Ah...yes. One moment." I had undone my straps, but the distance between myself and the ground seemed rather far and my equilibrium was still a little rattled. I went to perform the dismounting maneuver – which I had done successfully several times by this point – but slipped on Kezia's slick scales. With a cry I found myself falling – and then I was abruptly stopped by something soft.

"Oof." Steffyn muttered in my ear. "Are you alright?" I realized I had fallen into him, and he had caught me. Which meant he was currently holding me in his arms in a rather intimate position.

"Ah...yes. Thanks." He quickly put me on my feet. I had a strange tingly feeling in my stomach.

"Are you alright?" Now it was Kezia asking the question. "I apologize, did I descend too quickly?"

"Oh no, it was fine. I simply slipped on your scales. They were more slippery than I anticipated."

"Hmm." She examined herself. "Well, they need to be smooth to move through the water quickly."

"Oh, I wasn't blaming you. Merely making an observation."

"So, what now?" Neriah asked. I turned toward him, seeing that beyond him Barak had landed and Lissa and Rhodri were in the process of dismounting. I waited for them to finish and come join us before I answered Neriah's question.

I looked around at our group, making brief eye contact with each of them. "I'll call Dynin," I said. My gaze landed on Lissa. "Then, once Dynin is sure he can transfer back here again, Lissa, you two should go to Tairport. I'll try to contact Delwyn again and make sure he and his people are standing ready or almost there. Then, I suppose," I couldn't help glancing over my shoulder toward the coast, though my view was blocked by the rocks, "we must wait until close to dawn and...approach the island." I turned to Steffyn, trying to ignore the feeling of my stomach tying itself in knots at the thought of the sorceress so close. "How did you say that tunnel was accessed?"

"We will have to swim," he said, looking at Barak. "It will be best, Barak, if you three can carry us through the water in your wings. It is too cold for us to make the swim ourselves. The cavern is located on the southwest side of the island. There is a gap between the rocks. It looks small, but once under the island it enlarges quickly. All three of you will fit easily."

Barak dipped his head. "Of course. That is easily done."

"What do you mean, carried in the wings?" Rhodri asked.

"It is a technique we use when transporting things by water when we need to keep them dry." The older leviathan reared up on his hind legs and unfurled his wings. He then wrapped them around himself, and I could see that they made a pocket between the wing and his stomach where something – or someone – could go. "The cavity made is water-tight. It is quite safe."

"Ah. Alright." Rhodri sounded a bit dubious, but he didn't dwell on the topic. He turned to me instead. "So, will you be able to sense when she leaves?"

"I should be able to easily, considering the effect of the last time I sensed her approach," I said, remembering the way the twisted songs of her magic had pounded into my ears. "The question is, do we want to wait here until she leaves, or wait in this underground cavern near the tunnel entrance?"

"This feels a bit too exposed for my liking," Rhodri said, looking around the plain. "It's fine while in the dark, but if we wait until dawn then she could very well see us on her way out, and I doubt she would pass us by even with the thorns coming down."

"The prince speaks correctly," Steffyn said. "We can wait here for several hours, but we should be in the cavern before dawn starts to break. Your Highness," he turned toward Lissa, "you should leave at the same time. You need to have a place to safely hide while the leviathans attack the wall."

Lissa nodded, gripping Rhodri's hand and leaning into him. "I don't like leaving you all here, like this," she said softly. She looked up at her fiancé. "Especially after the last time we were separated."

Rhodri looked down at her, eyes filled with worry, but also trying to be reassuring. "I know, Lissa. But we have to."

"I'll make sure he doesn't fall through any more pathways, if that makes you feel any better," I told her, trying to lighten the mood.

It didn't really, but I could tell Lissa appreciated the attempt. "A little, I suppose."

"Aislinn." Steffyn. He was looking up at the sky, likely calculating how close it was to dawn. By my estimation, it was a little after midnight. Considering how far north and east we were, I thought we had about five and a half hours until daylight. Which meant we had more like four and a half hours until we needed to be safely concealed in the underground cavern. "You need to call Dynin now."

I nodded. "Of course."

"How are you going to call him?" Kezia asked.

"In my mind. Watch." I walked a bit of a distance from the others, making sure Dynin had enough room to slow down from his transfer without having to worry about running into anything or anyone. Then I closed my eyes and reached for my memories of him. I had called him this way before, but never from such a distance. *Dynin. Dynin, come.* I focused on my need for him, the danger facing us, the love between us, and sending out my need from my mind. For a few moments, I felt nothing. Then I felt a faint sense of acknowledgment, and I opened my eyes. A minute later, I sensed him clearly, and he burst onto the plain in front of me, seemingly materializing from thin air at a full gallop. I wondered once again how exactly the horses did it. When asked, they just said they ran fast with a place in mind and got there – not the most helpful explanation. However it worked, I, along with every other Brenwyd alive, was very grateful for it.

He quickly slowed and came toward me at a trot, letting out a whinny. *Hush*, I thought to him immediately. *We don't know what enemies could be around here.*

Oh. Sorry. But you are well? You came to no harm? By this point he had stopped in front of me and was nuzzling my face and hair to reassure himself of my welfare.

I smiled despite myself, my spirits boosted merely by his presence. *Yes. I am fine. Now come on, you need to look around to be sure you can return.* I turned, and he followed me back to the others, but with suspicious looks at the leviathans.

"How did you do that?" Neriah asked him, eyes wide. I found it somewhat amusing that he asked Dynin directly. Usually, the only ones who talked directly to the horses were Brenwyds.

I ran, Dynin answered simply. It was the best answer he had.

The next few hours were tense. I considered sleeping, as Lissa and Rhodri did, but found my nerves too tightly wound for it. I did successfully See Delwyn. I could not speak with him, but I could See that he was preparing a company of Brenwyds to ride out. Their numbers heartened me; I counted fifty. I also Saw Cerdic and Rhys milling about with Delwyn, asking him questions about the time frame. I slowly gathered that Cerdic intended to ride with them to the south, and he was bringing a larger company of his own soldiers to protect the Brenwyds from physical attack while they fought the magic of the barrier. It was a good plan, actually; I remembered that the downfall of Sir Eiwas and Lord Duke Ceredon's group had been that they could not fight both the physical and the magical at once. Rhys seemed to want to join them as well, but recognized that he needed to stay to protect the province. At the end of the Seeing, I was reassured that there would be Brenwyds waiting on the other side of the barrier.

When I finished Seeing, I considered talking to Steffyn again, but he was standing a fair distance off, and again there was a check in my spirit that told me I needed to leave him to Abba. So instead, I talked with the leviathans, giving them last-minute information on how Brenwyds fought and how they might best support them. Despite the length of time since Brenwyds and leviathans had last fought together, we each knew enough of our own tactics to figure out how they could work best together.

Finally, I could sense the approach of dawn. It was still a way off, but the songs in the air around me of the grass and waves began to alter subtly in the way they did when nature knew the sun was readying herself for another journey through the skies. I woke Lissa and Rhodri. Now I was the one marveling at how they had managed to sleep. Perhaps it was because they had been unsuccessful in doing so mid-flight. Steffyn reappeared in our midst as the two royals rubbed the sleep from their eyes.

I looked to Lissa. "Are you ready?"

She nodded. "Yes." I called Dynin and checked his neck strap, making sure it was still secure enough for Lissa to hold onto. She was not a very experienced bareback rider, but as long as she could hang on, Dynin wouldn't let her fall.

"Lissa, here, take this," Rhodri said. From his pocket, he took a ring. I recognized it; it was the ring that had the sigil of his father's house. He always had it, though he only wore it on his finger when needed on state occasions. He said that it got in his way when he was doing everyday things. I raised an eyebrow to see him offer it to Lissa, though. Signet rings were incredibly important to nobles, and giving one away was usually tantamount to transferring one's property to the recipient.

Lissa looked at the ring, then back at Rhodri. "Rhodri, I hope this does not mean you are planning any foolish heroics."

He smiled and pushed a tendril of hair behind her ear. "No. But...just in case, all the same. Please?"

For a moment I thought she would refuse. But then she nodded, blinking rapidly. "Very well. I will keep it safe for you." They looked at each other for several long moments, no doubt reading in each other's faces what was not said aloud. I looked away to give them a little bit of privacy and noticed Steffyn doing the same. He was talking quietly with the leviathans, giving them more particulars as to the location of the underwater cavern we were making for. I wondered what he had been about to tell me on Kezia's back.

I felt a touch on my shoulder and turned to see Lissa. "It's alright, you can look now."

I smiled. "Why, thank you." I hugged her. "Be safe. Come back quickly. May Abba watch over you."

"The same to you. I will be back as quickly as possible." She pulled back from the embrace and looked at me seriously. "Be careful. Please." I nodded. There was a tightness in my throat that kept me from speaking.

Rhodri boosted her onto Dynin's back. Dynin nudged me with his muzzle. *Heed the princess's words.*

I will, as best I can. I stroked his neck and looked into his gentle brown eyes. *I promise.* He nickered low in his throat, plainly unhappy with leaving me. But we both knew it was necessary.

"Good speed to you, Your Highness," Steffyn rumbled behind me. "Hopefully by the time you return we will have destroyed the rose and gained the boat. If not, Barak, Neriah, and Kezia will be here."

"Very well." She looked at us, opened her mouth, and closed it again. There really wasn't much left to say. "Abba protect you all."

"And you," Rhodri said. She nodded, blinked rapidly, then bent down and reached out her hand to him. He took it, drawing her closer, and they exchanged a last, brief kiss. Then Rhodri stepped back, Lissa turned Dynin around, tapped her heels gently against his sides, and he took off, achieving a gallop in a few paces, and then, after a few more, vanishing.

"That is a most useful ability," Barak said above my head.

I nodded, trying to push away the thought that I might just have seen my best friend and my horse for the last time in this life. I took a deep breath and turned to face the direction of the coast. "Shall we go then?"

⁓ᘓᙢᘐ⁓

The logistics of actually getting to the island turned out to be a bit trickier and more uncomfortable than we had thought. We walked the remaining distance to the shore. I could clearly see the dark island out in the ocean. As I had seen in my dreams, it had the shape of a tall, circular tower surrounded by a lower wall in the shape of a square with towers on the corners. Once we reached the coast, we had to get ourselves situated against the leviathans' bellies so their wings wrapped around us to protect us from the cold seawater. It was rather uncomfortable being pressed up against Neriah's hard belly. It was also rather hot. I began to understand why leviathans needed to stay close to water. If I was that hot all the time, I certainly would. I had felt some heat during the flight, but it was much more pronounced in this position.

Rhodri was riding with Kezia, and Steffyn with Barak. Once we were safely and firmly ensconced in the wings (though I still wasn't so sure about the arrangement), I sensed Barak and the two younger ones comparing observations about the shore, the distance, the choppiness of the water, and such. Then, I felt Neriah climb down the rocks, and he entered the water.

I stayed dry, but I could feel the cold of the water through Neriah's wings. Suddenly I was very glad of the heat radiating through his belly, and better understood why (besides the fire) leviathans were so hot; they needed the heat to swim through the depths of the sea. I also held my breath for as long as I could, but eventually I had to breathe. Barak had assured us that there would be air trapped in the little cocoon made by their wings, but I hadn't quite believed it. I was relieved to discover that was true.

Are you alright? Neriah asked.

Yes, I'm fine. Thank you.

In one sense the swim seemed endless, but in another, much too short. Before I knew it, I heard Steffyn giving the leviathans specific directions to this underwater cavern, and I sensed the creatures diving deeper, then coming back up and breaking the water's surface.

I see the small ledge you mentioned, Barak said. *It will be hard to get you onto it without you getting wet.*

We may just have to deal with that, Steffyn answered. *Could you rear up some and just partially unfurl your wings above the ledge?*

I don't think the ceiling is high enough, Kezia said doubtfully. *Barak, could we dry them like we do fish?*

What? I asked, a little alarmed by the question.

Perhaps, the older leviathan said thoughtfully. *And do not be alarmed, Lady Aislinn. Sometimes, after we catch fish, we dry them to preserve them, as humans do, I understand. We can blow hot air onto them and it dries them out quickly. What Kezia is suggesting is that we let you out into the water to get to the ledge, but then we blow on you to dry you off and warm you up. I think it would work.*

Are you sure it wouldn't cook us? I asked.

It won't, Steffyn spoke up. *I remember now. The leviathans would do that sometimes in the camp when it was very cold. It was very nice.*

So we're swimming to the ledge? Where is it in relation to where we are now? I asked.

It is just in front of me, Lady Aislinn, Neriah said. *All you have to do is swim upward along my belly until you breach the surface. Then, it is right there.*

Alright. You might as well unfurl your wings then.

Hold your breath, he said. I had several heartbeats to fill my lungs with air, and then I felt Neriah's wings unfurl, exposing me to the water. It was very cold, colder even than the deep spring near Kheprah where I often went swimming in the hot Ecclesian summers. I just barely managed to keep from gasping at the shock of it. My fingers and toes instantly went numb, and I began to move to keep my limbs from freezing in place. Now I was even gladder for the heat emanating from Neriah, for it enabled me to move. I quickly kicked upward, my only guide that of Neriah's belly. There was obviously no light source in this cave, for I could not distinguish the surface of the water from the seafloor. Still, within a few seconds I broke through the surface, gasping.

Where is the ledge? I asked, turning my head in various directions. I had never experienced such complete blackness before. Usually, even on nights when clouds covered the moon and stars, I could still make out the landscape around me with my keen Brenwyd eyes, but now I saw absolutely nothing. I finally felt like I had an understanding of Lissa's childhood fear of the dark.

Turn around. It's right in front, no more than a few strokes, Neriah answered. I did as he said, though leaving the reassuring solidity of his body was nerve-wracking. But sure enough, within ten strokes I hit rock, and extending my hand along its outline, discerned the shape of a ledge. I put both hands on the ledge and tried to raise myself from the freezing water. However, the cold had sapped me, and I struggled, nearly falling back into the water.

"Aislinn, here. I'll pull you up," came Steffyn's voice from the darkness. I raised a hand blindly. I couldn't see him at all. The darkness was disorienting. Fortunately, I felt his hand take mine in a strong grip, and he hauled me onto the dry rock.

"Th-th-thanksss," I managed, teeth chattering so I could hardly speak. "I-i-s Rh-Rhodri...?"

"H-here," Rhodri answered, voice shaking as mine was. "Th-that's really c-cold water."

"Neriah, Kezia, air, now," I heard Barak say. Suddenly I felt a blast of superheated air, and my shaking began to subside. After several minutes, it ceased altogether. Indeed, I started to feel too warm.

"That is enough," Steffyn said. The hot air ceased.

"Now that is some great heating," I heard Rhodri say. "Aislinn, after...we get this done, remind me to see about installing some real heaters in the castle."

"Rhodri, the castle already has a great number of fireplaces."

"No, I mean heaters...they have them on Earth. Heating without fire."

"Really?"

"Fascinating as that is, we have to defeat Morrian first," Steffyn interjected with a dry note in his voice. "Our first course of action should be to find the room with the rose and the sphere."

"Right. Of course," Rhodri said. "Is there any way to get light? My electric torch won't work after that soaking."

"Once we get into the dungeons, we can find a regular torch," Steffyn said. "Barak, Neriah, Kezia, thank you for your help. Now I'm afraid we must wait for dawn. You can stay here with us or patrol the water around the island until Aislinn senses Morrian is gone."

"A patrol would be a good idea," Barak said from the darkness. "Who knows what creatures may be lurking in this foul place?"

"As long as it is not another sea serpent," Neriah said in low voice.

"What? Did our first encounter with one scare you off?" Kezia taunted.

"Of course not, but I have no desire to wrench my wing again. It hurt."

"If we find anything, our task will be to avoid its notice, if possible," Barak said. "We want this sorceress to leave without suspecting anything out of order. Understood?"

"Yes, Patriarch," the two chorused.

"Very well. We will wait on your call, Lady Aislinn. May Abba go with you, before you, and behind you, and may we meet soon to put an end to this sorceress."

"Abba go with you as well," I answered. I heard sounds indicating he had submerged once again.

"Do not worry. We are sure to be victorious!" Kezia's voice echoed through the cavern.

"That sorceress will rue the day she stirred up the ire of leviathans," Neriah agreed. There was definite glee in his voice at the thought of the upcoming altercation. Then I heard more sounds of submersion, and the cavern fell quiet.

"Leviathans," Steffyn said once we knew they had all gone. "As I said, always eager for a fight, no matter the odds."

"Still, it is Abba's blessing that led them to cross our path so soon. They are a valuable asset," Rhodri said. "Mathghamhain, are you sure you remember the way to the dungeons through this passage well enough to do it without a light?" I started involuntarily at Rhodri's use of "Mathghamhain." Of course, he had no knowledge of Steffyn's true identity, but I had grown used to his true name. I made a note to talk to him about telling Lissa and Rhodri the truth once this was over...assuming we survived.

"Yes. I did it the last time in darkness. I can do it now, as well. But we should wait here until Aislinn senses her leave."

"Any idea how long that will take?"

I shrugged, though I knew he couldn't see the gesture. "No. Hopefully, not too long." We lapsed into silence. I reflected later that until that last wait, I had no true concept of what the word interminable meant. It is one thing to wait patiently for something out in the open air, with at least enough light to see one's companions. It is another thing entirely to wait in darkness so complete it makes no difference whether your eyes are open or shut.

Fortunately, Rhodri kept up a light conversation on mundane things. I was grateful for it. I didn't think I could have endured that time either in complete silence, or in discussing the task immediately before us. We knew what we had to do, and I felt that any further talk on the subject would only make us more anxious. Rhodri probably had the same thought, for his talk centered on his time on Earth, and what he had seen and experienced. I hadn't really heard details of his full story before, and several of his anecdotes, particularly from his first weeks on earth, made me shake with suppressed laughter. Steffyn, however, remained completely silent, and I wondered how much he even listened. I knew he was sitting near me, for I could sense his song. At one point, driven by an impulse I didn't quite understand, I reached out toward where I thought his hand was, and once I found it, grasped it with my own. The touch was reassuring to me, a physical reminder that I was not alone in the darkness. I felt him start at my sudden contact, but he did not pull his hand from mine.

For all Rhodri's conversational skills (which were considerable), eventually our talk lapsed as time continued with no hint of Morrian's departure. I could feel the stress begin to pump through my body. Had we overestimated the leviathans' abilities to bring down the wall? Had Morrian's servants at the border overcome them and Delwyn's Brenwyds? Had something else gone wrong?

My mind continued inexorably on these thoughts, despite my attempts to reassure myself. Suddenly, though, my head snapped up and my senses went on high alert. I could hear something now with my song sense; something powerful, something evil, was waking in the fortress above us.

"Aislinn? Can you sense her?" Steffyn asked quietly, clearly sensing something of my abruptly focused attention.

"I think so." I gasped as the sound of Morrian's song and magic – similar to how I had sensed her approach in Kheprah – seemed to explode inside my head. I released Steffyn's hand to grip the sides of my head. "Yes, definitely. She's awake. And she seems very angry."

"Is she leaving?" Rhodri asked.

I hesitated, waiting...waiting...waiting...then, the pressure in my head and inner ears eased and stopped as quickly as it had started. I cautiously probed the area with my song sense, alert for any whisper of Morrian's magic, but sensed none. The fortress now seemed devoid of life except for myself and my companions. I extended my reach, pushing to the outer limits of my range. I found the leviathans swimming deep below the surface, but nothing else. They sensed my mental probe, and eagerly asked me if it was time, since the sun was now half-way into rising.

"She's left," I said, saying the words mentally as well for the sake of the leviathans. "I don't sense her anywhere."

"Could you try to See Tairport, just to be sure?" Steffyn asked. I nodded, knowing he would sense my assent despite not being able to see the movement, and did so.

I gasped again at the image that filled my mind's eye. The sun had indeed risen in colors of flame, though perhaps it simply appeared so from the quantity of fire being spouted from many leviathan mouths to engulf the wall of thorns. I heard the familiar howls of shadow wolves as the flames poured down from the aerial assault, and above that I heard the sweet, hard strains of Brenwyd battle songs. Then, a pause swept the field, and the brightness coming from the dawn dimmed. I could not see her exactly, but I knew. Morrian had arrived. Our plan was working. It made me smile, confidence returning, despite my worry for those now in the south.

I rose to my feet. "The battle is joined in the south. We need to move now."

"Good," Rhodri said. By the sounds from his direction, he was also getting to his feet. "I was about to go mad if we had to wait much longer. Which way, Mathghamhain?"

I felt Steffyn's hand brush my arm, then take a hold of my hand. "Prince Rhodri, Aislinn is just to your right. Take her hand. That way, no one gets lost."

"May I assume you have her other one?" Rhodri asked as he did so. He squeezed my hand slightly, as if in reassurance. I did find it heartening.

"Yes. The entrance is over here. Come, we must hurry." Steffyn gently pulled me to my feet, with Rhodri after me, and away from the water's edge. "The door to the passage should be somewhere around here," I heard him say under his breath. Long seconds passed. "Ah, here it is." I heard a deep groaning from the rock, then a screeching, grating noise like a gate opening for the first time in years. It made me wince. But Steffyn pulled me after him, and Rhodri and I followed him into the darkness of the tunnel.

DAWN AND FIRE

Lissa willed herself not to look back as Dynin took off for the transfer. If she did, she was sure she would start crying, and she needed to be strong. For her country. Her family. Rhodri. Aislinn. Oh, Abba, keep them safe, her mind cried. Please, keep them safe. Dynin accelerated to the transfer speed, and moments later their surroundings blurred.

She breathed an internal sigh of relief as Helmond appeared a few moments later and Dynin began to slow. She had ridden bareback only a handful of times before when she was a young child and didn't feel at all secure in her seat. It would be a relief to saddle Dynin properly, even if it was Aislinn's astride saddle instead of a sidesaddle.

She dismounted, feeling a little wobbly. *Are you alright?* Dynin asked her.

She nodded. "Yes. It's been a long time since I've ridden without a saddle, 'tis all." She waited a moment for her legs to regain their strength. "Come, we must hurry."

He followed her silently. Lissa had him tacked quickly. She might be a princess, but her parents had insisted she learn how to care for her own horse. Before she mounted again, she found herself pausing, staring at the leather of the saddle.

Dynin turned his head toward her. *What is it?*

She took a deep breath, shuddering a little. "I...I think it is simply crashing over me what it is we are trying to do. What I am doing. It is...it is not exactly what I ever imagined myself doing. I have not been trained for battle like this, Dynin. Not like the others."

He regarded her with a large brown eye for several moments. It made her miss her own mare, Caramel, sleeping under the curse back at the palace stables. *No*, he finally said. *You have not been trained. But you are willing to do all you can anyway. That counts for more than training, I think.*

A small smile broke through, and this time the breath she took was calm and even. "Thank you, Dynin. Aislinn is right, you give excellent counsel."

I only say what makes sense. We animals do not think big thoughts like you humans.

"Thank Abba for that." Lissa lifted herself into the saddle. She was grateful for the pants she and Aislinn had made from her petticoats under her overskirt. They would protect her legs from chafing on the leather saddle and keep her modestly covered while still astride. Aislinn would have laughed to hear such a concern at such a moment, but Lissa found it comforting to still consider such mundane things.

Several minutes later, she found herself looking at the white and grey buildings of Tairport. She had been here often on trips of state, and it brought tears to her eyes to see it so still and silent. Swallowing down the emotion, she looked upward, scanning the sky for any sign of the leviathans. She saw nothing, and she began to worry that something had happened, that they had been delayed.

Then Dynin snorted and pricked his ears up to full alertness. *They are here. I smell them.*

"Where?"

Suddenly, not far above them, the night sky seemed to shift and move. "Your Highness, I am glad to see you. Your party made it safely north then?"

Lissa felt her eyes widen as Bityah seemingly appeared from nowhere in the night, Aliyah behind her. The two landed close enough so Lissa could feel the slight vibration that shook the ground even from her position on Dynin's back. *Of course, they can camouflage,* she told herself once she recovered from her shock.

"Yes, we did. It was an uneventful journey, thank Abba. And yourselves? Did you have any trouble?"

Bityah shook her head. "No. We mostly traveled by sea and have kept ourselves hidden, as you saw. The others are waiting in the sea just past the harbor. Dawn will come soon. Did Lady Aislinn confirm that there will be Brenwyds waiting on the other side?"

"She did. They were preparing themselves as she Saw them, a good number. She said there will also be a company of regular soldiers accompanying them, led by one of Rhodri's older brothers. They will serve to protect the Brenwyds from any physical attacks while they attack the barrier."

"Ah, that is wise," Bityah said approvingly. She turned her head toward the direction of the barrier. Even Lissa, with her poor human vision in the darkness, could make out the wall of thorns and fog. It was the first time she had ever seen it, and its enormity made her shudder. "I wonder, Your Highness, do you think if we approached the barrier we might be able to contact any Brenwyds on the other side mentally? It would serve us well to be able to speak directly about our strategy."

Lissa frowned. "I am not sure if the magic of the barrier would let us, but I think we could certainly try. Cautiously. Remember, there may be monsters patrolling the border. We do not want to alert them."

"No," Aliyah said. She also turned to consider the distant barrier. "I will try to approach alone, hidden. If I see, hear, or smell anything I will return immediately. Your Highness, for your safety, it would likely be best for you to stay here."

"Yes," Lissa said slowly, considering. "But if Delwyn has questions, I may be the one best able to answer them."

"Easily done," Bityah said. "Your Highness, if you will accompany me to the outskirts of the city, I will be able to hear Aliyah at the border, and she can relay any questions to you through me. It is a cumbersome means of speaking, perhaps, but it will work well enough."

Lissa nodded. "Very well. I need to find a place to safely wait out the battle in any case."

"Let us find somewhere to wait before making your approach, Aliyah," Bityah told her. "If the monsters are alerted, the princess must be safe."

"Yes, Elder. I wait for your order." Aliyah bowed her head respectfully.

"Where would you like to wait, Your Highness?" Bityah asked.

Lissa considered the question. "All the houses are within the city walls. There are three gates to enter the city from land, each with its own gatehouse. The western gate would be the best, I think. It is well protected but will let me see what happens at the border easily enough. And there will be enough room for you just inside the gate, Dynin."

"Very well. Aliyah and I will fly to the western side. Can you ride through the city to the western gate?"

"I should be able to. Aislinn and Rhodri said that the gates were open, as the curse struck during daylight hours."

"Good. We will see you in a few moments, then." The leviathans shifted their scales to match the darkness of the air and took off. This time, Lissa could make out the movement against the sky and hear the quiet beat of wings as they flew above. Still, she marveled at their ability to become nearly invisible. Such a useful talent.

Shall we go? Dynin asked.

Lissa shook herself from her consideration of the amazing creatures. "Of course."

He began walking toward the eastern gate. *If you wish, I could also go with the one to the barrier. I may be able to contact their horses if she cannot contact the Brenwyds.*

"Hmm. That may be a good idea...but you could be at terrible risk if more of those shadow wolves appear. I could not face Aislinn if something happened to you."

He snorted, as if in scorn of the danger. *I can outrun any wolves. Do not worry for me.*

Lissa had a feeling that he intended to go in spite of any arguments she might make. Aislinn often said the gelding was stubborn. "If you think you must, I will not stop you. It is a good thought."

They fell silent as they entered the city. Lissa felt the tears threatening to return at the sight of the citizens – her people – slumped in the street, no more than motionless lumps barely distinguishable from the night itself. Despite reassurance from Rhodri, Aislinn, and even Mathghamhain that the curse was in no way her fault, she still felt some responsibility for pricking her finger on the rose thorn. She was the crown princess; her job was to evaluate and judge people. How had she not seen through Morrian's mask?

Are you alright? Dynin had stopped and was looking back at her. Lissa realized she had tensed up on his back.

"Yes..." She looked around. "No..."

Dynin followed her gaze and then turned back to her. *It will be alright. We will wake them. Trust Abba, Princess. He holds us all. He will not let evil win. Not while those who follow him fight against it.*

Lissa stared in disbelief at the horse. Aislinn had often spoken of Dynin's surprising insights and wisdom, but she was astonished to hear for herself such clear understanding. "How do you know that, Dynin?" she asked, curious.

Why should I not? All animals know the One cares for us. He orders the world. It would not make sense for him to let it fall. He paused, then added, *Also, I have often listened to Aislinn's father telling her things. I learn from her lessons also, you know.*

"I see...well, thank you. I find your words very heartening." She really did. She looked around at her people with new hope, determination renewed. Yes, she unwittingly had a part in bringing this on her people. But she would give everything she could to save them from it. She was their princess; she would not let them down. As she looked around, however, she noticed that she was starting to be able to distinguish more of the details of her surroundings. Instead of just being chunks of black or grey, the buildings began to take on definite shape, and the colors of people's clothing were starting to become apparent. Alarmed, she looked toward the sea in the east, and saw a definite lightening of the horizon. "Hurry, Dynin; we haven't much time until dawn."

He said nothing more but broke into a brisk walk. It took them some time to traverse the city; Tairport was large, after all. When they did reach the western gate, Lissa saw that the horizon was starting to change from grey to white, signaling the imminent approach of the sun.

The leviathans were also keeping an eye on the rapidly brightening sky. "We must make contact quickly," Bityah said as soon as Lissa had settled herself in the gatehouse and explained that Dynin wished to accompany Aliyah. "It will be good for Dynin to go." Lissa nodded. It was a little disconcerting to speak with the leviathans while their scales were still shifted. It was like talking to empty air.

"I will simply make sure they are there, and tell them that we will begin our attack as soon as the sun begins to fully hit the walls," Aliyah said. "Even if the barrier blocks the sun on their side, they should be able to tell when we start flaming."

"Indeed. Go quickly." Aliyah took to the air again, but this time Lissa thought she merely glided a few yards from the ground. Dynin followed her, looking painfully visible in the pre-dawn light, but there seemed to be no movement to indicate shadow wolves or any other monsters nearby. Perhaps it would take the direct attack on the barrier to draw their attention.

Lissa took shelter within the gatehouse. There were several sleeping guards, but she ignored them, going to the narrow window. It was a good vantage point. The flat plain between Tairport's walls and the barrier was clear, though the narrowness of the slit meant she had to move around to see the full extent of the area. Most importantly, no one would know she was inside the building. She shied away from the thought of Morrian appearing. She knew that was the whole point of this southern venture, to draw her away from the north to give the others a chance to destroy the rose, but the thought of coming face-to-face with the sorceress again made her tremble. If she was honest with herself, she had been glad and relieved to be chosen as the one to come south, and to be kept out of the direct fighting. She just hoped that Morrian would also, as they suspected, immediately go back north when she felt her spell break. If not...well, there should be enough Brenwyds to defeat her here. And perhaps she should hope for such a thing; then Rhodri, Aislinn, and Mathghamhain would be safe.

She saw Dynin come to a stop in front of the barrier. Odd ripples in the air near him seemed to indicate that Aliyah had touched down. Now that she was closer to it, she marveled even more at its size. She prayed they had enough force to truly bring it down. If the force of Brenwyds that was (hopefully) on the other side could not get through...she avoided the thought. *Trust Abba,* she told herself sternly. *Dynin was right. He holds us all; he will not let us fail.*

As minutes began passing, she wondered if that meant Aliyah and Dynin hadn't been able to make contact with the other side.

Before she could get too worried, though, Dynin turned and began cantering back toward the wall. She squinted, and thought she could make out that Aliyah had taken to the air once again.

"I have heard from Aliyah," Bityah's voice came from just outside the window, making Lissa start. "They made contact. The Brenwyds are there, and they are ready. We will start the attack soon. If you are settled, Your Highness, I will return to the others to wait the remaining minutes."

"Of course, Elder Bityah. I am fine; go. May Abba watch over us."

"Indeed."

She heard noises indicating the leviathan had left. Several moments later, Dynin entered through the gate, his hooves making what seemed like a cacophony of noise as they hit the paved stone of the street compared to the silence around them. She winced, turning to go to the door to be sure Dynin was well hidden. There was a small stable behind the gatehouse for the guard's horses, and this was where he hid himself.

"Would you like me to take off your tack?" she asked him.

He turned his head as if surprised to find the saddle still there. *It would be more comfortable...but I think it would be better not. We must be able to move quickly.* He sounded decidedly glum at the prospect. Again, Lissa admired the horse's common sense. Aislinn had been riding Dynin since the age of twelve, but Lissa had never spent much personal time alone with the gelding. Caramel was also a Brenwyd horse, a privilege of royalty, but Lissa had never heard her say such things to her. Perhaps it was simply because she'd never been in such a serious situation.

Lissa decided to take some pity on him. "Let me loosen your girth at least. It will not take but seconds to tighten it again."

Thank you.

Lissa loosened the piece of tack and returned to her observation post. Looking to the east, she knew the attack wouldn't be long now. The sun was starting to rise.

And what a sunrise it was! Lissa wondered if Abba had designed this particular sunrise to give her new hope. For it certainly did. The sky lightened from grey to white, with streaks of orange, yellow, and pink dashed across it like how Aislinn sometimes streaked paint across a canvas when she was excited. The water gleamed blue and gold, the clouds taking on the color of lavender hemmed with white, again turning gold in the places the sun's rays shot through to touch the land with day's first light. Lissa's heart lifted more than she thought possible. This was why they fought at dawn; they fought for the light, and darkness could not overcome it.

As if summoned by her thoughts, a chorus of bellows and roars ripped through the morning's stillness, joined by the sound of many leathery wings beating against the air. Lissa moved to her right, and saw the full strength of the leviathans rising into the sky from her narrow view. Her eyes widened, her mouth gaping open in a fashion that would have made her mother cringe in horror. Outlined by the rising sun and roaring out their challenge for all to hear, they made an impressive sight indeed.

She knew there were twenty-five of the creatures altogether, and as she watched she deduced that they had organized themselves into two groups of ten and another one of five. She didn't know either of the leviathans who seemed to be leading the groups of ten, but Aliyah led the five. One of the groups of ten positioned themselves over the part of the barrier that touched the sea; the other flew to the part of the barrier closest to the forest. Aliyah's group paused over the center, and Lissa wondered if they served as reinforcements to go wherever they might be needed.

Then they started to breathe fire.

Lissa watched with fascination as tongues of orange-yellow flame, tinged with bluish-white, shot forth from toothy mouths spread wide. Their grey scales shifted to match the hues of the flames. The fire covered the thorns, and slowly the leviathans began moving along the barrier towards each other in precisely organized lines. Aliyah's group continued to circle overhead, watching, instead of engaging.

The amount of flame, after a few minutes, began to alarm Lissa. What if the plain between Tairport and the barrier caught on fire, and it swept toward the city? No one had given any thought to that, and she berated herself for it. Then, she noticed that Aliyah's group was beginning to swoop down towards the ground, near places of errant flames. They stomped them out, then took to the sky again. Lissa was impressed with their organization and forethought. If they continued to do that, then a natural firebreak would form between the city and the thorns.

She eagerly looked back to the barrier, thinking that surely even a magical blockade of thorns would have to catch fire from such a maelstrom. The sight of the barrier, though, dampened her enthusiasm. The concealing mist was gone, but the thorns were still very much there. The flames simply danced and crackled around them, unable to touch them. Morrian had woven her spell well. Then a new sound filled the air, one that gradually started drowning out the crackle and hiss of the flames.

Singing. Many voices joined together, bent to the same purpose. Men and women, sopranos, altos, tenors, basses, baritones, and all those in-between ranges that Lissa never quite understood despite the number of times Aislinn had explained them to her. They rose clear, high, and strong in the morning air, full of life, hope, and determination. A real smile found its way onto Lissa's face. The Brenwyds. They had begun their own attack.

The sound of the song seemed to encourage the leviathans, for the fire seemed to pour out more rapidly and intensely. The flames began leaning more toward yellow, blue, and white instead of orange and red. Lissa could start to feel some effects of the heat even from where she stood watching a mile away. She wondered how the troops on the other side were dealing with it. She noticed that some of the leviathans were leaving off their attack and winging quickly back towards the sea to plunge into its cooling waters for a moment. Whenever a leviathan left, one from Aliyah's group took their place.

She watched the barrier intently, convinced that at any moment the thorns would begin to crumble and fall. Before that happened, however, another sound came into her ears, one that made her heart feel like it would stutter to a stop. Wolf howls. Morrian's guardians had finally noticed them. Part of her thought cynically that it had certainly taken them long enough.

She couldn't quite see all the way to the edge of the forest from her narrow window, but she could tell that was where they were beginning to appear from the few leviathans that broke off from the main groups and headed in that direction. A few moments later, the howls took on the same fearful edge as the ones she remembered when Mathghamhain had finally set fire to the plain. She found her smile becoming one of satisfaction. Those horrible creatures didn't stand a chance against the leviathans.

Then a new worry appeared on the field. Suddenly, several people seemingly appeared from nowhere in front of her. She blinked, but they remained in her vision. They spread out, their movements rapid and jerky, as if frantic. They raised their arms, and then the sound of chanting joined the other sounds of the battlefield. She winced at the sound and covered her ears. She didn't have to be a Brenwyd to recognize it as magic. The syllables seemed to pierce the air like sword thrusts, and then their echoes remained as if painted. The barrier, which had seemed so close to burning, now looked more vigorous. *No, no, no,* Lissa thought frantically. *Abba, help us! Give us support!*

As if in response to her prayer, the song from the Brenwyds increased in volume, overcoming the sound of the spell-chant. It took on a more driving beat, and Lissa knew this was a war song. The wall began to waver again.

"Come on," she said under her breath, watching it. "Come down. Abba, please make it come down. Like the walls of Jericho. Let it come down." She had become so engrossed in the scene before her, that she forgot it was all meant, ultimately, as a distraction.

Until the sky darkened and the wind picked up. A cold sensation crept down her spine, making her shiver, and she thought she heard distant thunder rumble through the air. Her breathing hitched. *Morrian.* She was coming. The fluttery sense of fear began turning over in her stomach, making her limbs tremble. The plan had worked. The sorceress had come.

And then, abruptly, she was there.

She appeared in a twist of wind in the middle of the field, directly in front of Lissa's view. The air around her seemed to immediately darken. Unlike the last time Lissa had seen her, her appearance looked rather unkempt – her black hair billowed wildly about her face, buffeted by the gusts of hot air churned up by the leviathans' fire, as did her skirts. She was dressed in black, but it had the look of a dressing gown donned hastily. Beneath her fear and worry, Lissa felt a certain sense of amusement that it looked like they had roused her straight from bed.

Unfortunately, she did not seem unduly disoriented from her hasty awakening. She turned completely around to take in the scene before her, and Lissa had never before seen such an expression of pure fury overtake someone's face. Within moments, she adopted a position similar to the other magicians, who must be her followers. Her chants, however, began to make more serious headway against the Brenwyds' song. Again, the barrier seemed to stabilize, and indeed, parts of it almost looked like they started to move as if it was growing again. The fire from the leviathans, which had begun to catch in various areas, dimmed and started to die. The howls from the wolves came back without fear, and Lissa began to hear bellows from the leviathans that she feared were cries of pain.

Abba, please help us. Support your people. Don't let darkness win! She cried out in her heart.

So abruptly and smoothly that she was sure the leviathans were communicating with each other silently, several of them, including Aliyah, broke off from the others and began to circle right above Morrian. The sorceress looked up at them and thrust out her hands. A strong wind swept the field, nearly taking them down from the sky. More wind began to whip up. Multiple leviathans – young ones, if Lissa had to guess based on size – began to struggle to remain in the sky, much less keep up the concentrated attack on the thorns. Her heart leaped from her chest to her throat, her breathing coming in shallow gasps. She hated simply watching the battle that could very well decide the future of the whole continent, but she knew she could do no good on the battlefield

Aliyah and a few other leviathans were managing to overcome the wind gusts and began to spit fire directly down onto Morrian. The flames didn't reach her; instead, they stopped a few feet from her head and poured off the sides, so it seemed like Morrian was enclosed in a flaming bubble. Lissa remembered Aislinn and Mathghamhain discussing Morrian's shield and the necessity of pulling it down before any harm could be done to her. She assumed that was what protected her now. But though the leviathans could not physically harm her, after a few moments Lissa saw that the few who bombarded her shield directly had succeeded in distracting her from performing any great feats of magic against the whole force. The wind died down, and most of the other leviathans righted themselves to attack the barrier again. A few others broke away and headed to attack Morrian's followers. They did not seem so lucky in their protection, and the fire hit home. Lissa shut her eyes and clamped her hands over her ears against their screams as the fire bit into their flesh. She knew there was no other choice, but tears forced themselves down her cheeks. Such a terrible, terrible waste of life.

She only opened her eyes and looked out the window again when the screams died down and were replaced by the sound of the Brenwyds' song, once again dominating over the other sounds of the battlefield. Now it sounded even louder and stronger than ever before, and Lissa realized that now there were words in it, unlike usual Brenwyd songs. The singers were too far for her to make out any particular words, but she felt a new sense of hope overcome her, driving out all her fear. She felt goosebumps break out on her arms as if from cold, but this time her shivers came from a sudden, certain awareness of Abba himself drawing palpably near. The melody and harmony of the song, while still martial in beat, also communicated strains of awe and reverence for the Creator. The feeling enveloped Lissa like a warm blanket, and for the first time since that horrible birthday eve, she felt safe and free of worry. Abba was here.

As the thought crossed her mind, the barrier of thorns in front of her seemed to give a huge shudder, as if it was a living thing. Then, with a great whoosh of air and blast of heat, the thorns were completely engulfed and began crumbling to ash that blew away on the wind. Within minutes, the huge edifice was gone.

An abrupt calm came over the field. The leviathans immediately shut off their fire and chased after any flames still burning to put them out before any harm was done. The song that had filled the air so vibrantly a moment ago cut off. Even the leviathans attacking Morrian shut off their flames, as everyone stared at the place the thorns had just been. Beyond it, Lissa could make out a mass of people and horses. The Darlesians. Lissa felt her mouth gaping open again. They had done it.

She only had a moment to consider their success, however. Morrian let out a scream of rage and shock, and it brought everyone back to the very real threat she represented. She circled an arm around her head abruptly, and the strongest wind yet swept through the air, enough to disorient all the leviathans. "

"You think to challenge me?" the sorceress shouted. Lissa wondered if she was using magic to ensure everyone heard her. "Me, the Queen of darkness? Do you think knocking down my wall has won you anything? You have yet to test my real strength, and you have just won for yourselves a slow, painful death. I hope your precious Abba is worth it." She raised her arms to chant again.

Lissa swallowed nervously. Now what? She wasn't sure how long Morrian had been there, but surely enough time had passed for Aislinn to destroy the rose. Wouldn't Morrian have felt that? Or, had Morrian caught them before she ever came south? The thought made it hard to breathe.

Again, the leviathans moved to attack Morrian, but new roars from the direction of the sea distracted them. Lissa turned and saw new dragons taking to the air, but these were definitely not leviathans. They were smaller, not as streamlined, and their scales came in colors of red, blue, white, and brown. She guessed that these were elemental dragons, something confirmed when one of the brown ones dived down and seemed to summon a ball of earth to rise and smack into the side of a leviathan, a red one whipped the remaining flames into a new frenzy, and several white ones seemed to move the air to knock several other leviathans to the ground. The howls of the shadow wolves became more excited, and now Lissa could see them darting out from the edge of the forest's darkness and bringing their fog with them so they could safely pounce on the downed leviathans. Distracted, the leviathans turned to face this new, aerial threat and defend their fallen comrades, leaving Morrian free to work any enchantment she wanted. Lissa could tell the Darlesian group was rapidly approaching the plain to cross over the border. The sound of song began to fill the air again. Lissa was rapidly feeling more and more useless, stuck as she was in the tower.

Then Morrian screamed again. Lissa looked toward her, hoping it was one of pain, but nothing was attacking her. Morrian turned toward the north, her face seemingly permanently disfigured from rage. She hesitated for a few moments, looking toward the Brenwyd force rapidly approaching her, then back toward the north. Finally, she seemed to reach some decision, for she took hold of the side of her garment in the way Lissa remembered from the Khephrah courtyard, spun in a circle, and vanished. The leviathans seemed glad of her disappearance, for now they could turn their whole attention to the elemental threat.

Lissa eagerly looked at the guards around her. Surely Morrian's sudden departure meant Aislinn had been able to destroy the rose and lift the curse. As the minutes ticked by, however, her brow furrowed again in worry and confusion. The guards continued to sleep with no sign of waking. If Morrian hadn't been recalled by the destruction of the curse, what had happened? And what did it mean for Rhodri, Aislinn, and Mathghamhain? Fear reappeared in her stomach, and she pressed a hand to it to quell the sudden nausea. She had to get the Brenwyds north as quickly as she could.

She looked out the window again. Now that the leviathans could spare the elementals their full attention, they seemed to not be having much trouble with them. Several of them were down, and now that Morrian was gone, others were starting to flee, leviathans in pursuit. She couldn't see much of what was happening with the wolves, but it seemed that they, too, were being brought to bear between the flames of the leviathans and the help of the armed men and women now pouring onto the field. In all, the Darlesian force looked to stand a little over a hundred strong, with almost half being Brenwyds. After a few more minutes, Lissa decided the battle was winding down enough to ride out and join them.

She quickly ran from the gatehouse to where Dynin stood waiting. He didn't seem to have been waiting calmly. His whole being looked on high alert with head raised, ears perked forward, and muscles taut, though he stood stock still. *What has been happening?* he asked as soon as he saw her. *Did it work? Have we won?*

"We've won this part of the battle, at least," Lissa told him as she quickly tightened the girth. "The barrier is destroyed, and Morrian made an appearance. She has just left; the others must have been successful in drawing her attention back north."

But why is everyone still asleep?

"I don't know. We must hurry; Rhodri, Aislinn, and Mathghamhain need our help." She led him out of the stable and mounted. As soon as her weight settled firmly in the saddle, Dynin moved off at a fast walk.

He stopped as they reached the open gate. Lissa allowed him the moment to take in the field, and she also took the opportunity to survey the wider view she now had. As she had thought, the wolves had been killed or driven completely back into the dark depths of the forest. With the bright daylight, they should have no more trouble with them for the time being. The elemental dragons now looked completely scattered. Several of their still bodies lay on the ground. Lissa turned her eyes resolutely away from them. Others had been completely ringed by the leviathans and seemed to be prisoners. The Darlesian force had broken off towards the woods to help with the wolves, but were now starting to come back toward the center of the field. Many of them were looking at the aerial acrobatics overhead as the leviathans chased down the remaining elementals. Lissa imagined their expressions were ones of wonder and, possibly, wariness and fear. After all, those outside the kingdom had only been experiencing the bad monsters, not the good ones.

She spotted a fair head and focused on it, recognizing the stance of the rider and the horse a moment later. Cerdic. "Dynin, there. There's Rhodri's brother, on the bay mare." Dynin needed no other direction and began heading straight for him.

As she emerged from the shadow of the gate, she became aware of wings flapping close overhead and looked up. Aliyah. "Are you well, Your Highness?" she asked.

"Perfectly," Lissa answered. "I think I should rather be asking that question of you. Your troops took a beating."

"It was certainly a challenge, but the One was watching over us. Fortunately, there have been no fatalities. I believe several of our number had injured wings and bite wounds, but those are the worst injuries. I suppose the departure of the sorceress means that the second part of the plan worked?"

Lissa shrugged. "I'm not sure. They must have done something, but the people are all still asleep. I'm afraid I'll have to leave you to tend your own to lead the Brenwyds north."

"Do not worry yourself for our sakes, Your Highness. Until that sorceress is defeated, none of us are truly safe. I will go inform Elder Bityah of what has occurred, and we will start care for the wounded." Her words confirmed a suspicion Lissa had had that the older leviathan had sat out the battle. Given her age, it had seemed logical.

"Princess Calissa! Thank Abba, you are alright!" a familiar voice called to her as Aliyah pulled herself higher in the sky to go find Bityah.

Lissa allowed a smile to cross her face as she turned to face the man who had approached her. "Prince Cerdic, how many times have I told you to simply call me Lissa?"

He smiled back at her, his wide grin reminding her of Rhodri. "At least as many times as I've told you to call me Cerdic. So we are even, you see." He looked around, his smile dropping. "Is...Is Rhodri with you? Delwyn said Aislinn told him you found him."

"He is back, but he is not here with me. He is in the north, with Aislinn and Mathghamhain. We must hurry to them quickly; they are likely facing Morrian even now."

A grim look crossed his face. "I take it that delightful sorceress was Morrian?" Lissa nodded. "Rhodri always did know how to land himself in trouble. Oh well, I am used to pulling him out of it. It shouldn't be too hard." He grinned at her again in a clear attempt to lighten the mood.

Lissa shook her head, maintaining her serious expression but secretly amused. Cerdic was only older than Rhodri by two years, and both shared a similar sense of humor. "It may be harder than you think, and do not forget your father is also ensnared in her spell," she told him. "Where is Delwyn?"

"I am here, Your Highness." A Brenwyd man who had been listening to the conversation from a respectful distance urged his mare forward so he was closer to the nobles. "Lady Aislinn said you would be here to lead us north. Can you do it?"

Lissa nodded. "Yes. Dynin knows where to go and will tell your horses." At her words, Dynin stretched his head toward Delwyn's horse and nickered. The horses looked at each other in silent communication, and after a moment Delwyn's horse looked back at his rider.

Delwyn nodded in response. "Yes, he has given Arey the location. I will gather the rest and be ready in a few minutes, Your Highness." His face had settled into extremely grim lines. "Lady Aislinn did not exaggerate the strength of this sorceress. It will be a hard battle."

"Abba is with us, Delwyn," Lissa said. "We will prevail."

Delwyn gave her a small smile. She realized, then, that Delwyn was rather young, looking to be only in his late twenties. "So we know and pray." He left then to reorganize his force.

"So how are you, Princess? Really?" Cerdic's gentle question was for her ears alone.

She sighed. "I am...ready for this to be over." She glanced toward where Delwyn had gone and lowered her voice, though there was no chance of anyone overhearing her. "Have you heard what we suspect Morrian's real purpose is with this spell?"

"Demon's Gate?" At her nod, Cerdic gave her one in return. "Delwyn told me, in confidence. Most of the others don't know. We thought it better for morale. Nonetheless, Rhys decided to leave for Feingeld with his own contingent to speak some sense into my uncle. Hopefully, those with him will be able to overcome whatever malaise is gripping the capital and they will be ready in case...something goes wrong here. We also sent messengers to the other courts in the kingdoms. It's a risk to have so many of our forces out across the continent at such a time, we know, but Rhys left Gisila in charge of the province, and the other realms need to know what they might be facing." Lissa nodded, part of her feeling relieved that the rest of the continent would have some warning.

"How is Gisila?" she asked, given the reference to Rhys's wife. "I hope the pregnancy is progressing well."

Cerdic smiled. "She certainly seems well enough to me, though Rhys, as usual, is enough of a worrywart for both of them. It's almost as if he's forgotten she's already had two pregnancies that went perfectly well, despite the children being quite obvious about their existence each day. He didn't want to leave with her getting so near her time, but she quite firmly told him that she's pregnant, not ill or injured, and perfectly capable of keeping the province running smoothly until he gets back."

That won a short laugh from Lissa, as she could easily imagine the no-nosense Gisila doing just that. Any reply she might have made was cut off by Delwyn's return.

"We are ready, Your Highnesses. I have left a few Brenwyds here to help the leviathans with healing. After their efforts in bringing down the barrier, it does not seem right to leave them no help." He glanced up, a clear look of wonder in his eyes.

"Of course, that is a good thought, Delwyn," Lissa said. "We must treat our allies well."

Cerdic followed Delwyn's gaze to where several leviathans circled overhead. He shook his head. "I've seen a lot of unbelievable things over the past few weeks, but I think that these creatures are the most impressive. Especially since they are friendly to us. Once this is all over, I expect the full story, you know."

"Many people will, I expect," Lissa said, turning Dynin around and beginning to look for a clear space for the transfer. "And I will be happy to tell it...after we defeat Morrian." She looked back, evaluating the force gathered behind her. "Dynin, you've relayed the location?"

To enough, and they have told the others. They are ready.

She turned her face back to the open field in front of her, jaw set. She was the Crown Princess of Ecclesia, and she would protect her kingdom. "Then let us go."

23

Sneaking In

$\mathcal{I}$ lay on the dungeon floor, promising myself that I would never, ever travel in such complete and absolute darkness again. It had been hard to even tell that I was moving forward, and that made it much harder to bear than simply sitting in the darkness. Finally, though, we reached the end of the tunnel, Steffyn found the hatch leading into the dungeon, and we left the oppressive black. Not that the dungeons were any lighter, but at least they were large and not quite so closed in. "So, Mathghamhain," Rhodri said from my left, "you found that hatch, and then went through the tunnel and swam to the shore all by yourself?"

"There was a guard who became sympathetic to my plight and told me about the rumors of a hidden passage, but other than that, yes." I heard him walking around. I assumed he was looking for a torch.

"I'm impressed, especially with that swim."

"It was high summer and, as I've said, I come from Lamasia originally. You have not experienced cold until you've had to swim in those waters."

"Why in the Five Realms would you want to?" I asked in disbelief, raising myself to my elbows. While accompanying my father on a state visit to Lamasia, I had merely dipped my feet into the ocean and felt as if I would freeze all over.

"It is, or was, a tradition to hold a swimming race at the mid-summer festival in coastal areas. Whoever lasted longest won a place at the local nobleman's right hand for the rest of the day."

"Oh, that swim," Rhodri said. "My family visited Lamasia once at mid-summer when I was young. I remember very much wanting to try it, but my mother wouldn't hear of it. How long did you make it?"

"Never far enough to win, unfortunately," Steffyn admitted. I debated whether or not to insert a comment about how only men would think up such a challenge when Steffyn continued, "Ah, here we are." I heard the sound of flint striking metal, and then saw sparks fly and hit a torch. Instantly the dungeon was cast in better light. I looked around, blinking away the glare caused by the sudden source of light after being so long in the dark. It was made of black stone. Each cell was surrounded by walls of stone, the only break being the wooden door allowing passage in and out. We were in the center aisle of the dungeon. As I looked around and took in our surroundings, it began sinking in that we were really here, in Morrian's fortress. We were here. I got to my feet.

"Well, shall we go? We shouldn't waste time," I said, trying to keep my voice from trembling. I noticed Steffyn standing rigid, staring into a particular cell. I went to him and gently laid a hand on his arm. The muscles under the fur were tight with tension. "Are you alright?" I asked quietly.

"Fine," he ground out, spinning from my touch and striding toward the exit. "Come. Each moment we delay is an extra moment those in the south must keep her occupied."

⁂

The trip to the rose room was harrowing. Once we left the dungeon, it was clear that the fortress was inhabited. Lit torches lined the wall at regular intervals. The stairway from the dungeon led upward in a slow spiral. No doors opened off the corridor. There was no place to hide if anyone came upon us. And with every step I took upward, the sense of evil weighing on me increased.

"So will the rose's destruction mean the immediate reversal of the spell?" Rhodri asked in a whisper.

"Hopefully," Steffyn said. "But we'll have to consider the sphere as well. Though we must hurry, Aislinn needs time to fully evaluate any protection spells around both objects."

I frowned. I was in front, technically leading since I was the only one who had seen the rose room, so I couldn't see his expression, but he sounded worried. "Do you think that there might be a...backlash?"

"Perhaps. And because of that, you will let me deal with it."

"But you can't sing...can you?"

"Not in this form, no." I heard the sadness in his voice. I empathized. I had felt depressed enough to lose my voice for a week, but he hadn't been able to sing in over two centuries. I couldn't imagine it. "But there are other ways to deal with such spells. If I hear anything...concerning, I will let you know."

My mind got stuck on his "other ways to deal with spells," and remembered his description of how he had broken Morrian's mirror long ago. "Will you break the sphere, too, never mind the consequences?"

"Better me than you."

I turned to scowl at him. "You will do no such thing until we fully examine it. Promise me."

He frowned at me in turn. It really wasn't fair how he could make himself look so fierce. "And if a full examination takes too much time? What then? Aislinn, I won't have you suffer my fate."

"And I won't see you once again a victim of her machinations! Promise me you won't do anything impulsive regarding the sphere or the rose without fully analyzing the situation first."

Steffyn opened his mouth to reply, but Rhodri interrupted him. I could almost swear he sounded amused. "Mathghamhain, just agree with her. We'll move faster. And for the record, I do think she's right."

Steffyn shut his mouth and looked at Rhodri, then at me. "I seem to be outnumbered," he muttered. "Very well. But keep moving, shall we?" I turned and resumed the climb.

A few minutes later, we came to a wooden door. I pressed my ear against the door, but heard nothing. I extended a thought in Steffyn's direction, knowing he would pick it up. *Do you sense anyone?*

No one who is awake. There are many sleeping people on the other side of that door.

Rhodri's father and the Darlesian Brenwyds. But Morrian's lackey? Her servant, Pelagius, had been weighing on my mind during the time we spent in the dark. While we had planned for Morrian's distraction, I doubted that he would leave with her.

No. But Morrian knows how to conceal herself from Brenwyd mind readers, so she may have taught him. She had to learn, to be able to hide her true intentions so long.

But you don't think he's on the other side of this door, do you?

No. I would know if he was right there.

"Well, let's go, then," Rhodri said. I realized Steffyn must have been projecting his words into Rhodri's mind as well. Keeping a hand on his sword hilt, Rhodri carefully opened the door. It swung silently on its hinges. We crept out into the revealed room. It was full of raised beds, and each one held a person. I recognized the place. This was the room I had seen in my dreams, the one with the Darlesian Brenwyd patrol. The rose room was right off this one. But first...

Rhodri walked to the first of the beds and looked down at its occupant, his face tense. Then he moved on. I knew who he was looking for. *Is the rose room off here?* Steffyn asked.

Yes. I looked around, and saw the door on the other side of the room. *There.* I listened with my song sense. *Grindles. There's a protection spell on it. The moment I break it, her lackey might know it.* Beyond the protection spell, I sensed something else, a purer song from the room beyond. It sounded nearly like a cry for help. I began moving toward the door before Steffyn could respond, but a slight choking sound from Rhodri made me stop and turn to him. He had stopped by a bed. I went to him and looked down, already knowing who I would see. Rhodri's father lay on the bed, breathing easily, face calm but asleep. Rhodri had a hand on his father's arm, as if he could shake it and wake him up.

A pained expression was on his face. "All these months I've thought about seeing him again...but not like this."

"I know," I whispered. "Come on. Let's wake these sleepers." Gently, I pulled him after me. Steffyn had gone to the door of the rose room and was examining it, arms crossed.

"You are correct; breaking these spells will likely bring her servant down on us," he rumbled. "But I wonder...Aislinn, draw your sword."

I raised an eyebrow. "You think the sword can break the spell without him noticing?"

"Perhaps. Listen, and see what you think."

"Alright." I drew the blade. White flames glimmered to life along the blade, causing the diamond in the pommel to flash with light and brightening the whole room considerably. Instantly I felt better, more confident, better able to deal with the task in front of me. I listened. I heard the melody of the protection spell; it reminded me of the briar-spell that had surrounded Kheprah, though here there were no thorns. Still, it was strong, woven, like a fence. To break it with song, I would need to sing a winding melody that went fully up and down my whole range. Then I turned my attention to the sword. It, too, had a melody. The melody was light, seeming to dance its way from note to note like the flickers of flame danced over the blade, but there was also a deeper harmony that was strong, steady, and gave off a sense of the indomitable. I compared the two songs. Maybe, just maybe, this might work. I looked at Rhodri and Steffyn. "Well, I suppose we might as well try." I extended the sword toward the door. The spell wasn't a physical thing, per se, but I could sense it would keep the door closed and locked no matter what mundane methods we might try. I touched the point to the door. Instantly the sword blazed up and I nearly dropped it in surprise. Listening with my song sense, I heard the two songs apparently go to war with each other. I gripped the sword tighter, willing my strength into the blade. It seemed to work, as within a minute I heard the protection spell wane and break. I heard a click within the door, pushed on it with my hand, and it opened.

"That was dramatic," Rhodri said.

"Well, it worked," I said. I glanced up at the ceiling, briefly sending my song sense out for any sign of someone magical stirring. I sensed nothing. I caught Steffyn's eye, and he shook his head slightly, indicating he didn't sense anything, either.

"Will you go in first?" he asked quietly.

"Oh." I looked at the open door. "I suppose so." I pushed on the door to open it wider and stepped inside.

It was a small room, the far wall curved to match the shape of the fortress. My gaze immediately fell on the rose in the center of the room. The white was nearly gone, with only the upper fourth of the petals still displaying the snowy hue. The next thing I noticed was the white sphere next to it. Now that I saw it in person, I realized it wasn't floating; it was standing on a black pedestal to support it, but the poles blended in so well that it was hard to differentiate them from the walls.

Rhodri and Steffyn stepped in behind me, and I moved closer to the far wall to give them room – specifically, Steffyn. His bulk made the room feel much smaller. "So that's it," Rhodri said, eyes fixed on the rose.

"That's it," I said, stepping closer to it. I had to admit it was a gorgeous rose, perfectly formed. I delicately laid a hand on a petal, wondering if I might trip a spell by touching it. Nothing happened.

However, listening with my song sense, I sensed that this, indeed, was the anchor for the spell. The song of the spell was nearly overwhelming. I gasped and shut myself off from it.

"Well?" Steffyn asked.

I shook my head. "I don't know. The spell...it's very strong."

"How about the sphere?" He was standing next to it, paw-hand hovering just above. "This seems...wholesome to me. Do you concur?"

I listened. "Yes. It seems we are right about what it is." I stared at the sphere, bringing my hand to hover over it as Steffyn's was. He was right about it feeling wholesome...but at the same time, standing next to it, my vision seemed to go a little dim, and I started feeling a bit dizzy. I staggered, but Rhodri was right behind me.

"Easy," he said. "So this is how Morrian is collecting the Brenwyds' abilities."

It was a statement, not a question, but I nodded all the same. "I think so. In concentrating it like this, it becomes like any other collected power, and can be used for various purposes...theoretically."

"Like opening a legendary gate to let demons into the world." I grunted acknowledgment of his statement.

Steffyn was quiet, staring at the sphere. "She always was fascinated by that story," he said slowly. He almost seemed to forget mine and Rhodri's presence. "She always asked to hear it. I should have suspected..." Seemingly without meaning to, his hand actually came down on the sphere. White light blazed up around him – around all of us. I squinted at the harsh light, shielding my eyes with a hand. An urgent melody came to me, one of desperation, almost sounding like a last shriek for help. "Oh, grindles," I heard Steffyn mutter. "That will surely bring trouble. Aislinn, Prince Rhodri, draw your weapons. If this sets off a magical trap, you'll need the protection." My arm was already complying with his words before I was fully aware of it. The music surrounded me, nearly drowning me as the light ricocheted off the walls in all directions, nearly blinding me. I caught a glimpse of Steffyn bringing his spear down point first on the sphere, and it shattered, ringing in my ears like the highest flute notes, which was somewhat grating. In that moment, I sensed something, a harsh discordance starting to cut across the flute-like music, seemingly aimed at... No. I would not let Steffyn be the target of one of Morrian's spells again.

I tightened my grip on the sword, and it blazed up, clearing my head. Immediately I began singing. The Creation song was much suppressed here, barely audible to me through the other melodies and harmonies humming in the air, but it was there. I reached for it, bringing it back to the forefront of the competing songs, and it seemed to respond to me eagerly. Amazingly, it fell right into my comfortable middle range. The melody wasn't very dramatic, but it was steady, soothing, and slowly I could sense it bringing order to the spells going on around me, stopping them from causing their intended harm. The bright light decreased so I was no longer blinded.

"Should I set fire to this rose now? That has to have been enough to get someone's attention," Rhodri said, starting to lower the torch to the flower.

"Aislinn, what spells do you sense around the rose?" Steffyn asked urgently. "Quickly, we have no time-"

"I should say you don't," a new voice said. Nasal. Masculine. Her lackey, Pelagius. We all turned to see him standing in the doorway, a nasty smile on his face. However, it seemed a little strained to me, and there was something in the way his eyes darted about that conveyed nervousness. "Well, well, who do we have here?"

I decided my best course of action was to keep singing. It was foolish to lower one's defenses just as the real battle began. The man glared at me. "It was my understanding that you could not sing."

"Perhaps Morrian should double-check that her spells actually work," Rhodri retorted for me. He now had his sword pointing directly at Pelagius. I had never seen such a fierce, angry expression on my friend's face.

Pelagius glared at him. "The mistress's spells are impeccable, Your *Highness*," he snarled. "As you will soon see. You cannot defeat her, nor do you understand the full scope of her plan." He raised his hands and transferred his glare to me. "And if you wish to keep your voice this time, you had best stop - Ahhh!" This last was as Steffyn jumped on him, pinning his arms to his sides and him to the wall. I had a feeling he hadn't fully registered Steffyn's presence. With his dark fur and black clothes, he did rather blend into the walls. Pelagius's eyes fairly bugged out of his head as Steffyn bared his teeth and growled. I didn't really blame him, but it did look comical. "Who-*What-*"

"That is none of your concern," Steffyn growled. "If you want to live to see another sunset, you will disable any and all protection spells surrounding the rose. We might consider letting you live if you cooperate."

Pelagius still seemed speechless, mouth hanging open. A slight croak emerged from his throat. "I would do as he says, if I were you," Rhodri said.

But while he and Steffyn seemed focused on Pelagius, I turned my eyes to the open doorway. A trembling began in my limbs, and I sensed something evil coming. Or rather, someone. The shattering of the sphere had attracted her attention back north, alright. *No time!* I threw the thought to Steffyn. *She's coming! I'm getting rid of this rose* now. He shifted his concentration toward me. The break was enough (apparently Pelagius was getting his wits back) for the lackey to shout a word, and Steffyn crashed to the floor with a grunt. Instantly, though, Rhodri was on him, and Pelagius was preoccupied with fighting off the prince. Rhodri's sword flared up as it thwarted the spells Pelagius tried to throw at him. I turned to the rose. Morrian would be here in moments. There was only one course of action. Still singing the Creation Song, I thrust my sword at the rose, planning on cleaving it in two and (hopefully) lighting the thing on fire. However, I hit something invisible fingerbreadths away from the flower, and my blade turned aside, throwing me off balance enough that I fell to the floor.

And then we were out of time.

Morrian appeared in the doorway.

24

To Defeat a Sorceress

At least it looks like we got her out of bed, I thought abstractly. Her ebony hair flowed wildly about her face, loose of any restraint. She wore a black dressing gown, the white material of a nightgown peeking through at the hem and neck. Unfortunately, her eyes were all too awake and full of fury. I noticed that what looked like soot had fallen in various places on her face.

As she took us in, the fury in her eyes dimmed a bit, replaced by something like satisfaction. "Well, well, well, who have we here? A little Brenwyd and the valiant prince. What a lovely surprise." Then her eyes fell on Steffyn, who had just climbed back to his feet. He stared at her, glaring, but with deep pain in his eyes. His fist was clenched, and he pointed his spear at her. Morrian drew in a breath that sounded like a hiss and, to my surprise, I thought I saw a little uncertainty enter her eyes. She covered it so quickly, though, I couldn't be sure. "And who, or what, rather, have we here? I would not expect such noble personages as yourselves to travel with a *beast*."

"Oh, you know me, Morrian," Steffyn's voice rumbled. I noticed that Rhodri had succeeded in knocking Pelagius out. With his magic unable to harm Rhodri because of the flamestone sword, Pelagius was no match for Rhodri in fighting skill. "Or, you should."

She fixed her eyes on him, her glare softening a little to a searching expression. "Is that so?"

Steffyn stared right back at her, his silver eyes meeting hers without flinching. I frowned. His eyes...there had always been something familiar about them...A slight gasp from Morrian recaptured my attention. "Well, what do you know," she said softly. Then she began to laugh. Softly at first, but it quickly grew in volume, until she sagged against the wall, gasping for air. Rhodri and I just stared at her, too astonished to do anything. Then I began to get angry. She had no right to laugh so at Steffyn's- "The wolves said a beast attacked them, but I never thought...oh, this is rich."

"I'm glad you find this situation so amusing, since it is your doing," Steffyn said darkly. He advanced on her. "Now, Morrian, we both know what happened last time we met. This time, you won't be escaping."

"Really?" she asked. The threat didn't seem to cow her. "You will just kill me in cold blood, will you? Doesn't that go against all your precious principles and sense of honor?"

"Mayhap, if you hadn't laid a sleeping curse on an entire kingdom and set out to drain all the Brenwyds of their power, if you hadn't cursed me to *this*. Let me tell you, Morrian, I've had a lot of time to think about you, and no matter what I think of, every time I come to the conclusion that you. Must. Die." Rhodri and I exchanged glances. I had a bit of a better understanding of where Steffyn was coming from than he did, but I could tell in his gaze that he was thinking the same thing: there was something deeply wrong here. Well, besides the obvious, that is. The way they were talking... True, Steffyn had told me he had grown up in the same village as Morrian, and he had known her half-brother well, but nothing to indicate...

Morrian laughed again. "Such ferocity, such anger. I didn't think you had it in you, Steffyn. I'm impressed."

I saw surprise and confusion flicker across Rhodri's face at the name, but I was more concerned about the look I saw in Steffyn's eyes. I had heard the expression that someone's face could look like murder, but I had never understood it until now. Steffyn launched his spear at the sorceress, but she raised a hand and it flew through the open door and clattered harmlessly on the floor. "Tsk, tsk, I thought you would know better," she said mockingly. "I can't be felled by such a direct attack."

"It doesn't matter," I said, feeling the need to redirect events. "We will still defeat you. We have Abba on our side."

Morrian turned to me. "Your voice is back?" Her eyes latched onto my blazing sword. "Ah, I see. Well, I hate to ruin your delusions, but your Abba is useless. A weak god whose only defense is love, which is itself a weakness."

"And yet love has defeated you before," I countered. "With Nivea, her love woke her, and she then led her army to defeat you. Now, Rhodri woke Lissa, and we will defeat you again. Love is powerful, Morrian, if you but choose to admit it."

Her expression went cold, but a smile was still fixed on her lips. "You are right. Mistakes were made in the past. But I learned from them. You cannot stop this spell now, or what is to come." She paused, then continued, "And don't think those allies of yours in the south will do you much good. Even Brenwyd horses have to know where they're going first, isn't that right?" My heart leaped at the mention of allies. They must have been successful in breaking down the wall. It would explain why she had been so angry when she entered. I decided to not give her any indication that there was, in fact, one horse who did know where he was going. We simply had to stall her until help arrived.

"Well, the kingdom might still be sleeping for now, but we just destroyed your magic sphere," Rhodri said. "And Aislinn's right. We've got Abba helping us. We won't let you win."

I truly don't think that Morrian had realized we'd destroyed her sphere until that moment. The smile slipped from her face, replaced by shock, disbelief, anger. I felt like kicking Rhodri. I appreciated the brave words, but it was not what we needed at the moment. Morrian pinned him with her glare. "Then I suppose I will begin by finishing what I started in that courtyard," she snarled, starting to raise her hand. My mind immediately flashed back to the courtyard, Morrian magically strangling Rhodri in an invisible grip.

"No!" I cried out, starting to move, but Steffyn moved faster. He leaped on her, knocking her to the floor, and the two rolled through the open doorway into the larger room beyond. Rhodri and I followed. "Did you have to mention the sphere?" I muttered to him.

"I thought she'd noticed. Why'd she call Mathghamhain Steffyn?"

"It's his real name. He changed it when he changed. Come on, no more time for questions."

"Wait. Shouldn't we try to destroy the rose first?"

"It can wait. There's some sort of protection spell round it. Right now Steffyn needs our help more."

He cast me a speculative glance, likely trying to figure out the significance of Mathghamhain's real name and why I knew it, but he was wise enough not to pursue it at that moment. He nodded. "You had best start singing again. It's our best weapon. Get at-"

"Her shield, I know. While we're distracting her, you should get out of this room and try to get outside, get the lay of the fortress, and find the leviathans. It sounds like the leviathans and Brenwyds in the south were able to break through the barrier, so the Brenwyds should be arriving soon. They'll need to get here as quickly as possible."

He nodded, though he was clearly unhappy with the thought of leaving Steffyn and me to deal with Morrian alone. Still, it couldn't be helped. In this kind of battle, anyone not a Brenwyd could be more of a hindrance than a help. "Since she didn't say anything about Lissa, I suppose that means she's alright as well. If she had seen her or...done anything, she couldn't have kept from waving it in my face."

I nodded agreement. We entered the larger room and stopped, trying to take in the scene before us. Steffyn was no longer on top of Morrian, but the battle between them raged throughout the entire room. I worried for those ensnared in the sleeping curse. Steffyn had reclaimed his spear, and I could see the ghostly white fire around the blade, but it was nothing like the way my sword blazed up. At the moment Morrian seemed to just be fending him off with defensive spells. I couldn't see them, but I could hear them. Steffyn kept dodging, trying to get closer to her.

I saw the exit door Rhodri needed to take across the room. "I'll get her attention off that door," I muttered to him. "Take whatever chance you get." He nodded and began to creep in that direction.

I began to sing, loud and strong and clear, keeping my sword in front of me as protection. Morrian turned to face me. Her earlier equilibrium was gone in a mask of anger. "You think your silly little songs can defeat me?" she asked. "I just withstood dozens of your people. How could you hope to defeat me all alone?" I didn't bother to answer. The shield protecting her was very strong. I knew I couldn't attack it head on. I had to go with the indirect approach Steffyn and I had discussed: singing a melody in my range that didn't directly battle the spell-song, but weakened it steadily nonetheless. "You think that flaming stick in your hand makes you invulnerable?" I kept singing. *Don't think about anything else, Aislinn,* I told myself. *Just sing. Sing. Sing.* I saw Rhodri reach the door and slip through it. "You think you can succeed when my miserable excuse for a brother has failed? Do you want to end up like him? A beast for eternity?"

That brought me up short. I stopped singing. I couldn't help it. The flames from my sword seemed to die a little as I worked through the implications of that statement. I stared at Steffyn. "What...what does she..." But his eyes held the answer, full of shame. His eyes...silver grey eyes...Morrian had silver grey eyes... he'd told me her brother was half-Brenwyd...they'd been friends... she'd captured him...tortured him...could it be?

"So, Steffyn, it seems you have been keeping secrets. Did you not tell your fine new friends exactly how you are associated with me? How rude. Did you think you could keep it hidden, even now, when you face me?" Her voice had regained some of its smugness.

He glared at her. "You stopped being any kin of mine a long time ago, Morrian. They didn't need to know." He pointedly avoided my stare. I was still having a hard time understanding this information. *Steffyn* was Morrian's half-*brother*?

"Oh, truly? What do you think, Aislinn? Don't you think you deserved to know who you were really traveling with?" She turned to me, newly confident after having apparently regained the upper hand. Now Steffyn did turn his eyes to me, full of apology. I tried to organize my thoughts and feelings. Now that they said it, lots of things began to make more sense about Steffyn. How he knew so much of Morrian. Why he had been so leery of facing her again. Why it had been so hard for him to get past her tortures. And I found I didn't blame him for not telling me exactly how he was connected to Morrian. I wouldn't exactly want to be going around publicizing such a piece of information, either. I smiled at him, reassuringly. He blinked, surprised, but I turned to Morrian, still smiling. She, on the other hand, frowned.

"Perhaps," I said. "But you know what? I know I don't know everything about him. And that's alright. But I do trust him. And that's enough for me." I began to sing again. Calmly. Steadily. But ever-eroding the spells Morrian enshrouded herself with.

"Trust?" Morrian barked over my singing. "Trust?" For some reason, she laughed. "I'll show you what such blind trust gets you." She thrust out her hand and said some harsh words I didn't catch. My sword blazed up, but the magic was too strong for it to counteract. My vision went black, and I had the oddest feeling of my body dissolving. A moment later, I felt solid again, and I could see. I blinked, trying to make sense of my surroundings. Instead of being inside, I now felt a chilly wind brush against my body, and I was lying on my back on a cold stone floor, my sword lying beside me. Above me I saw the blue sky, colored that particular hue of early morning. Slowly, I realized that I was outside, and apparently on top of Morrian's round fortress. I tried to get up, but invisible bonds held me down. I turned my head with effort, and saw Steffyn lying near me. He also, apparently, couldn't get up. Of Morrian I could see nothing for the moment.

Aislinn? His voice came to me, weakly, in my mind.

I'm here. What happened?

I think...I think she moved us with a transport spell. I've felt it before.

Where is she?

I don't know. Prince Rhodri?

He managed to get out the door to go find the leviathans.

Good. Then, a few seconds later, *Aislinn, I'm sorry. I was going to tell you, before we landed, but then-*

It's alright, I told him. *I remember. Kesia cut you off. Steffyn, it's really alright. I understand why you didn't say anything.*

He turned his head so his eyes met mine. *Truly?*

I would not really wish to advertise such a relationship, either. Especially to people I haven't known very long.

We were interrupted just then by Morrian walking onto the platform. "Did you enjoy your trip? Such a useful spell, don't you think? You don't even need a horse." She considered us on the ground, then pointed a finger toward us. Abruptly I felt myself pulled to my feet, though I still couldn't move my arms or legs. In fact, I discovered that when I tried to sing I couldn't move my mouth either. *Oh, Abba, let Lissa and those Brenwyds come quickly,* I prayed silently. "Such a spell would be useful for many people,"

Morrian went on in a reasonable tone. "A horse is quite an expense, after all. They must be kept fed and watered, and when they are ill, they must be cared for. It is something quite out of many people's reach. But magic, as long as a person is born with it, is free. It does not need to be cared for. It's just there, like a jar on a shelf, ready whenever it needs to be used, and requiring no maintenance when it does not."

She looked at me. "Is it really wrong to practice such useful things? Magic could help so many people. Think about it. Instead of risking their lives with levers and ropes to lift heavy building materials, builders could simply move rocks and wood with a touch of their fingers. Instead of only relying on herbs and concoctions to fight disease, healers could kill the root of the infection and save many more lives. And instead of being forced to rely on messengers and wait for information, kings and princes could instead merely look in a mirror to see exactly what they need to. All without Brenwyd assistance, easily done by, well, nearly everyone. Is it so bad to want to teach people how to tap in to such potential? To want to make such advances to improve the lot of everyday people?" Her words were sympathetic, reasonable. "Don't you think that by outlawing magic, Abba has condemned people to a life that is much harder than it needs to be?" I didn't like to admit it, but her words stirred up seeds of doubt within me. I had wondered at various times, though never very seriously, why exactly magic was so bad. Some of the things – like sleeping curses, for instance – were obviously terrible and evil, but were all uses of magic inherently evil? I had heard many instances of people who strayed into magic use just because they were trying to improve their lives or someone else's, not because they were bad people. Why *did* Abba say that magic was bad?

Morrian's lips began to curve into a smile. She knew she was getting to me. *Stop thinking like that*, I chided myself. *That's what she wants you to think. Don't doubt Abba. He always knows best. Always.* Still, the doubt kept whispering.

Aislinn. Steffyn's voice, quiet and sure. *Don't listen to her. Abba outlawed magic because it does not come from him. It all comes from the Shadow Angel, and he excels at disguising himself and his works as good and right. But eventually, it all leads to evil and destruction. Morrian started working magic because she wanted to help comfort her father after her mother died. But when he married my mother, she saw it as having gone awry and so began to delve deeper to split them up. This she couldn't do, but her studies led her further and further from the Light. You see what she is now: this evil witch, after beginning to explore magic with the best of intentions.*

These words, coming from him after I'd been fighting with him half the trip to get him to acknowledge Abba's interest in him, immediately recalled my mind. I knew my lessons. The Shadow Angel and his followers were skilled deceivers, and the human heart easily turned toward evil. Our senses were perverted through the Fall so that which was actually evil seemed good and wholesome in our eyes. It was why followers of Abba had to be constantly vigilant in the faith and quick to discern false teaching. It was what I had been taught my whole life. Though the doubt still whispered to me, I consciously decided to ignore it. No matter what my natural inclinations might think were right, I would lean on the good understanding and faith I had been raised in. I would trust my Creator. I looked at Morrian coldly, defiance in my eyes, letting her know, even though I couldn't speak, that I would not be swayed by her. *I would not.*

Morrian's smile faltered and turned into a sneer. "Very well, then. Have it your way. Die knowing you have failed. You cannot save your kingdom from what is coming." She flung an arm behind her, saying more of those terrible words I couldn't understand. Smoke and mist came seemingly from nowhere, forming a tall figure. My heart seemed to stop in terror as my mind flew to the figure I had seen Morrian talking with in the castle after she cast the sleeping spell, the one I had suspected was the Shadow Angel. Was she calling him here? *Abba, help us!* I cried. I tried to move, sing, but I was still stuck in my magical bonds.

Suddenly I remembered the leviathans. *Barak! Neriah! Kezia! Come help us!*

The figure finished forming. I felt a wave of relief pass over me as I realized it wasn't real. Still, it was intimidating, at least nine feet tall, with wings behind it that reminded me of the leviathans' and glowing red eyes. "This image terrifies you?" Morrian said, sounding pleased. "Imagine a whole army of them, in the flesh. This is what your puny kingdom – indeed, this puny continent – will face in a few days' time. True, you have destroyed the power I was going to use to open the gate," irritation flickered over her face, "but I can always replace that...with your energy. Those of the Brenwyds downstairs. Others. The gate will open, and the world will fall." I felt my eyes bug out in shock. She really meant to do it. She really wanted to open Demon's Gate.

"Are you mad?" Steffyn said, echoing my thoughts. Apparently, he was not magically gagged. Then again, Morrian didn't have to worry about him singing. "You would open the Gate? This is truly your goal?"

"Indeed, brother. I'm glad you remember the tale. This time, I won't rely on mere human vessels. This whole realm will experience a freedom it has never felt before, the freedom of throwing off the rule of Abba and embracing the freedom of following the Shadow Angel." She smiled wickedly.

"There's a reason those creatures were sealed from the world, Morrian," Steffyn said. "To release them again will only serve to hasten the apocalypse. To what end is that a good thing for you?"

"Don't you remember where I banished the prince?" Morrian asked. "The world our ancestors first came from? Well, it has not clung so rigidly to antiquated beliefs about an all-powerful God and the need to obey him mindlessly. No, it has fully embraced the freedom of the mind, the knowledge that comes from freeing oneself from tiresome morals. *There* has been true progress. Only ask your friend the..." She frowned and looked around, seemingly just realizing Rhodri wasn't with us. "Where is the prince?"

She got her answer rather quickly, though not how she imagined. Suddenly all three of us started at the sound of three thunderous roars right overhead. Barak, Kezia, and Neriah seemingly appeared from nowhere in the sky and hovered just above the fortress's top. Obviously, they had used their camouflage to sneak up on us. Though not quite sneak, since I had sensed them coming. The volume of their roars still caused me to flinch, however. On Barak rode Rhodri, and behind him was Lissa with a man I recognized as Delwyn. Neriah and Kezia also carried three passengers each, all Brenwyds. I smiled as best I could. The Darlesian Brenwyds had arrived.

"Morrian," Rhodri called down to her. "We have you outnumbered, and there are more Brenwyds waiting to come. Surrender now, and give us Aislinn and Mathghamhain."

"Immediately, or we will torch you where you stand," Barak added, teeth bared.

For the first time, Morrian truly looked taken aback. She had not foreseen this. But I had a feeling she wouldn't give up this easily. The low sound of singing reached my ears, and a moment later I felt my magical bonds loosen and break. I immediately snatched up my sword. Steffyn stepped close to me. *Be ready*, he warned. *She won't be out of tricks yet.* I nodded grim acknowledgment. *Start singing, but quietly.* I had a feeling he'd sent that message to all the Brenwyds, as when I began, I heard other voices joining me. I took up the steady melody I had before, working to bring the Creation song back to the front of all the melodies in the area, as it should be.

Morrian glared up at the prince and princess, her face turning red. When she spoke, her voice was a shriek. "Surrender? You think I would surrender to you, a stripling prince barely of age?

A gullible princess who naïvely believes whatever anyone tells her? Who are you to think you can lead a country?"

"Morrian, please," Lissa called. "This is pointless. Give up now, and you will have a fair trial at least, I promise."

"Fair trial! Fair trial? You think that is what I want, girl? I have more right to the throne than you! My father was a nobleman of impeccable lineage, and I was married to a king! You come from woodcutter and dwarf stock, people not fit to serve as the lowliest of castle servants, let alone be sovereigns." She raised her arms. I increased my volume slightly. "You think the leviathans make you invincible? Well, meet *my* draconic allies!" I sensed some wild presence coming from behind me and I whirled.

"Look out!" I shouted before I even fully registered what I was sensing. The three leviathans jerked out of their hover and reared up, forefeet in a defensive position, sparks flying from their nostrils, passengers hanging on for dear life as several shapes dropped from the sky with wild shrieks and cries. They resembled the leviathans, but weren't as large, scales rougher, and from what I sensed with my mind, not nearly as intelligent. I needed no one to tell me that these were elemental dragons. They collided with the leviathans with a terrible noise, scratching and clawing with desperate abandon. I worried for the passengers, caught in the middle of the battle. Within minutes, Barak managed to send one tumbling by spewing a stream of fire into its face. Its screams were terrible to hear. "Barak, set your passengers down!" I called.

Suddenly I felt myself knocked sideways by a large, furry body. Steffyn. We hit the floor together, but he instantly rolled off me, brandishing his spear at Morrian. I assumed that she had tried to hit us with some magic while we were distracted. *Aislinn, get her shield down. Focus on nothing else. I'll get you the time. Just get it down.*

I gulped as he charged the sorceress again. "Morrian, you tried once before to force me to accept the brutality within myself," I heard him call. "Would you like to experience the results of your handiwork?" I forced myself to stop paying attention to the altercation. Steffyn was right, I had to get the shield down. Nothing else mattered.

I felt a touch on my shoulder and whirled, almost slicing Rhodri's hand off. Fortunately, he jumped back in time. "Aislinn, what needs to be done?"

"Her shield has to come down." I looked at Delwyn. Obviously, Barak had managed to offload his passengers, though the aerial battle was still raging above. In fact, it looked like more elemental dragons were joining the fight. Where in the Five Realms were they coming from? "Follow my lead. This will be tricky."

He nodded. "Of course." He stretched a hand toward me. "Here. It will help with focus." I nodded, and took it. I also shut my eyes, recalling every bit of magic-fighting my father had taught me. I drew a breath, and began to sing. This time, words began to pour out of me. I don't remember them; I was only half aware I was singing them. I do know the words formed a prayer to Abba, asking for his help for his people, praising him for being holy, being loving, being God. I remember speaking words against the workers of evil, invoking the authority I had as a follower of Abba to rebuke the Shadow Angel's followers. Delwyn followed my melody line, and I gradually became aware of other voices rising in song, some taking up my melody, others making a harmony. I opened my eyes. Neriah and Kezia had also managed to get their passengers safely down. Extending my awareness up for a moment, I realized that Barak and Neriah were taking on the elementals while Kezia was continuing to ferry Brenwyds to the island. My voice rose in confidence with the reinforcements, and the Creation Song rang out clearer and clearer with the added strength of the extra voices. I fixed my eyes on Morrian and Steffyn. She had realized by this time that Steffyn was merely serving to distract her, but he was doing too good a job of it for her to focus on the fact that we were weakening her shields. Her magical attacks he either avoided, or they seemed to roll right off him. I wondered if his curse actually gave him some protection. I began walking toward them, because I was concerned. Steffyn couldn't avoid her forever, and I wanted to be on hand if he needed help.

That turned out to be very soon, as Morrian unleashed a wave of magic that knocked everyone down like an earthquake had hit. Our song abruptly cut off, and she alone remained standing, a wild look in her eyes I didn't like. She picked up Steffyn's spear from where it had fallen and walked over to him. I rolled over onto my stomach and struggled to my feet. It was like trying to walk through a bog. Morrian stopped over Steffyn and raised the spear over his heart. "Any last words, brother?" she snarled.

My heart dropped. *No, no, no, Abba, don't let him die.* I couldn't move fast enough. Even with my sword helping me cut through the enchantment, I knew I couldn't get to him in time. "No!" I yelled.

Morrian jerked her head up and looked at me. Her expression turned calculating, then she began to smile. She opened her mouth to speak...but the words never came. I heard a whistling sound, and as I registered it, a streak of wood raced by me and planted itself firmly in Morrian's chest. She gasped and staggered, shock in her eyes. That arrow – for arrow it was – was followed closely by a second, which hit her in nearly the same place. I jerked my head around to see who was shooting, and my jaw dropped open. It was the last person I had expected.

Lissa stood tall amidst the others still struggling to their feet, bow raised, another arrow already notched and drawn. Her jaw was clenched in determination. I noticed that the metal arrowheads had the white flames around them that marked them as flamestone, which explained how they easily found their mark. We Brenwyds had weakened Morrian's shields enough that the flamestone arrows could punch through. "I'm sorry," Lissa said. "But you have given us no choice. Morrian, sorceress, for your crimes against Ecclesia, both past and present, I, Calissa, crown princess of Ecclesia, do sentence you to death."

Morrian was dying. Only a Brenwyd healer could have saved her now, and I certainly was not inclined to. But she had enough strength left to turn back toward Steffyn and jab the spear into his stomach. My scream of horror was drowned out by Steffyn's roar of pain. I started to run to the sorceress, intending to stab her through the heart so she was well and truly dead, but before I did a concentrated stream of fire shot down from the sky, catching Morrian squarely and...well, I nearly heaved up what meager contents were in my stomach. I glanced to where the fire had come from and saw a leviathan hovering just past the courtyard wall, looking very pleased with herself. Kezia.

And so Morrian, the ancient sorceress, died, felled by the arrows of a princess and the fire of a leviathan. But I focused on that later. At that moment, I just concentrated on getting to Steffyn and falling by his side.

To Wake a Kingdom

The spear had entered his stomach and I knew, based on the placement and angle, that many internal organs had been damaged. But he was still breathing. Putting pressure on the wound, I made ready to remove the spear so I could heal him. It would be tricky; the spear was keeping him from bleeding out, but it had to be pulled out for the healing. I would need to sing fast.

Aislinn, his voice came to me very weakly, like a whisper.

Whatever it is, it can wait, I thought back. *You're injured.*

I know. Let...let me go.

I stared at him, shocked. *What?*

Aislinn, I've...lived a long time. Longer than anyone should. I'm ready to die.

And how would you characterize your relationship with Abba now? We defeated her, Steffyn. We did. With his help.

A silence. *I will...take my chance.*

No, you won't. You still have a lot to answer for.

Aislinn. Please. You're right, she's dead. But I...I am still a beast.

Don't say that, I thought hotly. *You are not what your appearance makes you. So her death didn't free you. But now that she is dead, maybe we will be able to break it.*

*Aislinn...*his voice trailed off. I decided I wasn't going to spend any more time arguing with him. He needed to be healed, now. I was not going to let him die, to let Morrian have that one little victory. I didn't care what he thought. I was the healer. I would do this. It was my call.

I pulled out the spear, causing him to bellow again in pain, and immediately began singing. Since I had healed him before, I could now easily find his song. I was vaguely aware of Lissa, Rhodri, and the Brenwyds and leviathans talking behind me, but no one approached me.

It was not the easiest healing I'd ever done. With all the internal damage, it took precious minutes, and I was already tired. But I did it. When I finished, I looked at his face expectantly. His grey eyes were open, but veiled. I couldn't read them. He just said, "Thank you" in an expressionless tone, and drew his hood over his face to shield his features. I was pretty sure the other Brenwyds would have gotten a good look at him, but I didn't comment on it. He got to his feet, as did I. Then we both really took the time to consider Morrian's corpse. Or, Steffyn did. I spared it a glance, then quickly looked away. "She's really...gone." His voice sounded a little hollow.

I thought about that. The sorceress that had dominated my thoughts for nearly a month was gone, never to trouble my country again. We had stopped her. Ecclesia – all of Niclausia – was safe. It was hard to take in. Some part of me thought it should have been harder, while my more rational side recognized that it had been hard enough. But we had been blessed and protected by Abba, and had come out the other side of the confrontation alive. But Steffyn...this had been his sister, after all. Even if certainly not a good one.

"I'm sorry," I whispered.

He turned to look at me, eyes still unreadable. "Don't be. As I said, she died to me as a sister a long time ago."

"Oh, Mathghamhain, are you alright?" Lissa's voice asked. She and Rhodri had walked over, apparently judging it the right time to interrupt.

He inclined his head to her. "Your Highness. I am in your debt."

"Yes...think nothing of it, please." Lissa was avoiding looking at the body, her face pained. Rhodri had an arm around her and gave her a comforting squeeze. "I know she was evil and she had to die, but...it still feels so wrong."

"As it should, Your Highness," Delwyn said, stepping up to us and casting a curious look at Steffyn. "Killing a person, no matter who they were or what they did, is a terrible thing, and it is a terrible world we live in that makes us have to kill some people. But please, do not let your mind be too troubled about it. It was necessary, and it is done. No more."

Lissa inclined her head. "Thank you, Delwyn."

"And what did you think of that, Barak?" I heard Kezia say, sounding smug and proud. The older dragon had come back to hover near her. The elementals had either been killed or had fled once Morrian died.

"Very neat work, Kezia. Excellent flame control," Barak said. He turned his head to Steffyn. "Are you at all burned?"

"No."

Kezia smiled a toothy grin and poked Neriah with a wingtip. "Hear that?"

I could have sworn Neriah rolled his eyes. "Yes, I heard. I admit, well done. But did you see how I took on those two elementals at once?" He extended his left wing and grimaced. "I think I wrenched my wing again, though."

"Oh, did you?" I asked in concern. "Here, let me heal-"

I started to take a step toward him, but Delwyn put a restraining hand on my arm. "Lady Aislinn, you have been through a rough several weeks and just led the song to defeat a sorceress. You are more tired than you realize. There are plenty of other Brenwyds here who can tend to the leviathans."

I blinked, really looking around me. There were a fair number of Brenwyds milling about, and several were already approaching Barak as if to ask about injuries. "Oh. Alright, then." His mention of tiredness seemed to suddenly bring out the fact that I was feeling exhausted, and I swayed on my feet. "I suppose I am rather tired." Delwyn let out a low chuckle at my surprised tone. I turned to him with a smile. "Thank you for coming. Did you break the barrier?"

"We did," he said. "It was stronger than we anticipated, but between our numbers and the leviathans' actions, it came down."

"Good."

"But everyone is still asleep," Lissa said, looking at us anxiously. "Were you not able to destroy the rose?"

"Well...we got interrupted. We did manage to destroy the containment Morrian had for keeping the drained Brenwyd abilities, though."

"Ah." Lissa nodded thoughtfully. "So that is what got her attention."

"I should say it did," Rhodri said wryly. Then, more seriously, "Were there any casualties in the south?"

"Some of the leviathans suffered injuries from shadow wolves and elemental dragons, as did some of my people, but praise Abba there were no fatalities. I left several Brenwyds behind to help tend to the wounded," Delwyn answered him.

"How was the fighting there?" Kezia's voice broke in on our conversation. Neriah and Barak were being tended to, but she seemed to have escaped the conflict uninjured. "Could you see how well Doron or Ziva did? I cannot wait to tell them what I did here." From her smug tone, I guessed that Doron and Ziva were rivals of hers.

"Kezia," Barak said sternly. "You did well, yes, but do not let that inflate your pride. Too much pride is a dangerous thing, and no one enjoys a braggart." Kezia's head drooped at the rebuke. Barak continued, "You will have plenty of time to compare feats with Doron and Ziva for yourself. Now, though, we must determine what the humans and Brenwyds want to do next." He swung his head to us. "Shall we begin transport back to the mainland?"

Rhodri nodded. "I think that's a good idea. And we should check in with those still there." He turned toward me and Steffyn. "Once I got through the door, it was pretty easy to get to the main courtyard. I came across some other servants, but they were no more than men-at-arms. Neriah saw me and swooped down to get the news. I told him, and he said Barak had seen something moving on the shore and had gone to investigate with Kezia. After he picked me up, we went to investigate as well, and found Lissa arriving with the first of the Brenwyds. However, these...things started attacking."

"Ogres, Your Highness," Delwyn supplied. "We've had some experience with them in recent weeks in the Rimed foothills."

Rhodri nodded. "Right. Those. So some Brenwyds got on the leviathans, while others stayed to fight off the attack."

"And that's what you need to check on," I said. He nodded.

"I think I will go back now, if that is all right with you, Your Highnesses," Delwyn said. "Others will stay here if you wish to remain."

"Very well, Delwyn," Rhodri said. "And thank you for coming. Thank everyone."

"Yes, thank you, very much so," I said. "I couldn't have torn that shield down by myself."

"You're welcome, Lady Aislinn," he said. "But perhaps you underestimate your own strength. We had no luck in bringing down her shield until you were leading us." I blinked, surprised, and could think of no reply. Delwyn bowed to Rhodri. "And may I officially say, Your Highness, it is a great joy to see you again. We were all quite worried."

Rhodri smiled. A real smile with not a hint of concern or worry. "It's good to see you again, too, Delwyn. We'll be back on the shore soon. There's just a little unfinished business to take care of." Delwyn departed.

"Are we going down to break the sleeping curse?" Lissa asked.

I nodded. "Yes, but...I think it will require a specific sort of method for its destruction."

⚬⚭⚬

It's really amazing how the back of one's mind can think and make connections while one is in the midst of fighting for one's life. When I had tried to cleave the rose in two, some part of me had focused on the failure, trying to analyze it and determine why the flamestone blade hadn't been able to damage it. Once the battle was over and my thoughts returned to consider it, several things clicked in my mind. I had maintained a lingering suspicion for some time now that Lissa would be crucial to undoing Morrian's spell, even though she wasn't the actual anchor, and despite my surprise at her being the one to actually kill Morrian (she was the kind of person who hesitated to kill a spider), I believed I had now worked out exactly how she was linked to the spell's undoing.

Understandably, as I relayed my theory on the way to the rose room both Rhodri and Lissa had objections, though Rhodri was rather louder in his protestations. "Absolutely not, Aislinn! After all the trouble we've gone through I won't have her risk falling under the curse of that sorceress again. Especially since she's now dead!" he said, frowning at me. "Surely you can destroy it with song. We can call a few of the other Brenwyds from their survey of the fortress to support you." The Brenwyds who were awaiting transport back to the mainland had decided to examine the rest of the fortress for any magical traps or spells, or any other magically inclined lackeys of Morrian's. Pelagius had been nowhere to be seen, so he was likely still lurking. Steffyn had elected to join them instead of coming down with us to the rose room again. I had a feeling he needed to be alone to come to grips with the events of the past hour.

"I know," I said. "And with enough Brenwyds, that will work. But I truly think that this is the easiest, simplest solution. My father always taught me that when fighting magic, take the simplest approach you can because that's the best way to undermine a spell."

"But what makes you believe this will work?" Lissa asked, brow furrowed.

"It makes sense, Liss. I've long thought that you are somehow connected to fully undoing the spell because you were the starting point for it. True, you're not the anchor, for which I'm exceedingly grateful, but I think that the fact you are so connected with its start means that you are the best person to break it."

"By pricking my finger again? Would it not send me to sleep again and recast the spell?"

"A spell can only be cast once. To do it again would require a new anchor. At worst, you'll have a pricked finger and we'll just have to destroy the rose some other way. And at best, it would break the spell without much more effort and circumvent all the protections laid on it."

I could tell she was thinking about it. Rhodri was still glaring at me, but he wasn't arguing so I knew he understood the sense in my argument. In truth, I was a little worried myself about the implications of Lissa pricking her finger again, but I didn't really think anything drastically bad would happen. We reached the door in the stairway, and I opened it. "I'll do a thorough job of listening to the spells around it and seeing if there's any chance one could backfire on you. If there is, I'll call the other Brenwyds and we'll deal with it. But if not, I think you should do it."

"What if Morrian's death has completely disabled all the shielding spells around it and we can just destroy it with a sword or fire?" Rhodri asked as we walked across the room full of sleepers.

"Then we'll do that, but I don't think it's likely."

"Why not?" Lissa asked. "Don't spells usually die with their makers?"

"Yes, but there was nothing usual about Morrian." I stopped before the entrance to the rose room. The door was still open. "And considering Steffyn's curse is still in place..."

"Whose?" Lissa asked, sounding mystified.

I blinked and realized my slip. "Oh, grindles. I didn't mean to say that."

"I would like an explanation for that, all the same," Rhodri said. "Why did he tell you and not all of us? And why did he change it in the first place?"

I turned to him. "He didn't tell me, I figured it out. The dreams I've been having over the past month...they've told me a bit about his past."

"Whose past?" Lissa persisted.

"Steff...that is, Mathghamhain. His true name is Steffyn."

Lissa's eyes widened, then narrowed. "I see. He did tell us when we met him Mathghamhain was not his true name...interesting that you, out of all of us, should figure it out."

I gave her a look. "I told you, I've been having dreams, and I don't control what I See."

Suddenly Lissa's eyebrows shot up. "Wait. Steffyn...the name of Nivea's champion from the first war with Morrian?" I looked at her for a few seconds and decided there was no point in denying it.

"The same. Don't tell him I told you that, though; I told him I wouldn't."

Rhodri looked stunned. "He's *that* Steffyn?" I nodded. "Grindles and spindles...and I accused him of cowardice in facing Morrian."

"He paid a very high cost the first time," I said. "But regardless of who he is, the fact that his curse remains in place makes me think that Morrian's spells are more resilient than one would think."

"It is still in place," Lissa said thoughtfully, as if just then realizing it. "Poor man...Aislinn, there must be something that can be done. Perhaps now that Morrian is dead, you will be able to break the spell, even if it did not break upon her death."

"That's my thought as well, but first I shall have to convince him of it..." I sighed at the thought of that conversation. "But for right now, let's focus on this rose, since that can definitely not argue with me about trying to disenchant it. Come on." I didn't want to prolong the conversation on Steffyn's stubbornness.

We entered the room. Lissa looked at the rose warily, wrapping both her hands around one of Rhodri's as if to keep herself from moving toward it. I quickly listened to the rose with my song sense. Sure enough, the shielding spells were still in place, loud and strong. Then I listened to Lissa's song. I had been taught that a person kept the impact of having been under a spell with them, even after the spell was broken...ah. In comparing her song to the shields around the spindle, I could sense a slight similarity.

"Well?" Rhodri asked when I turned toward the two of them.

"There are spells still in place, but I think it will work."

"You're sure?" he pressed.

"Reasonably. The only spells I sense are the ones shielding the rose, nothing else. I think Lissa pricking her finger again will do the trick in reversing it."

"Like reverse engineering?" he asked. I frowned, unsure what that meant, but he saw my confused look and waved away the question. "Never mind. If you're sure it won't hurt her..." He looked at Lissa with concern.

She looked a little nervous, but nodded. "Very well. I will do it." Rhodri walked with her to the rose. She glanced towards me, and I nodded encouragement. I was half-paying attention to her and half-listening to the shield spells. Lissa firmed her chin, extended her hand, and after a brief hesitation she brought her finger down on the dark thorn point, almost exactly as I had seen her do in my vision several weeks before. I heard her bite back a cry, but my attention was more immediately grabbed by the extraordinary effect her action had on the spells. My father has since told me that breaking spells by using the instrument or instruments that had been used to cast them in the first place was an ancient way Brenwyds would use to break spells before they fully understood how to use their abilities, but at the time I had no idea. I just knew that it worked. Morrian had defended her anchor very strongly against any sort of Brenwyd intervention; clearly, the idea we might use her own method against her spell had never occurred to her. I had never heard a spell break so fast, or so spectacularly. (Though, granted, I didn't have a wide range of spell-breaking experience.) Not only that, but as soon as those spells broke, I heard the Creation song rise up to its proper volume – and past it, as it happens – as if wanting to cleanse the place of the evil that had occurred. It made me gasp.

Lissa and Rhodri looked at me inquisitively, but the smile breaking over my face – and the fact that Lissa was still obviously wide-awake – assured them that it had happened as I had thought. Noises of rustlings and movement from the outer room started to reach me, and I wasn't the only one. Rhodri, keeping his grip on Lissa, moved toward the door. I was quick to follow. A beautiful sight met my eyes: all the sleepers were waking, stretching, yawning, sitting up, looking around them in bewilderment as they tried to understand where they were and what had happened.

At that point, finally feeling overcome by the day, I collapsed to the floor with my back to the wall. "Thank you, Abba," I whispered. "Thank you." Simple words, but I had never said them with greater meaning.

I saw Lissa gently remove her hand from Rhodri's grip and usher him in the direction of his father, whom I could see just starting to sit up. Rhodri smiled at her, then hurried to his father's side, dodging awakened Brenwyds. "Father!"

Lord Duke Ceredon turned around in surprise at the voice, and continued to stare in astonishment tinged with joy as his son reached him and threw his arms around him. To my surprise, he returned the hug warmly. I had never really considered Duke Ceredon to be the outwardly affectionate type.

He gently pushed his son back so he could look fully into his face. "Rhodri! Heavens above, boy, where have you been?" He was trying for an exasperated tone, but I could hear the deep relief behind it. He regathered his son into his arms.

"There's something long overdue," Lissa said quietly, coming to sit beside me.

I nodded. "Yes. Now the celebrations can finally begin. The wedding is still on, I assume?"

"Aislinn!" she admonished, but with a laugh. "Of course it is."

"Good. I can't think of a better way to celebrate." I took her hand and sang a few quiet notes to heal the thorn prick.

"What? A sorceress? We suspected some magic mischief, but it seems to have been stronger than we realized." Duke Ceredon's voice penetrated my awareness. I looked toward him and found him looking my direction. "Calissa? Is that you over there?"

"Yes, Lord Duke," Lissa said, still sitting on the floor. "Pardon me for not standing to greet you properly, but I believe my exertions from the past few weeks are finally catching up with me."

"Yes, from the look of you I'd say you've had a hard time of things." Duke Ceredon had walked over and was scrutinizing our worn and travel-stained attire. Despite our fatigue Lissa and I did make the effort to get up, as it was a bit disconcerting to have him towering over us. "So, there was a spell cast over Ecclesia, as Sir Eiwas said?"

"Yes, your grace," I answered. I looked around and found Sir Eiwas. "It was a true vision you had, sir; an ancient sorceress cast a sleeping curse over the whole country so that everyone within the borders fell asleep. When you tried to cross the border, she sent shadow wolves to attack you and a couple of servants to cast the sleep over you as well."

Sir Eiwas nodded thoughtfully. "I see. Where is the sorceress now?"

"Dead," I answered.

"You killed her? Just the three of you?" The knight sounded surprised. I didn't blame him, but the idea made me laugh.

"No sir, not at all. We had several surprising allies turn up, and we managed to coordinate an attack that brought the thorn barrier down and allowed a force of Darlesian Brenwyds to join us for the final battle."

"You managed to bring down that monstrosity? Good for you," Sir Eiwas said approvingly.

"Well, not me personally, sir. I was here the whole time. It's...it's a bit complicated."

"I can imagine. Let me ask a simple question, then. Where is 'here,' exactly?"

"We are on an island off the northwest coast of Ecclesia, past the northern mountains, sir," I answered.

"I can see that you've a long tale to tell," Duke Ceredon interjected, looking between the three of us. "Not the least of which, Rhodri, is where in the Five Realms you have been the past six months and how you managed to get back, but I think the full tale will wait until we can arrive in more comfortable surroundings, yes?" he said kindly.

"That would be much appreciated, Father," Rhodri said. "And as it happens...what happened to me probably is of the least relevance in the tale."

"I think not," I protested. "Do you think we would have ended up here if I hadn't discovered where you'd gone and how to follow you and bring you back?"

He shrugged. "You would have figured something out."

"Father?" came a new voice from the doorway. I recognized it, and the person it belonged to. Cerdic. He was scanning the room and his eyes lit on his father first. He walked toward him. "Praise Abba, you are alive and well. You are well, are you not?" An anxious tone colored the query.

Duke Ceredon laughed. "Yes, son, very well."

"That's nice," Rhodri said, giving his brother an all-too-serious expression in my opinion. "How about me? I'm the one who's been gone for six months."

"Rhodri!" Cerdic crossed over to him in two paces and gripped him in a tight hug. "I did not see you in the shadows." He backed up to look his brother over but kept his hands on his shoulders. "Well, wherever you've been, it doesn't seem to have treated you poorly. Would it have killed you to at least send a message you were alive?"

"I would have if I could have, believe me."

"I don't mean to break up this reunion," I said. "But since the spell is now broken, I would like to get back to Kheprah for a reunion of my own, if you understand me, your grace, Your Highness."

"Then it *is* broken all over the country?" Lissa said anxiously.

I smiled. "Of course it is. I Saw it break. Everyone's awake. And I'm sure that your mother will go into one of her nervous fits if you don't get back within the next hour."

Lissa nodded, rolling her eyes a little. Her mother was a good, kind queen, but very prone to worrying and attacks of her nerves. "Likely."

"Then allow us to escort you home," Duke Ceredon said. "I'm sure the tale can be told there. Which way to the boat off this island?"

"Oh, we don't have a boat, Father," Cerdic said, a smile curving his lips.

"How did you get here, then? Swim?"

"No, we flew."

"Flew." It was a dubious statement.

"Indeed." Cerdic beckoned to everyone in the room. "Follow me, and you will see a being that is straight out of legend." The Brenwyds in the room exchanged amused and slightly bemused glances and followed Cerdic out. Rhodri, Lissa, and Duke Ceredon all went out together and I followed. Before we reached the outside, however, I stopped and turned back. I was listening for someone, and I wasn't finding him.

"Aislinn? Where are you going?" Lissa asked, stopping the other two with her.

"There's...something I need to see to. Hopefully it won't take long; simply tell Barak to have someone wait for me, will you?"

"What could you possibly have to do still in this fortress?" Rhodri protested.

Lissa, however, met my eyes, and I'm pretty sure she understood what it was I was going to do. "Very well. But don't be too long, and if you cannot make him see reason, tell him I will order him to."

That made me laugh. "I'd like to see that. Go on." Lissa turned and drew the two men after her, despite their puzzled expressions. Then I turned and once more descended into the spiral stairwell. Morrian may be dead, but there was one more beast I needed to deal with today.

❧⚭❧

As I had suspected, I found Steffyn down in the dungeon, standing in front of the cell we had come through. He turned his head as I entered, but upon seeing it was just me, he turned back and continued his contemplation of the cell. A lit torch was in a bracket on the wall, lighting the interior. I went to stand beside him. "How are you?"

For a few minutes, he didn't answer. "I...I'm not sure. I thought that having her finally defeated, dead, would impart a sense of triumph or finality, but...I only feel more adrift." He sounded lost, like a child who was wandering the woods in search of his family. On the last word he sat down on the stone floor.

I sat beside him. "My father says that we should never really feel triumph upon taking another person's life because, assuming they were not a follower of Abba, it means that their soul is lost forever."

"Hmm. And what do you say?"

I considered the question, drawing my knees up to my chin and resting my head on them. "I think he's right." I paused. "You know, I've never killed anyone before today."

"You didn't, technically. The princess did. And Kezia."

"You know what I meant."

"Aye...well, your father is right. I should have known better than to hope for a triumphal feeling. I should be ashamed I even thought of it." He sounded deeply melancholy.

"Do you have memories of her before she began practicing magic?"

He shifted, not answering right away. I thought he would refuse to answer the question, but he surprised me. "Some. I was much younger than she. Her father married my mother when she was ten. I was born two years later, when she was twelve. By the time I was old enough to really remember things, she was a young lady out in society. I remember, when I was very young, trying desperately to gain her approval. But she always kept herself distant. She preferred spending time with her mother's family." He paused, then said slowly, sounding a little bewildered, "I believe she killed my mother."

I gasped. "Oh, Steffyn..."

He took no notice of my exclamation. "I didn't suspect until long afterward. It wasn't long before King Llewelyn came to Lamasia and found her. I was twelve years old. My father had died two years earlier in an accident, and his death had caused Morrian to withdraw into deep mourning. The first time I really understood she held no great love for my mother was the day of his funeral. She shrugged off Mother's condolences and wouldn't even speak to her. Then she left to live with her mother's kin. However, one day she came back. She was very apologetic, and blamed her grief. She said she wanted to make amends. She was with us several days. Then, one night, I woke to the sound of my mother's voice, singing. She had a lovely voice, soprano. I had never heard it as I did then, but I recognized that it was raised in battle. Wanting to help her, I grabbed my small sword and went downstairs. But before I reached the bottom, my mother's voice abruptly ended, and I sensed a great wash of magic from the entry hall of our house. I rushed in, and found Morrian standing up from a body, blood soaking her dress. She turned to me. I stared back at her. Then she sank to the ground, crying out hysterically that she had tried to stop him, but had been too late to save her. I approached her, and I found her in front of two bodies. One was that of a man I didn't recognize. The other...was my mother.

"I was numb. I couldn't take it in. Morrian told me that she had been wakened, as I had, by my mother's voice. She said she had grabbed a knife and come to assist, but by the time she got there, the man – a magician – was standing over her body. She said that before she knew it, she had stabbed the man. I believed her. There had been some magical activity in our province recently. My mother had been part of a Brenwyd squadron who had discovered a cult believed responsible for it. It was reasonable. After that night, Morrian was much warmer toward me. Said we had been bonded by tragedy. With both parents gone, I needed someone to cling to. I couldn't help it. But then, in those later years..." He seemed to be speaking to himself and had forgotten I was there. His fists clenched. "I should have seen what she was earlier. How she was manipulating the king, taking control, shunting Nivea to the side. I knew her best. I should have seen it. I *did* see it. I just chose to be blind."

"It is reasonable," I said gently. "She was your sister. You were a child when your parents died, and when she opened up to you after years of coolness, it's only natural that you returned the affection."

"I'm a mind reader," he persisted. "I should have known."

"Is this what you've been telling yourself for all these years? If so, no wonder you're a pessimist."

At that he did glance at me. "Is that supposed to make me feel better?"

I shrugged. "Maybe a little. I'm more interested in why you're telling me all this after she's dead. And after all this time."

He grunted and turned his attention back to the cell. "I don't know. It's just...all coming back...I'm sorry for inflicting all of that on you."

"It's no burden. It's the most I've heard you talk about yourself since I've known you." A long silence. "So...what will you do now?"

He shrugged. "What should I do?" His tone was despairing. "What is there for me to do, Aislinn? I am still cursed."

"We can fix that."

"Can we?" He stared at me, hard. "Are you sure?" I nodded, taking the time to listen to the spell enveloping him. It was still rather overwhelming. But now Morrian was dead, surely, surely, we could- "No," he said out loud. "Don't raise false hope, Aislinn. If her death didn't break this, then nothing can."

"That is not true, and you know it. Remember Elfleda's prophecy. The only person really standing in the way of breaking this curse is you." I expected him to growl out an irritated response and turn away, but instead he kept his gaze on me. And it softened. But in grief. Then he turned away.

"I...I wish I knew how," he said helplessly. "How? Can you conceive how long two hundred and fifty years is, Aislinn? Can you even begin to comprehend it? All the long days, and dark nights, spent in isolation and solitude, cut off from any and all forms of...love?"

I considered him for several minutes. Obviously witnessing Morrian's death had unleashed a wave of emotion and turmoil that had broken many of the walls he had erected around himself. My mother had told me that traumatic events in people's lives could create such a response, especially those related to magic. Thus, another important facet of a Brenwyd's duties was not only to heal physical injuries, but to do the best we could to heal the mental and emotional ones. Mother...what would she do in this situation? She was not a Brenwyd, but she was an excellent comforter.

I took a deep breath. "No, I cannot imagine it," I answered quietly. "Or rather, perhaps I can imagine it, but I doubt I could come close to the true reality." He grunted. "What I do know is that just as you learned to wall yourself off from the world, you can learn how to be a part of it again."

He made a noise that sounded like a snort. "Really? In this form?"

"I never said that. We'll break the curse. You will."

He turned back to me then and shook his head. "You are nothing if not obstinate."

"I prefer the term dogmatic optimist." I smiled briefly, then turned serious again. "But, in all seriousness, what do you plan to do right now?"

He shrugged. "Go back to my mountain." He glanced toward the stairs, and suddenly seemed to realize what my presence in the dungeon represented. "You destroyed the rose, then? And the sleeping curse broke?"

"Yes. The others are getting ferried back to the mainland by the leviathans. Then I believe we will split between those traveling back to Darlesia and those going to Kheprah. And a few will need to go back to Tairport. There are many things that need to be explained." I had a sudden imagining of the citizens of Tairport waking up to find two dozen dragons flying about the city. "Yes, I must make sure someone goes down to Tairport. Someone official."

"Then what are you doing down here? You should be going home."

"I wanted to make sure you wouldn't do anything drastic."

"Such as?"

I shrugged. "Disappear into the mountains, never to be heard of again."

He grunted. "It...crossed my mind. But I've a sneaking suspicion that you won't let me."

I smiled. "You are correct. I assume it's too much to ask you to come back to Kheprah with us?" His eyes widened in incredulity. "I had to ask. So you will travel back to your mountain. On foot?"

"If I need to. Though I suppose I could ask one of the leviathans."

"That would seem wise. And I trust you won't mind visitors."

"Even if I did, I suspect you would ignore it."

"Very true." I reached out to him and squeezed his hand. "I am sorry for your sister, Steffyn. Evil as she was, she was still kin. In a way, you have lost her twice, and I am sorry. There is no shame in your feelings."

He stared at me, moisture rising in his eyes, and he blinked rapidly, though he seemed at a loss for words. Finally, he withdrew his hand from mine and turned, moving past me to the exit from the dingy dungeon. "I...thank you. I suppose we should get back to the rooftop to get back to the mainland."

"Yes," I agreed, following him. "But if you ever want to talk more, I'm willing to listen." His only response to that was a grunt.

Aftermath

$\mathcal{T}$he next few hours passed mostly in a blur, interrupted every so often by moments of vivid clarity that stood out to me as clearly as if painted. We reached the rooftop and received a ride from Barak to the mainland. Once there, we found that Cerdic and many of the Brenwyds had already gone back to Darlesia with the intention of riding to the capital and finding Lady Rhian. Understandably, Duke Ceredon wanted to go find his wife, but he wanted to make sure his son got safely to Kheprah first, and he wanted to hear the whole story explained. Neriah agreed to ferry Steffyn back to his mountaintop, despite Lissa's attempts to have him join our trip to Kheprah. He politely refused but gave his assurances that he would see us soon.

Before we left for Kheprah, the three of us made a quick trip to Tairport to tell Bityah and the leviathans there what had occurred, and to reassure the citizens that the large, fire-breathing dragons outside the walls had no intentions of ransacking the city. Two of the Darlesian Brenwyds kindly lent Lissa and Rhodri their horses so Dynin didn't have to keep making multiple transfers. Fortunately, the people of Tairport were all disoriented enough from sleep that by the time we got there, the guards were only just starting to gather weapons to attack the perceived threat. The sight of the crown princess, with her no-longer-missing fiancé, quickly smoothed things over. (Although the expression on the lord mayor's face was so astonished both by the sight of the dragons outside and the crown princess in tattered skirts that I was hard-pressed to keep from breaking into laughter that I had a feeling would have a hysterical edge to it.)

Once that had been taken care of, and assurances given that a more thorough explanation would follow, Lissa and Bityah spoke and agreed that for now, the leviathans would return to their islands to let the rest of their race know what had occurred. In two weeks, however, they would return to Tairport so that formal negotiations for the return of the leviathans and other friendly monsters to the mainland could begin. The meeting would also serve to renew the ancient alliance between humans and leviathans to fight together against the bad monsters, for none of us thought that Morrian's death would end their attacks. Once those arrangements were made, we went back north one more time to let Barak, Kezia, and Neriah know, and then, finally, we transferred back to Kheprah with Rhodri's father, Sir Eiwas, and several other Darlesian Brenwyds in tow.

The sight of the city so clearly bustling with activity and noise brought happy tears to my eyes. I noticed that Lissa teared up as well, and Rhodri made several furtive movements across his face that looked suspiciously like wiping away wet tracks. As we crossed through the gate, we were met by a bewildered crowd of citizens who were nonetheless overjoyed to see their princess and her prince riding into the city. They slowed our progress to the castle considerably, as they surged about us shouting well-wishes and queries. Like the people of Tairport, many still had the bewildered look of sleep in their eyes. Because of our slow progress, news of our arrival reached the castle long before we did, and we were met at the castle gates by King Cayden and Queen Alyessa themselves.

Lissa dismounted from her borrowed horse and ran to her parents, throwing her arms around them in an unusual public show of affection. They returned it, looking relieved and confused. "Calissa? What is going on?" Her father asked, at the same time her mother exclaimed queries about her health and the state of her clothes. Both were quickly silenced by the sight of Rhodri walking up to them with a smile, followed by his father. I missed their initial greetings and questions, for my attention was grabbed by the sight of several familiar faces pushing their way through the growing crowd around the gate.

Dynin saw the same thing I did, and pushed his way through the crowd, allowing me to tumble directly off his back and into my parents' arms. "Mother! Father! You're alright, it's all alright." The feel of their arms around me and murmured assurances broke down the last walls keeping my emotions in check and I began to cry.

"Are you alright, sweetheart? What's happened?" My mother brushed tendrils of hair back from my face and looked at me with concern. "Are you hurt?"

I shook my head, smiling through my tears. "No, no, I'm fine. I'm just so happy you're okay."

My father looked me over, an appraising look in his celestine blue eyes. "You've been around a lot of magic. Powerful magic. I'm not sure what has happened, but the last thing I remember was the feeling of powerful magic overwhelming us." He stopped there. My father wasn't one to ask direct questions; he preferred statements punctuated by searching looks.

I nodded. "It was a curse. It's...it's rather a long story from there." I looked around. "Where's Aiden?"

"I sent him to the house until we could determine what was going on," Father answered. His gaze on me shifted to one of concern. "You've been fighting a witch." My mother gasped and looked at me with wide eyes.

I smiled and shrugged. "I had help. You trained me well." Any further conversation was forestalled by an announcement from the king, saying that any imminent danger was passed, and that a herald would be dispatched to each of the market squares by noon with at least the basic information of what had occurred. In the meantime, it would be best for everyone to return to their homes and shops and make sure everything was in order. Then he firmly took hold of his wife in one arm and his daughter in the other and walked back through the castle gates. I and my parents followed. Once we were into the courtyard, I found one of the grooms and firmly instructed him to take care of Dynin as if he were the king's own mount. Dynin gave me an affectionate nuzzle with his nose and then followed the groom happily.

After seeing him off, I, along with Rhodri, Lord Duke Ceredon, my parents, and Sir Eiwas, followed the royal family to the king's private office. It was small compared to his official meeting room used for diplomatic affairs, but full of personal touches and had a cozy feel. King Cayden sat in the chair behind his desk, Queen Alyessa beside him, and the rest of us claimed the various chairs around the room.

The king passed his gaze slowly and carefully over me, Lissa, and Rhodri (who held a purring Boomer on his lap. I had no idea when the cat had joined our small party, but I was not in the least surprised to see him. The real question, in my mind, was when Rhodri would ever experience privacy from the cat again.) Everyone else in the room remained silent, waiting on him to speak. "It seems that you have quite the tale to tell," he said finally, eyes settling to rest on his daughter. "The most any of us can remember is that we were going about our business the afternoon before your birthday, Calissa, and then suddenly we were overwhelmed by sleepiness and lost consciousness until waking just a short while ago. Based on the time, at least one night has passed, yet your appearances suggest you three have been on a strenuous journey. And while I am overjoyed to see you again, Rhodri," he allowed a quick smile to flash over his face, "I am rather curious as to where you have been the past six months."

"As am I, Your Majesty," Duke Ceredon said, looking at his son. "I still have not received a satisfactory answer on that count, Rhodri. All I heard from your brother was some sort of nonsense about the pathways to the old world still being active."

"It's not nonsense, Father." Rhodri exchanged quick looks with Lissa and myself. "It's all a long story, and as it started with me, I'll tell my part of it first. When I left here six months ago, my company, as you know, made it safely to the middle of the Anianol Forest just over the border into Darlesia, which is important later. I left the others for a few minutes..." He went on to narrate briefly his encounter with Morrian and subsequent experiences on Earth. Then, I took up the thread of the story with Lissa's request for me to investigate the possibility of pathways, and how I was outside the borders when the curse fell. As the story went on, the three of us took turns narrating events. Though at various points throughout the story our listeners let out gasps or exclamations (mostly from Lissa's mother at the sound of the dangers her daughter had been exposed to), no one interrupted with questions.

Finally, after what felt like hours, we reached the end of the story and the room fell completely silent. Even Boomer had stopped purring in contemplation of the events. (I also suspected he was affronted at having missed them.) Looking at my parents, I saw their faces reflecting shock, incredulity, and pride. My mother reached out and wrapped me in an embrace, and I felt my father place a comforting hand on my shoulder.

King Cayden leaned back in his chair and breathed out slowly. "Well. That is quite the story." He focused on his daughter. "You are sure you are unhurt?"

She smiled at him. "I am perfectly well, Papa. I am only tired. And a little hungry." At her mention of hunger, I realized just how ravenous I was, and my stomach chose that moment to growl loudly. I felt a fierce blush rise to my cheeks, but the sound seemed to break the silence in the room, and everyone broke out in smiles and relaxed.

"Of course you are hungry, you brave dears," the queen said, rising from her seat to walk to the bell pull to ring for a servant. "I can only imagine the state the kitchens are in, but I am sure Maude can scrounge up something for you. You in particular must be starving, Aislinn."

She smiled graciously at me, alleviating my embarrassment.

I returned her smile. "Thank you, Your Majesty. I would love some food."

Sir Eiwas turned to where I sat with my parents. "I must say, Lady Aislinn, I most heartily commend you for your actions. Delwyn told me how well you led them in song. You've been trained well." I felt the blush return as he looked past me to my father. "You should be very proud of her, Brychan."

My father's hand squeezed my shoulder. "I most certainly am, Eiwas." The words ignited a warm feeling in my stomach that was welcome after all the uncertainty of our journey. After that, conversation flowed freely, and the three of us were bombarded with questions about the details of the past weeks. The plate of food the queen ordered arrived promptly, and it seemed that no matter how flustered Maude was with the condition of the kitchens after three weeks of inactivity, she was quickly pulling it back into order. The warm, flaky biscuits with butter and jam tasted heavenly after all the trail food, and they gave me the energy to keep up with the questions. Finally, though, the queen called a firm end to the questions and ordered us to go get some sleep. I had a feeling that the king and Duke Ceredon would have liked to continue questioning for a little while longer but they made no protest in the face of the queen's hard stare at her husband. Instead, the king said he would gather the heralds and tell them the basic details to relay to the people.

And so, at last I found myself back in my own house, in my own room, about to climb into a hot bath before tumbling into my own bed to sleep. It felt nearly like a dream, except for the layer of dust that had accumulated on my furniture. As I unwound my braid, my door creaked open and Aiden poked his head in. His eyes brightened upon spotting me and he pushed the door fully open. "Aislinn!" I opened my arms and he crashed into them. Our dogs, Elva and Conall, followed behind him and pressed against us as we hugged each other tightly.

"Aiden! Oh, are you alright? I've been so worried." More tears crept down my cheeks.

"I'm fine," he said, pulling back, looking a bit embarrassed by my emotional display. "Don't cry, I was just sleeping. Is Rhodri really back? Were we really all asleep for almost a month? Did you really fight an evil witch?" His eyes were wide. Apparently, the news was traveling fast.

"Well...yes," I admitted. "But I had help."

"Aiden," my mother said from the doorway. We both turned to her. "Let your sister bathe and rest. She's had a hard few weeks. You can talk to her all about it later."

He sighed. "Yes, Mother." He left the room, but reluctantly. The dogs kept their positions by my side, not really speaking but sending me feelings of assurance and love. Apparently, Dynin had filled them in on what had happened. Each of them sent their regrets of not being with me, but I did my best to reassure them I was alright and gave each of them a scratch and a hug.

Mother smiled at me as she walked over and wrapped me in her arms in the type of big hug the presence of the others had prevented her from giving me before. Conall trotted out of the room, going to look for my father, while Elva jumped up and settled herself on my bed. I relished Mother's embrace, enjoying the feeling that the weight of the world was now off my shoulders. "Oh, Aislinn," she murmured. "I'm so sorry you had to go through such a trial."

"Abba was with me – with all of us," I answered.

She sat next to me, keeping an arm around my shoulders. I laid my head against her. "I know. And I am also immensely proud of you."

"Thank you." I shifted so I could look her in the face. "Mother... why did you have clothes from Earth in your closet?" Elva raised her head from her position on the bed and pricked her ears forward.

Mother sighed. "Ah. That. I had a feeling you would ask. That's why I begged off helping your father work with the king and queen to make an announcement to send to the provinces explaining what happened." She shifted and hesitated.

Go on, Elva said. *You should have told her a long time ago. Aiden too. They both deserve to know where they come from. And the ones we lost deserve to be remembered.* Her voice turned sad at her last statement. I looked at the large wolfhound in surprise.

"I know, Elva," my mother's voice pulled my attention back to her. "Aislinn, the portals to Earth have never been completely forgotten by Brenwyds. There are...a few who know and have visited. They consider it a duty. Brenwyds are supposed to help guard normal humans from magic and dark forces. We were driven from Earth, but we do still feel responsible for it. Your father and I have discussed broaching the subject with you." She paused. "In fact, sometimes the Brenwyds who go...bring people back with them, usually people descended from Brenwyds but too far removed to have any Brenwyd abilities."

"Really? Why?"

"Because Earth is dangerous for them. There's a group that still hunts them, despite their lack of abilities." A shadow of pain crossed her face. Elva jumped off the bed and nuzzled her hand.

I frowned slightly, thinking. "So, did you help Father rescue people?"

She sighed. "Actually, Aislinn...he rescued me."

My eyes widened. Suddenly I remembered how my mother always tended to gloss over her past, how I have never met anyone from her side of the family, and I realized that I had never even had a straight answer as to where she had grown up. "Mother, are you from there? Earth?"

She nodded. "Yes, a long time ago. I met your father while I was in England – the country most of the portals open into – studying at a school there. He was there trying to get information on the group that hunted Brenwyds, and our paths crossed. I didn't believe him at first when he said where he was from. But then the Brotherhood came after my family and I had to run. So he brought me here."

"The Brotherhood? Is that the group?" She nodded. "And you never went back?"

She sighed again, and the sheen of tears came to her eyes. "I have nothing and no one there to go back to, Aislinn. Your father helped me escape, but we weren't able to save my brothers, or my mother." She dug her fingers into Elva's ruff. The dog leaned against her and sent comforting thoughts, though they were also tinged with grief. Looking at them, I realized that Elva must have come from Earth too, for she had been Mother's dog before she and Father married.

I renewed our embrace, this time with myself in the role of comforter. "I'm so sorry, Mother. That must have been awful."

"It was a long time ago." She smiled at me. "And I don't regret coming here. There are some things that I miss from there, but here...it's home now." She laughed suddenly. "Although I never bargained on becoming part of a fairy tale myself, much less that my daughter would bring down the wicked witch responsible."

"Fairy tale? What do you mean?"

"Well, believe it or not, there is actually a story on Earth about a princess who pricks her finger and falls into an enchanted sleep, and could only be woken by true love's kiss. That story has a spinning wheel instead of a rose, though."

I stared at her. "Truly? Has such a thing happened there, too?"

She laughed again. "Not that I know of. It's only a fairy tale there. But for that matter, it's not the only Earth fairy tale that I've seen happen here. We have a story called "Snow White" that I think is somehow based on Nivea."

I blinked, considering the information. "So you're saying that somehow, as we have tales of Earth that we discount as false, Earth has tales of us that are also seen as fable?"

"Apparently. Although since the original Sleeping Beauty story was told a couple hundred years ago, I have no idea how it could have originated since this just happened now." It was an intriguing idea the more I thought about it.

"Will you tell me more about these tales?"

"Later. Right now you need to bathe and then sleep." She shifted as if to get off the bed, but I held her back.

"Wait, Mother, one more question: Why didn't you think of Earth when Rhodri disappeared, if you knew about the pathways?"

A look of chagrin crossed her face. "We weren't aware of a passage that existed there in the forest. And of those who went and investigated the site, I don't think any would have recognized a pathway. Believe me, I'm disgusted with myself for not considering the possibility."

We really should have thought of it, Elva agreed.

I nodded, turning over the information in my head. Mother was from Earth! Earth had tales of us! But it was still dangerous... suddenly I remembered something Morrian had said. "Mother, when I first came back to Kheprah after the curse fell, I overheard Morrian talking with...her master. He mentioned that there is a powerful Brenwyd on earth who had killed a servant of his a couple of years ago. Should we try to find her to bring her here?"

Mother blinked. "What? Who?"

"I don't know. He didn't give a name, just mentioned it is a she. But she would certainly be in danger from this Brotherhood group, wouldn't she?"

"Yes," Mother said, frowning. "But also hard to find if she has managed to survive. When did he say this had happened? If somehow a Brenwyd with full abilities is still on Earth, I would be surprised if the Brotherhood hadn't yet found her, and assuming they haven't, I doubt we'd have much luck, either." She stopped for a moment, clearly thinking. "Hmm. I'll mention it to your father, and when all the excitement dies down, we'll see what we can do. For now, though," she smiled and got up from my bed, "go take your bath before the water cools. You've certainly earned it. And I don't expect to see you outside this room until tomorrow." She started toward the door and I rose to undress. Elva reclaimed her position on the bed. Despite my tiredness, I was eager to soak in the hot water and wash away three weeks' worth of travel dirt and grime. "Aislinn?" I turned back to her. "Just...one more question. This...Mathghamhain." I was instantly a little more awake. We had decided by tacit consent not to use Steffyn's true name in our tale – at least, not yet.

"Yes? As we said, he returned to his home."

"Yes, I believe you, but...I have a feeling that there is far more to him than what was said in your story."

I nodded slowly. I would like to talk to Mother about Steffyn, but at the same time the subject seemed...awkward. "It's...a long story."

"Alright. But I would like to hear it eventually." She headed out the door. "Now enjoy your rest, dear."

In hindsight, that was to be the best real sleep I got for the next few days. The whole kingdom was in an uproar, and it seemed that people wanted to make up for the weeks they'd lost to sleep by working twice as hard as usual. I repeated the whole story multiple times to many people, and traveled throughout the Five Realms to relay the story to other Brenwyd communities, who then spread it themselves. Lady Duchess Rhian and her party were found and safely brought back to Clunglasham. Apparently, the group had never even reached Feingeld, they had been so hounded by monsters. Rhys had arrived in the capital to find the whole place enmeshed in a spell of disinterest toward anything from outside the walls. The spell had fallen apart upon Morrian's death, but no one could say for certain where it came from. The best guess of the Brenwyds who had been there was a foreign lady who had arrived only a few days before Morrian cursed Ecclesia. No one had been expecting her or even knew where she came from, but she had very quickly won the good graces of the court. Too quickly, now that people were taking the time to think about it. The lady had since disappeared, but her general description was sent out and all Brenwyds would be on the watch for her.

In Ecclesia's own court, we soon found the man responsible for collaborating with Morrian, as the taint of her magic was with him and we now knew what to look for. It was the secondary stablemaster, and he had been motivated by resentment about being passed over for the primary stablemaster position several years before. He underwent a full Brenwyd examination to ensure no magic was found in him, then was sentenced to the dungeon to wait for his full trial. His wife immediately moved the rest of the family back to her home village.

Monsters were still very much a problem, and were even beginning to be reported in isolated areas of Ecclesia. Scholars in all the Five Realms were being urged to delve deeply into the older records of the kingdoms in the hope of finding the effective techniques our ancestors had discovered to fight the monsters. What the scholars couldn't find, the leviathans and other friendly races were already providing.

And of course, there was, at long last, the wedding. Though no one wanted to wait any longer, the final date was fixed to be three weeks from the day the curse broke so things would have a bit of a chance to settle and those who wanted to could travel to Kheprah for the day. It had already been going to be a big wedding, but with the curse and Rhodri's reappearance, I thought it was turning into the biggest wedding of the century. Everyone wanted to celebrate, and what better excuse than a wedding? Even the leviathans were sending representatives, which necessitated the use of creative logistics to clear the courtyard so they could listen to the ceremony there. Fortunately, the cathedral was located close enough to the castle and the leviathans could hear well enough that such a thing was possible. An invitation had also been extended to the leaders of the other races on the islands, which was accepted. It would be the first wedding in over a century to have so many different creatures mixing, but Lissa and Rhodri both felt it important in reestablishing relations between our species, something I fully agreed with. People were getting used to the bad monsters; they needed to know there were good ones, too.

The one thing that troubled me during this time was Steffyn, up alone on his mountain. I had managed to slip away twice, briefly, to tell him what was happening and to warn him it might be a little bit of time before things calmed down enough for us to really focus on breaking his curse. He seemed in good spirits (for him, at least) and told me not to trouble myself about him. But of course, I did. I prayed about him daily. I fretted about him being alone. Mother tried to pry information about him from me gently, but it was never quite the place nor was there ever enough time for me to really sit down and relay his history and my tumultuous thoughts about him to her. Still, the rapid hustle and bustle of the three weeks leading up to the wedding pushed him toward the back of my mind – though he always seemed to be lurking at the edges. I found that I missed his outlook and droll comments, and even constantly rebutting his pessimism. I found myself visiting the library more than usual and thumbing through the titles, trying to focus on them long enough so I could make out the letters, and wondering if he would like any additions to his library. I had taken a couple when I visited him, one a recent history of Ecclesia and another a work of fiction. He had been as excited as I had ever seen him. Yet whenever I tried to get away to see him, I was always interrupted by something or someone. Hence, I found myself, the day before the wedding, still having seen him only twice.

I was in Lissa's room, and the two of us were alone for the first time in what seemed like ages. She had just had her final wedding dress fitting, and the queen had bidden all the maids and seamstresses out of the room so she could rest. Lissa was sitting in her window seat, staring out of the window, with a look of blissful happiness on her face. "I can hardly believe it is finally happening," she breathed out. "It feels like a dream...like at any moment I'll wake up and find that it is still the day before my birthday and Rhodri is still missing."

I smiled. "Well, the good news is you never have to wake up to that reality again."

She laughed joyfully, almost giggling. She had been rather giddy of late, which was very unusual for her, but I understood why. At times I felt rather giddy myself, when I paused to stop and look at all the happy, bustling activity of awake people around me and remembered how still and silent the castle had been under the curse. "Oh, Aislinn. I know, yet I never get tired of hearing it." She threw me a mischievous glance. "Weddings are such joyful occasions, I think I shall pass an order that there shall be one at least once every month that I can attend."

"I'm sure that weddings happen so frequently throughout the continent, and I doubt anyone would deny you an invitation."

"Hmm. But it is so much more convenient to have them here, within easy reach. Hence, I have decided the next one shall be yours."

"Mine?" I looked at her incredulously and laughed. "Excuse me, but I think you've overlooked the part that requires a man to be the groom. I'm not being courted by anyone, and I have no wish to be at present."

"No, I haven't overlooked it. I know just the person. I think the only trouble with the affair will be convincing Mathghamhain – or should I say Steffyn? – that a large celebration with people is a necessity."

I stopped laughing and stared at her. "Steffyn? Marry me? Methinks your joy has addled your common sense. He is a friend, nothing more. And a prickly, obstinate friend at that."

She laughed again. "I certainly could not see you with a man who agrees with you all the time. You need someone to push and tease you as you do everyone else."

I was beginning to feel very uncomfortable with the conversation. Lissa was starting to sound serious. I decided I should retreat from the room before she went any further. I had an appointment with Master Ferghil to dictate my account of the past month so he could record it. I'd been working with him for days, but the man had an infuriating attention to each and every detail (Who really needs to know precisely how many shadow wolves attacked us? Or what the dimensions of the room with the hidden flamestone weapons were?). I found the sessions exhausting. I got up and made my way toward the door, shaking my head. "Think about it however much you want, Liss, but I very much doubt that will ever happen." In reply, she just laughed again.

As I pushed the door open, it abruptly ran into something on the other side that halted its progress. Something that let out a yelp of pain as the solid wood hit him. "Careful, Aislinn, I don't think Lissa would forgive you if you caused the wedding to be further delayed because you knocked me out with a door," Rhodri exclaimed, rubbing a spot on his head.

I winced in sympathy. Those doors were hard. "My apologies. I didn't know you were there. And what are you doing here, anyway? You know you're not supposed to be up in her room."

He neatly sidestepped past me into the room. Boomer strolled in behind him. "So?"

I rolled my eyes. "Oh, never mind. Just be sure to behave yourself. I'll see you later." I turned and walked out the door.

⚞⚭⚟

Lissa watched Aislinn leave, and Rhodri closed the door behind her. "Perhaps we should have asked her to stay for propriety's sake," she said as Rhodri turned back to her. "After all, we will not be married until tomorrow."

Rhodri shrugged and sat down beside her. "Oh, this close to the date and considering the circumstances, I think it's alright." He smiled at her. Boomer chose that moment to jump between them and plant himself firmly in that spot. He fixed Rhodri with his green eyes and meowed commandingly. Rhodri frowned at the cat. "For heaven's sake, Boomer, you can't be serious about still playing chaperone at this point." When he and Lissa had first started courting, Aislinn had had a long chat with the cat about proper human courtship and what was allowed and what wasn't. Boomer seemed to take a perverse pleasure in upholding the rules.

Boomer meowed again and slowly nodded his head up and down. Rhodri sighed. "Held hostage by my own cat. It's not right."

Lissa laughed and stroked Boomer affectionately. "Do not be upset with him. He suffered severely in your absence. Aislinn said she has never known a cat to be so depressed." Boomer shifted his regard to her. Though she could not understand the cat as Aislinn could, she was sure, based on his expression, that he was refuting the description most ardently.

A fond expression crossed Rhodri's face and he scratched Boomer behind the ears. The cat started purring in pleasure and stretched languorously. "I missed you, too, Boomer. I didn't realize how hard it is to sleep at night without your snoring." The purring stopped for a moment as Boomer lifted his head to look at his master, clearly debating whether to take offense or not. Apparently, he decided not to as the purring resumed and he relaxed again.

Lissa's expression grew eager. "How did the trip go?"

Rhodri's smile disappeared and he sighed. "About how I expected."

"He said no?"

"He said no."

Lissa frowned. "Bother."

"Were you really expecting anything different? He has good reason for his isolation."

"His circumstances will never change if he persists in making an outcast of himself. And he deserves to celebrate just as much as we do."

"I know, but I don't think we should push it."

Lissa stood up. "I think he could use with some pushing."

Rhodri shifted to follow her with his gaze. "Now you sound like Aislinn."

"It is Aislinn I am thinking of." She tapped her chin as she thought. "What she needs to do is face her feelings. Math – Steffyn, as well. In fact...perhaps that could be the key to undoing his curse."

"What, you think true love will break his curse as it did the sleeping curse?"

"No...not exactly. I think...I think what he needs is something to fight for, to motivate him to seek out a cure. What better than love?"

Rhodri weighed her argument. If, as Lissa said, Steffyn and Aislinn really had fallen for each other, then he could attest personally to how love was a powerful motivator. But that was the one thing he was still unsure of. He could see that they had become close, which seemed only natural after the journey they'd all shared, but that close? "You're confident that they do have feelings for each other?"

She smiled at him coyly. "Perfectly. Have you ever known Aislinn to be so fascinated by a man before?"

"No, but his circumstances are such that anyone would be fascinated."

"Then let us call it woman's intuition." She fell to pacing. "I believe his main problem is that he has been so long hopeless of a way to break the curse that he has fallen into complete apathy where it is concerned, and so hopelessness has become a habit. He needs something – something powerful – to break him out of it. From what I observed on our journey, I believe Aislinn has already made great inroads in breaking down that apathy, but he needs one last push."

Rhodri nodded slowly. "Which you believe could come from the two of them admitting love for each other."

"Precisely. Specifically, Aislinn confessing her love for him. If he has admitted his feelings to himself, he will never tell her because he will think she deserves someone better. She has to initiate it, because then she will push him."

Rhodri grinned wryly. "And Aislinn is nothing if not good at pushing people."

Lissa returned the smile, but it quickly became a sigh of exasperation. "Of course, she has to admit to her own feelings first, and I have not been successful in making much headway in that endeavor." She sat beside him. "Perhaps if they can simply get pushed together often enough, she will come to realize it."

Rhodri shrugged, putting an arm around Lissa's shoulders and drawing her close, enjoying the fact of her nearness. "That could prove somewhat difficult with Steffyn determined to stay cloistered in an isolated mountain fortress."

"Yes, I realize," she mused, leaning into him. They sat in peaceful silence for several moments. Rhodri put his other arm around her and rested his chin on her head. They had had precious little time to simply enjoy each other's presence recently, and he wanted the moment to last for as long as possible. Boomer, he noticed, had busied himself with grooming so he pointedly ignored the two humans in the room.

Lissa broke the moment abruptly by suddenly sitting straight up and turning to face him, excitement flashing in her eyes. "Of course! He lives in an isolated mountain fortress!"

"Yeesss," Rhodri said, drawing the word out, wondering what the significance of that was.

"Aislinn does not want him to stay up there, and by continuing to argue with him about coming down, she will be forced to admit her own feelings. Oh, Rhodri, you are brilliant!" She leaned over and kissed him eagerly. He wasn't quite sure what he had done besides state the obvious, but he wasn't about to argue. Unfortunately (to his mind), she broke the kiss off quickly and rose, striding toward the door.

"Where are you going?" he called after her.

She opened the door and glanced back at him. "To find Aislinn. I will see you at supper." With that, she disappeared into the hall. Rhodri wondered what in the Five Realms she was planning. Clearly, she had thought up some plan that, in her mind, would achieve the goal of getting Aislinn to admit she loved Steffyn. However, what that plan was, he had no idea. After several minutes of pondering it, he shrugged and rose to go out, his cat shadow immediately following. He'd find her later and ask for a more detailed explanation. For now, he had some last-minute plans of his own to see to, ones that involved his own love life and not someone else's.

❧⚛☙

I pulled Dynin up gently, mindful of the fact that Sirac was behind us and also needed to slow down. Sirac was the largest Brenwyd horse in the royal stables, and I had decided (with Lissa's gentle urging) that it would be a good idea to bring him along, just in case.

I was once more in Steffyn's mountain valley, and I halted the two horses to observe it. It was at Lissa's prompting that I had come here today. She had caught me on my way out of the library yesterday. "Ah, Aislinn. How was your session with Master Ferghil today?"

I let out a long breath. "I think we finally finished to his satisfaction, thank Abba. That man's attention to detail would try the patience of an angel!" She laughed, but I thought I saw something troubling her in her eyes. "Is everything alright?"

She seemed surprised by the query. "What? Oh, yes. Nearly everything, leastways." Her lips were slightly downturned and a faint furrow appeared between her brows.

"Nearly everything?"

She sighed and started walking down the hall. I fell into step beside her. "Oh, it is nothing really. I expected the answer, but I thought, maybe, with Rhodri going in person and asking in earnest and all...but never mind, there is nothing to be done."

"What?" I asked.

She shrugged. "Mathghamhain. Or, Steffyn, rather. Rhodri went this morning to invite him to the wedding – after all he has done, it seemed the least we could do – but he refused to come."

I frowned. Steffyn. Here we were on the subject again. At least this time she wasn't trying to convince me of my own feelings. Yet, anyway. "You're right. That would be his answer." The words came out a bit more heated than I intended, and I realized that, somehow, I had assumed he would be coming. Very irrational of me, but I couldn't deny it. "So that's where Rhodri was this morning?"

Lissa nodded. "Yes. I even had him ready Sirac and prepared a private place for him to stay, should he like to come, but, well..." She sighed again. "Not that I blame him, really, only I think it would be right for him to be there."

I considered her words for a few seconds. "You're right, it would. Where in the Five Realms did you find a private room in the midst of all these people?"

"The old storage rooms near the stable. No one goes in them anymore, but they are connected to the palace by the tunnel system, and the tunnels are plenty big enough for him to use to move about."

She had a point there. Like most castles and palaces throughout Niclausia, Kheprah's castle had secret passageways built for use in times of need. Most of the time, however, the only people who used them were children who wanted to explore their depths. It would be fairly simple for Steffyn to arrive here after dark, go to the storerooms, and then use the tunnels to reach the great chapel attached to the palace for the ceremony without anyone taking note. Of course, the ball and feast afterward were a different story, but at least he would be able to make the ceremony. Although, given all the species set to attend, it was possible he wouldn't stand out too much. "Rhodri explained all that to him?" Lissa nodded. "And he still said no?" She nodded again.

My frown deepened. I could understand him refusing on principle, but after Rhodri explained how Lissa had planned for him and accommodated his wish and need for privacy? That started to grate on me. And, I did have to admit to myself, I should like him to be there. He could meet my father, at least, and maybe he could determine some way to help him. But this sounded like he was preparing to isolate himself again. And that could not happen. I would not let it happen. *And why do you care so much?* some part of me whispered, but I batted it away. I could deal with the whys later. Now, I was more concerned with the overwhelming conviction I felt that Steffyn needed to come to this wedding. "That was this morning?" Lissa nodded again. "Hmm." I didn't know that I could get up to the mountain with what remained of the day. But if I got up early tomorrow morning, while it was still dark, and simply forced him onto the horse...

"Aislinn?" Lissa's voice intruded on my thoughts. "What are you thinking?" She was looking at me, her blue eyes soft and questioning.

I opened my mouth, then closed it. If I told her what I was thinking, she would simply take it as further confirmation that what she thought was true – that I cared so much because I was in love with him. What I really wanted was for him to open himself up to normal companionship. Nothing more. That's what I firmly told myself, anyway. "Nothing. Just a plague on the stubbornness of men, 'tis all."

Her gaze turned a little harder, a little more inquisitive. "Are you sure?"

"Positive." I stopped and turned toward another hallway. "If you'll excuse me, I have a few last things to do."

She nodded. "As you wish." She swept on down the corridor with a slight swish of her skirt. I remained standing there for a few seconds, wondering if I had really seen a satisfied smile flicker over her face as she moved off. Then I shook my head and went in my chosen direction, my mind churning with all the arguments I would need to get Steffyn off his mountain, and resolutely pushing away the uncomfortable thoughts that I was somehow deluding myself in my reasons for why I wanted to help him.

However, those thoughts were now starting to swarm again as I gently squeezed Dynin into a walk across Steffyn's mountain valley. Why, exactly, did I have such a vested interest in drawing out this cranky, prickly man? *Well, someone has to*, I reasoned. *Someone has to keep pushing him back to Abba. Someone has to help him break his curse. It might as well be me.*

Really, a little voice in my head seemed to respond back. *Is that really all?* It sounded suspiciously like Lissa.

Of course it is, I defended myself. *Why would it be anything more?*

Then how did you feel when he was about to die from that spear? The question came out of nowhere and made me swallow involuntarily. The memory came, sharp and clear, the spearhead being thrust into him, his cry of pain...

Dynin stopped and looked back at me. *Are you alright?*

I blinked, realizing that tears had started to rise in my eyes and that I had stiffened on his back. *Yes, of course.*

He remained stopped, and he seemed to be looking at me thoughtfully. *You really care for this...person, do you not?* he asked plainly.

I stared down at him, mouth agape. It was one thing for Lissa to accuse me of loving him, but my horse? "What?"

Dynin snorted. *I have heard your arguments. You disagree with him all the time. Yet you two keep talking to each other, and you make each other laugh, and I can sense that you have a great caring feeling where he is concerned.*

"Of course, I care, but...as a friend. Just a friend."

Hmm. Dynin started walking through the predawn darkness again, sounding unconvinced. *Then what are we doing out here before breakfast? You know he will never agree to come to such a big gathering of humans.* Dynin had not been excited about leaving the comfort of his stall in the wee hours of the morning without his usual breakfast of warm oats.

"I...I have to try, is all."

Why?

I let out a sigh of frustration. I did not need my horse interrogating my intentions right now. I was doing too good a job of that myself. "Because he's my friend and...I want him to be there." Dynin asked me no more questions, but my state of mind was now thoroughly frazzled. One part of it even started to think, could Lissa be right? *Of course not,* I was quick to answer. *I would know if I were in love with someone...Wouldn't I?*

I let out a huff and shook my head, trying to regain my equilibrium. Just for putting me in such a state, I was determined to get Steffyn to the wedding. If he was going to make me feel uncomfortable in my own mind, he could stand to be uncomfortable at a wedding.

BEAUTY AND THE BEAST

We reached the castle and walked straight up to the door. I halted Dynin and Sirac, who had mercifully remained quiet throughout mine and Dynin's exchange, and before I could have any further doubts I dismounted, marched up to the door, and firmly knocked several times as I tried to get my mind in order and a guard around it. I didn't need Steffyn reading my thoughts. As it was, I sensed him touch my mind and felt his surprise. *What are you doing here at this hour? Is something wrong?*

Yes, I thought very deliberately to him, *but I would prefer to discuss it verbally face to face.*

Several moments later the door opened and he looked down at me questioningly with some amount of worry. "Are you alright?" he queried, sounding careful in his tone. Likely he sensed some of my mental turmoil despite the tight block I had around my mind.

I frowned at him. "Actually, no, I'm not alright. I've had to get up at this *unseemly* hour of the morning and trek all the way up here to come in order to drag a singularly *obstinate* person to a wedding that he needs to be at despite any and all objections to the contrary."

He seemed rather taken aback by my outburst and glanced past me to take in the two horses several paces away. Then he sighed and leaned against the doorframe, crossing his arms. It occurred to me just then that he was wearing a nightshirt with a dressing gown over it, and I realized that if this were anyone else under any other circumstances, this would be a highly scandalous situation. Now, however, propriety was the least of my concerns. "Aislinn, please, you know why-"

"Oh, no," I said fiercely. He blinked. I myself was wondering about why I was being so snappish, but I didn't feel in any mood to apologize. Abba knew he had snapped at me countless times over the past month. "I know all your excuses, but they will not work anymore. Not when Lissa has so graciously given such thought to how to make you comfortable and respect your privacy and yet have you attend. She told me Rhodri told you about the old storage room and the tunnels. It would work, Steffyn. It would work perfectly. And they want you there. Not to mention I doubt you would stand out as much as you think with leviathans and centaurs and fauns and the like around. So, what gives you the excuse to refuse?"

He looked at me with the same old sad, resigned look I had grown so accustomed to during our journey. "Do you really think it would work so perfectly that no one would notice me? As tall as I am and all in black?"

"So? Maybe a few, but most everyone will be focused on Rhodri and Lissa, not other spectators. Besides, there are many other colors you could wear and you are known to some people, Steffyn. Those Brenwyds who helped us with Morrian, Rhodri's father and brother, Lissa's parents, my parents...They would like to meet you and thank you personally."

He clenched his jaw and crossed his furry arms. "If they wish to meet me, surely it can be arranged in a quieter manner."

"Oh, that's not the point, and you know it! Why can't you just come? Lissa and Rhodri want you there. If it wasn't for you, this wedding likely would not even be happening!" He opened his mouth as if to protest, but I forestalled him. "Don't deny it; it's true. Yes, I'm the one who found Rhodri and brought him back, but you led us to the flamestone weapons, you led us to Morrian's fortress, you taught me ways that could defeat her. Ways that worked. I know she was your sister, and that there is a part of you that grieves for her, but you have spent far too long in your own dour company. Let yourself relax and celebrate! Take some joy in life! Abba made us for joy, not eternal sadness! You want your curse broken? Let joy back in!" He was staring at me, utter shock in his eyes, lower jaw hanging slack. I realized, suddenly, that I felt a wetness on my cheeks. I lifted a hand to brush it away, and discovered it was from tears. Mortally embarrassed, I turned away from him and gazed into the distance, frantically trying to wipe the tears away. Why were they there? I didn't cry, not as a rule. But as I had already acknowledged, Steffyn caused new and uncomfortable emotions and thoughts within me, and perhaps this was just all my frustration with him boiling over at last.

I heard him slowly take a few steps and sensed him standing close behind me. I held myself in a rigid posture, arms crossed. "Aislinn..." he said softly – or as softly as he could, in his low, growly voice. "Why do you care so much about what I do?" He sounded decidedly unsure. I didn't turn around; I shut my eyes. There was that dratted question again. The one I had been pushing away every time it popped up in my head. But now it wasn't in my head, and I couldn't just push it away. Why did I care to the point of tears what Steffyn did? It was one thing to care as a friend, to keep gently poking and prodding until he once again saw the light of Abba's love. But this?... Now I recognized what Lissa had. These feelings I had went deeper. Much deeper.

The silence between us was taut with tension and emotion, the words of his question hanging heavily in the air. As I held myself rigid, I could tell he held himself the same way, and I was also aware of the horses watching so intently that they were deliberately sending thoughts my way about how *not* interested they were. At last I opened my mouth, still facing away from him. If I was facing him, I didn't think I'd be able to answer the question as honestly as I was about to. "Because…" I managed at last, "because I'm your friend and…I…I seem to have…to have fallen in love with you."

My last words were hardly above a whisper, but I knew he heard them. I heard his sharp intake of breath, sensed him move back a step as if I had physically struck him. I remained fixedly gazing into the distance, my breath coming in short gasps as I explored the words I had just said. And deep inside myself, I knew they were true. I had somehow fallen for this irascible, prickly, cursed, pessimistic Brenwyd, whom I had also seen on our journey to be resolute, brave, even humorous, and hurting. I had seen that hurt and wanted to help heal it, to lead him back to Abba where true healing is found. But had there been another reason I had so quickly picked up on his hurt? Was he the one whom Abba had planned for me?

This time the silence stretched so long that I finally turned to face him. He was staring at me as if he had never laid eyes on me before, a hand placed on the wall of his castle as if for support. I had a sudden fear: what if he didn't feel the same way? After all, what had I done but poke and prod him where he most hurt? I glanced away, staring fixedly at his feet. I had never seen his feet bare before. Like his hands, the nails on his feet were distinctly claw-like, and he seemed to have most of his weight balanced on his toes rather than his heel. How had I not noticed that in his gait before?

"*What?*" finally reached my ears. His voice reflected the shock that had been so apparent on his face. I dragged my gaze up to eye level – well, my eye level, which meant I was looking at his chest. I couldn't make myself face his eyes just yet – the only human part of him.

"You heard me," I said, my mouth feeling dry.

"But...how? You...you must be mistaken."

I let out a short, humorless laugh. "No. Lissa tried to tell me, but...these feelings are true. And I don't know how. Believe me, I'm trying to work that out for myself." I quickly glanced up at his face, then back down at his chest. He was shaking his head, eyes vague and unfocused.

"No, no, you must be mistaken."

That made me start to be irritated again, and I found the will to meet his eyes. "And why? Can I not know my own feelings?" I gestured to his body. "Are you so convinced that no one could love a beast?" I sounded bitter, even to myself. I felt tears welling up again. "Or is it that you cannot bring yourself to love anyone after spending so long alone and so think I'm just a foolish child, falling in love with someone who could never love me back?" Anguish came to his eyes, and he opened and closed his mouth, as if trying to find the words. Tears blurred my vision, and I blinked, shaking my head. "No, don't try to answer." I turned, looking wildly about for Dynin. I had to leave. Had to get away from this confusing man, these overwhelming feelings. I needed my mother. I needed someone to help me make sense of all this. "I'm sorry. I should never have come. What chance do I have of convincing you of the value of friendship and joy when you've shut yourself away from the one who is the source of it all?" I mounted and Dynin began walking quickly toward the valley's exit, which was the best place for transferring.

"Aislinn!" Steffyn's bellow wrenched my gut and I glanced back at him, checking Dynin. He came forward a few steps, then paused an arm's length away from me. "Please. I don't...That is, I mean..." He loosed what sounded like an irritated growl and ran a hand down the back of his head – which would have been him running a hand through his hair in frustration had he still had a human form. "Grindles, I'm making a mess of this. But you have to...to give me some time. I need-"

"Time?" My voice rose. "Haven't you had time enough? It seems to me you've had plenty. Time to determine that no one could love you. Not me. Not Elfleda. Not Abba. What hope have I of convincing you otherwise when you still lock even Abba out?"

"Aislinn..." He looked at me with his silver grey eyes, pleading... but pleading for what? I didn't know. I just knew I needed to get away. I needed to be alone. I turned away from him and dug my heels into Dynin's sides. He whinnied and lurched forward into a startled canter. I loved Steffyn. But he had not admitted to loving me in return.

⚜

Steffyn stared after Aislinn. Part of him said he should go after her, that he was being the biggest fool in the Five Realms for letting her leave like that, yet he could do nothing but stand rooted to the spot and watch as she transferred from view. I seem to have fallen in love with you, her words echoed in his head. And kept echoing. In love with him. Him, with his beastly body and moody temper. Who had tried to push away her probing questions, her counsel. Who had tried to deny his own feelings where she was concerned. For he most definitely had feelings for her. And now he could put a name to them: love. Something he hadn't felt in...oh, so long. *This can't be true*, he thought. *She cannot really love me back. She's mistaken friendship formed through hardship for love. We've only known each other a few weeks. She doesn't truly know me. She doesn't know what I'm capable of. She'd never had any real suitors.* Surely before long she'd meet someone else, someone who made her realize that what she felt for him wasn't that kind of love. *Are you so convinced no one could love a beast?* Her other words came back to him, jumbled and out of order as he tried to bring order to his frenzied mind. *How can I convince you otherwise when you have left even Abba out?* Something like that. And the question cut deep. Too deep.

An involuntary roar of pain ripped from him and he fell to his knees. For now he forced himself to admit it was true. He had, voluntarily, cut all love and joy from his life in his own misery, thinking he would be better off, even before he became a beast. But in fact, it had just made him worse. *Abba*, his spirit cried out, *Abba, Father, what have I done? What have I done?*

With that one heartfelt, anguished question, he felt the distance two hundred and fifty years of self-enforced isolation had placed between him and his Creator shatter. And then he knew. Abba had not abandoned him, as he had tried to make himself believe, and succeeded doing for so long. He had abandoned Abba. His God, his Father, the one who had loved him so much he sent his only Son to die so that Steffyn could cry out to him as he was doing now and be assured of being heard.

A deep peace filled him and soothed his spirit, bringing tears to his eyes as it also magnified the guilt he felt from pushing his Maker away. *Abba, Abba, forgive me. Please, forgive me. I have been foolish and stubborn and rebellious. I let my own hurt and pain and resentment blind me, and that was my real curse. Forgive me.*

He felt a soft wind blow over him, ruffling his fur and tugging at his clothing. And heard words whispered in his spirit, in a still, small voice: *But of course, my child. I have been here, throughout all these years, waiting for you to say those words, ready to give you my peace whenever you asked it. Take my love, my child. I give it to you freely.*

Love...he felt it pour into him, filling all the empty places in his soul, reviving his own heart like a parched land rejuvenated by a gentle, steady rain. He remembered his childhood, before Morrian made her sorcery known. He remembered his mother and father. The fond glances they would exchange. The kisses when they thought he wasn't looking. He remembered his mother singing him to sleep, telling the stories of Abba's love over and over and over. His father holding him on his lap, helping him learn to read and passing on his own love of learning in the process. Celebrating annual holidays with his province. Worshipping Abba at the weekly fellowship gatherings. He remembered Elfleda and felt a new pang of guilt. She had been prepared to offer him all her love, but he had rejected her as he had rejected them all. Fresh tears sprang to his eyes, and he didn't know whether they were of sorrow or gladness. *Oh, Abba, I have stumbled. I have failed. I let Morrian twist me more in my resentment and hatred of her than her tortures ever did. I have failed...so completely.*

Everyone does, came the answer quietly in his soul. *But you are not the beast your sister tried to make you. You are my beloved child, as you always have been and always will be, if you choose to remember it. It is your choice. Will you embrace my gift of love and grace and admit it can cover your failings, no matter how grievous? Will you come home, my child?*

A simple question. *Will you embrace my love?*

Steffyn drew in a shuddering breath and answered audibly in the only way he could. "Yes."

Pure joy suffused his being, filling his every fiber with a lively, tingly feeling that made him want to jump and dance. Abba forgave him. Embraced him. Called him *beloved child.* Before he could fully settle into that realization, tremors began to wrack his body, and he became aware of a strange pain in his chest, pain that seemed vaguely familiar but he couldn't remember why. He rolled over onto his back and let loose another roar as the pain spread and every nerve in his body felt like it had caught fire. The pre-dawn darkness seemed to grow darker and press in on him, and Steffyn lost consciousness.

❧⊗☙

It was the light that woke him. Light, and the sensation of a soft nose nudging his side. His brain sluggishly returned to consciousness, and he became aware of a bright light shining on his closed eyelids. His next thoughts were that he felt sore and also...cold. Not that it was unusual for it to be cold in the mountains in spring, but usually his fur kept him warm. He opened his eyes slowly, squinting against the light, and shifted simultaneously to try and find a more comfortable position. As he did so, the nudging stopped, and he became aware of the fact that his body felt very...odd. He lifted a hand to block the direct sunlight and shook his head, trying to remember what had happened, but his thoughts froze as his hand came into his vision. It looked like...it looked like...he tilted it this way and that, trying to verify what his eyes were telling him and to make sure it was, indeed, his own. For it was not the strange half-paw half-hand with claws and fur he had grown accustomed to, but an actual human hand. With growing astonishment and delight he moved his gaze from his hand up his arm and to the rest of his body. It was all human. There was not a trace of the beast to be seen, and as he lifted a hand to his head, his finger grazed the slight points on the tips of his ears.

Utter delight filled him, and he felt a grin spread across his face as tears of happiness fell from his eyes and he looked upward. "Oh, Abba, thank you. Thank you!" How extraordinary to be able to speak without discomfort rippling across his vocal cords, and to hear his own, real voice saying the words without a hint of a growl. In a burst of enthusiasm, he sang a favorite song of his from childhood, marveling and reveling in the way his tenor voice slid easily from note to note as if he had last sung only yesterday and not over two and a half centuries ago.

He stood and staggered a few steps, feeling a little dizzy, and went to the Searching Pool. He went to his knees beside it, gazing eagerly into its depths, and was rewarded by seeing a face he had nearly forgotten: his own. He still looked to be the same age he had been during that first battle with Morrian so long ago. He was glad to see that; it would make things go easier with Aislinn and her parents with him looking to be about her age. That thought drew him up short. Aislinn. He shut his eyes as the memory of her visit flooded him, and he groaned. He would be lucky if she still wanted anything to do with him after the mess he had made for himself. Still, he was buoyed by a strong sense of optimism that he hadn't felt since...he couldn't remember when. He opened his eyes and determined he would go to see her, beg her forgiveness, and ask if he could court her formally. He would not make the same mistake that he had with Elfleda.

A horsey snort interrupted his thoughts and he jumped, turning around to see the second horse Aislinn had brought with her standing behind him. He hadn't noticed that the horse had stuck around. It was currently surveying him with very alert ears and flaring nostrils. Belatedly, Steffyn realized that the nudging sensation must have been the horse prodding him with his muzzle. *You are the same that was here, and yet not,* it – he, Steffyn saw – finally said, sounding very confused. *You were asleep for a while. After it seemed long enough that you would not do any more...changing, I decided I should try to wake you.*

"Yes, thank you," Steffyn answered, holding a hand out for the horse to sniff. It was a handsome animal, a dark liver chestnut, and quite large. He reminded him, suddenly, of his own horse. Eliara had been a smaller, brighter chestnut and a loyal friend in those first terrible years of the curse. Her eventual loss years ago had driven Steffyn into such a depression that he had briefly considered taking his own life. Now, Steffyn brushed the thoughts away and focused on the chestnut horse currently in front of him, swallowing down the sudden emotion. "I was under a spell, you see, that made me look like a beast, and I finally...I finally surrendered to Abba to break it."

That seemed to satisfy the horse. *Ah. I see. So are you coming now?*

Steffyn started to nod, but then he stopped and looked up at the sun. Judging by its position, it was at least midmorning...and then there was the wedding. He'd forgotten about the wedding. He knew that it was in late afternoon, with a following dinner feast and ball, but there would be precious little chance of getting Aislinn alone at any point in the day. Not to mention all his clothes would now be miles too big and he had nothing suitable to wear to a royal wedding. He considered his options. He could just wait until tomorrow and then go to the palace to talk to Aislinn. But even as he considered it, he felt a burning inside that insisted on seeing her now, today. He supposed he could create some makeshift clothes. He did know how to handle a needle, since he had been on his own for so long, and Rhodri had brought over some things yesterday of good quality. He felt a smile tugging at his lips again. After all the shocks Aislinn had given him, he thought it was high time for him to truly shock her.

"Yes, I'll be coming. But I'll need a few hours to prepare first."

Most of Lissa and Rhodri's wedding day passed in a blur for me. Outwardly I made sure to smile and be happy – which wasn't always an act – but inside I was a roiling ball of emotions. What I would really have loved to do was crawl back into my bed and not come out for the day. But I couldn't let my own heartache spoil Lissa and Rhodri's special day, not after they had been through so much to get to it. My mother, however, had found me before I could put my happy mask in place, not long after I returned from the mountain and was still crying into my pillow. She had just been coming in to wake me and was rather surprised and concerned to find me dressed and crying into the pillow. "Aislinn, what's wrong?"

I quickly tried to regain my composure to reassure her. "Nothing. I'm fine. Just everything catching up with me, 'tis all."

She raised her eyebrows and sat on the bed. "Somehow I don't believe you. Now, come on. Tell me. I know there's been something on your mind. Something, I believe, that has to do with your friend Mathghamhain?"

I sighed. There was no escaping my mother. "That's not his name," I said shakily, sitting up and drawing my knees under my chin. "His real name is Steffyn. He changed it after...after the curse." I had told both my parents, privately, about Steffyn's curse.

My father had promised to help me find a way to break it, but said it had to wait until after the wedding.

I could see her thinking that over, and then making the connection. "Steffyn the war hero from the Battle for Kheprah?" I could see her surprise.

I nodded. "He didn't die."

"Apparently not."

"The curse, it included some longevity spell. He's been up on that mountain for over two hundred years. And he's completely shut himself away from...from love." My voice broke on the last word and I buried my head in my knees.

"Ah," Mother said softly. "So that's it." She moved closer, and I felt her arms circle me and a hand start to stroke my hair. "You went this morning to tell him."

"No!" I looked up into her eyes. "I didn't. At least, not that I knew. I wanted to persuade him to come to the wedding. Lissa had arranged for him to use the abandoned storage rooms, and he could get to the chapel through the tunnels, so no one would see him, but when Rhodri went, he said no so I thought that maybe I could...so I went...and when he said no I just...I just got so upset and angry and he asked me why I cared so much and...that's when... that's when I realized..." I buried my head back into my knees. I felt absolutely ridiculous. I had always told myself I would never be one of those silly girls in love that cry about it. Yet here I was. I began taking deep breaths to calm myself.

"That you love him," Mother finished. "So, you yourself just realized it." I nodded. "And how did he react?"

"He said...he said I had to be wrong...and he needed time."

"And?"

"I left."

"Hmm." There was silence for several long seconds. Finally, I looked up at her.

"Aren't you going to say something?"

"Well, yes, but I was trying to think through it first." She smiled at me. "This is rather a lot to spring on me this early in the morning, even if I have had my suspicions." My lips twitched upward involuntarily. "Now, you said he's shut himself away from love. What exactly does that mean?"

"He doesn't think anyone can love him. Not even Abba. And that is the real problem I've been trying to get him past, before I realized..."

She nodded slowly. "And he's a Brenwyd?" I nodded. "There's a deep trauma there, then, Aislinn."

"I know. He's talked about it some. It's...complicated."

"He opened up to you?"

"In bits and pieces during the journey. More so after I knew who he really was. Is."

She nodded again, and a smile came back over her face. "Well, then."

"Well what?

"Well, it seems very probable that he loves you as well."

"How can you say that after what I've just told you? You've never even met him!"

"Something I think I'll remedy as quickly as I can. However, if he has cut himself off from all love, it will take some time for him to realize the feeling. So I think his request for some time is a good one. And I would recommend it in any event. Men generally need some time to wrap their minds around such a pronouncement when it's unexpected." She laid a hand to my face and wiped away my tears. "Right now, Aislinn, you need to pray about your feelings, and him, and how to proceed, and that is the best advice I can give you. It might not be quite what you want to hear, but there it is. And do give him a chance to figure it out."

I considered her words. Really, it wasn't all that different from how I had been dealing with Steffyn anyway, save for the addition of my feelings. I nodded. "Alright." Then I released a short, rueful laugh. "Lissa told me I was falling for him. I didn't believe her." I sighed. "Ugh. She is going to hold this over me for years."

Mother chuckled. "She is rather perceptive when it comes to such things." She was quiet a moment. "This curse of his. You said it caused him to become some sort of beast, right?" I nodded. "Hmm." Her tone of voice made me sit up and look at her expression. It was the carefully neutral mask she used often in court to disguise her thoughts, but I thought I could make out some sort of amusement in her eyes.

"Are you laughing at me?" I demanded hotly, fresh tears coming to my eyes.

She started. "Oh, sweetie, not at all. I was just thinking about... well, I'll tell you later after this has sorted itself out."

"How do you know it will?"

"Affairs of the heart always do, one way or another. And besides, any good child can tell you that fairy tales always end in happily ever after. At least your gown isn't completely golden."

I blinked at that comment. "What does that mean?"

"As I said, I'll explain it to you later." She stood and moved on before I could process and respond to that comment. "Now, I know you'd likely prefer to stay in bed all day, but Lissa is expecting you. Time to face the day." She leaned in closer and whispered. "Tonight, when the festivities are done, you can come right back here and I'll bring you a whole tray of leftover chocolates. It's an unwritten rule that chocolate helps make everything at least a little bit better."

That made me giggle. Weakly, but it was still a giggle. "Very well. I'll change then."

Mother moved toward the door but turned back to me before going through it. "Oh, and I think you should wait to tell your father about this until tomorrow at least. He has enough on his plate for the moment, and it will likely take him at least a week to fully come to grips with the idea of your being in love with anyone."

That brought another weak laugh from me, but the idea of telling Father did make it more real.

"Yes, Mother." So I had gotten myself up and dressed and over to Lissa's apartments to perform my duties as first handmaiden. Fortunately, she was too preoccupied to question me about what was distracting me.

A Closing Dance

The ceremony went off beautifully and perfectly. Lissa looked absolutely radiant in her dress. It was made from pure white silk, with gold and silver embroidery around the hem, sleeve cuffs, and down the front of her bodice. Her hair was arranged in loose curls that flowed freely down her back, and her veil was secured with a crown of white roses, as she had decided to forgo the traditional coronet. Lissa refused to let her experience with the cursed rose influence her feelings about roses in general, and so her bouquet was also made up of roses. Oddly enough, in the three weeks since the curse had broken, all the rosebushes in our garden had burst into full bloom as if it were early summer instead of spring, so I had arranged the bouquet myself (being sure to strip away each and every thorn, no matter how small). I had never seen Lissa look more beautiful, and I didn't have to fake my smile as I watched her and Rhodri say their vows.

Rhodri himself looked dashing in his midnight blue tunic emblazoned with his family's crest in silver and bronze thread and his silver coronet on his dark hair. (I did wonder how many people noticed the cat-sized shadow near him. Boomer was taking his vow of never leaving Rhodri's side again quite seriously. I had had a somewhat awkward conversation with him earlier, per Rhodri's request, of the absolute necessity of leaving him alone on the wedding night. Boomer hadn't seen that his presence in the room would affect events, but I finally persuaded him that standing guard outside the door would be better to ensure no one interrupted the couple after they retired.) After they finished the vows and the archbishop gave them permission to kiss, Rhodri swept Lissa into his arms and kissed her so passionately that gasps could be heard throughout the cathedral, and there were also some cheers, clapping, and whistling, with jubilant roars from the leviathans outside – not exactly the correct protocol for such an important royal wedding, but no one cried foul.

After the ceremony came the feast, and after the feast (and some very long speeches by various dignitaries from all over Niclausia not only remarking upon the occasion of the wedding but also thanking Lissa and Rhodri – and myself – for our salvation of the continent, as one speaker put it) came the dancing. Normally I quite enjoyed dancing, especially the more active ones. But tonight I found myself more going through the motions and content to sit dances out when I could – which was rather easier said than done. Apparently, all the young men who attended wanted nothing more than to dance with the savior of the country (as several of them put it), and I found myself rather overwhelmed with attention. Oddly enough, I found an ally in Rhodri's friend from Earth, Ian, and his "girlfriend," as he termed her. My father ended up being the one to bring them over, and I had enjoyed getting to know them over the last few days. Understandably, they were rather overwhelmed with everything and whenever I could I stayed with them to explain things. So long as I was with them, I was mostly left alone. Eventually, though, they decided to try some of the dances and I lost my buffers. It was late in the evening when I managed to retreat to a quiet, dimly-lit corner and sat down gratefully, watching the other dancers twirl around the room in a dazzling array of finery and colors that appeared to be a living rainbow. I glanced down at my own gown and ran a hand over the skirt.

I did rather like it. In keeping with tradition, the style was exactly the same as Lissa's gown, but the colors were different. Whereas hers was completely white, mine was mostly a deep maroon that complemented the reddish undertones in my auburn hair. The color was broken on the front of the bodice by a panel of golden cloth with embroidery patterns in matching maroon as opposed to Lissa's gold and silver, and the long sleeves that extended to my wrists from under short puffed sleeved on my shoulders were also golden colored and fringed in more maroon embroidery. I had protested when Lissa and her mother ordered the dress that it was far too extravagant, but they had overruled me. My hair, like Lissa's, had been arranged into a cascade of curls, which was held back from my face with a gold brooch decorated with small rubies, and matched the necklace latched around my throat. The dress was the most extravagant one I had ever worn. And, despite my fussing over it, I could not help but love the final result. Still, it had been rather a shock to look in the mirror after the servants had finished getting me ready and feel dumbfounded by my own reflection.

With a few moments to myself at last, my thoughts involuntarily turned from my gown to my conversation –confrontation, really – with Steffyn earlier. It was certainly not how I had ever imagined telling a man I had fallen in love with him. But then, I had never really imagined ever falling for someone like Steffyn, either. *Oh, Abba, what in the Five Realms am I supposed to do now?*

I was wondering along these lines when a soft voice startled me. "You look deep in thought."

I started involuntarily and turned toward it. "Oh, it's nothing... much," I trailed off. It was yet another young man who had approached me, but this one seemed...different. For one thing, while his clothes were certainly suitable enough, they weren't quite the formal wear one usually wore to a royal event, and the tailoring didn't look expert, though it was well done. They were also nearly all black. Still, the man was very handsome – and looking closer at his ears, I saw why. He was a Brenwyd. I relaxed a bit. I found Brenwyd men my age less annoying than normal human males. They at least were accustomed to how fair Brenwyd women are.

"Are you sure? It looked serious." His outward expression was solemn, but some secret amusement seemed to dance in his eyes, which were silvery grey. I frowned slightly. I was fairly sure that I had never met this man before, yet there was something familiar about him. His hair, neatly tied back from his face, was a light shade of blond, and his skin was pale enough to make me think he might come from a northern kingdom – perhaps Lamasia. There were several Lamasian Brenwyds in attendance. His accent, too, suggested such an origin, and his voice echoed in my ears as if I should recognize it.

I shrugged. "Ah, nothing that won't wait until later."

He nodded. He was looking at me rather intently, and now there seemed to be a hint of nervousness in his face. I stifled a sigh. It seemed he wanted a dance. However, his next question took me by surprise. "Are you sure you don't wish to talk about it?"

I blinked. Asking what I was thinking while I was clearly in thought was one thing, but this was downright forward. Especially from someone who hadn't even given me his name. "If I do, I'll be doing it with people I know, not strangers." I didn't mean to be rude, but I didn't appreciate his probing.

Something flared in his eyes. It nearly looked like amusement. "Strangers..." he mused, moving his gaze out over the dance floor. "Yes, very wise of you. But sometimes, one can think someone a stranger, but then find it's someone they know...quite well."

Curious. As I gazed at him, the sense of familiarity grew ever stronger, yet I could not place him. "I'm sorry, but...have we met? I'm afraid I don't remember, yet you seem familiar to me, somehow."

He turned back to me, definite amusement lighting his face, but again, that flash of nervousness. "Considering the circumstances, I find that rather impressive."

I frowned. "Pardon?"

He opened his mouth, then closed it and glanced from me to the dance floor and back again. "Would you like to dance?"

I would have preferred to keep talking to him and figure out why he was so puzzling, but I knew the etiquette of a ball: A lady never refused to dance unless she had already promised a dance to someone else. And I had not. So I nodded. And it was a slower dance, anyway, so I would have time to continue talking to him. "Yes, if," I smiled, "you tell me your name."

He returned my smile with a secretive one of his own. "I rather think, given enough time, that you can guess at it."

"Truly?" He was intriguing me despite myself. "Very well, then. I've never been known to back away from a challenge."

"I'm sure you haven't." Now his tone was wry and almost bespoke personal experience. Yet I had never seen him before, I was sure of it...wasn't I?

I had been sitting in a chair talking to him, so I stood to take his hand and let him lead me to the dance floor. As I took his proffered hand, I caught an eyebrow raised in surprise, and he muttered under his breath, but I heard him. "I hadn't realized you were so tall."

"Well, you can blame my parents for that," I answered lightly. In truth, I was a bit taller than usual for a woman, but I was pleased to find that he matched my height and so I could look him in the eyes without tilting my head down.

His eyes widened as he realized I had heard him. "I didn't mean it as a criticism, I assure you."

I smiled. "Do not worry; it is hard to tell height while someone is seated."

"Yes...of course. That's what I meant." He led me to the dance floor and we took our place on the outer edge of the dancers. The dance required the participants to start by simply facing each other and holding hands. I noticed his hands trembled slightly, but he held mine in a firm yet gentle grip.

The music started and we began to dance. I found my partner to be a good dancer, if a little out of practice – curious for someone his age, but it was an older dance, so perhaps he simply wasn't as familiar with it. "So," I began as we started to move, "you think I can guess your name."

"I know you can."

"Have we met? You never actually answered the question."

We turned from each other and walked around the couple next to us as the dance dictated. As we came back together and joined hands again, he said, "I suppose I didn't. The truth is...we have met. Rather recently."

"Ah. So you came for the wedding? That probably explains why I can't quite place you with your name yet; there have been hordes descending on us." We raised our clasped hands and spun under them. I was immensely grateful that my partner was the right height for me for the maneuver. I had lost count of how many times I had been forced to crouch to make it through the movement.

"I suppose I did technically come for the wedding, as I did make the ceremony," he answered as we circled each other "But that wasn't actually my main reason for coming." I raised my eyebrows. Why else would...? "I really came to...to see you. To apologize for my absolutely abominable behavior."

I abruptly halted. The music continued, but as we were on the edge of the floor, we didn't impede any other dancers. I stared at him, hard, and he looked back at me with a serious expression, and a definite hint of nervousness. "Who are you?" I whispered, gazing into his silver grey eyes. Silver grey eyes...who did I know who had eyes that color?

"Can't you guess?" he answered softly in the same low tone. He paused, then whispered my name. "Aislinn..."

I drew in a sharp breath. Grey eyes. I knew those eyes. The whisper of that voice. But it couldn't be...it couldn't be... "Ste...Steffyn?" I breathed out, my heart suddenly feeling like it was in my throat and beating erratically. And my stomach flipped when he answered with a nod, a nervous smile lighting up his face. "But...how?"

"You," he answered. He glanced around. "Is there someplace private we could talk?"

Feeling dazed, I nodded. "Follow me." I turned, found the corridor I wanted with my eyes, and headed toward it. I was very aware of Steffyn following behind me. Steffyn. Human. In his true form. A rather handsome true form. And here. At the ball. It was pure memory that took me down the corridors and finally out into the rose garden, because my mind was still reeling.

When we reached the garden, I turned to face him. He was looking around the garden with wide eyes. "Incredible," he breathed, taking in all the different roses. "This is the garden you and the princess tend?"

I nodded. "Yes. It's why I rather liked yours."

He turned his gaze back to me. "I remember. You said you like roses because they have thorns, like how life is full of trials, but from it still comes beauty in the flower." I nodded, still taking him in. If he was human, if his curse was broken, then didn't that mean-?

"Yes," he answered, stepping closer – though not too close. Obviously, he was reading my mind. I was struck by how peaceful he seemed. Yes, there was uncertainty there, likely because he wasn't sure of my reactions, but he seemed undeniably at peace. "I have stopped blocking Abba. And you were right. That was all I needed to do." He let out a sigh and shook his head with a rueful grin. "I should have listened to you sooner. You were absolutely right, and I was an absolute fool not to pay attention." He glanced at me, then away and continued talking. "I had cut myself off from love and joy. I did let my condition govern my mind and attitude, instead of allowing myself to trust Abba despite my conditions. And I deluded myself into thinking I was fine. You forced me to confront very unpleasant truths about myself, and so I responded badly, and for that I am very, deeply sorry." He looked back at me and took a hesitant step closer. "And...I also thank you, for all your poking and prodding. Abba knows I needed it." He stopped, and just looked at me, looking for my reaction – and likely mentally probing for it, too.

However, now it was my turn to be struck dumb. I felt a bit more empathy for how he had been feeling that morning. At that thought, I saw a smile flicker over his face. "Didn't your mother ever teach you uninvited mind reading was rude?" I asked, trying to make a joke. Then I saw the solemnity that crossed his face and remembered how his mother had died. "I'm so sorry, I didn't mean-"

To my incredulity, he laughed. He laughed! It was a happy, carefree sound. I decided I quite liked it. "No, it's alright. And she did. I'm sorry."

I felt my own lips twitch upward. "Didn't I tell you to stop apologizing for everything?"

He nodded thoughtfully. "That you did. I suppose it's a bit of a habit."

"I mean, not that you should never apologize for something, but neither do you need to apologize for everything." I realized I was starting to babble.

He smiled. "I know what you meant." His smile slipped and he looked at me anxiously, taking another cautious step forward, so we were within arm's length. "So...do you forgive me?" His voice betrayed how anxious he was for the answer to be yes. I fully considered him. Human. I knew that couldn't have happened without a true change of heart.

I smiled, and nodded. "Of course I do."

A grin of relief lit up his face. "Really?"

I nodded. "I think you've punished yourself long enough."

"Aye, that's true," he acknowledged. He reached out and took my hand, caressing it as if enjoying the contact. Considering how long it had been since he could feel real skin to skin contact, he likely was. That tingly feeling I'd felt a few times before started up again in my stomach. "Now, about this morning...I realize I did not react how you would have liked."

I winced. "Nothing this morning went as I thought it would."

"Yet I'm glad it did happen." He looked at me earnestly. "I needed that last push, Aislinn. Badly. It pushed me right to Abba, and...well, you can see what happened." I nodded. My heart started hammering again. "After I...changed back, I realized that I had to come find you, and tell you something. Hence why I braved the wedding."

"You really were at the ceremony?" I asked.

He nodded. "At the back. I followed those directions Prince Rhodri gave me yesterday, through the tunnels. Then I had to wait to get you alone...which did take a bit longer than I thought. I...underestimated your number of admirers." He sounded a bit dismayed at that last part.

I rolled my eyes. "So did I. Apparently defeating a sorceress and saving a kingdom makes one popular."

He took my other hand. "I wasn't sure how to...break the news to you, so I thought having you guess at it would be best. The best way to get you to believe me."

"So you asked me to dance."

He nodded. "I used to like dancing, once upon a time. I was just thankful it was a dance I knew. But as I was saying, I came here to tell you something." He took a deep breath. "You told me, this morning, that...that you've fallen in love with me." I swallowed, my mouth feeling dry, and nodded. "I came here to tell you that...I feel the same way." I stared, holding his gaze.

My breath caught. "You do? Really?"

He nodded. "Abba broke the curse for me, and it was my own stubbornness that kept me from that for so long. I know that. But you pushed me until I got to that place. I suppose that means you're even more stubborn than I am."

I tilted my head. "Is that supposed to be a compliment?"

For a moment he looked nonplussed, then shrugged. "Well, I don't mean it as a criticism. But that's beside the point. What I am trying to say, is...quite simply...I love you." He let out a breath of laughter. "How could I not? You're the most incredible thing to have come to my valley in decades. Centuries, really."

I felt the smile break over my face at the words, but I couldn't resist a little tease. "Because I'm stubborn? You know, I've never heard of that word being used as a reason for affection before."

The expression on his face turned wry. "It's not traditional, but it suits you. Perhaps you would prefer dogmatic optimism?" I laughed at my own words being parroted back to me. His expression softened. "Truthfully, Aislinn, I have never met anyone with such a determinedly positive outlook as you. Not in two hundred and fifty years. You see the world with your artist's eye always looking for good, and those who are around you can't help but get swept up in it. Not even this cranky Brenwyd."

I felt my blush return full force as the tingle in my stomach increased. "You're hardly being cranky now," I whispered. He looked a little bashful, but returned my smile. I tentatively leaned into him, and was rewarded by feeling him place his arms around me. "This is nice." I giggled. "Not that I object to cuddling with furry animals, but..."

He made a coughing noise in his throat. "I beg your pardon?"

I pulled back to look him in the eyes. "Oh, come. If you want to court me seriously, then I'm afraid you'll have to put up with some teasing."

"Ah," he nodded. "I suppose I'll get used to it." He didn't sound enthused.

My smile widened. "Now, there's the grumpy man I know. For a moment I thought he had completely disappeared into this handsome prince in front of me. I would miss him if he did, you know. Who would I argue with then?"

The corners of his lips twitched as he suppressed a smile. "Who indeed? Fortunately, I'm no prince."

"Perhaps not technically, but I do enjoy a bit of fantasy." A thought struck me. "Wait. Don't you have some sort of noble rank? From your father being a duke? At least...Morrian mentioned her father was duke, and since you shared the same one...but if your father died when you were young, wouldn't that make you-"

"A duke?" he finished for me. He sighed. "Yes, I did inherit the title. But since I was so young, I was at first under my mother's guardianship, then under...Morrian's. When she married Llewelyn I came with her and the province was overseen by a steward until I reached twenty. I was about to leave to formally take possession of the duchy when I finally discovered what Morrian was up to and confronted her..." His voice trailed off and a pained expression crossed his face.

I took his arm in mine and squeezed his hand. "I'm sorry. I didn't mean to bring up painful memories."

"No, don't be." He looked at me and a small smile returned. "I need to learn to live with my memories instead of being burdened by them."

I nodded. "I see. So, are you still a duke?"

His smile grew bigger and turned wry again. "Is it important to you? I wouldn't have taken you for a title-hunter."

I gasped in mock outrage. "How dare you, sir! Shall I challenge you to a duel at dawn?"

He laughed. "Please don't. You would win easily. The answer to your question is no, I'm not. After the curse took hold and it became apparent there would be no easy cure, I formally abdicated to a cousin. His line still holds the duchy; I check on it every so often. Thus, I am a mere common Brenwyd, I'm afraid."

"No, that's good. Since you don't have a title, I can officially hold to my fantasy of you as a grumpy prince. As long as you don't mind that the image of the flawless beauty is a little upset by my freckles. I'm afraid I can't abdicate those."

He leaned a bit closer to me and whispered, as if telling me a serious secret. "I love your freckles. They suit you completely. Anyone who thinks they detract from beauty is a fool."

I felt the blush coming back and I glanced down. "Good. Because I am rather fond of them, myself." He gently tugged on my arm and began to lead me in a walk through the spiral.

"Aislinn...there is something else I need to tell you." His tone had become serious again, and so I looked back at him with a quizzical frown.

His face looked uncertain, but his eyes held determination. "I...I think, before we make...any further decisions about what the future might hold...for us, specifically, that you deserve to know..." He paused and took a deep breath, pain entering the expression on his face. I was quickly growing concerned. "You deserve to know... the full circumstances of how I became...how I was."

"You mean there's more than you've told me already?"

"Yes...and it's the part I have never told anyone." He pulled me to a stop and turned me to face him, pleading in his eyes. "You Saw the conversation Elfleda and I had before the battle all those years ago, and you Saw how I pulled myself away from her. I do not want to do that to you, so I have decided...I must tell you..." He shut his eyes. "I have to finally tell someone what it was that Morrian did to me." His voice had dropped to a barely discernable whisper.

My eyes widened. "Oh." The magnitude of what he wanted to do was not lost on me. And yet... "Steffyn, I hope you're not telling me this from the noble intention to let me know the worst of you in case I decide that I don't want to...pursue something with you after all."

His eyes opened, and they held a wry look. "I would be lying if I completely denied that statement, but...I remembered today the importance of sharing burdens with others instead of relying completely on myself. Abba has freed me from the curse, and I do not want there to be any chance I might become that person again, in any way. So, if you would be willing, I would like to share it with you. Not all of it, not every detail, but...I know, now, that I need to be able to trust my friends to support me instead of only pitying me."

I nodded slowly. "I understand. And I am honored that you should choose me to share your confidence. But, would you let me take a guess first?" I took his raised eyebrows as an invitation. "Steffyn, Morrian tried to force you to join her, didn't she? She used your gift of mind-speaking against you to try and show you a reality where you joined her in her power and enjoyed it." I said the words gently, tying together long-held suspicions and half-guesses, but his eyes widened and he took a step back from me as if I had punched him in the chest.

"How did you...Did you have a dream about that, too?"

I shook my head. "No. It only seemed logical, based on what little you did say, and then what she said to you. You were her brother, after all, and she must have had a reason for keeping you alive. The only one I could think of was a desire to have you join her."

A wary expression overtook his face. "And...does this bother you? I...I sometimes did think that perhaps I should just give in to her." He shut his eyes again. "It is impossible to fully express the pain of having your own mind used against you. She...she confused me, planted false memories, false scenarios, imposed her own joy in causing suffering and partaking in evil on me, trying to show me that I was only denying my natural desires." His jaw clenched. "I managed to escape her that time, but...she was already halfway towards making me a beast."

I looked at him, feeling horror and anger about Morrian's actions towards him – if she wasn't already dead, I would have marched off right then to run her through – but made sure that only sympathy, compassion, and love showed on my face. I took his hands in mine, bringing his eyes open again. "Steffyn, everyone has a capacity for evil in them. That's why it's so hard to fight. It's only natural that, now and again, we fall victim to our own darkness. What's important is that we recognize it, and humble ourselves in repentance before Abba and accept his love and grace on our behalf. We are all of us beasts, on some level, because of sin; only Abba has the ultimate power to turn that to beauty once again. And remember, you did resist Morrian. She certainly affected your mind, but you didn't waver in your core beliefs. You didn't join her. You fought her. Twice. And besides," I added with a smile, "you have clearly come to recognize and claim some of this for yourself again. If you didn't, you wouldn't be standing here before me right now in your natural form."

He was staring at me with an expression of wonder. "How is it that everything you say goes right to the truth of things?"

I shrugged, and couldn't resist giving him a cheeky grin. "It's because I'm so wise, of course. I have lived a full eighteen years, don't you know?" He laughed. I continued, more seriously. "But honestly...I think Abba sometimes whispers to me and I don't quite realize it until later. I just blurt it out. I do sometimes have trouble keeping my thoughts to myself."

"I would believe that," he said softly. He raised a hand to my face and tucked an errant curl behind my ear. "I only hope that you don't tire of reminding me of those truths often. I have embraced them today, yes, but I know that I still face a battle to overcome so many years spent alone." He paused and looked at me intently. "I will not be an easy person to love, Aislinn. I hope you realize that."

I snorted. It was a very inelegant sound for the setting, but I couldn't help it. "Steffyn, I knew you would be a difficult person to be around, let alone love, after spending that first hour in your company. You haven't scared me off yet, so I would say there's a rather good chance you shan't ever be able to."

His slow smile returned. "Good. Because I let love and beauty slip through my hands once, and I have no intention of doing so again. I have gleaned that much wisdom, at least."

I returned his smile, but the reference to what I could only interpret as his relationship with Elfleda made me pause. "Steffyn... this may be an indelicate question, but...do you still have feelings for Elfleda?" It was awful, I know, to feel even a little jealous of a woman who had been dead for centuries, but I couldn't hold back the question.

He looked at me thoughtfully for several long moments. "Part of me, I think, will always sorrow for what might have been," he said finally. "But...it was not only my experience with Morrian that ended things between us. Things had already started to change, but neither of us was willing to admit it. I did love her, a long time ago, but..." An intense fire came to his gaze and he looked nearly fierce, "...that has no bearing on the love I have for you, here and now."

This time when I blushed, I held his gaze. "Well then," I said, "I think that settles things." I began to laugh. "Lissa will hold this over me for the rest of my life."

"Pardon?"

"She told me I was falling for you over a week ago. I didn't believe her. She kept badgering me about it, though. In fact," a sudden realization shot through my mind, "she's the one who's responsible for my visit to you this morning! Oh, how could I not see it?" I quickly narrated our conversation from yesterday to Steffyn.

"I see. It seems I have much to thank the princess for, then. She will make a great queen."

"That she will," I said, smiling up at him. I leaned into him again, and he brought his arms around me. We stood like that for several minutes, content to simply be silent and draw strength from each other. I quickly understood why Lissa and Rhodri enjoyed this position so much.

Gradually, though, I became aware of the music spilling faintly out into the garden from the great hall and realized that we had been away for quite a while. People would be starting to look for me before long, especially with the end of the ball coming into sight. I reluctantly extricated myself from Steffyn's arms. "We should go back. I'll be missed before long."

"Very well." He took my arm and started leading me back inside. "I suppose you'll have to placate your admirers." He sounded decidedly glum, which made me laugh.

"Not as long as you claim all the next dances."

"I likely won't know them. It's been rather a long time since my last ball, you know."

"I know." I cast a curious glance at him. "How old are you, anyway? It seems the sort of thing I should know. Two hundred and sixty? Two hundred and seventy? You certainly don't show your age. Probably a good thing." I had a sudden image of trying to explain to my parents that I was in love with a Brenwyd who appeared as ancient as Methuselah.

Steffyn laughed. "You know, I had the same thought earlier. I was twenty-one when I was cursed, and I look no different from then. Why don't we simply go with that? I don't really feel centuries old, to tell the truth." He shook his head slightly. "Already it feels more like a long dream from which I have finally awakened."

"An apt metaphor considering recent events," I said wryly. Mentally I was adding the numbers. He was technically two hundred and seventy-one years old. "I think twenty-one will work quite well. Especially when it comes to introducing you to my parents."

"Ah. Yes." He sounded markedly unenthusiastic. "Have you... told them anything about me?"

"Well, I told both of them about your curse, since I wanted to enlist my father's help. But I've only told my mother about my feelings for you. She...she found me in my room this morning, soon after I arrived back from your castle."

"Ah. I see." Now he sounded uneasy.

I halted and turned to him. "Don't worry; it'll be fine. They will like you, I promise. So will my brother."

"So you say. I'm beginning to remember why I like the mountains so much."

"Don't you dare run back there," I said vehemently.

He smiled, pulling me to a stop near the garden gate, and tentatively touched a hand to my cheek. "Small chance of that," he said softly. He began to lean toward my mouth, pausing a few fingerbreadths away. My heart pounding and nerves fluttering in my stomach, I sent him a shy but encouraging thought. His hand moved to cup the back of my head and his lips touched mine. When they did, a sense of rightness flooded my mind and I felt as if I flew on a leviathan's back again.

When we came apart, I knew I was blushing madly and smiling like a fool. Steffyn had a similar expression on his face. Before either of us could say anything, however, we both heard running feet from the corridor and quickly put a foot of space between us, looking guiltily toward the gate. To my relief (and somewhat annoyance) it was only Aiden. I closed my eyes and took a quick breath to maintain my composure. He was no gossip, but he would not hesitate to go straight to our parents if he got any idea of my having just kissed someone in a darkened garden. Oh, dear. That did sound rather condemning when I thought of it like that. I needed to speak to Father first thing tomorrow about Steffyn. At least Mother had some forewarning.

Aiden paused when he saw the two of us, looking curiously from me to Steffyn. "Aislinn, Mother sent me to look for you. Lissa's asking about you; it's nearly to the last dance, and she needs you to see her and Rhodri off. What are you doing, and who's that?" He was nothing if not direct, and I saw his eyes narrow slightly as he looked at me. He knew me well enough to know when I felt flustered.

"Aiden. Hello." I finished gathering myself together. "This is my... friend, Steffyn. I was just showing him the garden. He is quite fond of roses and a gardener himself. Steffyn, this is Aiden, my brother."

Steffyn bowed to Aiden, to his amusement. "How do you do?"

"I am well." He looked between the two of us again, no doubt noticing the fact we were unchaperoned. I could see vague suspicions beginning to form in his mind, and he frowned at Steffyn. "How do you know Aislinn?"

Steffyn looked at me, then at my brother, and smiled. He held out his arm for me and we walked toward Aiden. "Well, Aiden, your sister happens to have helped me very much recently, and I was just thanking her for it." I stifled a laugh at the description of the conversation, but fortunately Steffyn distracted Aiden by continuing to talk to him as we walked back to the hall. By the time we got there Aiden had the idea that he had been one of the Brenwyds involved in the fight with Morrian, but not exactly sure how. Fortunately, his suspicions seemed to have been calmed, though I wasn't sure if it had more to do with Steffyn's conversation or Aiden's own belief that I had no interest whatsoever in courting. Which, up until this morning, had been entirely true.

I realized that it was the break right before the last dance when the bride and groom would begin the dance alone, and then slowly be joined by everyone else in the room, beginning with their attendants. No wonder Lissa and Mother had been starting to look around for me. Even now I saw Lissa searching through the crowd until her gaze landed on me. She smiled in relief, noticed my partner, and sent me a quizzical look. I just beamed at her, feeling ridiculously happy. I could find her tomorrow before she and Rhodri left on the honeymoon and explain. Now, there was no time as Rhodri was leading her onto the floor and the musicians were beginning to play the opening bars. It was a very old, traditional dance, the Ecclesian waltz, one of the more romantic of the dances and so a fitting choice as the last dance for the happy couple before they went to their wedding chamber. Traditionally, the first handmaiden danced with the first gentleman for this dance, but not always.

"I know this dance," Steffyn said. "I used to rather like it."

"Do you remember it well enough to give it a go?" I asked, using a phrase I had often heard my mother use, and which I now assumed was a saying from Earth. I could see Cerdic, whom Rhodri had appointed his first gentleman, starting to move toward me, but I could also see the young lady he was courting looking after him wistfully – no doubt she would rather be dancing with him for this dance, and he with her.

"Aren't you supposed to dance with the first gentleman?" Steffyn asked, blinking.

"Exceptions can be made," I said as Cerdic came up alongside us. He looked curiously at Steffyn but addressed me.

"Well, my lady, shall we dance?" he asked, holding out his hand.

I smiled and curtseyed slightly. "My thanks, Prince Cerdic, but I think there is another young lady who would much rather have this dance with you, and you with her."

He raised his eyebrows and appraised me and Steffyn more closely. "And you?"

"I have a partner, if he'll say yes." I turned raised eyebrows to Steffyn.

He nodded. "Anything to please the lady," he said, smiling.

"And you are?" Cerdic asked him.

"My name is Steffyn, Your Highness," he answered quietly.

"Prince Cerdic, unless we wish to delay the other dancers, we must join the dance now," I said to forestall any further questions.

"Ah, yes. Quite right." He turned, and his young lady quickly came to claim him, throwing a grateful glance in my direction.

"Are you sure?" Steffyn asked me quickly, even as we moved toward the open dance floor to join Lissa and Rhodri. "No one knows me, and these clothes aren't exactly tailored to undergo such scrutiny."

I shrugged. "Of course I'm sure. And no one will take note of your clothes while you're dancing with me. This dress is fancy enough for both of us. If they do, I shall ask them if they could tailor their own clothes so well. And you said you liked this dance."

"So I do." We reached the open space in the floor. He bowed, and I curtseyed; then he placed one hand on my waist, took one of my hands in the other, waited a moment for me to gather my skirt, and swept me into motion. I noticed Lissa and Rhodri looking at me with questioning glances, no doubt trying to figure out who my partner was. I heard some whisperings from the crowd and figured that most people would assume I had graciously offered to take another partner to allow Cerdic to dance with his lady, but they would still be wondering who I was dancing with. I pushed the whispers out of my attention and focused on said partner, letting him lead me through the spins, turns, and twirls involved. At one point, I noticed my parents joining the dance and met my mother's eyes. She smiled at me, and I back at her. I was sure she would somehow have figured out who my partner was.

"You know, you dance very well for being two hundred and seventy-one years old," I remarked to Steffyn partway through. "Not at all stiff and creaky."

He let out a short laugh. "I should have known you would calculate my true age. I should have left you guessing."

I laughed. "I would have figured it out eventually. I might not be much for reading, but I am still fairly intelligent, you know."

"I know. And you should know, I fully intend to convince you of the joy to be found in reading."

"That could be possible...if you agree to read the books to me."

A turn in the dance allowed him to meet my eyes. "Now that sounds like an excellent compromise." I smiled back before following his lead into a spin, enjoying the feel of my silk skirts as they twirled about my legs with a soft swish.

As we continued the dance, I sent a heartfelt thanks to Abba. Now I felt like the task of defeating Morrian was truly complete, with the breaking of this last spell, and I could look forward to new adventures, whatever they might be. But I had a feeling, as the dance ended and I made my final curtsey, that one of them was called Steffyn, and it would be an adventure it would take me the rest of my life to complete. And that was fine with me.

ALSO BY
ROSEMARY GROUX

Brenwyd Legacy

Epic trilogy about the unseen battle between good and evil

FINDING TRUTH

Cassie Pennington discovers that she is descended from the Brenwyds, an ancient group of gifted people. When a mysterious organization of the enemies of the Brenwyds kidnaps her parents seeking to thwart Cassie's destiny, she hides her pointed ears and special talents, and embarks with her friends on a great rescue adventure.

FINDING SECRETS

Cassie and her friends journey to Glastonbury, where they meet a mysterious woman who holds the key to their past – and their future. Suddenly thrust into a kingdom ruled by the legendary King Arthur, the four friends discover they are in a race against time.

FINDING FREEDOM

An epic spiritual battle ensues in the conflict between the Brenwyds and their enemies. King Arthur's treasure, the Brenwyds' future, and Cassie's safety are all at stake. Cassie has not forgotten the prophecy foretelling her role in this great battle. Can she possibly live up to such an extraordinary destiny?

www.BelieveBooks.com